AN ANCHOR
ON
HER HEART

AN ANCHOR ON HER HEART

MENDED HEARTS SERIES

By

Patricia Lee

An Anchor on Her Heart
Published by Mountain Brook Ink
White Salmon, WA U.S.A.

The website addresses shown in this book are not intended in any way to be or imply an endorsement on the part of Mountain Brook Ink, nor do we vouch for their content.

This story is a work of fiction. All characters and events are the product of the author's imagination. Any resemblance to any person, living or dead, is coincidental.

Scripture quotations are taken from the King James Version of the Bible. Public domain.
ISBN 9781943959-30-3
© 2017 Patricia Lee

The Team: Miralee Ferrell, Nikki Wright, Cindy Jackson
Cover Design: Indie Cover Design, Lynnette Bonner Designer

Mountain Brook Ink is an inspirational publisher offering fiction you can believe in.
Printed in the United States of America

First Edition 2017

1 2 3 4 5 6 7 8 9 10

To Loren who believed in me from the beginning and has
continued to encourage me to see this through to the end.

I love you.

Acknowledgments

As a member of various critique groups in past years, I have learned many minds collaborate to create a competent work of fiction. Saying thanks to everyone who made this journey possible makes me fearful that I will forget someone important. Hopefully not.

I am grateful to my family who endured my absence at home to attend conferences where I could learn how to fine-tune my story, make connections in the writing world, and seek the wisdom of those who had gone before me. I'll never forget the words of my husband, Loren, the first time I was gone for almost a week: "I didn't realize how much you have to do around here!" That kind of appreciation warmed my heart to the fullest. Thank you for standing in my place. Thank you, too, for the witticisms you share at the most appropriate times. Your sense of humor is threaded through the voices of all my male characters

To my son, Jonathan, thank you for sharing your adventure in Alaska with me and for reading all the onboard scenes to correct my mistakes. Any mistakes are mine alone. To my daughter, Rachel, thank you for being you and teaching me how to be a better mother as we worked through your problems together.

My longtime friend and encourager, Mary Ellen Spink, receives my deepest thanks. She suggested I write a book years before I ever considered it. She paved the way by having her own novel published by Bethany House almost four decades ago. She has been my grammarian and critique editor for all my works.

I'm grateful to my current critique partners—Karen Barnett, Tammy Bowers, Rebecca DeMarino and Heidi Gaul—for their willingness to advise, react, and suggest changes as this book took shape.

My agent, Sarah Joy Freese, with WordServe Literary, played a big part in securing the contract with Mountain Brook Ink and my wonderful editor, Miralee Ferrell. Thanks, too, to Nikki Wright, MBI publicist, who came alongside and suggested a series name as well as offered insights into the cover and marketing strategy.

Classes at Mount Hermon Christian Writers Conference, Oregon Christian Writers, and American Christian Fiction Writers gave me first-hand contact with successful authors who shared their knowledge and writing secrets. Thanks to Lauraine Snelling, Deborah Raney, Lynn Austin, James Scott Bell, Davis Bunn, and Jane Kirkpatrick for their individual contributions.

But most of all, my praise and thanksgiving goes to my Lord and Savior Jesus Christ who makes all things possible in His time.

CHAPTER ONE

SHE'D MISSED THE OCEAN. PAUSING AT the water's edge, McKenna Nichols stared out over the rolling waves, letting the saltwater, the incoming breeze, and the cry of the gulls welcome her home. Nothing had changed since she last stood here, yet everything had. She let the scene renew her, while her gaze fell on the handful of beachcombers ambling at the water's edge. A lone swimmer emerged and caught her eye.

Sea water dripping from his wetsuit, he stepped out of the rolling surf. Sand churned as he sprinted toward the beachside park's public area. A face mask hung from his fingers. He'd tucked rubber flippers beneath an arm. His gait suggested something amiss, as if trouble drove him. He scanned the horizon, continued up the rise, then disappeared among the vehicles at the park's perimeter.

Alarm bells chimed in McKenna's head, as automatic as a fire drill, worry intruding like an uninvited guest. The ocean demanded respect. Ignoring its power brought trouble. Grim details from her husband Dane's sea stories ripped through her imagination like a hook caught in a wind sail. She looked again for the swimmer, but he'd gone.

She redirected her attention to her six-year-old daughter who played close by in the silt of the incoming tide. Sydney jumped, splashing everything within a four-foot radius, leaving a trail of grit down the side of McKenna's capris. She shivered and took her daughter's hand, leading her to the slower current of a freshwater stream running through the oceanfront wayside. The creek's mouth ended in a swirl of incoming tidal foam and provided a quieter place to play. "Try this, sweetie."

Sydney stared into the clear ripples of the narrow waterway, her toes flashing pink. Feet still submerged, she plunked herself on the sandy bank and sifted through pebbles scattered along the surface, tiny rocks washed by a thousand tides.

Satisfied her daughter would be content for a few minutes, McKenna's gaze again skimmed the park, seeking signs of the distraught swimmer. The beach's serenity mocked her. Nothing appeared out of place. Like a kite without string, a gull fluttered, hovering in the gusts of wind, his squawk muted against the roar of the waves. A handful of climbers explored the rock piles surrounding the cove's northern tip. Two shrieking girls hopped swells in the rolling Pacific, each jump making them wetter, their cold skin no doubt covered in goose bumps.

McKenna smiled, having done the same—before marriage, a child, and Dane's departure. Countless journeys along this stretch of shoreline bounced around in her mind—every step imprinted with a different memory, each piece of gravel proof she'd come home.

Why do I feel as if I'm starting over?

Staring upward, she implored heaven to hear her cry. Today, though, God remained silent.

She circled back toward Sydney, her line of vision fixed on the footprint trails making paths to the pavement. Assorted sizes dotted the shore, hers and Sydney's fresh in the wet sand, a larger groove pressed alongside a smaller one. The earlier swimmer's prints sank deeper—his determined steps, his haste—eerie reminders she shouldn't let down her guard.

She breathed deep, cleansing the ache in her middle, and let it out. The refreshing mist smelled of saltwater and seaweed. She welcomed the breeze's reprieve like a long-lost treasure. The air brought renewal after the weeks of hot, dry, valley weather they'd endured until they'd moved here at the end of July. Nothing remained for her there anymore—journalism degree finished, her reputation as a photographer launched. Still packed in a box with his things, her husband's engineering degree hid behind its green diploma cover, waiting to be used.

Would she ever stand on this beach and hold his hand again?

Sydney stood, moving out of the stream, and shuffled back to the ocean's edge. The miniature ripples of the tide made fizzy, foaming noises at Sydney's feet, their former strength now spent. She giggled and stomped the bubbling water as wave after wave washed over her ankles. Face lifted toward the wind, she shook her head, the mass of auburn curls bouncing in every direction. Amber eyes squinted as she sniffed the sea's breeze.

McKenna forgot her earlier unease and basked in her daughter's beauty. Sydney served as a souvenir from a different life—an ever-present reminder of the man who'd made her a mother and the family they'd been. She never tired of watching Sydney. Or thinking of Dane. What danger might he encounter today? She didn't want to know. Yet she wished she could.

"Look, Sydney." McKenna grabbed her daughter's hand and led her to a large crab hurrying to rebury itself after exposure by a breaker. Loose debris shifted beneath the pincers as the crustacean struggled to disappear. McKenna stepped back and let the animal entertain Sydney's curiosity.

Her daughter stared at the creature, flapping her hands from her wrists. She squatted to watch as the crab dug deeper. As if by magic, the sand stilled, a small hump the only evidence something hid beneath the surface. Sydney flapped harder, her excitement too difficult to contain.

McKenna grimaced at the hand motion, a self-stimulating behavior that helped Sydney process whatever was before her. Like a hummingbird's wings, the flapping grew faster the more her daughter studied her subject. The action mimicked a camera clicked over and over, capturing every detail. McKenna accepted the action as part of her child's persona, saddened that the calming affect the ocean possessed over her daughter couldn't somehow erase all traces of the disorder with which she'd been born.

But that wasn't to be, experts said. She reassured herself, knowing today Sydney played with abandon in the salty water, a pretty little girl whose delighted squeals pierced the air.

If only Dane could see her this way.

Glancing at the spot where she'd left her camera on its tripod, McKenna scouted out possible photo opportunities. Capturing the coastline's beauty had prompted today's jaunt, her first trek to the park since she'd returned to Newport.

Boulders rose like watchmen on either side of the small bay. The rugged terrain protected the area from the ocean's fearsome power. Like a firecracker sparkling on the Fourth of July, the water's crash against the granite sent spray fifteen feet in the air. Shots of the rocks and the waves, once matted and framed, would add a nice variety of prints to the work of other coastal artists at her gallery.

Dane would be proud—if he ever saw them.

"Aaah!" Sydney's scream jolted McKenna out of her reverie. The swimmer she'd spotted before ran back toward the surf, his wetsuit re-zipped and face mask in place. His stride kicked up gravel as he swished by the child, spattering saltwater and grime on her shoulder. Sydney sprang to her feet, jumping up and down as if she'd been burned.

With her gaze directed to the tide line where the man had run, McKenna reached for her daughter. Several other beachcombers hurried toward the water's edge, shaded their eyes with their hands, and pointed. She looked out over the waves, intent to see what others watched. A dark form broke the surface.

"It's a harbor seal." She lifted Sydney, quieting the child's cries against her shoulder, and walked to where she could get a better view. Only then did she realize the dark image was an additional swimmer in a wetsuit a great distance from the shore, well beyond the protection of the inlet.

A beachcomber stopped and leaned on his cane. "Bad riptides on this beach."

"He's out too far." A nearby woman raised shaking hands beside her head.

"Saw a novice drown here last spring." The man stared at his feet, shuffling the sand as though wiping away the memory.

Fists clenched beneath her daughter's legs as she drew Sydney closer in her arms, McKenna's attention remained on the drama unfolding in the surf. Beads of sweat prickled her brow, breathing shallow.

The second swimmer paddled to the edge of the inlet, yelling something into the wind, his words carried away like brittle leaves falling from a storm-threatened tree.

The stranded man's arms arced over the water, propelling him ahead of a giant wave. The breaker crashed in a spray of white, swallowing his form like a whale gulping krill. He bobbed up an instant later as if he were a tethered cork on a fishing line, a few feet further from where he'd been. He again swam toward the shore, his long powerful arms reaching out over and over, stroke after stroke, yet he drew no closer.

"Someone call the Coast Guard!"

"Is there a phone at the lighthouse?"

"I've got my cell with me."

"He'll be gone before they arrive."

"You might want to get your daughter out of here, ma'am." An elderly woman touched McKenna's arm. "This may turn out to be a tragedy."

Wanting to run, but unable to move, McKenna prayed. "Help him, Lord. You have always been my heart's anchor in times of trouble. Be his today. Now. Guide his strokes and give him strength to swim to shore."

She set Sydney down, tears still wet on her daughter's face, and led her back toward the tripod. If only she could remain calm while McKenna shot a few pictures. Hiccups brought a giggle, and Sydney sank into the sand, digging with her toes. McKenna whispered thanks.

Needing to keep busy, she picked up her camera, snapping pictures of the crowd as they waited for the dark figure to emerge from the blast of yet another wave. Her heart fluttered like a sandpiper skittering ahead of the swells, the seconds stretching to minutes as she held her breath.

Finally, the man's head popped out of the water, face mask askew.

The second swimmer brandished arms above his head, as if trying to guide his friend toward shore. He threw out a rope, only to have it fall short and bounce into the water.

McKenna focused as quickly as she could and snapped the rescuer's picture.

The struggling victim struck forward again, a yard ahead of yet one more surge. Several bystanders had waded into the water up to their waists, as if they might somehow reach the endangered man. Yet he remained a hundred feet beyond their grasp.

McKenna shuddered. How many times could someone be sucked under and still reemerge?

Alive.

As another huge wave slammed his body, Rudy Taylor resisted its power when it plunged him toward the ocean floor. He kicked with precision to the surface, strength draining with each effort. Though he'd considered himself strong and capable, his energy would soon be spent if he kept fighting against this undertow. Zigzagging in the direction of the beach had proven futile. The last breaker had taken one of his flippers. Now only one leg propelled him forward with any efficiency. As he reached the surface, he gasped for air. A few more waves like those last ones, and he wouldn't survive. If he did, his swimming buddy, Kurt, would throttle him anyway.

He was too experienced a diver for such an amateur mistake. How had he not noticed the water carrying him this far out to sea? Absorbed in exploring the underwater life here, he'd left Kurt behind in the cove and forgotten to exercise caution. He rested for a moment, lungs burning from the exertion. He waited for the next breaker. He'd swim with it, hoping its power would carry him closer to shore.

Lord, help me swim. I'm out of strength.

Inhaling as much air as he could, Rudy dipped below the surface. The churning water around him made it impossible to breathe, but dropping too low in the surf caught him in the riptide. He couldn't see he'd made much progress, but as the roller washed over him and spiraled his body down to the ocean floor again, the sting of a submerged rock jabbed his side. He reached for the protruding slab. The water sucked at him, trying to tow him further into the sea. The weight of the wetsuit pulled against him. His legs cramped. As the tug of the breaker ebbed, he made one final attempt, plunging forward, swimming as hard as his weakened body could manage.

Lungs screaming for air, Rudy stretched his hand out, grazing the sea floor. An underwater rise, higher than the rest of the sandy bottom, collided with his knees. Mustering all his strength, he propelled himself forward from the mound with a swift kick, resurfacing. The angry water bubbled around him, as if it sought prey, its drag yanking at his legs and ankles. He advanced a few more yards. His legs threatened to surrender to the cramps, but he willed his feet to kick harder. He swam with deliberate, long strokes—the noise deafening, the surf's foam blinding. Taking a couple of deep breaths, he forced his arms to move in rhythm, body parallel to where the breakers churned along the shoreline. *Always swim parallel to the shore in a rip tide.* The warning pounded his subconscious.

An unexpected figure rose out of the surf, its black outline unfocused as Rudy struggled to see. A man, not ten feet from where he bobbed, faced him—Kurt. His friend reached forward and offered his hand, pulling him upright.

"Thanks."

"Thought you almost bought the farm, buddy." Reflecting the tension of the last few minutes, Kurt's eyes narrowed as though scolding a small child. "This cove has a reputation for widow makers." He spat into the water. "What were you doing out so far?"

"I wasn't—" Rudy's breath came in gasps and sputters, "—thinking."

"You've got that right. I went ashore assuming you'd left the water, only to find you beyond the cove." Kurt steadied him with his arm. "Let's get to shore. I can't take any more excitement."

"Sounds good." Rudy leaned into the warmth of his rescuer. Gazing toward the beach, he noticed a small crowd of people dispersing in pairs and triplets, individuals who must have gathered to witness his ordeal. A woman with a camera caught his eye. Her lithe form scrambled toward a young child who jumped up and down in short bursts of energy, hands flapping wildly at the wrists. He stared, the scene dredging up images from his past. He shook away the memories and sat down on the sand, putting his head between his knees. Fatigue messed with his mind.

Thanks, Lord.

The phrase, though not much, proved all he could manage. As Kurt headed toward the parking lot, Rudy took several deep breaths and let his body recoup from the nightmarish swim. Glancing around, he again saw the woman rocking the little girl in a musical rhythm. Something had frightened the child.

His gaze spanned the beach. No one lingered except him, a tired man in a black wetsuit. But to a small child, he might well be a creature from a sinister lagoon. He remembered another who'd seen him that way. Perhaps he could help.

McKenna replaced her camera on the tripod and reached for her daughter. Sydney's fright returned as the swimmers emerged from the water, looking every bit the part of aliens in a sci-fi flick. One man straightened, mask and black wetsuit covering him from head to foot. The other sat, head in his hands. Seeing the men through the child's eyes, McKenna scooped Sydney up to prevent another meltdown and sang to calm her, backing away from the water. "Old MacDonald had a farm…"

Body trembling against McKenna's shoulder, Sydney quieted, but her gaze remained on the black blob as the man walked up the beach.

The second swimmer stood, glanced their way, and stopped before proceeding up the beach a few more feet. Cautious. Careful. He waved.

McKenna arched a brow.

Eyes on them, he removed his headgear and unzipped his wetsuit. Lean muscle peeked from behind the zipper. He walked closer, halting within ten feet of where they stood, and spoke. "Did I frighten you?" He waited, keeping his distance.

Sydney buried her face in McKenna's shoulder.

"I'm sorry. I probably seem very scary when I'm dressed all in black."

McKenna looked at the man and smiled, feeling a faint twitter in her heart as she took in the stranger's jade green eyes and copper-colored hair.

"I'm Rudy Taylor." His broad grin drew dimples on either side of his mouth. He stuck out his hand, and McKenna moved closer. Returning the grasp with her free hand, she felt the man's strength rippling through his arm. Interesting. Dane's grip emitted that same kind of power.

"I'm McKenna. This is Sydney." She studied the man's features. "I took pictures of you, um, swimming to shore. I'm glad you're all right. You had me worried for several minutes."

"I was kind of worried myself." Rudy's smile spread like a sun rising, a lopsided grin teasing his dimples. "I had no idea the undercurrent here was so strong. I'm usually more careful about such things."

"Several people told me to get my daughter out of here because they were certain you were going to drown."

Not to mention my own concerns.

"Another wave and I would have. I prayed for help, and the next minute I found a rock to grab."

"You had me praying, too."

His eyes widened. "Appreciate it."

McKenna shifted Sydney to her other side and rolled her head to relieve the cramp spreading across her shoulders. "Want down, honey?"

Please say yes.

Sydney shook her head with a vigorous no.

Of course not.

"I'm Rudy, Sydney." The man angled around to where Sydney

still hid her face on McKenna's shoulder, keeping a safe distance away. "Don't be scared."

Sydney peeked up at him, lifting her head by inches. When she had straightened enough to sit in McKenna's arms, she gaped at the man as she had at the crab, her eyes transfixed in a cold, blank stare—appearing to analyze his face, wetsuit, and words. She dropped her gaze to McKenna's necklace and played with the beads.

"Won't talk to me, huh?" Rudy glanced back to McKenna, tugging on the collar of his wet suit. He rubbed the reddened skin, as if his circulation needed warming.

"Words and language are very difficult." McKenna dreaded explaining her circumstances as she had to so many others for what seemed like the millionth time.

"With strangers?" Rudy inclined his head, piercing her with his gaze. "Or is speaking part of a larger problem?"

McKenna stared into the man's earnest face, wanting to trust him with the truth, though not certain why. He seemed genuine in his attempt to help. "She's autistic."

"I guessed as much."

His response startled McKenna.

He must have read the surprise in her face. "I considered speech pathology as a career before I became a biologist. Autism is one of the areas I investigated. But now I work part-time out of the Hatfield Marine Science Center when I'm not prowling in the water, trying to drown myself, and scaring little girls and their mothers." His eyebrows lifted, face expectant, as if he waited for her reaction.

McKenna resisted the temptation to laugh, aching to set Sydney down. Though the child was small for her six years, she still sat like a lump in McKenna's arms. "I should let you go. You're cold and probably tired. I'm sure you'd like to get going somewhere nice and warm." She extended her free hand. "I wish you well." When he returned the gesture, McKenna pivoted toward her tripod, Sydney still on her hip.

"McKenna?" Rudy's voice sounded hesitant, and she turned once more. "Did you say you were taking pictures?"

"I was doing a photo shoot for my gallery when your friend dashed into the water." McKenna's face grew warm. "I don't normally photograph someone's tragedy."

Rudy glanced down at his feet as if he were embarrassed, then gazed at her, his mouth set in an amused smile. "I'd like to see those pictures you took of me almost drowning. Believe it or not, I also teach safety to scuba divers."

"You're kidding, aren't you?"

This guy must have a death wish.

"No, I'm not." Rudy grew sober, his green eyes narrowed as if she'd slapped him. "Even professionals make mistakes. Those pictures could be grim reminders of what might have been. Showing my mistakes to someone less experienced might save their life."

"I hadn't thought of it that way."

Rudy's grin returned. "Could you email me some of them?"

"Sure." McKenna fumbled in her bag for a notepad and pen. "Write your address here." She waited as he wrote down the information, intrigued by his muscular shoulders and well-formed biceps. Little wonder he'd been able to swim to shore.

"Let me pay you something for your trouble."

"Let's see if anything I took came out, and then, maybe, we can discuss a fee." She dropped the notepad into her tote.

"Understood. I'm glad I'm alive so you can collect."

"I'll bet you are." McKenna ignored the odd fluttering in her abdomen. Something about this guy left her flustered, and she didn't know why.

CHAPTER TWO

Alone in her home office, McKenna booted the computer and inserted the memory card linking her camera to the hard drive. With a whir, the file opened and yesterday's shots appeared. A breeze rippled in through an open window, the blast chilling. She grabbed a sweater from the highboy against the wall and slipped the sleeves over her shoulders. Gripping the mouse once again, she scrolled through the individual pictures, studying the coastline she'd spent the morning catching with her lens. Not bad for a first visit.

She congratulated herself for capturing Rudy's facial expression when he emerged from the surf to breathe. Eyes wide and mouth agape, his head poked above the surface and tilted back as he gasped for air. Another angle caught him swimming, long arms stretching out over the water as a huge wave threatened to crash above him. In the final image, he stood on a rise of sand as though walking on water, body bent at the waist, hands on his knees. His head drooped from his shoulders, a defining picture of strength spent.

The frames were good, focusing in on his face and seizing those long, tense moments in the water in a way which told the entire story. If Rudy would agree to an interview, she'd convert these into a photo essay—a winning combination for both of them. He'd have his pictures for his safety class. She'd write another piece for her portfolio. No reason not to take advantage of a good opportunity.

Choosing the best photos to send, she opened her e-mail account, perusing the inbox for anything needing attention today. One message stood out—a notice from the Vancouver payroll clearinghouse that distributed her husband's paycheck. Clicking the message, she found the usual balance of funds deposited into her account every tenth of the month. On time like the tides. A poignant reminder of her marital status and the façade she refused to surrender.

Staring out the opened window of the small bungalow her parents built so many years before, she caught a glint of sunlight on the distant water. Once she could have viewed the ocean from where she stood, but new construction amid a burgeoning coastal population obscured much of the original landscape. Gulls floated in the wind above the beach, screeches piercing the afternoon air. The ever-present roar of the waves against the shore filled the background.

As teenage sweethearts, she and Dane used to race down this street toward the ocean. She'd hold his hand at the top of the berm separating the beach from the town, letting the turbulent air tangle her hair around her face and neck. Dane would lead her to the sand, and they'd sit, his fingers straightening the unruly locks, his kisses tickling her ears. Nothing separated them, all of life waiting like a well-written fairytale.

Until Sydney changed the story for Dane.

Her husband had been gone from her life the past two years, and though he preferred to live away from his family, he paid their bills without complaint. She couldn't fault him for his attention to their needs. Generous by nature, Dane's protective spirit was what first attracted her. Sending money now assuaged his guilt.

The small gallery her father signed over to her when he retired and flew to Europe with her mother had drawn McKenna back to the coast—the place of her fondest memories as well as the source of heart-breaking pain. She'd sent word to Dane about the move, though he never responded. She'd even blind copied the message to herself to be sure it arrived. Why he never answered, she didn't understand. Dad's artsy shop anchored her to the sea and happier times, but in darker moments thoughts of Dane and his tales swept in like a black cloud.

What kind of a life did she have married to a man who refused to spend time at home? Who never answered her e-mails? Whose location she didn't have a clue about, except north?

Empty and alone.

Remaining true to her vows grew more difficult each day Dane didn't return.

If only he'd come to his senses.

McKenna's eyes burned. God expected her to be faithful to her husband, but the day was coming, like a shark in murky waters, when she'd have to find some way to confront him about their relationship. When she'd last seen him, he'd made excuses about his return, hedging the details about his work responsibilities, conveniently avoiding his home life because of something beyond their control. Did God require her to stay in this relationship alone? Marriage shouldn't be like this.

Shoving her hurt aside, she reached in the top drawer of the secretary her father always used to pay bills and found the slip of paper on which Rudy Taylor had written his e-mail and phone number. As she typed the message and attached the picture file, Rudy's warm smile and his attention to Sydney filled her thoughts. How different this man's reaction to her daughter from that of the child's own father. Did Dane really have no heart for the sweet, sleeping girl in the next room? She toggled the send button and hit enter, breaking her fingernail in a ragged mess. Fitting.

Sounds of Sydney waking from her nap drifted through the door. McKenna turned off the computer monitor and walked to her daughter's bedroom.

"Hi." McKenna stroked the mass of auburn curls and tucked a strand behind one tiny ear. "Sleep well?" When Sydney said nothing, McKenna ran her fingers up an arm and smiled. "Itsy-bitsy spider."

Sydney's mouth widened to a half grin, gaze on her pillow while McKenna sang the song, moving her hands in time to the music. Sydney listened, giggling only when McKenna's spider moved under her chin. Then she laughed.

"Let's get you up and put your shoes on. You want a snack?" McKenna waited for the almost imperceptible movement of her daughter's head. "I need to go to the gallery to work today. You can bring your new sticker book."

"Book?"

"Um-hmm." McKenna reached for Sydney's shoes and helped her daughter dress. "I have to make a file of some photographs I took at the beach."

"Beach." Sydney reached in her closet and grabbed her plastic bucket. "Beach."

"Oh, honey, we're not going to the beach today. We're going to the gallery." She punched in Rudy's number.

"Beach." Her daughter's blue eyes stared at her, not seeing, as if McKenna were a piece of furniture. Invisible.

McKenna stroked her daughter's head and smiled, attempting to ward off a meltdown while she waited for Rudy to pick up on the other end.

The phone rang as Rudy loaded tanks and scuba gear into his truck for an afternoon of diving with Kurt. He hurried back inside the cabin to check the caller id. Sheridan and Marie Danielson. He didn't recognize the name displayed, but picked up anyway. Most salesmen presented unknown on the screen. He avoided those rings.

"Rudy Taylor?" The woman's voice sounded tentative, but lilting as she spoke. "McKenna, from the beach yesterday. I have your swimming pictures downloaded."

"Oh, McKenna! Yeah, hi!" Rudy nodded his head as if she were present in the room. He could still see her standing in the sand, rocking her daughter, long black hair framing her face. His pulse quickened. "How did they turn out?"

"Actually, I'm quite pleased. I just sent the file to you. I'd like to turn them into a photo essay if you would agree to an interview. I'm a journalist by trade, and the photography is a sideline."

"Interview?" He could see the headline: *Drowned Swimmer Rises from the Dead.*

"Yes, I'd write about the incident and scuba diving. You'd have a set of the pictures for your safety classes, and I'd have a piece for my active portfolio."

Rudy glanced around the interior of his home. The small living area needed cleaning, and he didn't want to miss today's dive. But seeing the raven-haired beauty with the ice-blue eyes again would make for an interesting afternoon. Perhaps he could do both. "Say, McKenna. I was about ready to head out with my diving partner, Kurt, to Beachside State Park. Would you and Sydney care to join us? That way you could see what I do and interview me at the same time, at least until I get in the water."

"Um, I'm not sure. Sydney set her heart on the beach ever since I mentioned the pictures to her. Showing up and leaving soon after might trigger a reaction I don't need."

"I don't mind, really. Maybe I can help."

Her sigh resonated into the phone. "We'll be there in forty minutes."

"I'll be driving a maroon and silver pickup with a crew cab." He checked his whiskers in the mirror. "We park in the Day Use area."

"Got it."

"You could ride with us if you wanted." As soon as the words were out of his mouth, Rudy regretted them. He'd have to take the woman home.

"Uh, no, thanks. Sydney does better when she's familiar with the car. Thanks anyway."

"Okay, I'll see you there." Rudy started to hang up the phone, but thought better of it and added, "I'm the one in the black wetsuit."

"You should be easy to spot. We've glimpsed that outfit before."

McKenna's tone sounded way too serious. Did she not know he was teasing? Rudy hung up the phone and whistled on his way to the pickup. This had all the earmarks of a great day.

McKenna held Sydney as Rudy slipped his wetsuit up his torso and gathered his goggles. His friend, Kurt, attached the weight belt around his middle, and the two men inspected each other's gear.

Sydney remained calm in McKenna's arms as the man climbed into his ocean paraphernalia. Today, as he prepared to dive, recognition dawned on her daughter's face. Body relaxed and face blank, her gaze never left the man, like evidence of wheels spinning in her head.

The sand warmed McKenna's toes while the backdrop of the cool ocean breeze lifted her hair. She struggled to focus on the interview and not on the man. Rudy's rugged face, wide cheekbones, and bushy eyebrows made a handsome combination. His ready smile and the glimmer in his green eyes completed the package. His answers to her questions revealed an individual with a keen mind. Only a coma could have kept her from feeling some attraction. She guarded her feelings, knowing this was the first time in a long while she had spent an afternoon at the beach with a man for any reason. That she came for an interview didn't stop her wandering and lonely heart.

Sydney provided the perfect buffer. McKenna's attention to her child hid her inward appraisal of the man, allowing study of Rudy without being caught.

"How do you two know each other?" McKenna had listened to Kurt's input, his accounts of their escapades filled with humor and juicy tidbits.

"I taught Rudy how to dive." Kurt grinned at his friend. "This guy didn't know which way was up when I met him."

"Hey! No telling family secrets there, McKintrick." Rudy frowned, his eyes twinkling in spite of his protests. "I can tell a few of my own."

McKenna laughed. "Sounds as if there's more to the story."

"Actually, we attended diving school together." Kurt tossed Rudy his diving belt. "I recently discharged from the Marines after spending two years in Afghanistan. I stopped to see Rudy before I move to Central Oregon."

"What will you do there?" McKenna wrapped an arm around Sydney.

"I'm going to assist a friend's mother running her rescue facility." Kurt's face grew sober, his eyes narrowed as if in memory. "Her son died in an explosion near Kabul."

McKenna didn't know how to respond. She returned her focus to Rudy, enjoying the interview as he told her about the safety classes he taught and his work at the science center up the highway. When he mentioned his adventures in Alaska where he worked as an observer biologist in the Bering Sea, McKenna froze. This interview needed to end. She glanced at her notes again and lifted the camera, hurrying to wrap up her materials and be gone from this place.

Rudy slipped his fins on his feet, letting Sydney touch one. The little girl ran her fingers up and down the webbed part, and the man pretended to be tickled, his silly sighs and exaggerated shrieks mixed with giggles as Sydney enjoyed the game.

Her daughter's interactions with the diver transfixed McKenna, something she'd never witnessed between the child and a stranger. Why Rudy? When countless other people marched through their lives—from therapists to friends—why would this red-haired fellow with the dancing green eyes capture her daughter's attention?

"Think you have enough for an article, McKenna?"

The question startled her, and she jumped. She'd been so preoccupied with the game the pair played that Rudy's voice shocked her back to the moment. She glanced at her notes, skimming her shaky finger over what she'd written. She looked up at Rudy and nodded. "I have enough to write a competent article. May I call you if I find any gaps in my information?"

"Sure." Rudy zipped his wetsuit to the neck. "I'd be happy to fill you in."

"Thanks for doing this."

"Glad to be of service." He focused on her daughter. "I'm going into the water now. Will you wave to me?"

Sydney stared, wide-eyed, her gaze taking in his every movement as he waddled, duck fashion, toward the shore where Kurt waited. Once he reached the water's edge, the ocean bubbled around his feet. He pivoted, his tanks and webbed feet making him look every inch the part of a creature from another planet. Using his thumb and pinky finger, he made the gesture for "call me" on the phone.

Awestruck by the man's unfettered acceptance of Sydney's problems, McKenna gaped after him. He'd talked to her daughter as though interacting with an autistic child was an everyday occurrence. McKenna anticipated their next encounter with an inner excitement she hadn't experienced since Sydney's diagnosis.

Not even Dane's obvious disdain for his daughter's condition could squelch the sudden infusion of hope flooding McKenna's spirit. Maybe she could feel something other than she'd joined the mothers from hell.

Sydney's hands lifted, her palms flapping from the wrist to the ends of her fingers, her attention on the men entering the waves.

Rudy raised his arm in a farewell gesture and disappeared into the ocean. A massive wave spouted behind him, the splash like a cymbal in an orchestra's final movement.

Sydney stood there entranced, her eyes fixed on the spot where Rudy had last been seen.

McKenna watched as well, the ocean's ability to swallow up a person leaving her with a sense of dread. An uninvited shudder rippled up her back. Dane's stories had crept from her memory again.

Soon, though, Rudy and Kurt surfaced about fifty yards north of where they had entered the water. He waved, then flipped over and dove again, a human seal investigating the depths beneath him.

McKenna stood and picked up her notebook and camera, loading them in the pack she'd carried to the beach. Now that Rudy and Kurt were in the water, part of her wanted to stay while the men explored the coastline, but the common-sense side of her said it was time to leave. The interview completed, she had no reason to linger. If they returned and conversation ensued, she might have to field questions her heart refused to address. Keep this professional. Leave now.

"Sydney, pick up your sand tools and put them in your ocean bag." McKenna lifted a small pink shovel and poked it in the mesh carrier.

Her daughter followed her example and soon all the toys were tucked away. McKenna grabbed her daughter's hand, leading her toward the parking lot.

Twice Sydney jerked away, turning to scour the horizon and pulling McKenna with her.

Rudy was nowhere to be seen. His dive today would be a long one.

"Rudy?" Sydney pointed at the water. "Swim?"

Stunned by her daughter's question, McKenna gasped. When had Sydney ever used a person's name without coaxing? Rudy must have left quite an impression for her to call him by name. Was this a breakthrough of some sort? Who could she tell? Nibbling on her lower lip, McKenna smiled at Sydney, who stood looking at her, waiting an answer.

"Yes, Rudy went for a swim." McKenna knelt and cupped Sydney's face in her fingers. "He'll be back another time." *I certainly hope that's true, Lord, for Sydney's sake.*

That night Rudy sank into bed, his thoughts restless and uneasy, turning a direction in sleep that they'd gone so often in the past. He stroked murky water, his arms weighted down, leaden in the darkness. "Romelle, Romelle, where are you?" Ahead he glimpsed a pair of feet paddling rhythmically in the swirling water.

"Wait for me to catch up!" But the swimming figure continued to surge ahead, bubbles gurgling in the force of her kick. Rudy struggled against the weight of the surf, his breathing labored, strength sapped.

"Romelle, I'll never find you if you don't slow down. Wait!"

Suddenly the figure disappeared. Rudy turned in circles, searching for some sign of the fleeting swimmer. But he couldn't move. The swirling water encircled him; the oppression of the darkness choked off his air.

With a gasp, Rudy sat up, blinking, his breathing swift and

shallow. Confused as he peered into the dark room, he fought to make sense of his surroundings. His blanket and sheet were wrapped around him, drawn taut against his arms and legs. He groaned.

As always, in the wake of trouble, the dream had come again. And, as before, it ended the same—his voice beseeching Romelle to turn around. Instead, she disappeared into the abyss right before he awoke. Only this time, as he stared into the darkness, an image of the dark-haired woman with the ice-blue eyes holding her daughter filled his head.

CHAPTER THREE

RUDY PARKED HIS PICKUP AT THE dock and walked toward Newport's Old Town. He'd awakened this morning with a plan of finding McKenna and paying her for the pictures. She'd done him a favor and as yet hadn't charged him a fee. Even though she'd come to the beach to interview him, she'd not breathed a word about payment the entire time. The photos were professional shots—he would not let his responsibility slide.

As his enthusiasm for the idea grew, so did his frustration. McKenna had his number, but he didn't have hers. He'd deleted the record of her call on his cell without thinking. He didn't know the name of her gallery, nor was he absolutely certain of her last name. He could contact her through the e-mail address she'd used to send him the pictures file, but he didn't want her to put him off. He planned to ask her in person.

The shops along the thoroughfare hadn't changed much since he'd been here. The wax museum still waited at the end of the street. The smell of ocean water, fish, and tackle permeated the air. Sea lions brayed from the pier. Clothing and crystal stores, interspersed with candy shops and knick-knack boutiques, filled every corner. If McKenna's gallery were new, she might be in a different part of Newport. He'd start here and move on.

He passed two blocks of various commodities before he spied a cluster of galleries across the street next to the public plaza. One held kites, another angels of various sizes, and a third pictures. Prints—matted and framed. Bingo.

Heart thrumming like a metronome set on three-quarter time, Rudy entered the shop, a wind chime tinkling in the wake of the door's opening. He glanced around at the wall displays, seeking evidence of a raven-haired photographer's handiwork here. Lighthouses and coastal beaches dominated the collection. A corner display of wetland flowers and seagulls caught his eye. A shelf of books on coastal life lined one wall. Nothing shouted back at him.

"May I help you find something?"

Rudy jerked around to the source of the voice.

A plump, middle-aged woman with long grey hair hanging in wispy bunches about her head smiled from an easel in the corner. Two of her front teeth were missing. "Most of our offerings are matted prints, but we do have an assortment of paintings."

"I'm looking for the gallery of a friend I recently met. She mentioned she's a photographer and a journalist. But her gallery features matted prints."

"Name?"

"I don't know the name of the shop." Telltale warmth worked its way along his ears, Rudy's only information on McKenna was she took pictures and wrote articles. Not much to go on. "I know her name is McKenna. Black hair." *And ice-blue eyes.* Did he say that aloud? He swallowed and cleared his throat, daring a glance at the shop owner.

Analyzing him head to toe, the woman laid down her brush and stood, her tie-dyed t-shirt and faded jeans bagging around her middle. She waddled to the counter where the cash register sat and pulled a soft-covered book from beneath. Flipping through several pages, she stopped, her long nail sliding to the center fold. "I'm fairly certain this is the gallery you want. Sheridan Danielson and his wife ran it for years, but I heard through the grapevine his daughter recently returned to Newport and is running it for him now. It's called *Lady Marie's* and it's located in the Nye Beach section of town, up near the motel development along the beachfronts." She held out the book to him and pointed. "I can't remember the daughter's last name. She married and moved to the valley right out of high school. Been gone about eight years. So she's about twenty-six or so. That sound right? But her first name is McKenna."

"May I copy the address?" At her nod, Rudy dug in his pocket for his phone. This had to be her. How many women named McKenna could there be in Newport? He entered the address and the phone number. Looking up, he nodded at the woman. "Thanks for your help, ma'am."

"You a friend of her husband?" The woman stowed the directory beneath the counter and ambled back to her easel. "I'd like to paint him yellow."

Husband? McKenna had never mentioned the man in conversation. Rudy straightened his shoulders, storing this tidbit of information in his mind. "No. I work out of Hatfield Science Center as a dock inspector. I study coastlines and aquatic habitats."

Picking up her paintbrush, the woman dipped it in a pallet of maroon. "Stay ahead of the tsunami, then." The woman chuckled, the gap between her teeth black. "Never know when it's going to hit."

"I will, and thanks." Rudy nodded at the lady and left, the wind catching the door and closing it with a bang. He winced.

Paint him yellow?

McKenna glanced to the clock above the door, its white, life-preserver shape with the red anchor for hands pricking at her subconscious like a nail in her shoe. Though she lived in a coastal town, anything reminding her of sea rescues, hazardous oceans, or fishermen at risk made her shudder. She needed to find a new clock. Until she did, McKenna was forced to read this one, and right now it said lunchtime.

"Sydney, are you hungry?" McKenna walked to the back corner where her daughter sat stacking interlocking building blocks at a bright green table. McKenna kept the area stocked for exuberant children to use while their parents browsed the gallery. The tower her daughter had built stood three feet high and wobbled precariously on its narrow base.

"Christmas tree." Sydney shoved several larger blocks nearer the bottom and stacked them at random angles.

"Burger?" McKenna waited for her daughter to affirm her favorite lunch.

Sydney placed another block on top of her creation. The fragile structure teetered, but it remained upright. "Presents."

The bell over the door jingled, and McKenna turned her attention to the front of the store. Seeing the man who entered, she gasped, her hand grazing Sydney's masterpiece as she stepped away from the table. With a loud bump, the tower toppled, sending building blocks in every direction.

Sydney scurried to snap the disconnected mass into place, her fingers working as fast as they could to relock the pieces into position.

"Time for lunch." McKenna bent down and scooped a pile of blocks into their container.

Her daughter wailed.

"McKenna?" Rudy followed the noise to the back of the store. Red, yellow, and blue blocks lay everywhere, Sydney in the middle of them, crying as if her heart might break. Screaming had a new rival.

McKenna stood off to the side, hands on hips, her face an

unreadable layer of frustration. "Your timing is skewed." Her words, laced with anger, belied the pointed look she aimed at Sydney.

"Let me help." Rudy squatted beside the sobbing child, took a large section of her broken structure, and stood it upright. He steadied it with several smaller chunks as he built a new base. When he had the lower half secured, he pushed the colorful edifice Sydney's way. He handed her a red rectangle, guiding her hand to the space he'd left open for her to finish. Locking the piece into its grid, he picked up a blue square and laid it in the child's palm.

Sydney stared at him for a minute, holding out the blue piece like a newfound treasure. "Christmas tree."

"Christmas tree." Rudy tucked the blue section into the base. "Present for Sydney."

Sydney picked up the piece, hiccupped, and cracked a half smile.

He offered her a yellow block. "Coloring books."

Behind him, McKenna's voice rasped. "How did you know to do that?"

He gazed up at her stunned expression. "I've known an autistic child or two." He smiled, before stroking Sydney's cheek. "They aren't too hard to figure out."

"I wish everyone felt that way." McKenna folded her arms across her middle and leaned against the shelving beside her. "So what really brings you to my gallery? Could I interest you in a couple of paintings at half a grand?"

"Not in my current position." Rudy stood and faced her. "But I might be interested in buying lunch so we can talk about your professional fees."

"You don't need to do that." A flush crept along McKenna's jaw. "I happened to be in the right place at the right time. Those were lucky shots."

"I insist." Rudy's knee bumped a block that had rolled beneath the table. He placed the green piece on the top surface and shoved it toward Sydney. "This is for lunch."

The little girl stood and waved the piece at her mother. "Lunch."

"Sydney is a die-hard burger fanatic." McKenna tilted her head, as if waiting for his reaction. "If you eat with us, you can't think outside the bun." She gestured for Sydney to come take her hand.

"Perfect." Rudy pointed beyond her. "My mother helps out at a sandwich shop across the street and two doors down."

"The Tidewater Takeout?" McKenna's mouth popped open, her gasp audible. "Sydney and I visit the place every time I'm in the gallery."

"Great." Rudy stuck his hands in his jeans pockets. "I needed to check in with Mom while I was on this side of town. She's been begging to go see her sister."

McKenna straightened, dropping her hands to her sides, grasping Sydney's fingers. "Which one is your mother?"

"Make your best guess." Rudy raised an eyebrow and tilted his head.

"Olivia?" McKenna covered her grin with her hand. "The red-haired sandwich maker?"

"The very same." Rudy rocked on his shoes, not surprised she knew his mother. "Most people call her Livy."

"I adore her." McKenna opened a drawer and retrieved her wallet. "She takes so much time with Sydney. Always makes sure the sandwich is right. Leaves off the tomato. Sneaks her a treat when I'm not looking." McKenna patted Sydney's head. "My parents are touring Europe right now. That's why I have the gallery. But it leaves Sydney with no grandparents close by to love on her. With Livy, it's like having a third grandmother handy."

"She's crazy about little kids, that's for sure." Rudy paused and gazed out the window for a minute, a memory sliding through his mind. He snapped back and grinned. "With her hair color, you have to admit Sydney would fit into our family."

McKenna laughed. "You'd be surprised how many people ask if I adopted her. My husband's grandmother had her coloring. Not many believe Sydney's my child."

"DNA has a way of playing tricks on people." Rudy strode to the door. "Shall we begin our sandwich adventure?"

"I'm sure Livy has ours already made." McKenna grabbed her key and slipped through the opening, Sydney in tow. Flipping the sign to closed, she double-locked the doors, turned, and smiled. "Lead on, Livy's son."

The shop alarm, designed to alert people working in the kitchen, buzzed when McKenna led the way into The Tidewater Takeout.

Beside her Sydney giggled, her hands moving up and down as her excitement grew. She broke away from McKenna, heading to the corner table. Mounted on the wall above her hung a ship's wheel. Sydney stared at the giant spokes.

McKenna pivoted to where Rudy waited behind her. "Think we know our way around?"

He grinned and shrugged. "Doesn't surprise me a bit."

Livy came out from behind the curtain hanging over the kitchen door, the fabric dotted with anchors and stars in red, white, and blue. Seeing Sydney, she burst into excited little squeals. "It's my Sydney, come to see Livy today. I have your burger ready, sweetie. Just waiting for the fries to cook." She glanced around and spotted McKenna. "And we have to feed your mama, too. She's way too skinny."

"Good morning, Livy." McKenna followed the aisle her daughter had taken to the table. "We brought someone with us you might know." She angled her head back toward Rudy and smiled. "He says he knows you." McKenna waited for the woman's reaction.

Livy's jaw dropped, and she raised her hands in the air. "I know that one all too well. He's full of baloney and will probably eat one, too—with cheese." She stretched her hands out toward her son. "Come here, and give your mama a kiss."

Rudy strode forward and wrapped his mother in a hug "I thought I was drumming up a little business when I suggested McKenna and Sydney join me here for lunch. But then I found out you've already adopted them and made them regulars."

"Sydney is a regular, for sure." Livy poked Rudy. "You be kind to McKenna. She's a lovely girl. Too bad she's already married. Sydney would make a perfect granddaughter."

McKenna gasped at the woman's boldness. Nothing like being put on the spot. Heat crept along her jaw and inched up her cheeks. She doubled up her fists and pressed them into place to cool her face.

"Mom." Rudy folded his arms across his middle. "McKenna and I have barely met. She took some pictures I plan to use for my scuba diving safety class." He stepped back a pace and eyed the older woman. "And I wanted to see if you are ready to go to Astoria with me this week."

"To Carrie's? Yes, I'm eager to see my sister." Livy glanced over at Sydney. "But first, I have to get this little munchkin's lunch." She turned back toward the counter. "She is hungry."

Rudy gazed at McKenna. "Does she know what you want?"

McKenna shook her head. "I never order the same thing. But don't worry. Sydney is a slow eater, so there's plenty of time for me." She gestured for him to follow her, and they sat at the table Sydney already occupied.

A few minutes later, Livy ambled to their table carrying food. She smiled at Sydney who sat playing with her dinner knife and fork, standing them up on end and making them march across the surface like soldiers, the sound of pretend boots clicking on the table. The woman set a large plate in front of her, a hamburger on one side and a generous serving of fries on the other. She reached in her apron and produced a bottle of ketchup and a straw, then set down the large drink she carried in her other hand. "There, Sydney. Burger, exactly as you like it." She glanced up at McKenna. "Have you decided?"

"I'll have the turkey and Swiss on sourdough today." McKenna braced herself for the woman's comments. "With a glass of iced tea, please."

"Good. Sandwich, not salad." Livy waved her hands in the air. "You eat too many salads, you blow away in the wind, which in Newport there is plenty of. Rudy, you want your usual?"

"Yeah, Mom. Can I have as many fries as Sydney?" Rudy's lop-sided grin fell into place. "You don't want people to think you play favorites."

"Ah, you tease. You want me to count the fries to make sure you get the same?"

Rudy laughed. "I don't have that much time."

With a wave of her hand dismissing her son, the woman disappeared behind the curtain. Within minutes, she reappeared, balancing a plate in each hand.

McKenna's sandwich had two layers of turkey with cheese parked beneath a blanket of lettuce, tomato, and onion. How would she get her mouth around the bite, let alone finish the meal? McKenna smiled, sniffing in appreciation of the woman's outpouring of love. She glanced at Rudy's plate and stared. "I thought you wanted fries?"

"Nah. Mom and I were sharing a joke." He angled his plate so she could get a better view. A polish kielbasa, split in half, nestled in the bend of the bun, the opening filled with sauerkraut and a dollop of mustard. Bits of red pepper and chopped onion ornamented the top. Appealing, but way too much food for her. Not to mention the need for antacids afterwards. Rudy grinned at her. "When in Germany, eat as the Germans do."

"That's Polish." McKenna quirked an eyebrow, still feeling the need for something to soothe her stomach. "Do you wash it down with antacids?"

"No. I like ginger beer." Rudy smiled. "Quite a kick to it."

Livy brought McKenna's tea and set it in place. She raised the glass in her other hand. "You want to try the ginger beer?"

McKenna lifted her tea. "I think I'll stick to a tamer menu, thanks."

Livy put her hands on her hips. "Now we talk about Carrie. What day will you travel to Astoria?"

"Tomorrow. I have business with Jim." Rudy bit into his bun. "Can you get the day off?"

"Yes. Patrice traded with me. She wants to be free on Fridays for the rest of the summer." Livy glanced at McKenna. "You ever been to the Astoria Column?"

McKenna nodded. "My parents took me there when I was in middle school. It's quite an unforgettable view."

"You should travel with us." Livy's gaze bounced between McKenna's and Rudy's, like a lighthouse beam probing the darkness for signs of life. "Rudy, you have room in the club cab, don't you?"

"Uh, yeah, but Mom . . ." Rudy's jaw dropped open, and his eyebrows popped up like two crescent moons suspended in space. "McKenna might have her own plans."

"You have plans?" Livy's gaze pierced hers. "You don't work the gallery tomorrow, do you?"

"No." McKenna fought the giggle growing inside her throat. The last thing Rudy Taylor needed in his pickup tomorrow was a strange woman and her even stranger daughter. His mother would be enough to handle in and of herself. A glance at Rudy's face suggested he needed rescuing. "But I really need to work on the gallery's books."

"They wait—those books." Livy bobbed her chin as if all was settled. "You and Sydney need a day of adventure. You'll go?"

McKenna couldn't decide which person anticipated her answer more—Livy, Rudy, or herself. Words she didn't believe she was saying came tumbling out. "I'm sure Sydney would find the trip fascinating. May I bring the lunch?"

Rudy swallowed the bite of frankfurter with care. He couldn't have asked McKenna to go with him tomorrow with more flair and flawless audacity if he'd tried. He'd never thought of his mother as a mover and a shaker, but the last few minutes proved otherwise. She either kept her agenda well-hidden, or she was completely clueless about the feat she'd accomplished. McKenna had agreed to go without so much as a polite whimper.

She's married, you idiot.

His mother knew she was married, a fact which alone presented a dilemma. Why would his mother invite the woman? Unless she sensed, like he did, McKenna needed friends. Loneliness hung on her like a giant spider web. Her beauty put Rudy on guard—she could attract any man she wanted—but perhaps the hesitation around people stemmed from a need to protect her daughter. McKenna lacked the inner pride and haughtiness which usually accompanied women who possessed such good looks. He'd let her prove him wrong.

"Rudy?"

He blinked and returned to the discussion. "Sorry. I didn't hear the question."

His mother folded her arms about her middle. "I asked what

time I should be ready tomorrow?"

He glanced between his mother's suspicious grin and McKenna's wide-eyed smile. "If you ladies can give up a little beauty sleep, your chariot will be ready at seven."

McKenna's gasp, though slight, didn't miss his ears.

He studied her. "Can Sydney get up that early?"

"She's not an early riser, but if need be, I'll bring her in her pajamas and dress her on the way."

"No need. I know Mom, here, won't be ready until eight, no matter what the rest of us do." He winked at his mother before returning his gaze to McKenna. "I'll pick you up at eight-thirty. Sound better?"

"Eight-thirty is good." His mother walked back to the kitchen.

McKenna nodded, her pursed lips spreading to a grin. "You two always spar like this?"

Rudy feigned innocence. "Like what? We know each other well, is all."

"Got it." McKenna picked up her sandwich and took a bite. "Tomorrow should be interesting."

CHAPTER FOUR

THE NEXT MORNING MCKENNA'S HANDS SHOOK as she spooned potato salad into a large plastic bowl. Snapping the lid closed she lowered the container into a Coleman cooler she'd retrieved from her father's storage building. When Livy asked McKenna and Sydney to join them for a trip to Astoria, McKenna's brain jump started, offering to make the picnic lunch. Rudy seemed delighted with the idea. Livy merely smiled.

Her heart thumping like a parade drum, she spoke to the ceiling. "Lord, I don't know why I said yes. I hardly know these people, and Sydney's bound to make trouble. I don't even know what they like to eat! Please don't let them regret their invitation."

As she spread mayonnaise across eight slices of bread, all the possible scenarios this trip might bring played widescreen in her head. If Sydney stayed calm, they'd share a wonderful day of sightseeing. But if something triggered a meltdown, as so often happened, she would no longer be McKenna with her young daughter, but McKenna, mother of the monster. Behind quiet smiles and silent nods, Rudy and his mother would withdraw, embarrassed by the public display of behavior Sydney had perfected when she couldn't cope. McKenna shuddered. Was it too late to change her mind and simply stay home?

Returning to the task before her, she layered slices of turkey breast, Swiss cheese, pickles, and chopped lettuce on the bread. A squirt of brown mustard finished the job. Joining the tops with their bottoms, McKenna wrapped the sandwiches and stacked them next to the potato salad. She added a six-pack of juice and a package of cookies. Placing paper plates, napkins, and a box of plastic silverware on top, she closed the lid with a pop. Done.

Glancing at the clock, she gasped. Rudy would be there in fifteen minutes. She hadn't checked on Sydney's progress. Hurrying down the hall, she found Sydney sitting on her bed, still in pajamas, sifting a dozen rings through her fingers. Sydney didn't look up when McKenna entered the room.

"Sydney." McKenna yanked a tank top from the dresser drawer. "We're going on a picnic."

"Picnic." Sydney continued to play with the rings.

"Rudy's taking us on a trip."

"Rudy. Rudy swim?"

"Not today." McKenna picked up her daughter's clothes. "Let's get you dressed to go."

Sydney whined as McKenna scooped up the rings and dumped them back in their container.

"We have to get you ready." McKenna kept her voice controlled though frustration rallied at the edges of her temper. No need to start the morning with a tantrum. The next few minutes she dressed Sydney and filled her backpack with a change of clothing. Gathering up the box of crayons, McKenna added coloring books to take along. On their last trip to the valley Sydney discovered sticker books and enjoyed finding the page where the sticker belonged. McKenna packed one of those and grabbed a couple of talking storybooks. The backpack bulged when she zipped the flap closed. If Sydney napped part of the journey, there would be enough here to entertain her while they drove.

Stopping in the bathroom, McKenna ran a brush through her own hair, and then applied a layer of lipstick. A knock sounded at the front door. She gave herself one last glance in the mirror before crossing the living room.

Rudy stood at the opening, lop-sided grin in place, green eyes twinkling with mischief. "I understood there was a picnic lunch to be had here. Thought I'd stop by to have some."

"That depends on whether you like potato salad and turkey sandwiches." McKenna smiled in spite of herself.

"Potato salad sounds heavenly." Rudy licked his lips. "Turkey sandwiches are great if they have brown, spicy mustard."

"This is your lucky day, then, I guess." McKenna looked beyond his shoulder. "Livy's in the cab?" At his nod, she placed her hands on her hips and sighed, fixing her gaze on him. "Rudy, I know your mother roped you into this trip without discussing it first. If you're uncomfortable having me along, I understand."

"Mom wouldn't have it any other way." He hesitated, hooking his thumbs in his jeans pockets. He raised his chin, eyes narrowed. "I won't lie to you, McKenna." He shifted his weight to his other foot. "I inquired at a couple of galleries in Old Town yesterday since I didn't know where yours was, and one woman asked if I was a friend of your husband. I was surprised, because you'd never mentioned him, but I respect whatever reasons you have for not bringing him up."

"Having a six-year-old daughter didn't tip you off?" McKenna searched his face. "Or did you think I was a girl in trouble?"

"Honestly, I hadn't really thought about it." He straightened, arms hanging at his sides, his expression serious. "I'm a Christian. I believe those vows you made are sacred." He paused. "When I offer you my friendship, I want you to understand that anything I do for you and your daughter is made on that basis and nothing more."

"I appreciate your friendship." She blinked back the moisture threatening her eyes. "I understand your concern." She glanced beyond him through the doorway to where his mother waited in the truck. "When I arrived in Newport last month, I didn't know anyone anymore, even though I grew up here. With my parents in Europe, and my husband's parents uninterested in their granddaughter or her troubles, I had no one to connect with. Then I met your mother and she kind of swept me under her wing. I really needed her kindness."

"Mom has made that verse about helping strangers her life's passion. She always wonders which angel she's entertaining when she meets someone new."

"Well, I'm no angel, but I can assure you your mother is."

"She has her moments, trust me." Rudy's grin slipped back in place.

Her curiosity bubbled to the surface. "Which gallery shopkeeper knew me?"

"I don't remember the name. But the woman looked like she'd survived Woodstock."

McKenna couldn't stop her giggle. "That has to be Birdie Bettelheim. Long, stringy, grey hair and tie-dye shirt?"

"That's her."

She shook her head. "She's been a Newport fixture since before I was born. Friends with my parents."

"She said something very peculiar." He glanced away at a distant wall as if the memory were confusing.

"Like what?" McKenna tilted her head. "Nothing Birdie said would surprise me."

"She wanted to paint your husband yellow." He looked at her now, eyebrows raised. "Why would anyone paint someone yellow?"

"We'd need another day to discuss that one." When she felt a tug on her legs, McKenna looked at her daughter. "Somebody's anxious to go." She resisted crossing her fingers.

"Hey!" Rudy bent down to speak to Sydney as she clung to McKenna's capris. "Ready for a picnic?"

"Picnic." Sydney said. "Rudy swim?"

"We might have time for the water later." Rudy offered his arms, and Sydney let him lift her. "Want to ride in my truck?"

"Let me get the car seat." McKenna moved past him in the doorway and went to unlock her car, lifting the child seat out of the back and setting it down. She inhaled to settle her nerves. How many other days had begun like this? Beautiful weather, great trip ahead, a fun outing planned. Until Sydney came apart at some minor irritation and spoiled the time for everyone. Fighting her child every other minute had become commonplace. These people had no idea what they'd invited themselves to share.

Having followed her out, Rudy handed Sydney over, took the carrier, and transported it to the truck.

Sydney didn't say anything, her eyes wide as she watched the man transfer her car seat to the truck. She wrapped an arm around McKenna's neck, her body rocking in a slow, tense motion. McKenna swayed with her, smiling and humming to assure her daughter everything would be okay.

Rudy wiggled the carrier into the small space behind the driver's bucket seat, buckling it to the extra bench. Once he had it secured, he walked back to where she waited with Sydney.

McKenna held her breath as Rudy took Sydney, set her down, and led her to the cab of his pickup. If only she would crawl in without a fuss. With everything still peaceful, McKenna hurried back to the house. She brought out the backpack and cooler and locked the front door. Clenching her fists, she waited for the first wail.

Livy leaned out of her front seat window. "Good morning, Sydney. We shall have an adventure today."

Rudy turned to her daughter and opened the door. "Ready to climb in?"

Sydney moved forward, letting Rudy lift her to the center of the cab and buckle her in. She flipped through the coloring books Rudy offered her, the box of crayons perched in one of the compartments of the car seat.

McKenna blinked back the burn in her eyes. What had happened here?

"Let's put the cooler behind you, McKenna." Rudy popped the passenger seat forward, the hinge registering a complaint when it squeaked, and stowed the lunch. A mischievous grin on his face, he whispered in her ear. "I think Sydney likes me."

"I've never seen her so complacent." McKenna shook her head. "Usually any little change in routine, like moving the car seat, would set her off."

"Maybe it's my hair." Rudy stuck his fingers in the fox-colored curls. "If she hasn't seen a red-head before, she might be a bit baffled."

"She plays occasionally with a little boy in Eugene who has red hair and freckles."

"Then it must be my overwhelming personality." Rudy winked at her.

McKenna snorted, holding her hand over her mouth. She had to admit she didn't understand the connection between this man and her daughter. Somewhere he'd learned to deal with an autistic child's nonconforming behaviors. Life with Sydney had been a learning curve, a sharp one McKenna wasn't always sure she could navigate. Yet Rudy seemed to take it all in stride, anticipating the child's next move as though they played chess. She smiled at Rudy's comical expression. "I'm sure it is."

Livy grinned at her. "He's letting all of this go to his head."

"Literally!" Rudy laughed, setting the step stool on the ground. "Mom likes this to climb into the seat. I thought you might, as well."

"Thanks. That's very thoughtful."

"Will you be comfortable in the back?"

"I'll be fine, thanks." McKenna blushed as Rudy gave her a hand up into the cab, the step to the seat a longer stretch than she anticipated, even with the step stool. "Wow. This is certainly above the ground, isn't it?"

Livy turned in her seat and nodded. "I really stretch my muscles climbing into his truck." Her voice grew conspiratorial. "Can you imagine wearing a skirt and tackling that step?"

McKenna shook her head. "Never."

"I need the extra height because sometimes I get called into territory where the axle of a small car or truck wouldn't clear." Rudy closed the pickup door and walked around to his side and climbed in. Turning the key in the ignition, he buckled his seatbelt.

"Does your job take you into brush and forest?" McKenna hadn't met a marine biologist working somewhere besides an ocean habitat.

"Once in a while, I have to check a stream or drive into a remote lake front, and the roads aren't always improved."

"Sounds interesting."

"Interesting is putting it mildly." Rudy shifted the truck into gear. "When I travel into remote areas, I'm there to observe the fish habitat." He glanced at her from the rearview mirror as he moved onto Highway 101 and headed north. "However, others have vested interests in the terrain, and the sight of a government truck makes them jumpy."

"By vested interests, do you mean they own property?"

"No, I mean people are growing pot and don't want to be discovered." He stared at her again, raising one eyebrow.

"Did you find marijuana in the forests?"

"On a number of occasions. Now, with the change in the law, people can grow up to four plants per household. Those with a medical license may have fourteen. That's small potatoes to the drug dealers, so in addition to the hemp gardens, these upstanding citizens have moved in little camp trailers set up to make meth." Rudy's jaw clenched. "That's why I always pack a gun."

McKenna shuddered.

"Those cooking the stuff don't care how many fish I came to see, they only know that I have seen their operation and am obligated to report it."

"That gives me such worry." Livy shook her head. "What's a mother supposed to do?"

"Will you stay in this position?" McKenna could think of a lot of jobs without the extra danger involved.

"I want to work using my degree, if I can. I'd also prefer to stay on the coast." Rudy glanced at her in the rearview mirror. "But nobody told me employment in marine biology can be hard to find. So I keep taking part-time, seasonal positions to stay afloat. It's also why I teach scuba diving safety on the side."

"Something will turn up." McKenna tilted her head, watching him in the mirror. "Persistence will pay off."

"Hope you're right." Rudy rolled his shoulders, straightening his back against the seat. "I worked three seasons in Alaska. If nothing changes, I can always go back there."

They drove in silence for several minutes, McKenna figuring out what made Rudy tick. First, he nearly drowned and now she discovered he carried a gun. His nonchalant demeanor about it all was intriguing, his ability to handle Sydney fascinating. Yet he remained so ordinary, so human in a little boy kind of way. That Sydney liked him only complicated matters. Even if she were single, as dangerous as his job sounded, Rudy represented a long drive to nowhere. McKenna had already been down that road.

CHAPTER FIVE

FOLLOWING HIGHWAY 101 KEPT EVERYONE ENTERTAINED as the road paralleled the coastline in several places. Rudy enjoyed pointing out the waves and the surf to Sydney as they drove along. As more of the coastline appeared, Sydney's agitation grew. Behind him, McKenna tried to distract her by changing activity books and reading. Nothing appealed to the child's growing frustration.

"She likes the ocean?" Rudy aimed his question at McKenna.

"Yes. She'll stand in the surf until her feet turn red, if I let her."

"Beach." Sydney pointed, kicking her feet against the back of the driver's seat. "Ocean."

"We'll get you some beach, little one." Rudy caught Sydney's eye in the mirror. "Hang on."

Sydney quieted at his tone, relaxing in her car seat. When she drifted off to nap a half hour into the ride, Rudy smiled. He glanced at McKenna in the mirror. "I expect she's got a lot more going on in her mind than she lets on. Right?"

McKenna's voice carried to the front of the cab. "True. Her intelligence is locked behind her inability to speak, so people don't see the bright young girl she is."

"What does her father think of her?" His mother twisted in her seat to look at McKenna, the blunt question bringing silence to the cab. "Is he involved in her life?"

Ever since McKenna's attempt to put him at ease this morning, he'd wondered about Sydney's dad, not certain what the rapport between the three of them had been. McKenna had told him the man wasn't around, but the circumstances of their relationship had been withheld.

"Dane didn't handle her diagnosis well." McKenna didn't return his gaze in the mirror, focusing instead on something out the window. "He hasn't come to terms with the fact that his beautiful little girl might never carry on a conversation or amount to anything. His job used to let him come home every six months, but he's used it as an excuse for him to stay away longer and longer stretches. He provides for us, but we rarely see him."

His mother frowned. "How long has he been gone?"

"Two years last month." McKenna continued to stare at the scenery, her jaw flexing as if she were hiding tears.

His mother shook her head and mumbled something under her breath.

Rudy let the silence between them grow, sensing that the subject of McKenna's husband still stoked raw feelings like a poker flames in a fire. The highway was bending inland, carrying them toward Tillamook, and he decided a break in the driving might be a welcome respite.

"Does Sydney like cheese?" He studied McKenna in his mirror.

"Grilled in a sandwich sometimes. Why?"

"The Tillamook Cheese factory is up ahead. I thought we could take a short break from riding." Rudy raised his eyebrows as if he asked a question. "We can't stay long."

"Is it noisy?" Tension spread over McKenna's face like a gate across an open pasture.

"Depends on the size of the crowd." Rudy glanced at her. "They have a glass wall where you can watch part of the process from a balcony. I know it's still early in the day, but if you agree to it, I'll buy all of us a treat at the café."

"That's very nice, Rudy." A small smile broke McKenna's deer-in-the-headlights stare. "Let's try it, at least."

Rudy directed his truck into the parking lot and killed the engine.

Sydney's eyes popped open when the motor died, and she glanced around her. "Beach?"

"No, cheese factory." Rudy unbuckled her from the car seat. "Let's go have a look, shall we?"

The four of them walked across the parking lot, pausing before the old sailing ship docked in the lawn. "The only way to transport their cheese to Portland used to be by ship." Rudy pointed to the placard at the front. "This is the boat that carried it."

McKenna walked around the vessel, holding Sydney's hand, reading the sign. *The Morning Star of Tillamook.* She touched the boat and closed her eyes. "I'm surprised this has survived. Rough water has a way of making dead men."

"Amazing, isn't it?" Mom ran her hand over the wooden surface. "People so determined to deliver cheese."

Rudy directed McKenna toward the building. Once inside, he led them to a wall with pictures from the factory's history. He lifted Sydney and showed her each one, speaking in simple sentences the child might understand. Sydney grew restless in Rudy's arms as McKenna hurried to absorb the history of the cheese-making facility.

"Let's go watch them make the cheese." Rudy nodded toward the stairs.

Other children stood close to the window, fingers and noses pressed against the glass. Sydney stayed back, hands covering her ears. She stared at the floor instead of the huge glass partition that separated the visiting public from the cheese production on the floor below her.

Rudy bent down, offering his arms. Sydney leaned against him as he lifted her where she could see. She studied his shirt collar, ears still covered, as he pointed to the large stainless steel containers, complete with computerized dials and hair-netted attendants, lining one corner of the main floor. He moved to where she could watch the conveyor belts. Blocks of cheese rode the belts to a machine that cut, wrapped, and boxed the product. After a few minutes, Sydney's hands dropped, flapping slowly in front of her. He squeezed her shoulder as he set her down, well away from the glass wall.

"Interesting process." McKenna's forehead leaned against the glass. "I wonder how long they cure it."

Rudy directed her attention to a monitor playing at the back where each step of the process was described in detail. "Sharp takes the longest." He turned toward the little girl. "Sydney, ready for some ice cream?"

Sydney looked at him, her stare non-committal as she headed toward the stairs.

McKenna speared him with her gaze. "She doesn't like ice cream."

"Why am I not surprised?" He glanced at his mother. "Sydney doesn't like ice cream."

"We should have remembered that, shouldn't we?" Livy shrugged her shoulders.

"There's no way you could have known." McKenna reached for the child's hand. "Hold on to me, sissy."

"What can I get her?" Rudy shared a look with his mother. "I don't want to eat in front of her."

"Something without sugar this early in the day. Do they have that kind of thing?"

They walked into the café and discovered many different cheese-based items offered. McKenna and Sydney shared a sandwich, Livy chose a cup of coffee, but he ordered an ice cream cone. He sat next to Sydney and produced a tiny spoon. "Care for a taste?"

Sydney studied the chocolate mound in the spoon and turned her head away.

"You don't have to lick this, Sydney." Rudy held the spoon nearer. "You can bite it off the top."

Sydney stared at Rudy, then at the spoon. She leaned forward, pressing her lips around the plastic utensil and slipping the ice cream into her mouth. Her eyes widened as she swallowed.

Rudy waited.

Sydney leaned forward again, and popped her mouth open.

Rudy scooped up another little mound of chocolate and gave it to her.

As Sydney worked on the small bit of food in her mouth, McKenna shook her head. "Why is it you can make a difference with her?"

"I suspect licking the ice cream is too cold for her tongue." Rudy took a bite of the ice cream for himself. "I've noticed she's sensitive to touch. Processing her world is a delicate dance between seeing, touching, and tasting without overpowering her sensory abilities."

McKenna grinned at his hand. "I'd say your ability to eat that cone is soon going to be put to the test."

Rudy looked at the ice cream which had melted enough to threaten the edge of the cone. "I'd better get busy." He scooped up a mound with the spoon and offered it to Sydney, then gave a lick around the edge himself, trying to catch each drop before it landed on his sleeve or on the floor.

His mother shook her head. "You're going to lose this battle."

"You wait and see." Rudy dipped the spoon again into the top for Sydney, then licked the sides for himself, determined to stay ahead of the ice cream melting in rivulets at the rim of the cone.

Sydney stared, her somber amber eyes fixed on his tongue, hands flapping softly as he slurped around the ring of the cone. He offered her another spoonful, but she refused, so he hurried to catch up to the melting confection. Soon the mother and daughter's stares had Rudy in stitches, and he laughed his way through the rest of the cone, intent on not making a mess. When the remaining ice cream was contained at the top, Rudy sighed, making a victory smirk as he conquered the dessert.

"Never doubt the determination of a man who loves ice cream to win a bet about it." Rudy wiped his mouth with a napkin. "And I think Sydney enjoyed her portion as well."

He glanced at his watch. "We'd best be on the road. I have to meet someone in Astoria at one o'clock." He led the way to the parking lot, helping Sydney buckle up. He retrieved the stepstool and helped his mother and McKenna climb into the cab.

"You're a good son, Rudy Michael Taylor."

"Yes, Queen Olivia." He bowed at the waist. "And you owe me a kielbasa." Glancing toward McKenna, he rolled his eyes upward into his lids and shook his head.

His mother giggled, patting him on the head as he stepped back and shut the door.

"We're off." Rudy started the engine. "About an hour's drive from here."

From the back seat a small voice chirruped. "Ocean?"

CHAPTER SIX

McKenna rode in the back seat in silence, appreciating the trip with her newfound companions. As though they were family, Rudy and his mother accepted her without question. Nothing fazed them, both content in their relationship with each other, a loving bond poised to conquer the world. Perhaps there were other family members. She'd learn more as she got to know them better. McKenna relaxed, the nagging loneliness which so often rode on her shoulder gone. They'd made her their companion for the day. She'd accept their gift of friendship and enjoy herself.

By noon they reached the Astoria Column, a high tower that looked out over the city and across both the Columbia and Young Rivers. Rudy parked, hopped out, and offered to assist his mother while McKenna helped Sydney climb down. They stood looking up at the Roman structure for several minutes.

"I remember this from my childhood." McKenna's gaze lifted to the images covering the column to its top. "The outside paintings tell a story."

"Like the totem poles the natives used to preserve their histories." Rudy motioned her to follow him around the structure in a slow circle.

McKenna surveyed the parking lot, noting that few tourists had arrived. "Livy, do you think you'd like to go inside?"

The older woman nodded, looking at her son. "Do we have time to climb it?"

At Rudy's nod, Livy set the pace. McKenna guided Sydney up the stairs, taking turns with Rudy holding the child's hand while she climbed the one-hundred sixty-four steps to the top. Several times Sydney stopped and covered her ears.

Rudy signaled McKenna above Sydney's head. "She hears the voices echoing against the concrete walls above and below us. Let's hurry."

Surprising her again with his insights, she nodded and quickened the pace.

Reaching the top, they stepped out into the sunshine. Below them the Columbia River Maritime Museum beckoned, sitting alongside the harbor which stretched to the West.

Sydney stared at their high perch, her hands softly flapping as she walked around the top of the tower and studied the view.

"Amazing air." McKenna inhaled deeply. "Nothing like coastal breezes."

"Do you think Sydney would enjoy the museum?" Livy pointed to a building below them. "There's stuff to look at and boats to climb in."

McKenna gripped the rail. "Let's give it a try. So far today she's cooperated more than I ever remember her doing on an outing."

"Must be all the things to see." Rudy glanced at his watch. "After we have lunch, I'll have to leave you three there. I have business to attend to on the marina, part of why I came up today."

Pulling a seaman's cap from his pocket and tucking it over Sydney's head so it covered her ears, Rudy lifted the child to his shoulder and descended the stairs, leaving McKenna behind to help Livy. When they reached the bottom several minutes later, Rudy stood holding Sydney's hand as they stared up at the column. McKenna caught her breath. "How did you go down those stairs so fast?"

"The echo was bothering Sydney, so we played horsey and galloped."

"I'm glad you didn't trip and fall." His mother frowned.

McKenna bit back a chuckle. Rudy couldn't get away with

anything.

"I held the rail with my right hand and Sydney with the other." Rudy tilted his head and shrugged. "We were safe enough to have fun." He opened the pickup door for them. "Let's see if there's a picnic table at the museum."

A few minutes later, Rudy pulled into the parking lot and pointed.

McKenna spotted the tables near the water. "Perfect place for our lunch." After she filled the paper plates with the sandwiches and potato salad she'd prepared, they ate while watching boats maneuver out over the water. Several gulls strolled nearby, heads bobbing as they searched for a handout.

"Any salad left?" Rudy had finished his second helping. "That really hit the spot. I haven't had salad that creamy in years."

Livy agreed. "Were those red potatoes?" At McKenna's nod, the woman smiled. "Good choice."

"Glad you liked it." McKenna handed the container to Rudy with the serving spoon. "Go ahead and finish it."

"Sydney didn't touch her salad." Rudy scooped out the container.

"Or her sandwich." Livy held out her hand. "Give me the bread crusts. I know a few gulls who might be hungry."

McKenna reached for the plate to clean off the leftover food, handing the sandwich remains to the woman. "I only give her a taste of everything. She's a very picky eater and rarely ventures into anything new or different, but I always try."

"I'm glad you do. She doesn't know what she's missing."

While Rudy and Sydney finished their juice, McKenna repacked the cooler, listening to Livy talk about her potato salad recipe. A breeze wafted over the harbor, bringing with it the smells of fish, traps, and salty boats. In different circumstances, they might well have appeared as a family unit, enjoying the day. Images of Dane and Sydney on another picnic interrupted her thoughts. Those outings had always been disasters. She shoved the unwelcome memories to the recesses of her mind.

Rudy stood and stretched, bending to retrieve the cooler. "I'll go finish my business and be back." He dug in his pocket and handed her a set of keys. "I shouldn't be gone more than an hour."

"Are these spares?"

Rudy searched his pockets. "I might have another on me, but I trust you." He made a face. "Sydney may need a nap before I return, and I'd like you to be able to get into the truck."

"I'll be careful."

"Just don't leave without me."

Livy laughed. "After all that ice cream and potato salad, walking home probably wouldn't hurt you."

"Oh, low blow, Mom." Rudy grabbed his shirt and feigned pain in his chest. "I'll probably work it off diving next week, especially if I get careless and swim out too far."

"Please, let's not have a repeat of that scenario." McKenna shivered at the memory. "*My* heart would be the one needing a defibrillator."

He studied her a moment before responding. "Wouldn't want to damage that. Hearts weren't meant to be broken."

McKenna stared, feeling heat creep up her neck and behind her ears.

Sydney tugged on her jacket. "Potty."

Rudy grinned. "See you soon."

McKenna reached for her daughter's hand.

McKenna jingled the keys in her pocket, lifting Sydney against her hip. The ocean air along the dock teased her nose, whiffs of saltwater and fisheries mixing together in a coastal soup. The museum visit had been brief. Sydney's need to inspect every boat, net, and piece of tackle the exhibit offered kept McKenna on guard, exhausting her. She'd had enough.

McKenna and Livy exited outside and crossed the wooden planks of the pier to find Rudy's truck. Their footsteps made soft padding sounds above the water as they passed over the aging walkway.

Livy ambled at her side, tossing crumbs from Sydney's uneaten sandwich to the gulls waiting motionless along the rails, some sitting atop boats bobbing in the current. The birds fluttered in silent swoops to where the crusts landed, their bobbing heads and flipping tails graceful as they gobbled up the morsels.

From her perch on McKenna's hip, Sydney stared at the hungry birds. Her tiny arms clung to McKenna's neck, her head wobbling as she struggled to stay awake. Soon she gave up the fight and collapsed against her mother's shoulder. McKenna shifted the child's weight to her other side and squinted into the sun searching for the pickup.

"McKenna!"

She twisted to the sound of the voice and saw Rudy's arms waving above his head from the street. "Rudy's here."

Livy nodded, taking the lead.

McKenna followed, her shoulder burning where Sydney lay like a dead weight on her collarbone, fatigue throbbing at the back of her head.

Rudy strode to where they stood and held out his arms. "Let me carry Sydney."

McKenna lowered the sleeping girl into his embrace. Once he had Sydney balanced in his arms, McKenna rolled her head in a circle to relieve the cramping. "Thanks."

Opening the passenger side, he lowered Sydney into her car

seat and fastened the safety harness. "McKenna, why don't you get in next, and I'll help Mom into the front." Setting the crate on the pavement, he handed McKenna up to her seat and then helped Livy while McKenna adjusted her seat belt. "Are you ladies hungry or shall we go see Carrie now?"

McKenna gasped. "We only ate a half hour ago. Are you hungry again?"

Rudy grinned. "I can always eat."

"Carrie will refresh us." Livy reached for the door handle, closing her door. "I don't want to miss seeing my sister."

McKenna studied the streets of Astoria as Rudy drove. They passed through newer sections of housing and then rounded a corner where older, more stately homes waited. Pulling up in front of a two-story Victorian with double upper windows, Rudy parked and hopped out. He hurried around to the passenger door and helped his mother climb down, then assisted McKenna.

A lady dressed in a lime green housedress and pink bunny slippers appeared at the top of the massive stairs which reached from the street to the front door. The main level sat above a daylight basement. "Livy! You're here."

"Carrie. We come at last." As though infused with new life, Livy scrambled up the steps to the porch where Carrie waited. Wrapping their arms about each other, the two sisters squealed, chattering like magpies as they disappeared into the house.

McKenna watched them go. "They seem happy to see each other. Is your aunt close in age to your mother?"

"Mom's fifty and the youngest of six. Carrie is next in line at fifty-two." Rudy reached in and lifted Sydney from her car seat as if she were a rag doll. "I'm sure Carrie will have an extra bed where we can lay her down."

"Can you carry Sydney all the way up those steps?"

"Hey, I did the Astoria Column today, didn't I?" At McKenna's nod, he led the way up the steps and through the door.

"Welcome, my dear." Carrie plodded to where McKenna had entered. "Rudy, introduce us?"

"Aunt Carrie, this is McKenna Nichols, who manages *Lady Marie's* gallery in Newport." Rudy gestured toward the older woman. "Carrie Hinrichs, my aunt."

"Nice to meet you, my dear." Carrie fixed her gaze on Sydney, who slept on Rudy's shoulder. "What a beautiful child." She pointed to a door on her right. "Rudy, lay the little one on the trundle bed. I've already pulled it out." She shifted her attention to McKenna. "Feel free to check on her."

"Thank you, Mrs. Hinrichs."

"Carrie will suffice. The mister in my life never materialized, so I'm a missed blessing." She chuckled and cupped her fingers around Livy's elbow. She nodded at the door to her left. "Livy and I will wait for you in the parlor." She pressed her lips together in a satisfied smile. "I made fresh scones this morning. Blueberry." She winked and led her sister away, the doorway allowing a glimpse of a polished wooden floor that reflected the sun's rays in every direction.

McKenna swiveled to the other doorway where Rudy had already entered and laid Sydney down on the low bed. A handmade quilt covered the single mattress, clusters of pink and yellow flowers stitched into each square. "This bed looks made to order."

"Let's leave the door open so you can hear her." Rudy patted Sydney's head. "I think we wore her out." At McKenna's smile, he stood and gestured toward the other door. "You need to try one of Carrie's pastries. Blueberry is my favorite."

Rudy ushered McKenna into the expansive room. Windows lined

an entire wall, allowing a spectacular panorama of the Pacific in the distance, the Astoria-Megler Bridge over the Columbia barely visible through the trees below them. He drew McKenna to the view, her appreciative gasp making him smile. "I've always enjoyed this spot."

"Who wouldn't?" McKenna stared for a moment, her gaze sweeping the scenery beyond the windows. The fatigue he'd noticed at the dock had faded. Like a deflated sail suddenly caught in a second wind, McKenna billowed to life, ready to navigate new waters. He admired her tenacity, a strength of character much greater than her diminutive form.

His mother and Carrie were seated at the claw-foot table, the teapot in the center emitting a trickle of steam from its spout. As he and McKenna joined them, he spied a basket of wrapped goodies waiting near dainty china plates. Carrie always insisted on using the fragile tableware. She knew he trembled every time he handled one. "Testing my etiquette again, are you?"

Carrie smiled. "Practice makes perfect, Rudy dear." She puckered her mouth. "That woman you'll marry someday may like dinner parties."

"May *that woman* marry the man of her dreams." Rudy pulled out a chair for McKenna. "And may he *not* be me."

As she sat, McKenna giggled. No doubt she wondered if all the Hinrichs clan and its subsidiaries teased each other. First his mother. Now his aunt. As quiet as McKenna was, the constant tossing of one-liners must be draining. Yet she managed their quirkiness with amusement.

Carrie rose and poured a cup. "Would you care for Earl Grey?" Setting it on a saucer, she extended the drink to McKenna, who nodded her thanks. "Allow me to offer you a scone." She lifted the basket and unwrapped the towel around it. "I'd let Rudy do it, but he's liable to scarf them all down with nary a bite for the rest of us."

"You make me sound like a heathen." Rudy reached for a plate. "I can't help it if you are the best baker this side of the Rockies."

"Flattery will get you everywhere." Carrie laid two scones on a plate beside her and handed another to his mother. "Now that you've left that fishing boat behind, I guess your civilized side will return once again."

"Not for long." Rudy dug into the basket of scones. "My agency supervisor in Seattle had two recruits fail their training, and a third observer broke his arm, so he started the season short-handed. Desperate, he contacted me. I told him I'd come and finish out the early pollock season for him. I leave Labor Day weekend for Dutch Harbor."

"Back to the Bering Sea?" His mother paled. "No, Rudy. You told me you wouldn't do such dangerous work again. What about your job here?"

"I told my boss of the need yesterday, and he said he could get along without me for a month. I checked in at the marina today with one last inspection. I've covered most of the remote lakes in the county, so the easier ones will wait for my return." He bit into his scone and let the soft pastry linger, then pressed his lips together as he devoured the last bite. "I'll be loading my duffel bag one more time. I wonder how many scones I can pack in it."

Grinning at his aunt and enjoying her chuckles, Rudy glanced at McKenna.

Her face drained of all color, she stared at her plate. The fork wobbled in her fingers.

"McKenna?"

She jumped, and the fork spun its way to the floor. The clatter silenced the conversation like a gong in the middle of an aria. Both his aunt and his mother stared at the offending utensil. "I hear Sydney. Please excuse me." McKenna stood and set her plate on the table, the scone untouched. She zipped from the room before anyone could speak.

"Rudy?" His mother's forehead creased in a frown.

"I'll go see if she's okay."

In the bedroom, he found McKenna gripping the bedpost, knuckles white, face pressed against her hands.

"McKenna?" He whispered her name lest he startle her. "What's wrong?"

She looked up, but didn't respond for a minute, her gaze aimed at the ceiling as if she prayed for answers. She dropped her chin and smiled. "I'm sorry. I overreacted."

"To what?" His forehead tightened. He raised his eyebrows so she wouldn't think he was frowning and forced a smile. "What did I say?"

Her sigh could have flown a flag. "Dane is a fisherman in Alaska."

He sucked in a quick rush of air. "Oh." He popped his mouth closed. "That's why he's not around much."

McKenna nodded, her black hair bouncing on her shoulders. "He's alive, I know that. I still get a deposit in our account every month. But as I told you on the ride up, I've not had a letter, a phone call, or a text in two years."

"What company does he work for?" Rudy pushed aside the need to throttle the creep.

"He worked for Trident Canneries for quite a while." She paused, face scrunched in a frown. "And I think his last company was Pacific Fisheries, but I'd have to look at my bank statement."

"Big companies with lots of ships." Rudy doubled up his fists, then let them relax. A lone man in a fleet of manpower. "You probably don't know what ship he's assigned to."

"No. Every time I hear of a ship that's gotten into trouble, I hold my breath, because I have no way of knowing which one he's on."

Rudy folded his arms across his chest. "If it's any consolation to you, most seamen are a rugged bunch who have had safety drilled into their skulls." He dropped his arms to his sides and shoved his fingers into his jeans pockets. "The outfit I work for stresses safety and practices emergency drills routinely."

"That's good to know." She bent to adjust the quilt covering Sydney. "The danger doesn't scare you?"

"I won't lie. The Bering Sea is a formidable foe. Many have lost their lives. But most of the big rigs carry rescue boats. There's usually one ready to move in a hurry if trouble happens."Rudy's jaw tightened. "My job as an observer is often at the bottom of the boat. I'd be more likely to be stuck if the boat capsizes than one of the fishermen. They are usually on top deck."

"Your mother would be devastated."

"Mom didn't want me to ever go back. I didn't plan on returning, either." Rudy looked down at Sydney, who whimpered in her sleep. "That's why we both spend time in prayer."

Sydney yawned and turned over. "Rudy? Swim?"

He chuckled, leaning down and touching the child under her chin. "Definitely a possibility." He glanced up at McKenna. "Before I leave, I'd like to see a picture of Dane."

"Why?"

"I want to meet him." He helped Sydney sit up and wrapped an arm around her waist. "Tell him what a great little girl he has."

"Rudy? Pictures?"

"And while you're at it, McKenna, I'd like one of Sydney, as well."

"I have both."

Rudy's priorities had just pointed north.

CHAPTER SEVEN

McKenna caressed the edges of the scrapbook she'd opened. Rudy had asked for a snapshot of Dane and as she sat at her kitchen table poring over the scores of photographs, the memories tumbled off the pages. Images which belonged to another lifetime filled the spaces on the sheets, proof of the many happy moments she and her husband had shared together.

Sydney sat in her booster chair, playing with her sticker dictionary. She flipped through the colorful illustrations and matched the printed object to the duplicate in her fingers. Peeling the sticky label off, she pressed the colored one over the black and white drawing on the page. "Orange?"

"That's right. You found the orange." McKenna pointed to a brown and white horse. "Find the pony."

"Pony." Sydney turned the pages with meticulous effort, her tongue caught in her teeth as she concentrated. She stopped and pointed at a donkey. "Pony?"

"No, look again, sweetie." McKenna returned her gaze to the scrapbook. A wallet-sized print of her engagement portrait lay loose on top. Dane's boyish face made her giggle, his dark brown hair long about his ears, deep-set, caramel-colored eyes twinkling. His chin rested against her cheek as if he were ready to whisper something mischievous in her ear. He'd always been a tease, making her laugh at the silliest things. At eighteen, they hadn't known anything outside their own private world. But eight years had passed. She hadn't seen him in two. Did Dane still look like his picture?

A knock sounded at the door. McKenna cautioned Sydney. "Stay in your chair. I'll be right back."

As if the words had bounced off the kitchen walls, Sydney continued scanning the pages for the pony.

McKenna hurried to the living room, opening the door to a smiling Livy. "Hi! Come in. To what do I owe this pleasure?"

"Sorry to drop by like this, but I went to your gallery when I got off at the sandwich shop and the girl said you were home. You're not sick, are you?"

"No. Please come in." McKenna stepped back and gestured for the older woman to enter. "Some of the artisans who display their work in my shop volunteer to work there in exchange for a smaller percentage taken from their sales. It's a lifesaver for me. Gives me time with Sydney." She closed the door and led Livy toward the kitchen. "Sydney's working on a sticker book."

"You have your priorities straight."

"I'm glad you think so. Running a business is a full-time job in itself, but this way I can pop in a morning or two a week, bring the books home, and still have time for my daughter." She pushed the swinging door open and locked the hinge.

"There's my sweet munchkin." Livy pulled a small bag from her tote. "I brought you something to taste." She glanced up at McKenna." Do you mind if she tries a pretzel?"

"A bakery pretzel?" McKenna closed her eyes. "I haven't had one of those in years. I'm almost jealous." She offered a chair for her guest to sit.

"In that case, I have two." Seated, Livy reached in her tote, pulled out another white sack, and handed it to McKenna. "You need a little spoiling, too."

"Thank you!" She laid one of the bags on Sydney's tray before opening the other and breaking off a piece to sample. Taking a bite, she tilted her head back and savored the soft texture. "Perfect."

Sydney glanced up from the book and seeing her chewing on the pretzel, examined her own bag. She sniffed it, and peeked inside, but she held it up to McKenna. "No."

"You don't want to try a pretzel?" McKenna pulled the treat out and held it in front of her daughter. "It's good."

Sydney turned her head, a frown forming above her brows.

McKenna broke off another piece of her pretzel and offered it to Sydney. "Little taste?"

Sydney shook her head.

McKenna apologized for her daughter. "I'm sorry. As I said at the picnic, she doesn't do well with new foods." She popped the bite in her mouth. "But these are the best I've eaten in years." Licking the salt from her lips, she smiled. "Did you make them?"

"Yes, we made a batch this morning." Livy patted her arm. "Don't you worry about offending me. Sydney knows her own mind, and that's a good thing."

"Thank you for being so understanding." She held out the second pretzel. "You want to finish this? I have my own, you know."

"No, put it aside and save it for later." Livy stood, looping the strap of her bag over her arm. "What did I interrupt? You organizing photographs?"

"Not exactly. I scrapbooked when Dane and I were first married. Rudy asked for a picture of Dane to take to Alaska. Since Rudy's leaving Labor Day and I'm going to be gone to shoot a wedding in the valley that weekend, I thought I'd better get this done." She held up the engagement photo. "I was eighteen, Dane twenty. Do you think Rudy will recognize my husband from that long ago?"

Livy took the print and studied it. "You haven't changed much, except for maturing. If your husband has aged to the same degree, Rudy will recognize him, should he see Dane." She laid the photograph on the table.

"Will you see Rudy soon?" McKenna added a snapshot of Sydney to the image of Dane. "I doubt I'll see him again before he leaves."

"He'll be at the aquarium tomorrow." Livy touched Sydney's shoulder and smiled as she talked to McKenna. "He's part of a back-to-school program. I wondered if you and Sydney might like to go."

"Actually, I'd already planned to take her, but thank you for thinking of us. I saw the write-up in the paper and thought it sounded like a great day." McKenna glanced at the calendar. "I don't have to work."

"If you want to go with us, Rudy will pick you up about ten-thirty and drop all of us at the front gate. He has to lead a children's program, so he will disappear after he leaves us, but if we enter with him, our admission is paid. He'll join us after his program."

"That's a wonderful offer, but I'd rather take my own car." McKenna glanced at her daughter. "I hope Sydney will like the aquarium, but in case she doesn't, I want to be able to leave."

"I understand." Livy stood and gathered her things. "Well, maybe I'll see you there."

"Thanks again for thinking of us." McKenna walked the woman to the door. "The pretzels were wonderful."

Returning to the kitchen, she picked up the photos and held them side by side. If Rudy were involved in a program with lots of children, the room would probably be too noisy for Sydney to get anything out of the presentation. They'd more likely spend their time outside viewing the live animal exhibits. Running into Rudy might not happen. *I should have given Livy the pictures.* She put the prints in her bag. *I'll have to find him somehow.*

She spoke to Sydney. "Tomorrow you can watch fish swim."

"Fish." Sydney rifled through her dictionary. She stopped at a page where a goldfish sticker glistened in the light. "Fish."

If only the day would be that easy.

Rudy lifted the letter from the envelope. The contract he'd expected from Pacific Seacoast Observers had arrived. His supervisor from PSO had called him two weeks ago with a short-term vacancy for a biologist observer beginning September first. The agency filled requests from the National Marine Fisheries Service for applicants to work aboard boats that fished out of Dutch Harbor, Alaska.

He'd been reluctant. Rudy had spent three previous seasons with PSO and had determined he wouldn't work for them again. But this assignment only had forty-five days left in its fishing season. Because his boss was desperate, and the season would end mid-October, Rudy had agreed to go. Leaving early meant missing the start of the cold Alaskan winter. Fine by him.

He had completed his final port sampling work in Astoria last week, and now his responsibilities at Hatfield Marine Science Center would be put on hold. With the new information he'd learned about Dane, Rudy anticipated making the trip, certain God had a part in putting this all together. The fishing boat assignment had taken on new meaning.

He glanced at his watch. After picking up his mother, he'd check with the aquarium to see where they planned to host his presentation. He tightened his belt and checked for his wallet. Keys in hand, he paused in front of the mirror long enough to comb through his hair. Normally worn very short, the hair hanging around his ears shouted haircut back at him. Soon. Haircuts were expensive in Alaska.

Minutes later, with his box of presentation materials stowed in his truck bed, and his mother comfortable in her passenger seat, Rudy breathed deep as he drove to the staff parking lot.

When his mother suggested inviting McKenna, Rudy nodded assent, letting her think this was her idea. But Mom said McKenna had already made plans to take Sydney, and she'd see them there.

The thought brought a smile to his face. The aquarium should interest Sydney. He'd always found the excursion through the waterways and holding tanks fascinating, but he'd never taken a six-year-old disabled child through the maze. Would the adventure prove overwhelming?

He tried to picture the tanks from Sydney's perspective. Some fish were as big as she. Some were ugly enough to appear as monsters. If Sydney became agitated, he wanted to help. Though McKenna didn't know anything about him, experiences from his past had a lot to offer.

But he had to be cautious. They were becoming friends. He didn't want to step over a line he shouldn't cross with McKenna. To truly help her, he needed to learn a little more about her husband before leaving for Alaska. Finding Dane and sending him home to his wife was his mission. Rudy would have to keep reminding himself of his goal to maintain his focus. Maybe today she'd have a picture of Dane for him. That would make his search easier. If not more painful for her.

Parking at the end of the lot nearest the auditorium, he held the truck door as his mother climbed down. He reached for the supplies in the back, gesturing for her to follow the gravel path around to the staff door. While his mother headed for the theater, he organized his presentation materials and greeted other members of the team.

With ten minutes until the program began, he scanned the theater to locate his mother. He searched the room for a minute before he discovered her talking with McKenna and Sydney at the back wall. He approached the threesome, allowing his eyes time to adjust to the dark interior. "Morning."

McKenna smiled and nodded, her attention focused on what his mother was saying.

"Sydney." He bent down to where the little girl stood clinging to her mother's leg. "Ready to see some fish?"

"Fish." Sydney held up her sticker dictionary, the book opened to a page where a goldfish shone in the sunlight. "Fish."

"That's right. Fish." Rudy looked beyond the girl's book to McKenna behind her. "Think this place will keep her engaged?"

"Never know until I try."

McKenna remained at the back of the small auditorium while Rudy and his colleagues entertained the children with their silly costumes and wily antics. Using the audience as participants the aquarium team introduced concepts about ecosystems and wetlands, preservation of species, and human responsibility in language the children could understand.

Sydney's concentration lingered when Rudy pranced about as a shark, but the discussion moved quickly. Within minutes the look on her face was one of confusion and disinterest. With limited language skills, Sydney's ability to absorb the information was questionable. She turned her attention to the textured wall behind her, rubbing the pebbled surface with her fingers. As she became more restless, McKenna took her hand and led Sydney out to the passageways where other exhibits waited.

Sydney had just discovered the jellyfish tank when McKenna heard her name. Twisting about to find the caller, she giggled when she looked through the tank of jellies and saw a distorted image of Rudy and his mother grinning back at her from the other side. Rudy appeared nine feet tall, the outline of his body a series of wiggling curves. Livy's image stretched sideways, making her wider and lumpier than her lean son. McKenna pointed them out to Sydney who stared, hands flapping at the indistinct images moving in the glass. The mother and son pair circled the tank and met her, the smiles on their faces suggesting they shared a joke.

"Let me guess." McKenna shifted her gaze from mother to son. "The tank made me look like a squid, or a sea lion."

Rudy stared at the floor, his grin deepening the lines around his mouth. "Squid is a good comparison."

"Thanks." McKenna reached into her purse and pulled out the wallet photo she'd brought with her. "I found a picture of Dane for you. It's our engagement portrait." She handed the print to Rudy, the heat of embarrassment creeping along her chin. "We look like little kids."

"Handsome fellow." Rudy studied the photograph for a minute. "May I keep this?"

"Please do. Here's the one of Sydney you asked for. It was taken at pre-school last year." McKenna swallowed before she continued. "Don't judge Dane too harshly."

"Why not?" Rudy's jaw went rigid, and he gestured for McKenna, Sydney, and his mother to exit the building, holding the door while two giggling girls hurried past. Outside in the sunshine, he tucked the prints in his wallet. "The man has left you alone. For reasons I consider a cop out."

"It wasn't always that way." McKenna walked with him to the side of a graveled path leading to more exhibits, as Livy led Sydney to a nearby tide pool. Sydney stared as the water rushed in and receded. Her gaze on Sydney, McKenna continued. "When we married, he would leave for a season and come home. He made very good money. We'd spend his time home like we were a couple on vacation—he didn't need to work. We both went to school, garnering college credits to finish our degrees." The tension in her expression reflected in Rudy's eyes. "Sydney was born two years after we married."

"That's when he left?"

Rudy's frown made McKenna tremble. Why did he care? She

wasn't the first woman whose husband found home life too much of a burden. "No."

She followed his gaze as he glanced at his mother. Livy had led Sydney to a rock formation with ebbing tidal waters flowing in and out. With the determination of a curious cat, the child stuck her foot in the tide pool. The cold water splashed, and she jumped down with a squeal.

Looking back at her, Rudy's jaw muscles clenched. "You're not helping his case."

"He adored his little girl—as a baby. She made him more determined to provide for us. He'd fish an extra month or do an extended season. We always had enough money, thanks to Dane."

"So he started out a devoted father and husband."

She nodded. "He was. In many ways, he still is. Until Sydney turned four. She still wasn't talking. The tantrums and behaviors accelerated." She stiffened as the pain she'd buried crawled to the surface. "He blamed himself for not being around and disciplining her, and he blamed me for not being a better mother."

"Oh, McKenna—" Rudy frowned again, his mouth pressed to a straight line and eyes narrowed. "Autism can baffle even the most experienced counselors."

Again, he had surprised her with his knowledge. McKenna held up her hand. "Don't misunderstand. He was as confused about his daughter's behavior as I was. Sydney didn't come with a special training manual." McKenna closed her eyes as the memories surfaced, lips pressed tight to stem the emotional roller coaster she held inside. "Have you ever witnessed a child *trying* to get spanked?" She searched his face. "Sydney would deliberately do something she knew not to do and then bend over and wait for a swat."

"Only to make her behaviors worse." Rudy folded his arms across his chest. "Autistic children often learn about emotion by watching those of the people around them."

"It was as if she was egging us on." McKenna forced a smile, a stray tear threatening her cheek. "We had her tested. Dane agreed we should get her help, but he saw his role as provider as more important. I could sense his frustration, but he didn't voice it. He spent less time interacting with his daughter. After he received his degree, he left for another fishing season and never returned. He always had one more fishing tour to do. No time to come home, he said. Even the excuses stopped."

"You don't know what happened to him?"

"Like I told you, he's alive." McKenna wrapped her arms about her middle, holding the hurt close. "And he still supports us with a check every month." She faced Rudy. "I've made attempts to e-mail him, sent texts—even contacted his last known supervisor—but that's where the contact ends."

As Rudy slid his billfold into his back pocket, a series of expressions flitted across his face. He glanced up. "Dutch Harbor isn't a large place. The terrain, the businesses, the lifestyle all center on surviving in a frozen wasteland. Fishing boats come and go depending on the catch they seek. Schedules vary for every person there. Finding one fisherman will be difficult, but not impossible."

"That's why you want the pictures?"

Rudy nodded. "Dane needs to know what a great little girl he has. And come home to you."

McKenna smiled. "He may not want to be found. He's good at disappearing."

"We'll see what kind of a detective I am." Rudy squinted at her. "If I'm as bad at surveillance as I am at acting, we're doomed. Today's performance at the aquarium certainly tested my skills."

McKenna shrugged, trying to appear nonchalant. "I enjoyed the presentation, though Sydney didn't get much out of it. She was more interested in feeling the walls. The texture intrigued her. "

"Thanks. Mom said I made a convincing shark." He glanced away, his eyes aimed where his mother stood with Sydney running her hands along the rocks. "Any time her son is on the program, she's there to cheer him on."

"I can tell she's proud." McKenna moved closer to her daughter, Sydney glancing up at her. "What will she do when you leave for Alaska?"

"Pout. Pace. Pray." He shrugged, inclining his head to the left. "That's what she always does when I leave town."

"She didn't seem too happy about you leaving." McKenna stretched her hand toward Sydney, signaling her to come closer.

Rudy smiled, tickling Sydney's chin as she leaned against McKenna. "No. Mom saw a program on television about crabbing in the Bering Sea and realized I was in the same place. She's terrified something awful will happen. She can't watch the program any more. Gives her nightmares." He squeezed Sydney's shoulder. "I promised her I wouldn't do any more stints in Alaska, so she's upset that I agreed to this one. But I'm only going for six weeks this time to help finish out the season. The contract came this morning. My supervisor is stuck, and I feel obligated to help him out."

"I'll check in on her while you're gone." McKenna lifted Sydney against her shoulder. "I enjoy her company. With my mom halfway around the world, it's nice to have someone her age to rely on."

"By the time I get back she'll have you pouting, pacing, and praying."

Livy approached them. "You two want to see more of the aquarium or talk about a mother concerned for her son's safety?"

McKenna grinned. "Sydney will enjoy the otters in the pools. Shall we head there first?"

Rudy nodded. "And then we can visit the puffins. There's plenty of those where I'm going."

"Not what I want to hear, Rudy." The older woman squinted at him, her mouth set in a pout.

"It's only for six weeks, Mom." Rudy dipped his chin, as if trying to appear sympathetic. "I couldn't leave the agency hanging."

"Instead, you break your promise to me by going again to Alaska. The agency gets their man, I get more grey hairs. Soon I will look like an old woman."

"You'll always be young and full of life to me."

Livy shook her head. "You are in God's hands."

CHAPTER EIGHT

"Sydney, look. Otter!" Leaning on a rocky promontory, Rudy pulled the little girl close to him and pointed through an opening in the cave wall surrounding the otter tank. All of the outside aquatic exhibits were situated in a series of rock formations made to look like scenes from the shoreline, boulders arranged as if the ocean had set them in place. "He's floating on his back for you!'

The child stared at the foggy glass as the otter floated by, the animal's eyes and whiskers turned toward his audience, a seasoned performer playing to the crowd. Sydney touched the glass and the otter flipped over, letting his sleek backside slide in front of the window separating him from the onlookers. He turned once again in a graceful rotation and swam back up to the opening in the rock.

Like most otters Rudy had seen, the animal's mouth curved upward as if smiling at his adoring fans.

Sydney remained spellbound, hands flapping as the animal finished his performance. With a flip of his tail, he slithered away in the water, head emerging at the surface several feet beyond where he'd been.

"Otter." Sydney pressed her hands flat against the Plexiglas, her breath leaving a cloud on the surface. "Otter swim."

"That's right, otter swim." Rudy stood and smiled at McKenna, setting Sydney down. "Did you hear the state of local otters in the presentation this morning?"

"Sad." His mother stooped and squinted at the otter chasing his mate near the bottom of the enclosure. "I didn't know otters were in danger here."

"I think the kids were really listening to that part, though I missed much of it." McKenna reached for Sydney's hand. "I had to stay near the exit when the children arrived. I feared they'd get too noisy for Sydney."

"The sound levels come with the territory." Rudy led them out of the damp rock outcropping, their shoes crunching on the gravel path. "Something about a shark chasing its prey makes them shriek."

"Which was my signal to take Sydney out." McKenna smiled. "But your advice about protecting wetlands and natural habitat was quite interesting. I learned a lot."

"If we can educate the public, fewer animals will wind up like these otters."

"I wonder if they hate their captivity." McKenna adjusted the tote on her shoulder. "Always swimming in a figure eight."

"Considering otters on the north Pacific coast are non-existent, I doubt it."

"Non-existent?" His mother frowned and pointed. "Those aren't figments of my imagination."

"There hasn't been a native otter seen on our coast since the turn of the last century." Rudy thumbed toward the animals gliding by the glass. "These otters are imports."

"That's the part I missed. What happened?" McKenna's brows rose. "Were they hunted?"

"Yes, but more tragically, the otters were hit by plagues. They died out."

"That's sad."

"True, though." Rudy gestured down the path. "Shall we try the bird pen next?"

"Do they fly around inside?" Worry lines inched above McKenna's eyebrows, her cheeks pink.

"They're seabirds mostly. They flip and dive in the water."

Rudy led them to the enclosed aviary. He opened the wired gate and let the women pass through with Sydney, then followed them inside, closing the second gate behind him.

Inside, aquarium volunteers instructed visitors about the differences in the birds. A tufted puffin strutted along a rock eyeing Sydney as she stared at him. Caught in his game, the bird raised his wing and tucked his knobby orange beak inside. When his head reappeared, Sydney's hands flapped in excitement.

"Look at the bird swim." Rudy pointed to a common murre at the edge of the pond emerging from a dive in the water.

Sydney watched as a second bird plopped and disappeared beneath the water's surface. When the murre's head popped up again, Sydney's hands flapped nonstop as the feathered swimmer slipped out of the water and climbed up beside his mate.

"Sydney is enjoying herself." McKenna smiled as they continued around the enclosed aviary, weaving in and out of the path of other aquarium visitors.

When they reached the gate, Rudy let them pass and took Sydney's hand. "Do you think she'd get claustrophobic in the underwater exhibit?"

McKenna frowned. "Underwater?"

"You walk through the aquarium in a Plexiglas tunnel with water all around you. Fish swim above, below, around and through."

"Is there an easy exit?"

"You can leave by way of a side tunnel or go back the way you came, but you pretty much have to walk all the way through "

"I don't know." McKenna's brows sagged, lines carving tracks in her forehead. "We can try it, I guess. Is it as noisy as the program this morning?"

"Only people noise."

McKenna didn't speak for a minute, obviously unsure of what to do.

"Tell you what." Rudy moved toward the woman, arm outstretched. "If Sydney starts to have trouble, I'll whisk her out." He extended his hand. "Deal?"

"You haven't carried her out screaming and kicking." McKenna's eyes darkened, her expression filled with warning. "You may not know what you're getting into."

"I've a pretty good idea." Rudy popped a smile. At her questioning expression, he grew uncomfortable. How much of his history should he tell her? Though she would learn of it eventually, now wasn't the time. He opted for a change of scenery and stood. "Let's go explore the undersea exhibit."

The crowd had thinned when they entered the long, concrete passageway leading to the Plexiglas channels. Sydney quieted, the walls of the tunnel looming large around her small frame as they walked through.

Rudy kept his gaze on the child, watching for signs of distress.

Her face stoic, Sydney moved forward into the area of transparent windows, an unreadable storm in her eyes as she glanced about. Below her feet, sharks swam along the aquarium floor. Sydney minced her way along the tube, hand clutching her mother's. She'd tucked her chin against her shoulder like the puffin had buried his beak earlier.

His mother followed behind, whispering quiet persuasion to the little girl.

Rudy led McKenna toward the smaller tanks, smiling at Sydney and encouraging her. The child stared, unseeing, her small face set as she watched fish glide beside her, flashing their tails as they swam up over the top of the tunnel.

"So far, so good?" Rudy forced himself to sound positive.

McKenna didn't look convinced. "I'm waiting for the other shoe to drop." Her smile remained frozen, an anxious sag tilted her mouth.

"Have faith, McKenna." Rudy relaxed as they neared the end of the Plexiglas tunnel. "She's doing all right."

As if she heard him, Sydney covered her ears, spun on her heel, and ran back the way she'd come. Her feet slapped the ground as she hurried, darting in and out of clusters of people milling along the tanks.

"Sydney, wait!" Rudy sprinted after the child, McKenna right behind him.

Sydney didn't look back, her legs at full speed. As she left the Plexiglas floor she slipped and fell, catching herself before she hit the concrete full force. Someone nearby held out his hand to help, but the girl wailed, jumped to her feet, and started running again.

Rudy darted through the crowd, excusing himself as he hurried to catch the crying child. Right as she was about to leave the tunnel and run up the ramp leading to the rest of the exhibits, he caught her and swooped her up into his grasp, holding her close to his chest. She continued to scream as he carried her out the entrance, face red and tear-stained. Two people entering the exhibit stared. Others exchanged watchful glances as he turned the corner at the top of the passageway.

"Sydney, let's find a beach." Rudy kissed her cheek, though the chance of being heard in the midst of the crying seemed impossible. He tried again, this time a little louder. "Sydney, beach." As if a switch had been flipped, the child stopped sobbing and stared at him, her rigid body relaxing in his grip.

"Rudy, beach." She hiccupped, a sniff making her eyes water.

"Good girl." He kissed her forehead. "Good, good, girl." He pivoted in the direction they had come and found McKenna walking up the ramp behind him, lines of mascara streaking her cheeks. He held out his free arm to her, keeping Sydney close to his chest with the other, and wrapped McKenna in a quick hug to assure her. "You were right." He gave her a gentle squeeze. "I do have a lot to learn."

She swiped at her eyes, smiled up at him, and shook her head. "No. You always seem to know what to do." Her body trembling, she leaned into his shoulder, cheeks pink as she stumbled over her words. "You need to be gift-wrapped, like a present I always wanted, but never got." She reached for her daughter, her gaze averted. "I'm sorry. I shouldn't have said that. Thank you for the rescue."

He gazed into her eyes, the temptation to comfort her and let her know he cared making his heart pound. He couldn't do that. She was another man's wife. He breathed deep, fighting to control his racing pulse. His resolve deepened. He'd find Dane Nichols and send him packing. For home. As soon as he could.

"Is she all right?" His mother came hurrying up the corridor, shoes clicking on the pavement. "I thought the place caught on fire, the way you two hurried out of there."

"Sydney got scared, Mom."

"Poor child." His mother glanced around. "What's next on this excursion?"

"Beach." Sydney stared at Rudy. "Beach."

Rudy laughed. "She's like comic relief, isn't she?"

McKenna nodded, setting Sydney down. "I warned you."

Rudy knelt before Sydney. "How would you like a sandwich with that beach?"

"Beach." Sydney repeated.

"Okay, let's grab a bite at the cafeteria and walk down the hiking path." Rudy lifted Sydney and gestured for the other two to follow him. "We'll find a beach there."

"Hiking path?" The two women echoed him in unison.

"There's an exploratory trail we can follow which will take Sydney to the sand and a little water. I believe there's a bench to sit on and we can have lunch while we *beach*." Rudy tipped his head the direction of the cafeteria. "I'm hungry after that sprint."

McKenna smiled. "Only if you let me buy."

"Nah, I'll take care of it." His mother reached in her purse. "Lunch is on me."

McKenna protested. "It's the least I can do for you after rescuing my child from the tomb of terror!"

"Never argue with Mom when it comes to food." Rudy winked. "You'll lose every time."

McKenna blushed. "Let's go find lunch."

The concrete bench sat gathering sunshine as Rudy led them to the edge of the small wetlands area nearby. Setting the drink carrier down, he pointed. An egret stood, statuesque and looking suspicious, his eyes trained on the four strangers. Sydney flapped her hands at the sight of the bird.

McKenna and his mother found places at the end of the seat while he and Sydney stepped into the small circle of sand surrounding the structure.

Rudy bent down and lifted a handful of pebbles for the child to inspect. "Look. Beach." He rubbed his fingers in the small mound, making a circular pattern.

Sydney took the sand and let it drift over her palm, each grain part of the veil of tiny rocks that splayed from her hand. She squinted, eyelashes blinking rapidly as if she counted each piece of gravel. When the particles were gone, she stared at Rudy. "More?"

Rudy scooped another handful and funneled the sand into her waiting palm. This time Sydney sifted the sand through her fingers, her free hand flapping slowly as she watched. Rudy hugged her and pointed. "Lunch time."

McKenna patted a spot beside her, rattling the bag of food in her hands, and Sydney joined her.

Sitting at the other end, his mother let out a contented sigh. "Such a peaceful spot."

"Most visitors miss this little hideaway." Rudy squeezed in between them, a curious gull squawking nearby.

"The concrete is warm." Mom swept her hands across the rough surface. "Perfect place to relax."

"Not to mention eat our sandwiches." Rudy rubbed his palms together, ridding his skin of any remaining debris. "Hunger is rumbling in my middle."

McKenna opened the bag, removed a wrapped sandwich, and handed it to him. She reached in again and offered his mother a second bundle.

He inspected the tops of the drinks and found the root beer soda he'd chosen for himself and stuffed the straw into his lid. He passed the other cups to McKenna. "Aren't you going to eat?"

"As soon as I find my chicken salad sandwich." She turned to Sydney. "Corn dog?"

The child glanced up from where she was swinging her legs, kicking sand with her toes. Her amber eyes squinted at her mother, the sun directly above McKenna's head, then gazed at him. Eyeing the offered food, Sydney snuggled closer. She took the corn dog from McKenna and nibbled at its end.

"Yummy?" Rudy gave the child a hug. Though she stiffened at his touch, a twinkle glimmered when she looked at him. "Do you like mustard?"

"Mustard?" McKenna reached in the bag and pulled out a packet of the yellow condiment. "You thought of everything, didn't you?"

Mom nodded. "With Sydney, I'm learning to anticipate the next challenge."

"You're both fast studies." McKenna grinned at Rudy and pulled the corner off the packet, dribbling mustard on the end of the corn dog. "Or you have secret training I don't."

Sydney watched, fascinated, as the yellow spice inched its way along the side of her lunch. With a tenuous lick of her tongue, she lapped the mustard off, and then puckered her mouth. Her eyes glistened as she swallowed and reached for her drink. She held her corn dog up for more.

McKenna emptied the packet. "Take a bite, Sydney, and the mustard won't taste so spicy."

Rudy grinned at the scene before him and bit into his turkey sandwich. "Are you anxious for school to start?"

McKenna paused, giving herself time to chew. "I haven't let myself think too much about it. First, I have to shoot my friend's wedding on Labor Day weekend." She nibbled at a second bite. "After that, I can concentrate on school." She gazed out over the wetlands. "Sydney does so much better here at the ocean, I'm hoping she will do well in school, too."

"I'm willing to bet she'll do fine." Rudy popped the last bite in his mouth. "I'll check in for a full report when I get back."

"You leave Monday?" His mother tossed her wrapper into the waste receptacle.

"Yep, Labor Day."

"Sydney's birthday is that week, too." McKenna thumbed the mustard off Sydney's chin. "She missed the kindergarten deadline by five days, for which I was glad. But that set the stage for the grades to follow. She needs the extra year."

"It's a pivotal day for all of us." Rudy smiled. "I leave for Dutch Harbor, McKenna attends a wedding, and Mom pouts, paces, and prays."

"Smarty pants." His mother made noise with her straw.

"The stories I've heard about working in the north make me nervous. Dane told me his, and you've shared a few of your own."

McKenna wrapped the rest of her sandwich and tossed it in the garbage. "You're sure you want to do this again?"

"No, if the truth were known, I don't. But the agency supervisor is in a bind and needs me. I'm helping a friend."

McKenna grew silent for a moment as she sipped her drink, her straw making raspy noises as it neared the bottom of the cup. She glanced at him. "Well, I hope you stay safe while you're on the Bering Sea." She wiped Sydney's mouth with a napkin. "When you return to the coast, we want to have you over to dinner. We can celebrate Sydney's birthday together."

"I'll look forward to it." Rudy glanced out over the rocky shoreline. The reunion he planned when he returned, with another man in tow, grew in his mind. Finding Dane would be his gift to McKenna and Sydney.

CHAPTER NINE

Warm air greeted McKenna as if she'd driven into the mouth of an active volcano almost the minute she drove over Badger Mountain and descended toward the valley floor, headed away from the coast. She'd only left this area in July, but already she'd forgotten how high temperatures could soar here, having been spoiled by the cool coastal breezes. The throng of people gathered outside the chapel for her friend's wedding kept McKenna busy snapping pictures before the service. What Julia had deemed a small, intimate affair among her closest acquaintances had morphed into quite a solid body of supporters. Clusters of well-wishers took advantage of the church's manicured grounds, the grass and trees offering a reprieve from the valley's hot temperatures.

McKenna wasn't surprised by the crowd. Julia's long journey to this special day had filled the prayers of many for a long time. Widowed while pregnant with her second child, Julia had resisted all attempts to help her heal. Resolved to go on alone, Julia returned to the University about the time McKenna had enrolled. Both majoring in journalism studies, they'd become fast friends. While Dane spent time away fishing, she and Julia had often taken time out for dinner and a movie. When Sydney came along, Julia offered tips on mothering, and often the two of them swapped babysitting nights, giving each other a reprieve from the challenges of single parenting. When Doug walked into their classroom the beginning of winter term, McKenna picked him out for Julia, long before her friend showed any interest in the man.

McKenna left the garden area and entered the small worship center, lifting her camera to shoot images of the flowers and the candelabras. The windows were opened along the side walls, allowing a slight breeze through the room. Two fans ran near the front. Once filled with people, this room's temperature might become uncomfortable, especially for the wedding party dressed in formal attire.

As if on cue with her thoughts, Doug entered from the side door, dressed in a tux. The tall, former soldier laid a guitar on a chair before glancing up and noticing her. He raised a hand in greeting, walking her direction. "McKenna. How's life on the Oregon coast?"

"Breezy. Cool. Smells like ocean." McKenna lowered her camera to her side and approached the stage. "Are you ready for the valley to cool off?"

"We've had quite a summer." Doug stopped in front of her. "Julia is wishing for rain. I spent enough time in the Middle East that I don't notice this weather as much."

McKenna nodded toward the guitar. "You sing?"

"In the shower." Doug wiggled his fingers. "But I do play, so Ricky and I planned a surprise for Julia."

"Sounds terrific." McKenna's attention shifted to a boy a few years older than Sydney who came in through the side door and joined them. "Is this Ricky?"

At Doug's nod, Ricky's smile broke into a crooked grin. "Hi." He took Doug's hand and beamed up at him. "Today we begin life as a family."

Doug wrapped an arm around the child. "Yes, now you and I will join Julia and her kids as one unit."

"We wrote a song." Ricky beamed, a confident miniature of his father. "It's called 'We are the Allen clan.'"

"How wonderful." McKenna lifted her camera. "You want to play a little for me with your dad, so I can get a picture?"

Doug nodded. "Sure, we could use a warm-up. You might recognize the tune from "We are family, brother, sister, mama and me. We sort of borrowed a few bars." He moved back to the platform and sat on the stool, one knee propped up on a crossbar, guitar in his lap.

Ricky stood to his right, hand on his father's shoulder. With an instrumental introduction, the duo broke into song, "We are the Allen clan. Mother, sister, brother and Dad."

McKenna laughed. "You're right. I do recognize it. Great choice."

"We're going to blend into one big melting pot." Ricky spread his arms wide. "You won't know where the Hughes family stops and the Allen family begins."

"Your mom and dad might even add a few to the clan." McKenna winked at Doug. "You never know what God has planned for your family."

Ricky's eyes grew round. "I never thought of more." He glanced at Doug beside him. "I'd take another brother."

Doug's laughter filled the room. "No more sisters?"

"Because Heather is three years older than me, she thinks she's in charge." Ricky's face sported frown lines along his forehead and around his mouth. "It isn't fair."

Doug hugged his son. "We'll get things sorted out after the wedding. You'll see."

Sounds of people finding their way to seats drew McKenna's attention. She glanced back at Doug and Ricky. "I better go finish shots of Julia and her bridesmaids. Can't have a wedding without them."

She followed the hallway leading to the ladies dressing room. Giggles and shrieks sounded through the door. She knocked. "Photographer here. Is everybody decent?"

Julia opened the door. "You made it." She linked arms with McKenna. "Ladies, I want you to meet McKenna Nichols, one of my dearest friends and a great photographer."

Greetings stirred from different parts of the room. A young girl, dressed in sea mist blue and white eyelet, stepped from behind a screen. "Hi, McKenna."

"When did you grow up and become a lady?" McKenna set her camera on a chair and wrapped her arm around Julia's daughter, Heather. "I remember when you helped me rock Sydney to sleep."

"That was a while ago." Julia laughed. "She's thirteen now. She's my junior bridesmaid and her brother's chaperone."

"They say time flies." McKenna gazed back at her friend, dressed in a simple, off-the-shoulder gown with tiny seed pearls adorning the bodice. "You look absolutely ravishing."

"Think Doug will like it?"

"If he doesn't, he needs his eyes checked." McKenna squeezed Julia's hand. "I just saw him in the worship center. He looks every bit as handsome as you are beautiful."

"Who's got Sydney?" Julia's brow rose in a question.

"I left her with the mother of one of her school friends from here. They'll be fine."

"Is she going to like the Newport school?"

"We'll find out on Wednesday." McKenna folded her hands. "Pray hard." She retrieved her camera from the chair where she'd left it. "I need to get a few dressing room photos. You and the girls together."

Julia nodded, gesturing for the maid of honor, the two bridesmaids, and Heather to gather around her. For the next ten minutes, McKenna shot many different poses. In one Julia sat, with her bridesmaids helping adjust the garter on her thigh. In another the three women encircled Julia, hugging each other like sisters. When McKenna had twenty images, including one with Julia's daughter leaning into her mother's shoulder, she stopped. "I better go find my place in the worship center. Wouldn't want to miss your grand entrances."

The women waved, dispersing to their personal areas, adjusting hair ribbons and gathering up bouquets.

McKenna found her reserved spot on the front row and laid her equipment bag on the chair. She edged herself into place along the back pew, waiting for Julia's appearance. Soon the string quartet broke into a musical bridge and the first bridesmaid entered, fingers on the groomsman's forearm. As the wedding party proceeded to the front, McKenna scooted to the side and knelt, catching several angles of each couple.

When Julia arrived on her father's arm, McKenna focused her lens on Doug, delighted when the groom's face lit up like a candle-laden holiday wreath. His smile could not have stretched any wider.

Julia's cheeks were flushed, her eyes moist with tears, a white-knuckled grip on her father's elbow. She stared back at the man at the front of the church, a tiny smile on her lips.

Ahead of her, Heather took the lead down the aisle, dropping flower petals to the right and left, pausing every step or two to pull her younger brother back up beside her. The boy's red hair and freckles captured the crowd's attention, people in every pew smiling as he passed their row. He beamed back, the bow tie at his throat and the satin pillow in his hands both bouncing like the comb on a turkey strutting across the barnyard.

McKenna followed at a discreet distance, walking on the far side of the pews, catching the action one frame at a time. When all were standing in prim order at the front of the church, McKenna found her front row seat and snapped pictures as the bride and groom exchanged rings. She swallowed, the words of the pastor falling like hailstones on her fragile heart.

"God made man and saw he needed a helpmate. He didn't create another plant, nor another animal. He didn't give him another man. He created woman to be at his side, to support him through life's trials, to share the joys life's journey brings. She was not his servant, nor his master. She was his equal, a gift to be treasured, cared for, and loved. He was to lead her, watching out for her every need—physical, emotional, and spiritual.

"Julia and Doug, you both have faced some of life's most difficult lessons, each losing your first loves to tragedy. But God, in his mercy, has looked down and offered you love again. Cherish this second chance at happiness, blend your families, and make them into one unit, a strong and capable household that will weather future storms together.

"Therefore, God said, let a man leave his father and his mother and cling to his wife and they will become one flesh. What God has brought together, let no one put asunder."

McKenna sniffed, holding the camera close to her face to hide the moisture trickling down her cheeks. She needed Dane's protection, strength, and love. The pastor's words cut deep, the knife of her pain stemming from Dane's absence. He only saw the physical side of his responsibility—keeping her fed and sheltered. Emotionally and spiritually, she lived in a state of drought. Her heart ached to be held. Her prayers seemed to fall on deaf ears.

What am I supposed to do, God? I'm so alone. So forgotten. I want to honor my marriage vows by remaining faithful, but I don't know if I'm strong enough to endure the everlasting loneliness in which I am imprisoned. I need to be freed of these bonds. Please bring Dane home. Sydney needs a father in her life. Help us. I'm falling apart.

The strum of a guitar string brought McKenna back to the service. Doug and Ricky were at their place on the stage, as they'd been earlier, grinning at Julia as they sang. The bride giggled, covering her mouth with the back of her hand. Beside her, mouth agape, Julia's daughter Heather clapped her hands in rhythm to the familiar beat. Her brother wiggled with abandon, his pixie grin and freckles lighting up his entire face. The satin pillow in his hand waved like a tambourine in the air. McKenna grinned as the scenario unfolded, catching every moment with her lens.

The crowd clapped when the pair finished, and Ricky joined his grandparents on the first pew.

Julia dabbed at the corners of her eyes as Doug wrapped her in his arms. Knowing the woman like McKenna did, her friend's happiness overwhelmed her.

"I pronounce you man and wife, husband and father, mother and helpmate. You may kiss the bride." The pastor chuckled as Doug tipped Julia, pressing a kiss to her lips. "The Allen clan is now joined together."

McKenna snapped a picture as the couple kissed, then slipped down the side aisle. Standing at the back, she snapped several shots of the newlyweds as they came down the aisle. Satisfied, she walked out the side door and hurried to get ahead of the bridal party before they entered the reception area. Snapping picture after picture, she followed the group to the fellowship room where smells of hot coffee, spicy cocktail sausages, and other undeterminable delicacies wafted from the serving tables.

The bride and groom took their places in the receiving line, with the rest of the wedding entourage following suit. McKenna found a place to the side where she could catch both the face of the bride and groom as well as their well-wishers with her lens.

"Julia, you did it!" A woman dressed in a bright blue suit with a matching hat and feathers, found her way to the head of the line and wrapped the beautiful bride in a hug. "I'm so happy for you."

McKenna put the lens to her eye, capturing the exuberant guest as she appeared to swallow up Julia in one big embrace. Beaming, the older woman strutted on down the line, her hat bobbing in time to her steps. Her chattering aimed at no one in particular, she laughed and exclaimed at each new group of people, as if she were reacquainting herself with old friends.

Julia looked up and caught McKenna's attention. "As soon as

this line dwindles, I want to talk with you more." Julia nodded toward the corner of the room. "Come to our table. I made sure you had a place to sit near me."

"I doubt I'll be sitting any time soon, Jules." McKenna flashed her camera. "Your wedding guests won't wait for you and me to talk."

"Just try. Okay?"

McKenna nodded and wandered through the crowd. Clusters of guests gathered here and there around the room. She snapped pictures of friends in conversation, people in line for food, and children with their hands in the candy dish. The noise of the wedding party rose in volume as guests reacquainted themselves with people they hadn't spoken with in a while. The cacophony of sounds pressed in on McKenna, making her head ache and her hands tremble. What was wrong with her? She'd always loved big parties and cheerful people. But the activity and the noise made the room blur around her, as if she stood alone in its center.

Is this how Sydney feels?

Her daughter couldn't stand crowds like this, would turn inside out if taken into a room full of chattering people. Avoiding those kinds of situations for the past few years for the sake of her baby girl had left McKenna unconditioned for the chaos a gathering like this could create. She longed for the quiet of a windswept beach, the soft murmur of an ocean as the tide receded, and the occasional cry of a lonely gull. How different her view of the world had become.

As the wedding party lulled to a low roar, McKenna slipped through the crowd to the corner where Julia and Doug were sharing a piece of wedding cake.

Julia's attention diverted when she glimpsed McKenna coming toward her. She pressed the wedding cake to her groom's mouth, missing by an inch and smashing the icing into his chin.

McKenna caught the shot a split second before Doug grabbed a napkin and wiped his face clean.

Giggling, Julia motioned McKenna closer, drawing her to the side of the table as Doug finished cleaning up the frosting. "I wanted to get an update on life in Newport." Julia touched her hand. "You were as much of an influence on this wedding as anyone, putting up with all my whining about this new man in my life." Julia smiled. "Have you heard anything from Dane?"

McKenna shook her head. "Nothing. But I believe God put someone in my life to help me find Dane. And even more unbelievable, he leaves for Dutch Harbor on Monday."

"Monday?"

"Yes. It's a long story. One you will have a hard time believing, trust me. He's got Dane's picture, and he took a recent one of Sydney with him. He works as an observer biologist for the government, sampling the fish catches on the boats."

"No kidding?"

"Nope. He will be on and off several boats and said he'd keep an eye out for Dane."

"He won't punch Dane in the nose, will he?" Julia cast her a sly smile. "That's what the lame brain deserves."

"No. Rudy is a true-blue kind of guy. He loves Sydney and thinks her daddy should love her, too."

"Well, he should!"

"I know, but convincing Dane he can have any influence on his daughter's condition will take another man's influence." McKenna dipped her chin up and down, thinking of Rudy's gentle way with people. "If any man can change Dane's attitude, it's Rudy. He's really one of a kind. I am blessed God put him in my life."

Julia studied her. "You have feelings for this guy?"

"Not in the way you mean." McKenna shook her head. "He told me the first week we met he would do nothing to violate the sacred vows Dane and I made to each other. And he's kept his promise.

Julia, you have no idea."

"I'd like to meet him sometime." Julia smiled as Doug came up beside her and wrapped his arms about her shoulders. "He sounds like the kind of guy we all need to know, because he's a straight shooter."

"Well, maybe you will." McKenna sighed. "Better yet, we need to find him a wife."

"Whoa. Does he know you're already playing matchmaker?"

"No. But I'm kind of protective. He needs a very special woman." McKenna nudged her friend. "And we know how good I am at finding people who are meant to be together."

Doug leaned his chin on Julia's shoulder. "I'd say you are very good at what you do. I'm glad I had you on my team when Julia and I met. I didn't ever think I'd break through the door to her heart."

"You simply needed an accomplice from the inside, Doug." McKenna grinned at the groom. "My bill is in the mail."

"You are worth every penny."

"Now if Rudy can do the same for Dane, I'm repaid."

Julia squeezed her fingers. "Doug and I will be praying."

McKenna forced a smile. If only God were listening.

CHAPTER TEN

THE DUFFEL BAG HIT THE BEDROOM floor with a thump. Rudy bent to unzip the wrinkled canvas, pulling out the corners in order to cram each vacant space. He grabbed a stack of flannel shirts and tucked them into a deep pocket. Socks and bars of soap were stuffed into boots wrapped in plastic. Folding his heavy coat into the container's end, he wedged three stocking caps and two pair of heavy gloves into the empty folds of the jacket. Thermal underwear and a medical kit lay across the bottom.

A knock sounded at his front door, followed by the squeak of the hinge as someone stepped inside and called from the entry. "Rudy, you here?"

"In the bedroom, Mom."

The sound of footsteps padding down the hallway made him glance up.

His mother's small frame paused at the doorway. "You leave tomorrow?" A frown wrinkled her brow and the fixed smile suggested she was trying to be strong. "I will miss you."

"It's just for six weeks." Rudy finished packing the duffel and zipped it closed. "Hatfield expects me back the third week of October to start port inspections."

"Want me to check on your house while you're gone?"

"Not much to keep an eye on." Rudy's gaze skimmed over the sparsely furnished room—bed, dresser, and closet. The rest of the house contained more of the same. "No plants to water or fish to feed."

"No, just fish to catch, along with cold, pneumonia, and flu."

"The snowy season probably won't get much of a start while I'm there. I won't even get a good wind burn."

Mom bit her lip. "You'll still be on the Bering Sea."

Rudy turned and went to her. "It's a lot safer than you think." He wrapped his arms around her shoulders. "I expect to be on a catcher processor. They're bigger and more stable. I will return."

"From your lips to God's ears." She touched his chin and tweaked his cheek. "I will pray every day. I couldn't bear to lose you."

Rudy glanced away. His mother had already endured enough losses in her life. He didn't want to complicate things by becoming a victim himself. He stepped back and gazed into her eyes. "I *will* be careful."

Sea-Tac was bustling when Rudy's plane landed, the airport's congestion annoying him as he dodged travelers on his way to the shuttle. The duffel didn't fit on the luggage cart and his sleeping bag kept tipping over, dumping his belongings in a thud against the floor. When at last he boarded the transport, his body relaxed as the vehicle wound through familiar streets to Pacific Sea Observer headquarters near the Seattle harbor.

The apartment the company maintained for its employees while they waited for planes to Alaska appeared dark. Was he the only one shipping out in the middle of the fishing season? Probably. Hoisting his duffel to his back, he grabbed the sleeping bag in his free hand, climbed the stairs to the door, and punched in the entry code. With a click the lock opened and Rudy entered. The place appeared to have been cleaned, which meant the last crew of observers had been gone a while, confirming his earlier suspicions.

He checked the fridge and found it empty, as well as the pantry. Stashing his belongings in one corner of the back bedroom, he retraced his steps out the door and down the street. A good Asian restaurant stood two blocks away. Rudy's mouth watered at the memory. Maybe Chan still worked there. He and the short, plump cook had gotten acquainted on his last trip to Seattle. Chan loved to hear the stories about catching fish on the Bering Sea, as if he lived the adventure vicariously through Rudy's tales. The more Rudy told, the bigger the plate of food Chan dished out. Rudy never left hungry, giving new meaning to the old adage of singing for his supper.

The bright red and green neon sign glittered in the late afternoon dusk as Rudy hurried to the restaurant's door. The place seemed quiet, but he'd arrived ahead of the evening crowd. If there were no observers waiting to ship north, the eatery might not hold more than a dozen patrons. The screen door squeaked as he entered and once his eyes became accustomed to the dimly lit interior, he saw Chan striding toward him.

"Hey, Chan. Long time no see."

The small man smiled, his grin lighting up his round, wrinkled face. "You on your way back to Alaska?"

Rudy nodded, the earnestness of the question making him grin. "Yep, my agency is short-handed, so they begged me to come work the end of the fall season."

Chan inclined his head. "By going in September, you'll not see snow?"

"Fine with me." Rudy pointed to the corner, moving that direction. "Is my favorite table still available?"

"Make yourself at home." Chan lifted his order pad. "You want the special?"

"Please." Rudy pulled out a chair and sat. "Your cooking is the only reason I agreed to work again. I knew I'd pass through Seattle and get to eat one of Chan's famous platters."

Chan laughed. "I'll be right back." The cook rushed to the

kitchen, his apron strings fluttering in his wake.

Soon a small Asian woman appeared in the doorway, a tray with a teapot, cup, and bowl in her hands. She approached his table, smiling, setting the carrier down and raising the teapot. She poured a tiny round teacup full and set it before him. Lifting a large bowl from the tray, steam rising from the soup inside, she set it beside the tea.

"Thank you, miss. Your egg flower soup is the best along the harbor."

A dimple graced her cheek. "Enjoy."

Rudy glanced up at the squeak of the screen door out front.

Two men, dressed in flannel shirts, jeans, and boots, entered the restaurant and found a table. They both wore knit caps, pulling off the headwear when they sat down. One sported blond hair, cut short, and the other, salt-and-pepper black, the caps a sure sign of seasoned fishermen.

Rudy looked them over, trying to decide if they might be part of a skeleton crew the agency had put together for this last month of fishing. He pulled the photo from his wallet and studied Dane's face, comparing the image to the two men across the restaurant. If Rudy were to guess, Dane rarely left Alaska, spending his free time in Anchorage. Though Alaskan winters were beautiful, a person could only appreciate so much white, and the temptation to venture to the lower forty-eight would be difficult to resist. Dane might be near.

Chan came through the kitchen door, a platter in his hands. He set it in front of Rudy with a flourish. "There you go—mar far chicken, almond chicken sub gum, pork fried rice, a pot sticker, and sweet and sour pork for my Alaskan fishing buddy."

Rudy smiled. "I'll sleep well tonight."

"When will you ship out?"

"Wednesday, if all goes as planned. I have to check in and get my orders tomorrow, review any new procedures, and pick up my hazard suit." Rudy sighed. "Then it's off to Anchorage and if the weather cooperates, I'll be in Dutch Harbor Wednesday night. More likely sometime Thursday."

"Not much time for adventure stories."

"Not this trip." Rudy thrust his fork into the almond chicken. "But when I come back, I promise you I will bring new stories and share them."

"You make me happy. You and your stories."

"You make me happier. You and your platters."

The cook beamed. "I have two more fishermen who come in. I go. I cook. You eat. Be full."

"Before you leave, have you seen this man in your restaurant?" Rudy handed Dane's photo to the cook. "I have a message for him from his wife."

Chan's forehead wrinkled above his nose. He shook his head, giving the photo back. "He's not familiar. But many fishermen pass through here. Can't say he didn't."

"Thanks, Chan. You're a good man."

As Chan turned to wait on the other table, Rudy returned the photo to his wallet and picked up his fork. The flavors of the rice and the sweet and sour pork melded in his mouth. Rudy closed his eyes and savored the taste, letting each bite last as long as possible. He picked up a chicken strip and dunked it in the special sauce, then stuck his fork in the pot sticker. If his mother could see him now, she'd know he wasn't suffering—at least not yet.

CHAPTER ELEVEN

When Rudy landed Thursday morning, Dutch Harbor hadn't changed much since he'd last worked here. Situated on Amaknak Island, in the heart of the Aleutians, the town of Unalaska rimmed the harbor's shores. The Grand Aleutian Hotel stretched majestic and red in the distance, a sharp contrast to the long, low structures lining the main road. The smell of fish permeated the air. Every other structure, it seemed, waited for a fishing boat's catch, making Dutch Harbor one of the most important fishing ports in the world.

The green hillsides struck him as the most noticeable difference. He'd always worked the winter pollock season and sometimes garnered an additional tour through the spring. During those stints the landscape stretched white in all directions. But landing here the first week of September, everything previously buried under a deep snowpack now lay exposed—green and beautiful.

Dutch Harbor had been a military outpost during the Second World War, a place where troops could keep an eye on any Japanese who might drift through. The older buildings which greeted visitors may have been military barracks and had done nothing but age since his last visit. The area had been bombed. Rudy could still see the bunkers built against the hill.

Aleuts were the original inhabitants and made up the majority of natives. Rudy looked forward to visiting the Russian Orthodox Church in the center of town, a trek he made every time he worked a season. Now a national landmark, the structure once served as a bastion for missionaries sent to reach the indigenous people.

He lifted his duffel and sleeping bag and sauntered toward the

National Marine Fisheries Service office, the government group which everyone shortened to NMFS. In an often-complex triangle of interdependency, the fishing companies hired agencies like Pacific Seacoast Observers, which in turn recruited observers like himself, which were supplied to the government to train. The interrelationships reminded Rudy of the song which he remembered from his childhood—the knee bone connected to the thigh bone, which connected to the hip bone, and so on. Keeping it straight made him dizzy. He quickened his pace, anxious to get this stint started. His crew assignment and lodging accommodations needed confirmation.

To his right, bald eagles fought over garbage in a dumped can. The regal birds, whose wingspan could stretch as much as eight feet, looked more like dirty vagrants fighting for food among the leftovers discarded outside a popular restaurant.

A fox, an animal once imported for sport, disappeared behind the building, the fluff of its tail barely visible as the small creature headed for the hillside. Once winter settled in, their reddish coats would stand out, as this species didn't change color like some. No chance of camouflaging them against the frozen landscape.

In the harbor two fishing trawlers floated alongside a catcher processor. Surprised to see the larger vessel, Rudy glanced around the port looking for signs of a crew. The late pollock season didn't start until January—the bigger ship must be in port for maintenance. With that many ships in the bay, Rudy would have a difficult time checking out all the fishermen on shore before their boats left for fishing grounds again. He didn't want to disappoint McKenna, but his quest seemed daunting. Maybe he'd land a boat where Dane was a crewman. The odds were against it, but still he hoped.

As Rudy neared the NMFS headquarters, voices permeated the walls of the building, and he recognized Hawk Bishop's drawl inside. He shoved the door open and allowed his eyes to adjust to the dim interior.

A chuckle sounded somewhere to his left. "If this day wasn't bad enough, look what the cat dragged in."

"Hawk." Rudy nodded at his former instructor. "You're every bit as ugly as the last time I worked for you." Hawk Bishop had trained him in Seattle the first time Rudy went north. The man had traveled on to Dutch Harbor after the training program had been completed. Rudy considered Hawk one of his best contacts and a great friend.

"Probably uglier." Hawk slipped off his stool and traipsed to where Rudy stood. His right arm shot out, hand extended for a shake. "Nice to see you again."

Rudy eased the sleeping bag down on his feet, stopping the bulky mass from hitting the floor, and returned the man's grip. "How are things?"

"Except for being short-handed, fishing season is about up to par." Hawk pulled a chair out from a nearby table and nodded for him to do the same. "Mackerel started this week. We expect our tonnage to be above our predictions. But the bycatch is at five percent."

"Whoa. Talk about a dirty catch." Rudy's stomach lurched. A dirty bycatch meant a lot of fish would have to be thrown back because they weren't mackerel. "Us observer types will work our rear ends off." Rudy sat next to the big man. "My mother said she'd send a care package every week, but I told her I'd never get to eat it."

"What can I say?" Hawk leaned back in his chair. "I'm a slave driver endorsed by the US government. I can't control the fish who want to swim with strangers."

"Very funny." Rudy leaned against the table top. "Have you and the agency confirmed my assignment?"

"I'm putting you on the *Northern Star*. She's in the harbor now."

"Processor?" Rudy held his breath. Catcher processors were larger boats, but the catch almost always meant heavier deposits of fish to sample. An observer on those boats could work a sixteen-hour shift.

"No, it's a catcher only. We won't use the catcher processors for mackerel." Hawk's grin revealed a missing tooth since Rudy's last visit. "Which means you'll come ashore almost every evening."

"Who's the catcher processor out there sleeping?"

"The *Bering Explorer*. In port for supplies. They've already got an observer on board." Hawk drummed his fingers on the table. "Ninety ton a haul."

"When does the *Northern Star* leave?"

"Six bells."

"Tomorrow?"

"You can stow your stuff tonight. Captain's already on board and knows you're coming."

Rudy walked to the water's edge, keeping an eye out for any fisherman with brown hair and deep brown eyes. Not that he expected Dane to pop out of the lineup and extend his hand, but if the man were here, Rudy wanted to find him. He prayed he'd have the right words, should the opportunity arise—words Dane would accept, words Rudy wouldn't regret. He'd have to be careful.

The *Bering Explorer* bobbed in the water, its bow lapping against the tide. Though empty earlier, now crew members came and went up the gangplank, several carrying crates like ants stocking a nest. The galley probably needed supplies before the ship returned to sea. If the fishing went well, an observer could spend the entire month aboard this one boat and never see anyone but a handful of men.

More likely, the boat would stay out a week, return, and orders would change. Rudy preferred that scenario—giving him more opportunity to scan the sea of faces walking the shore. He didn't frequent bars at home, but in Dutch Harbor bars were often the only places with restaurants decent enough to serve good food. Crowds crammed the few eateries the town boasted. Impossible to find one fisherman in a chowder made of many.

He studied the crew members, hoping for a glimpse of a Caucasian male, but this boat teemed with African Americans, Samoans, and a handful of Hispanic origin. If nothing else, Dutch Harbor blended all nationalities into a force of fishermen.

His boat, the *Northern Star*, lay quiet in the water. Manned by no more than five fishermen, the smaller boat fished for shorter periods, routinely coming to shore to unload its catch. Working the smaller boat, he would have a better chance of seeing more people because he'd return to Dutch every day. Though his chances of encountering Dane remained a remote possibility, he held out hope. He might even get shore duty, which meant he'd see all the fishermen coming and going for the next month. If that happened and Dane were here, Rudy would find him.

CHAPTER TWELVE

Even though photographing her friend's wedding wrapped romance around McKenna's heart like cellophane on an Easter truffle, the drive back from the valley left her drained. Like a slow seep in a clogged sink, each mile brought her back to reality—her marriage, as empty of its joyful beginning as a shell tossed aside by a gull. Too many forgotten dreams. Dozens of unfulfilled promises. Only Rudy's quest to find Dane rekindled her hope. She clung to that.

Hitting her mattress as if she were a corpse, she slept in late Tuesday. When she heard Sydney stirring, she sat up, her fingers brushing sleep from her eyes. Today meant a visit to the school—playing the power struggle game with specialists who thought they knew the best classes for her daughter. Already her temples throbbed.

First, she had to drop by the gallery, pick up the weekend receipts, and check how Livy fared, now that Rudy was gone. The woman's depression had hovered like an impending storm when her son announced he was leaving for another tour on a fishing boat. Livy's unconditional love had harbored McKenna when she'd first arrived this summer. Repaying the favor and rescuing the woman from sorrow now fell to her—a deed she welcomed.

Sydney padded into the bedroom, smelling like she'd slept in a stable. Ick. Would the child ever outgrow the bedwetting?

McKenna led her to the bathroom and ran water in the tub, stripping off the soiled garments. She added raspberry bubble bath and left to change the bedding. Sydney's happy squeals as she created mountains of suds helped McKenna keep track of her daughter's play.

Breakfast ready, McKenna coaxed Sydney from the warm tub. Wrapping her in a big bath towel she carried her to the bedroom. "You smell much better." She dried Sydney and helped her shrug into clean clothes. Twenty minutes had disappeared when she finally led her to the kitchen. "Upsy, daisy." Once Sydney sat in her booster chair, McKenna zapped the stack of now cold silver-dollar pancakes in the microwave and set the warmed plate in front of her. "We'll visit your school today and see what kind of classes they found for you."

McKenna had attended public school in Newport, but she'd never needed special education from the district. She didn't know what to expect. In the valley, specialists hovered around every corner, waiting like hawks seeking prey. Sydney shuffled from one program to another. Names of speech therapists and trained aides loaded Sydney's Individualized Education Plan, but more complaints about her daughter's refusal to cooperate than progress reports found their way home. If Newport played by the same set of rules, McKenna resolved to teach Sydney herself.

Sydney finished eating, leaving two of the three pancakes untouched, and with a hand from McKenna, climbed down and trotted to her room. The sound of plastic rings clattering on the floor wafted down the hall. At least she was consistent. When ready to go, McKenna would find her plunked in the middle of the circles, soft babble barely audible as she sifted the colors through her fingers.

McKenna ate a quick bowl of cereal, dressed, and had applied her makeup when the phone rang. She hurried to the kitchen where she'd left her tote and dug in the bottom for the device before it stopped ringing.

"Mrs. Nichols?" The voice wasn't one she recognized. "This is Claire Simpson from Yaquina View Elementary. I'm the learning specialist."

"How can I help you?" A tingle spirited its way up McKenna's spine. "Did you receive Sydney's school file?"

"Yes, I did." The woman paused as the sound of papers shuffled in the background. "With school starting tomorrow, I wondered if you might be able to drop by today so we can discuss educational options for Sydney."

"I planned on coming by after lunch. Will one o'clock work?" McKenna glanced at the digital readout on the microwave. Not much time to get her errands done. "I have a couple of stops before I get there."

"One will be fine." Claire's voice rose in pitch, as if she were fighting to be polite. Or was McKenna's imagination playing tricks? "Check in at the office and the secretary will direct you."

Returning to her bedroom, McKenna slipped into shoes and grabbed a sweater. With the wind howling, the ocean's chill always found its way to her bones. She rummaged through her tote, checking the completed registration materials still tucked in the side pocket. Satisfied, she fingered the ignition key as she sought Sydney.

The rings spread in a pile at her feet, Sydney sat on the floor. She held a blue ring aloft, jabbering nonstop nonsense at the object. Suspending it at arm's length in front of her face, she bounced it in a half circle around her. She pulled the ring to her eye, squinting against the surface before tucking it against her chin.

McKenna cringed. She hadn't seen this behavior before. Would this be the self-stimulator to replace the flapping hands? Or would Sydney adopt both for different occasions? These tics, as they were called, were often progressive, manifesting themselves in different ways at various stages of an autistic child's life. Sydney had so far only exhibited one—the hands flapping at the wrists—but McKenna had been warned there'd be more.

"On to bigger and better things." With a sigh deep enough to fill a windsock, she reached for Sydney's jacket in the closet and held it out. "We're going for a ride."

Sydney grabbed another ring and smashed it against the blue one in her hand. She made both dance in front of her, completing the half-circle path she'd made before. She picked up a third.

McKenna held her temper, impatience boiling right below the bursting point. She held out the garment and counted. "One, two, *three.*"

On three, Sydney dropped the rings into the pile and stood, holding out her arms for the jacket sleeves.

McKenna zipped the coat and gave her daughter a squeeze. "Good girl." Her efforts to teach her daughter had paid off. On three, Sydney knew she meant business. A small victory in a sea of battles, but for McKenna the win represented a giant vote of confidence. She'd avoided a meltdown. Maybe she *could* succeed in her daughter's future. She grabbed her tote, lifted Sydney, and prayed her way out the door. *May all our other challenges today be this easy, Lord.* Locking the door and hurrying to her car, the warmth in her soul offset any chill in the air.

The gallery beckoned McKenna first. Parking in her private space, she dashed in to collect the receipts she needed while Sydney hurried to the children's table. The sound of crashing blocks filled the room. Why did her daughter always dump everything? McKenna caught herself, the upcoming meeting making her nervous. Wrestling with her weariness, she sighed. One more mess to pick up. She could do this.

Today Sasha Turner, a painter who created coastal landscapes with acrylics, managed the store. She stood when McKenna entered, her smile bright enough to rival any sun she might paint.

"What's up?" McKenna could only guess.

"My lighthouse sold." Sasha brought both hands together, her effort to contain her glee reminding McKenna of a puppy trying to stay seated. "The big one. With the storm scene."

"Fantastic!" McKenna raised her palm in a high five. "That was one of your higher-priced canvases and worth every penny." She rifled through the receipts. "Here it is." Pulling out the invoice, she faced Sasha. "Do you want an advance on your commission now or wait until I balance the books and make payment at the end of the month?"

"I could really use an advance." Sasha's smile sagged. "This is my only sale at any of the galleries so far this month."

"My standard advance is fifty dollars." McKenna studied the painter. "Will that hold you until the end of September?"

"It's better than nothing." Sasha stared at the floor.

"Tell you what." McKenna thumbed through the checkbook. "Since this is such a big sale, I'll advance you double. It's the best I can do until I check the bank statement and verify the buyer's funds."

"You're the best." Sasha hugged her. "You really care about those of us trying to survive as artists."

"The creative spirit is the heart of my business, don't forget." McKenna squeezed Sasha's shoulder. "Without artisans, *Lady Marie's* would be just another *for lease* sign in the window." She wrote the check. "I'm doubly glad you decided to leave some of your paintings here to add variety to our offerings. It's a win for both of us."

Handing Sasha the check, McKenna extricated Sydney from the box of blocks and they walked to the Tidewater Takeout. The pace quickened as her daughter realized where they were headed and pulled against her hand, the downhill trek a familiar one. Laughing,

McKenna held the door so they could both enter. Glancing around for some sign of life in the tiny café, McKenna found none.

Disappointment wrote notes on Sydney's face as her smile faded and her frown etched trails between her eyes.

McKenna led her to their table and they sat. Perhaps, with Rudy gone, Livy had traded days with another employee.

Soon mumbling sounded from behind the red, white, and blue curtain and Livy emerged, carrying a bundle of napkins and a package of paper towels. A cobweb hung from her right ear like a nightmarish piece of costume jewelry. Glimpsing Sydney and McKenna, she brightened. "Girls! How nice of you to come see me."

"Is that why you're mumbling back there?"

"No, the light is out in the pantry, and I had to stumble around in the dark to find napkins and paper towels. The storage area is kind of spooky without a light bulb."

McKenna reached up and picked the cobweb out of the woman's hair, shaking it off her fingers. "Yes, another month and you'd be ready for Halloween."

Livy stared at the grayish mass on the floor. "I hope that didn't come with any residents attached."

Startled, McKenna wiggled in place, swiping at her clothing like she was dusting an attic. "I don't see any eight-legged visitors crawling around."

"Thank goodness for that." Livy dug in her apron pocket for her order blank. "You girls want lunch?"

"Yes, please. We have to be at the elementary school by one o'clock. Sydney will have her usual, and I'll have a cup of soup and half a grilled cheese."

"What are you doing at the school, if I may be so nosy?"

"The learning specialist is meeting us to explore options for Sydney's education."

Livy raised an eyebrow. "You think they'll be able to

accommodate you? Sometimes these *options* the school offers are like placing a round peg in a square hole. Lots of corners to collect troubles."

"I hope not. I've been in that situation before." McKenna studied her daughter. "Sydney struggles with big classes and lots of noise. A smaller school district and fewer children may be the ticket for her success."

"Maybe so." Livy turned toward the counter. "I'll make your lunches. Be back soon."

While her daughter played with a couple of toothpicks, McKenna leaned against the soft, cushioned chair. She drummed her fingers against the table top, taking deep breaths to steady her racing pulse. The meeting ahead could go two directions. The specialist either had a heart for children with special needs and would work to place Sydney in the best possible situation, or the woman had a job to do and Sydney would land wherever it was easiest for the school district to meet its obligation. McKenna prayed for guidance, the choices falling to her. *I'm glad you're near, Father. All these decisions are difficult, and I have no one to help me.*

Livy appeared a few minutes later carrying Sydney's hamburger and fries as well as McKenna's sandwich on plates, one of which also balanced a cup of soup. "Here you go. I'll get your drinks and return."

When she reappeared with full glasses, Livy sat down in an adjacent chair. Her face, damp with perspiration, aimed at the door. "Rudy called last night. Said they hadn't had any snow yet, but a polar vortex was reported forming on the Bering Sea. They could see as much as a foot in the next few days."

"I thought the wind felt awfully cold for September." McKenna sipped her soup. "Don't we get the breezes off their storms here on the Pacific?"

"We do." Livy shook her head. "But he works in these storms.

They can't be safe. Fifty mile an hour gusts sometimes." She glanced up at McKenna. "I can't lose my boy."

Nor can I lose my husband. McKenna shivered. Dane fished on a boat, too. Any storm Rudy might encounter would also affect Dane. Would the title of widow be more complicated than the one she now wore? She didn't want to find out.

CHAPTER THIRTEEN

THE ELEMENTARY SCHOOL COULD EASILY HAVE passed for a shoe box, the long modular structure ending in a larger addition McKenna remembered as the gym. Except for the bright red lettering at the front of the building, the colors of gray and white rivaled a sea gull's feathers.

She parked in the visitor's slot and opened the back door for Sydney. Unbuckling the car seat, she helped her climb out. Taking her hand, she led the way into the building, stopping at the main office. Same double doors. Same beige paint. Same smell of little bodies and dirty tennis shoes.

"I'm here to see Claire Simpson." McKenna glanced around the busy office. With school starting tomorrow, a flurry of people worked at various tasks, from sorting files to inputting data on two computers in the corner.

The secretary picked up her phone and punched in a number. "Your name?"

"McKenna Nichols."

The woman repeated the information into the phone before hanging up. "Mrs. Nichols, let me grab your file and then you and your daughter can walk straight down the hallway behind you to the end and make a right. Claire's door is open and she's ready for you."

"Thanks." McKenna took the manila folder and led Sydney back out the door into the familiar hallways. When they arrived, a tall woman in khakis and a green shirt waited. "Hi, I'm Claire. Come on in."

The office, cramped for space, held two file cabinets and a small table encircled by four chairs. Claire pulled one out and offered it to Sydney, gesturing for McKenna to take one as well. Claire reached behind her and grabbed a stack of cardboard puzzles. "You want to pick one, Sydney? You take the pieces and put them back in the frame." She dumped one puzzle and handed the frame to Sydney who picked up a piece and locked it into place. "Good. Your mother and I need to talk, but when you finish that one, you can have another puzzle."

McKenna sat in stunned silence. So far, so good. This woman knew autistic children and their penchant for working puzzles. The simple act gave her hope that maybe here Sydney would find a niche to fill, a place to belong. She leaned back in her chair and relaxed.

"Mrs. Nichols, we have several options available to you for your daughter's education. We can offer her speech and language training with our specialist once a week. We have offsite tutors who work with our children in their homes. And we can place Sydney in the smallest first grade class with an aide."

"How large is the class?" McKenna squirmed in her chair, afraid of asking the wrong question. "Sydney is bothered by noise."

"We saw that on her transcript." Claire handed Sydney another puzzle, transferring the finished puzzle to the bottom of the stack. "We also noted her teacher labeled her bright." Claire ran her finger down the file in front of her. "Unlocking that potential will be our highest aim."

"The size of the class will make the difference." The power struggle hadn't shown up yet. Coming to Newport may have been the right decision, after all. McKenna's defensive armor whooshed, like a balloon losing its air.

"The smallest class is twenty students." Claire indicated a room across the hall. "We have two other challenged students in there, each with their own aide. There should be plenty of help."

"How new is the teacher?" The early education teacher in the valley had been touted as a highly educated professional, only to call McKenna on the first day and ask what made Sydney tick. The woman had been clueless when it came to the nature of autism, not to mention lacking experience. Kindergarten hadn't been much better.

"Her name is Andrea Mallard." Claire's eyes twinkled as she spoke the name. "She's been teaching here since she earned her credentials four years ago."

McKenna started. "Is she married to a guy named Stewart?"

"Yes. She came back to teach in the school where she grew up." Claire picked up her phone. "She said she knew you. Let me get her in here."

A minute later a woman with dark, curly hair and a thick middle stood in the doorway, her gaze fixed on McKenna, lips curled upward in a cheery smile. Though she'd matured, the cheerleader with whom McKenna had run around during their days at Newport High still wore the mischievous grin she'd sported in school. Graduating a year ahead of McKenna, she disappeared when she went to college and they'd had no contact since. "Surprise!"

"Andrea!" McKenna stood and greeted her former buddy and mentor. "I had no idea you had joined the staff."

"I know." Andrea giggled as she squeezed McKenna tight, gesturing to the classroom across the hall. "Claire, I'll take them with me."

The other woman nodded and extended her hand. "Nice to meet you, Mrs. Nichols."

"Thanks. Same here." She leaned over Sydney and whispered. "Come, sweetie. I want to show you something."

Sydney whined and pointed at the puzzle. "Pieces."

Andrea scooped up the leftovers and laid them on the cardboard frame. "She can take the puzzle with her and finish it there."

McKenna nodded her thanks and followed her friend across the hall.

"After all the antics you and I got into during high school, I was afraid they wouldn't let me teach here once I got my degree. But this makes my fourth year." Andrea patted her abdomen as they walked. "I'll be here through January and then I'll be joining the ranks of motherhood."

"Congratulations." McKenna figured the months in her head. "By the time your maternity leave begins, we'll know if Sydney is going to fit in a classroom or if I have to find an alternative."

"Well, just so you know, I plan to work as a tutor after I give birth." Andrea pulled a small chair out from a low table and offered it to Sydney. Taking the puzzle, she plopped it upside down in front of the child. She pointed to a larger table nearby. "I will be available to continue whatever programs we get started here at the school." As they sat side by side, Andrea fixed her gaze on McKenna. "I have some great curriculum ideas to help her learn."

"That sounds like an answer to prayer." McKenna's eyes burned. "Who's the aide?"

"A woman named Janice with whom I've worked before and who understands my methods. She will act like a tutor for Sydney under my direction." Andrea pressed a finger against McKenna's shoulder. "I plan to involve you in her education as well."

"I have considered homeschooling her."

"Great. As her mother, you understand her better than any of us." Andrea glanced Sydney's way, smiling as she worked the puzzle pieces into place. "Except for Dane, of course."

Lowering her gaze to avoid Andrea's, McKenna feigned fascination with the color of her shoes against the floor tiles.

"Dane's still in the picture, isn't he?" Andrea's tone held worry as McKenna struggled to answer, but the teacher pressed on. "With his love for little kids and Sydney being such a doll, I can't imagine you two not together anymore."

"He's a fisherman in Alaska." McKenna perused the tidy classroom, avoiding eye contact with her old friend. *I can't tell you anymore.*

"So you're doing the teaching." Andrea sounded relieved, though a glance at her face said she still had questions. "I know how resourceful you used to be."

"You mean at getting us into trouble?"

"Let's make that our secret." Andrea pulled out a day planner. "Tomorrow Sydney will start in this room."

McKenna nodded, the regimen of a school day fixed in her mind. A great beginning. If only the ending were guaranteed to be as smooth.

CHAPTER FOURTEEN

THE TRAWLER ROCKED AGAINST THE WAVES as the ocean tides ebbed around the ship. Rudy stood on deck gripping the rail, stomach lodged in his throat. He hadn't ridden in a boat in two years and had forgotten how the sea tossed its occupants like riders on a roller coaster. The Bering Sea's depth couldn't compare to larger bodies of water which made its swells far less massive, but still the rises and falls were great enough to make him nauseous.

As the boat heaved upward on the wave, his belly plummeted to his groin. The next instant the ship pitched downward like an anchor into the depths of the surge, his innards left clinging to his esophagus. The sudden lurches from empty to full and back again forced frequent swallows as he attempted to keep his breakfast. What a waste if he didn't. The meal had been a good one.

"You doing okay, Taylor?" The captain's gaze probed him from head to toe. "Lost your sea legs since you were last here?"

"I'll regain them in a couple of days." Rudy swallowed again, midsection fluttering as the ship descended into the surf one more time. "The tilt of the sea hasn't bothered me much before."

"We'll be fishing in another hour." The captain's focus scouted the horizon. "You'll be off the deck then, the roll of the waves out of your vision. Won't help, but you'll be out of the wind." He lifted his hand to shade his eyes as he stared out over the water. "Unless we get more bad weather and have to port out the storm."

"I heard there were twenty-foot rollers here last week." Rudy studied the dark, black surface beyond them, the menacing coldness sending a shiver along his spine. He pulled his knit cap lower over his ears. "Must have been some storm."

"Earliest I've seen so much turbulence." The captain clasped his shoulder. "Makes the mackerel that much harder to find."

"And the bycatch that much dirtier." Rudy groaned to himself, thinking of the work involved in getting a good sample. What kinds of peculiarities would he discover in this year's hauls? Sometimes the mix of fish and the numbers of species not meant for the net were astounding. He could feel the fatigue already mounting, and he hadn't even begun.

When the trawler slowed, Rudy found his station in the wheelhouse. The first catch arrived, the cable straining under the weight. Fish soon covered the deck and spread into the tank as the fishermen struggled to contain the haul. Rudy walked into the fray, carrying his waterproof worksheets and his scale. He lifted what he considered a reasonable sample and counted the various species, checking for mammals and other sea life not meant to be caught. He weighed the mass, recording his estimate of the first drag's overall poundage. A salmon poked out of the heap of wiggling bodies. He cut a section of the scales, taking them off close to the lateral lines, then flung the fish overboard. He collected his samples carefully, recording the statistics, and putting the tissues into a collection envelope.

The next haul lacked anything significant. A lump sucker lay round and pale on top of the mass of fish. The grotesque mouth and eyes protruding from the oval body reminded Rudy of something from a recent horror movie, its sinister music playing in his head. He gathered a tissue sample and recorded the size. The trawler creaked under the weight of the catch, and the morning passed in a blur.

"Taylor! Grub!"

The captain's call came as welcome relief midday. Rudy's abdomen still lurched at the toss of the boat, but warm food and company sounded like a much-needed reprieve. He joined the three other crewmen in the galley and filled his plate. Sitting at the end of the table, he greeted his companions.

"How's the catch looking today?" A black man spoke around a mouthful of food. His white-toothed grin in the middle of his windswept face emphasized the redness rimming his dark eyes. He leered at Rudy, a gaze that anywhere else might have meant don't mess with him. But sailors on these vessels worked in cooperation with one another, following an unwritten code which hung over their heads. Getting along kept your job. Troublemakers didn't fish long.

Rudy shrugged and pointed at his plate. "About as good as this food, which is quite tasty."

The man's eyes fixed on Rudy for a minute before he smirked and cast a glance at his companion across the table. Rudy had seen controlled animosity in crews before. Observer biologists like himself were government employees and therefore open to mistrust. Fishing was big business and nobody wanted any flags laid on their profits. An observer's report could foul a lucrative day's efforts, which meant loss of revenue and time. He'd have to be careful not to rile the man.

"How's the chow?" The captain sat beside him, his plate heaped with ham, eggs, fried potatoes, and onions. He plunked his coffee cup on the table and sank his fork into his food.

"Hot meals out here are always appreciated." Rudy grasped his mug, warming his fingers around the steaming brew. "How many more dips today?"

"Have you looked north lately?" The captain pointed his fork at the darkening sky. "We're dragging now and as soon as we put this net in the tank, we're heading for shore. We'll be outrunning what looks to be a sizeable storm."

Rudy studied the mass of angry black clouds riding the horizon. Not something any of them needed to see. Storms on the Bering Sea were not infrequent, but suffering through one on a loaded trawler didn't appeal to him. He scraped his plate clean and stood. "Guess I'd better get my work done, then. I don't want to hold us up from going home."

Outside, the net strained under the load, and Rudy waited for the cable to lift the bulging lump of sea life aboard. The crane hovered over the middle of the stow only seconds before it dumped the contents into the tanks. Rudy pulled away a sample from the middle, groaning when what looked to be a Northern Rock Sole plopped out on top. He'd hoped the catch would be nothing but mackerel, but in an ocean this size stray species were bound to find the net. Reporting those anomalies fit his job description.

The sea grew rougher as the *Northern Star* chugged as fast as it could back to Dutch Harbor. Rudy had collected all the samples time allowed before the tanks were closed. When he reached port, the rest of his observations would begin. He anticipated a full day of standing over the catch, sorting out the keepers from the throwaways, getting exact poundage, and sizing up any other anomalies he found in the haul. The storm would buy him time, forcing the *Northern Star* to remain at port until the seas calmed. He could use the layover to explore the pubs and other eateries in hopes of glimpsing Dane. McKenna and Sydney's future depended on Rudy's success.

Sleet hit two hours into the trip back, bits of ice hammering at the window of the wheelhouse and making the deck slick. The sailors grabbed for anything that could keep them safe aboard ship. As the temperatures dropped, hazards rose. Rudy gave thanks he could stay inside, the sailing of the ship not connected to his reason to be on board. The swells grew deeper, propelling the boat higher in the water and dropping it lower into the waves. Rudy's stomach remained agitated, the threat of losing his meal a constant companion.

Darkness settled over the horizon as the *Northern Star* sailed into the bay. A collective sigh of relief passed through the crew, the hours of battling the storm and staying afloat reflected on their drawn and chapped faces. The gangplank was lowered and those not involved in the transport of the fish to the cannery clamored for solid ground beneath their feet. Rudy followed, certain his legs had turned to rubber en route to shore. Someone clapped him on his shoulder.

"We'll see you on board Monday." The captain studied him, as if weighing his next words. "Hope to ship out again early."

"Yes, sir. I'll be finished with this haul tomorrow morning, and then I can catch some winks before I'm back on board with you."

"You observer types are a dedicated lot." The captain hoisted his britches up on his hips. "Losing sleep over a tank full of fish."

"Comes with the territory. We were warned when we signed on." Rudy extended his hand. "Nice sailing with you."

"See you Monday."

Sunday night, Rudy poked at his fish and chips, his fatigue competing with his hunger. He'd worked all Saturday night and well into the dawn of Sunday before he'd finished his reports for the *Northern Star*. Sleep eluded him at first, his overtired body aching from the repetitive motion of slicing open specimens and recording their last meals. Or gathering their fins. Or whatever procedure each species not part of the intended school required. Hands throbbing and eyes as dry as sandpaper, he finally drifted off about noon and slept until his empty middle woke him.

He glanced around the pub, studying the faces of those who were there chowing down or collecting news of the most recent hauls and fishing spots. About half were fishermen who had weathered many a season, laborers dedicated to bringing home the catch. Others were younger colleagues like himself, guys who hoped to make a decent living while they put themselves through school in the off season. Those from other countries filled in the rest—South Africans, Hispanics, and Samoans here to make money. Lots of it.

A rowdy group caught his attention. The leader, a tall and broad-shouldered blond, cracked a joke about something they'd witnessed on a previous tour. The guy described how a halibut landed in the middle of the boat, presumed dead, only to come alive when the load had been lowered into the brig. Rudy had heard of that happening, though he'd never been on board when the giant creatures resurrected themselves. He'd only witnessed the huge halibut who got caught in the wrong net and wound up being thrown overboard to the seals as food.

A taller, thinner fellow joined the laughter with his own version. He lifted his knife and proceeded to slice the air as if cutting fillets, only to have the creature jump off the conveyor. With short claps of his hands, the man mimed the marine animal hopping away from him, the slimy mass squirming like a writhing snake across the boat. The rest of the crew howled. The man pulled off his cap and dropped it, stomping with his foot. "He tried to get away from me, he did, but I had the last grab."

Rudy's head jerked up. The man, Caucasian, glanced his way for just a second while describing his encounter with the halibut, returning to face his friends. The nose, the eyes, the chin, caught Rudy's attention. He pulled his wallet from his pocket and slipped Dane's picture out into the light. Though he couldn't be certain in the dim surroundings, Rudy's gut churned at sight of the second fisherman. Had he found Dane?

"Do you need more coffee, sir?" The waiter stood beside him, pot in hand. He eyed Rudy's uneaten food. "Do you not like your meal?"

"Yes, I like it. I'm just tired." He feigned a smile, picking up his fork. "I'm moving slow today."

"You want me to warm it up for you?" The waiter extended his arm. "Take a minute."

"Uh, sure. That would be nice." He leaned back and waited as the fellow reached for his plate. When he returned, Rudy pointed at the noisy sailors. "You know which boat those fellows are working?"

The waiter followed where his outstretched fingers indicated. "Yeah, they're from the *Bering Explorer*."

"I thought that boat wasn't fishing yet." Rudy wrinkled his brow at this information. The news conflicted with what Hawk had told him his first day here.

"I heard they were called in yesterday after the ship went out for a test run." The plate clattered as it settled on the table. "This is a little warmer. Didn't want you to burn your tongue."

"Thanks. That's thoughtful of you." Rudy focused his attention on the rowdy men still cracking jokes across the room.

"Enjoy."

Rudy lifted his fork, scanning the sailor group again for a certain dark-eyed man.

The next morning Rudy woke to the sound of his phone ringing. Checking the caller ID on the screen, he sat up. Hawk. At this hour? "Sending me home already?" Rudy yawned into the speaker. "I thought I was leaving with the *Northern Star* this morning."

"Change of personnel. I've already cleared this with your agency." Hawk sounded weary, his teasing tone missing, no doubt shed in a flurry of responsibilities. "Lost another observer to influenza. I'm assigning you to the *Bering Explorer*."

Rudy blinked awake. No way. "When do they board?" The news couldn't have been better. He sat on the edge of his bed. Goosebumps covered his arms.

"Today at noon." Hawk coughed into the phone. "Sorry about that." He cleared his throat. "You'll report to the captain, Lance Rogers, as soon as you can get your gear together." He coughed again.

"You're not getting the flu, too, are you?"

"Nah, I'm too briny." Hawk managed a snort before he wheezed. "My problem is one too many smokes."

"Be careful, Hawk." Rudy couldn't imagine the big man sick. "Cigarettes and influenza are a deadly combination."

"So are observers and the Bering Sea." Hawk paused, clearing his throat for the third time. "This boat is an old catcher processor and has had problems, so keep a watchful eye on exits in case of an emergency."

"Well, if it tips over, I'll be at the top." Dead, but at the top. The reality niggled at him.

"Not funny, Taylor. Not funny at all."

For once, he agreed with Hawk.

An hour later, after lifting his duffel and sleeping bag into the trunk, Rudy rode in a taxi to the waterfront. As the vehicle pulled up in front of the *Bering Explorer*, he paid the fare and hopped out. Grabbing his gear, he climbed the gangplank, glancing around for someone who might be the captain. He spotted the man minutes later, a clipboard in his hand as he inventoried the contents of a stack of boxes near him. Rudy approached and the man looked up.

"Captain Rogers?" He extended his hand. "Rudy Taylor, Pacific Seacoast Groundfish observers."

"Taylor. Right. Hawk said he had a replacement for me." The man shook hands and pushed his cap back with the tip of his pencil. "Have you worked a catcher processor before?"

"Yes, sir. The *Aurora Borealis* was my last ship."

"Great vessel. This one's about the same as the *Aurora*. Your work station is on the bottom. Galley's in the middle. Day shift is yours, if you want it. Stow your gear in the last cubicle."

"Thanks." Rudy shifted his belongings to his other shoulder and twisted toward the stairs. Crew members busy about the boat allowed him to pass on his way to the sleeping quarters. He found his bunk, the small quarters he would share in rotation with the second observer, each missing the other en route to their shifts.

Confident he'd secured his stuff beneath the bunk space, he followed the smell of coffee and cooking food to the galley. Tables were half-filled as he entered, the lunch rush midway in progress. He studied the other crew members in the room, trying to guess which of them was the one other observer and which were new recruits. The group he'd seen at the pub huddled together in a corner, an occasional outburst of laughter coming from the same blond fisherman who'd kept the stories flowing the previous evening. Rudy scanned the faces of the others with him, looking for the darker fellow he'd thought resembled Dane Nichols. Today the man had vanished. Maybe he wasn't part of this crew. Disappointment gnawed at Rudy. Finding a lone fisherman in a city filled with them would be no ordinary task.

He headed to the food line, picked up a plate, and considered the various choices before him. Plate full, he zeroed in on a corner table near the door where he could be invisible. He bowed his head, picked up his fork, and ate at leisure, all the while keeping his attention on the sea of bodies in the room.

A heavily tattooed fellow, head wrapped in a red-and-yellow bandana and left ear sporting an earring, approached from the back of the room. Though Rudy didn't know him, the man's gaze penetrated his and the purposeful stride toward Rudy made him nervous. He glanced around to see if any others sat in the vicinity, but he remained the solitary diner in the corner. The sailor spoke to different ones as he passed them, but his attention remained focused on Rudy. As the big guy reached the table, he broke into a wide grin, a day's growth of beard shadowing his jaw. "Hey, there. I'm Gonzales." He stuck out his meaty palm, the little finger missing its top joint.

"Taylor." Rudy stood and grasped the outstretched hand—muscled, calloused, and confident. "Nice to meet you." *Where did these characters come from?*

Gonzales gestured for him to sit, grabbing a side chair beside him. "I saw you bow your head over your food a few minutes ago, and I said to myself, you must walk in faith."

"Yeah. I'm a believer in Christ." *Last time he worked a boat, his beliefs hadn't created any trouble. Nor should it this time.* Pulse rising, Rudy waited for the big man to get to his point.

"I lead a Bible study every night after dinner, here in the galley, and I wanted to invite you to join us when you can."

Rudy fought the urge to gasp, forcing a smile. "Hey, thanks. I'm one of the observers on board. My shifts don't always coincide with those of other crew members, but I'm glad to be included." He inclined his head. "How many from a crew like this attend?"

"You'd be surprised. Up here we face life and death situations all the time. We think about our destinies a lot more when eternity could find us tomorrow."

"I hadn't thought of it in those terms before." Rudy swallowed, stunned by the man's honesty. "I'll be there whenever the fish let me escape."

Laughing like a jolly giant, Gonzales stood. His intent, dark chocolate eyes sparkled beneath eyebrows that locked like caterpillars ready to cocoon. He grinned as if he'd crawled inside Rudy's head. "I like you, Taylor. You'll be good for the crew."

"Thanks, I look forward to knowing all of you better." Rudy picked up his fork. "Thanks again for the invitation." As the man walked away, Rudy resisted asking him if he knew Dane. If Dane were aboard, he didn't want word of his inquiry to get back to the man and put him on his guard.

Waving his hand, Gonzales turned and headed out the galley door, his big bulk making clunking noises as his feet crossed the floor. At first glance the man wasn't someone with whom anyone would want to tangle. Yet beneath the colorful exterior lived another believer and he seemed like a decent guy. Maybe Gonzales would prove to be a friend. A fisherman and an observer—friends. Stranger things had happened.

Not realizing he'd been holding his breath, Rudy exhaled a rush of air. He lifted a bite of scrambled eggs to his mouth, the cold, greasy forkful a reminder of how soon the food aboard ship cooled. He washed the remainder of his plate down with swallows of hot coffee. The dark brown brew remained a staple among the men, if he could escape the observer post long enough to get any. Rudy slumped as he recalled the long hours of other tours. Not always possible to get away. Truth be told, coffee almost never happened for him.

CHAPTER FIFTEEN

McKenna drove Sydney to class the first day of school, hands white-knuckled as she gripped the steering wheel. Though a bus was encouraged and provided, her daughter's confidence needed bolstering any way possible. With the trials of last year's schooldays fresh in her memory, McKenna determined to help her child cope if it meant sitting in the classroom the entire session. She parked, killed the engine, and stepped out. She took Sydney by the hand, then they entered the building and marched to the end of the hall. When they reached Andrea's classroom, McKenna ushered her daughter into the room with a firm grip on the back of her coat collar. Only then did she breathe.

Andrea smiled, crossing the room at a brisk pace and bending down to Sydney's level. "Good morning, Sydney. I'm glad you came. Coat off?"

Sydney leaned into McKenna, gaze on the floor. Her hands flapped in an erratic rhythm, and her head bobbed left to right as she rocked.

When Andrea stretched her hand to touch Sydney's shoulder, McKenna winced, waiting. Here we go. Meltdown pending. Prepare to plug your ears.

"Coat off?" Andrea repeated, giving the collar a little pull and managing to slide the coat off Sydney's shoulder. "Let's hang it." Andrea stood and took Sydney's hand, leading her to the coat hooks. Professional. Empathetic. Friend. Andrea pointed to one dowel painted bright blue. "Sydney's." Guiding the child's hand to the hook, Andrea helped her snag the collar on the balled end. "Good."

McKenna relaxed as Andrea took charge. She used short sentences, met Sydney at eye level, and waited to let each direction be absorbed by Sydney's brain. If they made it through today, tomorrow Sydney would repeat the routine without prompting. Like saving a file on a hard drive, an autistic child followed procedures verbatim. The teacher had to get everything in the exact order she wanted things done because the child would repeat each step like a robot. The phenomenon never failed to amaze McKenna.

Andrea had read the memo.

She led Sydney to a school desk near the front row. The chairs faced the white boards and sat in the middle of the alcove. "School supplies?" Andrea glanced at McKenna, eyebrows raised.

McKenna jolted to life, the bag in her hand filled with the necessary materials. She hurried to the front of the room and handed the sack to her daughter.

Andrea opened the top of the desk and let Sydney peer inside. "Let's put your supplies in here." Popping the bag open, Andrea lifted out a ruler. "Nice ruler." She pointed to the rest of the contents. "Put your crayons away."

Within minutes, Sydney had emptied the sack into the desk.

Andrea helped her arrange them in neat order, then handed McKenna the bag. "Mommy is going to take the bag home." Andrea pointed. "Here comes Sydney's special friend, Janice."

McKenna turned and waited while a woman in her mid-forties walked to where they stood. Round-faced, with hair graying at the temples, she studied Sydney, a quiet smile in place.

"Good morning." Janice knelt, as Andrea had, in front of Sydney. "I'm Janice." She paused, waiting for Sydney to glance up. When nothing happened, Janice lifted Sydney's chin. She stared off to the right, but Janice continued to hold her gaze. "We'll have fun together."

McKenna's eyes watered. This just might work. Blessed by the two women's expertise, and at Andrea's nod, she backed away from her daughter. "Have fun." Before Sydney could turn this into a meltdown, McKenna pivoted away from the threesome and walked to the door. She glanced over her shoulder. Sydney had climbed into her chair. Hope beat a new song in McKenna's chest.

That afternoon McKenna waited on the corner for the school bus like a fisherman with a line in the water, hoping the hook would produce a live one.

Andrea had called at noon to reassure her Sydney had made it through the morning with only one meltdown. A boy next to her had rushed past her desk and knocked her watercolors on the floor. "She left the room with Janice." Andrea continued to calm McKenna's fears, telling her Sydney was spending time in the project corner, building a tall edifice she called a Christmas tree.

McKenna closed her eyes, imagining the scene, and smiled. No surprise there.

A half hour ago, Andrea called again and asked if she could put Sydney on her special bus for the ride home. "The more routine we build into her first day, the easier the rest of the year will be for all of us."

McKenna agreed, unable to swallow the lump in her throat as she waited for the bus to arrive. Above her, clouds drifted in lazy patterns and the unmistakable smell of a changing tide wafted from the beach, the shifting wind carrying the scent of rain in its wake.

Soon the short, yellow vehicle rounded the corner and chugged down the street to her stop. A piercing wail split the calm, the familiar pitch zapping her heart. Any remaining hope McKenna might have had fluttered away and joined the crows begging at a sand-covered picnic table right down the street. The bus doors opened and an attendant stepped out, helping Sydney climb down. "You show your mother what a big girl you are and stop your crying." The attendant pointed at McKenna and gave Sydney a slight push on the shoulder before climbing back aboard.

Tears covered Sydney's face. Sobs wracked her body. She stomped past McKenna and headed up the driveway. Reaching the car parked near the garage, Sydney banged it with her fist, letting out another loud wail. Her hands went wild as she continued to hit the vehicle, her cries growing louder and more desperate. A minute later, she stepped onto the sidewalk leading to the house, trotted up to the porch, and plopped down on the steps.

McKenna followed, sitting on the cement beside her. She wrapped an arm around Sydney, feeling the heat of her daughter's frustration through the yellow capris and green tank top. She let her cry, singing their bedtime lullaby to calm her. Half an hour passed before the tears subsided and the sobs stopped. Sydney drew in a ragged breath, sighs punctuated by a hiccup. She stared into the yard, unseeing, the spasms of her diaphragm and the deep intakes of air the only sound telling McKenna she still breathed.

McKenna stopped singing and waited.

Sydney remained silent, head nodding against McKenna's arm.

She stroked her daughter's forehead and rocked the trembling body. The ache in her mother's heart threatened to tear her in two.

Why?

For a day Andrea had said went well, the child in McKenna's arms suggested a different scenario. What had happened?

Sydney sat beside her limp, spirit spent, breathing irregular.

In the time between the phone call from Andrea at noon and the bus ride home something traumatic must have happened.

Her imagination taking flight, McKenna's phone vibrated in her pocket. Taking it out, she grimaced. Andrea.

"How is Sydney this afternoon?" Andrea's voice was cheerful and upbeat. "Did she manage the bus ride okay?"

McKenna bit her lip, not sure what to tell her friend. Both of them had so wanted this experience to be a good one for Sydney. "I don't know what happened. Sydney came home totally upset. I've spent the last half hour sitting on the porch listening to her cry. She's still shaking."

Andrea's groan resonated into the phone. "I shouldn't have pushed her to ride the bus. I thought she'd like the adventure. But I could tell as she boarded she didn't want to go."

"Why? What did she do?"

"She kept saying, 'blue car'." Andrea's sigh sounded as defeated as Sydney looked beside McKenna. "Is your car blue?"

"Yes." McKenna closed her eyes, angry at herself for not having thought of this before. She should have known. "She rode to school in the car. She expected to ride home the same way. That's the way she is."

"Can you transport her every day?" Andrea's tone had returned to the professional one McKenna had heard at the school. "The inconvenience won't be overwhelming?"

She's not giving up? McKenna couldn't believe what Andrea was saying. Dane could learn a lesson or two from their friend. "If riding in the car makes the difference between Sydney having a good day at school and a bad one, driving her is the least I can do."

"Is she always an independent spirit?" The fatigue in the woman's voice punctuated the question. Sydney hadn't been the only one who suffered today.

McKenna glanced down at her daughter, now asleep against her shoulder and smiled. "She wrote the book."

A couple of hours later, a knock sounded at McKenna's door. She reduced the heat under the pot of spaghetti and went to see who'd come. Opening the door, she greeted Livy who had tucked a bag under her arm. The troops had arrived.

"Come in." She stepped back and gestured for the woman to enter the kitchen. "I've got spaghetti cooking. It's Sydney's favorite. Would you care to join us? I'm sure there's plenty."

"I don't want to interrupt your dinner. I wanted to see how the little munchkin's day at school went."

Seeing Livy's kind face, McKenna wanted to fall into her arms and bawl. She trusted her friend to understand if she described the nightmare of her day. To listen as she whined about her disappointment. Anything to unload the pain she carried inside.

Instead, she forced a smile. "You aren't interrupting us. We could use the company." McKenna pointed to Sydney sitting in the corner of the living room, sorting a stack of books. "She's still recovering."

Livy walked to the corner, bent over Sydney, and smiled. "Hello, precious."

Sydney didn't respond. Her sober expression remained, a pair of eyes locked in a sea of frowns as her face scrunched up to cry. Wetness covered her cheeks and strangled sobs made her shake.

"Oh, sweetheart." With amazing agility, Livy dropped down on the floor beside the child and drew her into her arms. "McKenna, you get the dinner. Sydney and I need a little cuddle time."

McKenna fought the tears forming at the corners of her eyes. Can I have some, too? Sydney had spent the last two hours withdrawing—from McKenna, from her favorite things, from life. The happy child who had searched her sticker book yesterday had transformed to the sullen creature now sitting on the living room floor. All she'd done for two hours was push the stack of books around on the floor, not one of them opened to a page or a picture. If one day at school had done this to her, what would be left of the child by the end of the week? McKenna needed to scream. This was too hard. Dane, why aren't you here?

The spaghetti simmered on the stove when she returned to the kitchen, the noodles plump and tender. McKenna drained the pasta, and set the colander aside while she found three plates. Placing the dinnerware on the table, she dished out portions for Sydney, Livy, and herself, adding spoonfuls of sauce to the top of each mound. She retrieved the salad from the refrigerator and the garlic bread from the warming oven.

McKenna stuck her head into the other room. "Dinner's on the table, if you two are ready to join me."

Livy stood and offered her hand to Sydney.

When the pair walked to the kitchen, Sydney climbed on the stepstool to wash her hands, looking at Livy.

The woman nodded her approval, handing Sydney a towel to dry.

"It's spaghetti, your favorite." McKenna smiled at her daughter, hoping to get some reaction, a ray of sunshine in the midst of her gloom. Even a glare would be nice.

Sydney climbed into her chair and picked up her fork. "Sghetti."

Livy winked at McKenna, a lift of her eyebrows speaking volumes.

McKenna fought the tears all over again.

Livy left after dinner, her parting words still echoing in McKenna's ears as she put Sydney to bed. "School can happen anywhere. Sydney is bright, but the communal classroom may not be the best choice for her."

"I'm not a teacher, Livy." She stared in the hall mirror. A wilted, bedraggled shell of a woman she didn't recognize stared back. Today she wasn't anything.

"Nonsense, you are a smart and clever woman." Livy shrugged into her coat. "You said Andrea is willing to help you when she starts maternity leave. I'm available for respite. I've been known to write a letter or two myself."

"You'd teach?" McKenna lowered her chin and frowned, certain her suspicion was evident on her face. Not the response she'd expected.

"I'll teach kitchen duties. I'm off-duty most afternoons and no one comes in." Livy smiled, making sweeping motions with her hands as if she buttered bread. "Sydney can help me sort containers. We'll work outside of the food preparation area."

"But the gallery needs me there at least three days a week." McKenna's argument sounded feeble, her resistance to the idea of teaching her daughter losing ground in the woman's knowing gaze. "What do I do those days?"

"Teach Sydney from the paintings. Let her experience her world through the pictures." Livy nodded as if she could already see the outcome and reached for the doorknob. "Autistics learn through their eyes." With a wave and a grin, she turned to the door and left—argument suspended.

McKenna smiled at the memory as she pulled the blanket up over Sydney and sang her goodnight lullaby. She kissed her daughter on the forehead and prayed she'd have a better time tomorrow. Snapping the night light on, she left the room, unsure what morning would bring. Another day like this one and Livy would win her argument, hands down.

Once inside her office, McKenna booted the computer and launched the internet search engine. She typed 'home school curriculum' in the browser and surfed the sites which popped onto the screen. Dozens. Too many choices to count. Already overwhelmed, McKenna prayed again for the school situation. It had to work.

The kitchen phone rang, the wall device on which McKenna had learned her numbers. The square white box had hung to the left of the cupboards since her parents built the house twenty years before. Most of their friends reached them through that number. Mom and Dad insisted the landline remain in the house while they were touring Europe. They'd wanted a phone they could always call and be assured of getting through, even if they reached the answering machine and had to leave a message. Mom had set pickup on the eighth ring. She hurried to answer anyway. "Hey, Mom."

"Hello, darling. Are you enjoying Newport again?"

McKenna hesitated. This was not the time to be truthful. Play nice. "It's great to be back, though I don't know anyone anymore. How are you and Dad doing, seeing the world?"

Her mother laughed. "All we've seen so far is London. We leave for Paris tomorrow. Your father's cough returned about a week ago, and we had to find an inhaler."

"Must be all the London fog." McKenna pressed her lips together, enjoying the chuckle she heard returned in the phone. "Is he all right?"

"He's much better. We're scheduled to relax on the Mediterranean in two weeks. I'm sure the climate there will clear up his lungs." Her mother paused. "If not, we'll head for home."

McKenna detected more than a hint of worry in her mother's voice. What wasn't she saying? Her parents had anticipated this adventure for so many years. To cut it short for health reasons didn't seem fair. But Dad had always breathed better in a coastal climate. Could he be in danger?

Her mother hurried on, as if anxious to change subjects. "How's

Sydney doing in school?"

"She just endured her first day. And to say it didn't go well is an understatement. I'm so depressed I can't think straight."

"You have done an amazing job with that child." Her mother's voice sounded ragged, as if she were experiencing McKenna's grief. "Your father and I are quite proud of you. Don't give up, sweetheart. Sydney's worth the effort."

Like healing balm from a decanter of oil, her mother's words soothed her aching heart. "Thanks, Mom. I'm so glad you called." McKenna straightened, strength returning to her lifeless spirit. "The good news is my old friend from high school, Andrea Miller Mallard, is Sydney's first grade teacher. The district has provided an aide. I'm praying for better times tomorrow."

"As will I. I know it's tough going for you." Her mother's voice grew more serious. "Have you heard from Dane?"

"No." McKenna lifted her chin, rolling her head from side to side to release the tension needling her neck. "I talked with his parents briefly when I first arrived. They haven't heard from him either." Dane had made vanishing an art form.

"He still supporting you?"

"Yes." McKenna fought the urge to tell her mother about Rudy's search. But if his trip to Alaska produced no results, she'd raise her parents' hopes only to dash them one more time. Though they never voiced their opinions to her, they worried about her future with Sydney alone. McKenna tucked that information away for later. Maybe then she'd have better news.

"Well, darling, I better get off here. Your father says hello. We'll call you from the beaches of Italy next."

"Tell Dad to take care of his health." McKenna fought to speak, pulse pounding in her throat. "This trip is important, but not worth an asthmatic flare-up."

"He'll be okay. Don't worry."

Hearing her mother hedge, McKenna bit back a sudden wave of fear. "The coast here will clear him up in no time. He can come home whenever he wants." She'd end on a positive note. "Tell him the gallery is still making a profit, even though I'm not as adept at running it as he is."

"I'm sure you're managing well, McKenna. You've always been the independent one, clever at figuring out whatever needs to be accomplished, and then seeing it through. You're able to achieve whatever you put your mind to. Talk to you soon. Give Sydney a hug for us."

McKenna hung up the phone, her mother's last words echoing in her ears. *You're able to accomplish whatever you put your mind to.* Even teach my daughter? Mom, you don't know how much those words mean to me.

She returned to her computer where the homeschooling resource sites she'd researched before the phone call remained on the screen. She scrolled through a dozen or more, amazed at the information. Mind boggling. She opened a document to record the sites which seemed most suitable.

A half hour later, she awoke, her face pressed against the computer keyboard, a page of zzzz's marching across the screen. McKenna shook her head to clear the feeling of being besieged. Too many choices. Sorting through all the information available would take forever. Making the right decision for Sydney remained her highest priority. Her daughter's future might depend on it.

CHAPTER SIXTEEN

Hawk's words still echoing in his head, Rudy spent his first afternoon aboard the *Bering Explorer* familiarizing himself with the new vessel and scouting out all the exits. In the bunk room he opened his evacuation suit and practiced pulling it on. No matter how many times he'd done this, the task never got any easier. In an emergency, his struggles with the gear might cost him his life. Blocking the consequences from his mind, he headed out to orientation.

He followed the medic through the equipment stations, making notes of the protocol this crew followed. Now as he descended to the hatch, the familiar smells of human body odor and fish from previous seasons overwhelmed him. A catcher processor never rid itself of the stink of the cargo, all aspects of preserving fish done on board. This boat, being old, reeked. Nose burning and eyes watering, his acclimation to the stench would have to be fast or he'd be one of those leaving for medical reasons. Neither his agency supervisor nor Hawk would be pleased.

As the ship rocked on its journey to the designated fishing area, Rudy studied the hold around him, standing next to the observer table to get a sense of his surroundings. The conveyor belt lay silent, waiting for the first haul. The motion-compensating sensor scale stood nearby, and the pit for the fish stood open. He put his cache of forms and data recording sheets in a safe space near his table. Empty and silent, the area seemed to stand at attention awaiting orders as the crew prepared to get the tour underway. Rudy lingered in the quiet, aware this spot would never again be as undisturbed on this trip as it was right now.

Footsteps.

Rudy glanced over his shoulder. A young fellow, hair net in place and beard covered, nodded as he drew closer. Ah, the other guy.

"You Taylor?" The kid, whose youthful face suggested he'd recently graduated college, pulled off his glove and extended his hand. "I'm Jackson, the second observer. Captain said you'd be joining us on this run."

"Nice to meet you." Sensing the guy's hesitation, Rudy continued. "The captain didn't say which shift you preferred. Do you have one?"

Jackson gave a non-committal shrug. "Didn't think I had a choice. I'm a night owl by nature, but I can work days as well." He peeked up at Rudy. "You?"

"I'm happier with days than nights."

Jackson's face brightened. "Great! I'll work the nights for you."

"Have you met the bleeder yet?"

"Yeah, the day guy is experienced. Been fishing since high school. Nice enough." Jackson looked beyond Rudy's shoulder, lifting his chin in a jerk. "You can meet him. He's coming this way."

Rudy turned his gaze in the direction Jackson's glance indicated. A man in his late twenties approached, dark hair, darker brown eyes, and a knit cap the color of sable. Coming around the platform scale, he stretched to his full height, face lacking emotion, shoulders filling out the worn flannel shirt covering them. Rudy didn't need the picture in his wallet. Dane Nichols stood before him.

"You the new observer?" The man extended his hand, the calloused grip rough and dry against Rudy's fingers. "Dane Nichols. Bleeder."

"Rudy Taylor." Searching his mind for something to say that wouldn't suggest his quest, Rudy stuck with something simple.

"Been working the boats long?"

"I'm a permanent part of the scenery." Dane adjusted his cap, drawing the knitted band lower on his ears. "I came here out of high school, paid my way through college, and returned like I didn't know any better."

"You must love the ocean."

"Or I'm just plain stupid." Dane made a face.

"Experienced, at the least." Rudy nodded toward Jackson, smiling to reassure the other man of his jest. "Not like our little college preppie here."

"Hey. I resemble that remark." Jackson fist-bumped Dane. "Rudy's going to work days, so I'll be on nights now."

"You'll team with Chaffey, then." Dane frowned, his gaze aimed at the floor, as though thinking. He glanced at Jackson. "He doesn't speak much English, but you can figure out some hand motions to help him run the conveyor for you."

"Samoan?" Rudy looked between the two men, seeking confirmation of his assumption. "I've worked with a number of those in the past. They're good workers, but hard to communicate with."

"Yeah. Chaffey's pretty bright." Dane pulled a knife from a table and held it out. "I shared one of my better blades with him. He said he liked the way it made him faster."

The boat lurched and the grind of slowing engines interrupted their conversation. The crank of machinery and activity on the deck above drew sighs from all three.

"Sounds like we've hit the fishing hole." Rudy pivoted toward his work table and retrieved his papers. "Won't be long now before we're up to our knees in goo."

"I'll see you guys later. Got to get my beauty sleep." Jackson waved a farewell before disappearing into the equipment, leaving the hold.

A siren sounded. Rudy jumped, stashing his papers back in their spot.

Dane glanced at him, moving toward the stairs. "Know what that is?"

"Are we sinking already?"

"Safety drill." Dane pointed up the narrow corridor. "Captain is timing us. We better bust our behinds."

Winded when they reached the upper deck, he and Dane hurried to roll call. Men swarmed around the life rafts, listening for their names. The captain stood off to the side, watching the drill unfold. Rudy heard his name and proceeded to the line of men near the bow. Dane's name was called a few seconds later, and the man moved to a group on the other side of the stern.

"Hey, look! We got the observer on our raft." One of the fishermen let out a whistle and clapped Rudy's shoulder. "You bring your Coast Guard beacon?"

Rudy pretended the beacon resided in his pocket and patted the spot. "Don't leave your station without it, so they tell me."

"Just think, guys. If we sink, we'll be rescued faster." A chorus of good-natured cat calls erupted around the boisterous sailor.

Rudy held up his palm. "Only if our life raft inflates when it hits the water. And if I make it into the boat. I can't turn the signal on until I'm on the raft."

"We'll make sure you're on board. Trust me." Gonzales drew beside him, wrapping an arm about Rudy's shoulders. His olive skin gleamed in the sun. "Remember that I'll be hard to see in the dark. Don't float away and leave me behind."

Rudy bit back a snort. "You've got me there."

The captain stepped up and whistled for the men's attention. "This drill went fairly smooth for the first run. In an emergency, I expect all of you to cut at least two minutes off your time. An explosion or a fire could sink the ship in under a minute. Your lives depend on speed. Take note of the location of your assigned raft and the men in your group. Everyone is responsible for the safety of the others around him."

Murmurs rumbled through the crowded deck. Rudy shuddered at the dangers this exercise implied. In the event of a tragedy, all would face the same fate, dependent upon their lifeboat. If something went wrong, though, safety procedures didn't guarantee he and Dane would both make it home. *Please, Lord, make sure Dane makes it home, even if I don't.*

"All right men, let's get back to the reason we're out here. Fish!"

Sobered by the drill, Rudy descended into the belly of the ship, deep in thought. He approached his work station with a renewed sense of danger, each turn around a piece of equipment a reminder of how low in the boat he worked. All the men aboard depended on a quick and efficient exit. In an emergency, the tangle of machinery down here could mean a death trap. He squared his shoulders, resolved to be ready whatever the circumstances. This tour had yet to begin and he already regretted coming. The drill reaffirmed his decision not to return to the Bering Sea. If not for Hawk, and his promise to McKenna, he wouldn't be here now.

"You okay?"

Dane's question jerked Rudy out of his reverie. When did he arrive? "Just thinking of the consequences of engine failure. Not a promising scenario."

"I've fished these waters for almost nine years. I've never had an emergency where we abandoned our vessel." Dane shrugged, as if assuring them both. "Catcher processors like this one have the best track records."

"Thanks." Rudy moved into position as the conveyor rumbled forward. "I want to return home in one piece." *With you in tow.*

Dane nodded and started to say something, but the engines squealed and the nets groaned, drowning out his words. He moved nearer and shouted. "Let me know if I'm moving the fish too fast or slow." He held up his fingers and made gestures indicating both. "I'll help you gauge the haul as best I can."

"We'll make a good team." Rudy yelled back, covering his hair with a hairnet and adjusting his ear plugs. He yanked on his gloves. Chains rattled as the fishermen prepared to lower the nets and retrieve the first drag. As the sounds of an awakening catcher processor filled the silence, Rudy fell into the familiar rhythm his position required, aware of the man beside him. Working next to Dane, maybe he could help McKenna. He'd promised, after all.

Three days later, Rudy stumbled toward the galley, exhausted after working one sixteen-hour shift after another. He'd entered his data for yesterday's haul late last night, sent the computerized information to NMFS through cyberspace, and dropped into bed like he'd died there, skipping dinner. With this day's work waiting an hour away, his empty stomach protested, driving him to find something to eat.

The morning rush filled the galley when he joined the food line and Rudy glanced around for a place to sit. He lowered his plate of ham and eggs to the table, back aching from the twelve-hour stretch of standing while inspecting fish. At least he'd been able to sit while he did the additional four hours of paperwork. The only person he'd really talked with in the past seventy-two hours was Jackson whom he'd passed in the stairwell as they changed places. Neither time nor opportunity presented itself to get to know Dane.

Soon, though, the processor would meet its quota here, and he'd have free time between fishing stops to converse and get acquainted. What little Rudy had observed, Dane kept to himself. Moody and brooding, Dane hid his thoughts from the public eye. If

Rudy were any gauge of character, he'd wager Dane wrestled with hidden demons in his past, wary of revealing too much. What Rudy knew about Dane could hurt him. Or worse, embarrass him. Either would make the man defensive. Rudy wouldn't go there. He prayed he could remain sensitive to the man's needs.

He savored his ham and eggs, smiling when the cook carried a tall plate of toast out to him. "Thanks." He lifted his cup of coffee and studied the half-filled room. He grabbed a couple of slices from the stack and folded the buttery glob in two. He'd just bit into the wad when Dane sat beside him.

"How's the grub?" Dane set his own plate down, a stack of pancakes drowning in a puddle of butter and syrup. Bacon swam on the side. Scrambled eggs filled a second plate, a sprig of parsley dangling over the side.

"Not big on greens, are we?" Rudy rolled his gaze to Dane's plate, smiling as he looked back up. "Pop-eye would frown."

"Nah, old Pops liked his spinach." Dane stuck his fork in the eggs, scooping them aboard his toast like a backhoe in a landfill. His mouth opened as if it were a dump truck bed, ready to load the fluffy, yellow mixture. No room for vegetation with that maneuver. "I'm more of a green beans kind of guy."

"They grow a lot of those where you're from?" Rudy chomped another bite of toast.

"I grew up on the coast of Oregon." Dane eased a second scoop of eggs between his lips, drawing the fork out in a slow, even slide. He chewed, unhurried, as if the memory suspended his thinking. "Beans were grown inland. I met friends in college who worked the fields driving truck and loading boxes." He shoveled more eggs onto his toast and ate, sandwich style.

"I'm from Newport, but my childhood was spent in Astoria." Rudy held his breath, waiting for the other man to react. "Where were you?"

"No kidding? I grew up in Waldport." Dane stopped, fork poised in the air. "What a coincidence. Two beach bums on the same fishing rig."

"I paid off my college loans working up here." Rudy picked up another slice of toast. "Nice to be debt free."

"Yeah." Dane pinched a piece of bacon between his fingers. "I'd work a couple of seasons here and then attend school the other half of the year. It was like being on vacation for six months."

"Where did you go to school?" Rudy concentrated on his ham while Dane demolished the stack of pancakes.

"University of Oregon." Dane shoved his plate aside, crunched the last of the bacon, and wiped his fingers. "Land of the Ducks."

"Family?"

Frowning, Dane scooped the final bite of eggs from his other plate. "I better go report to the captain." He stood and scooted his chair beneath the table. "See you in the underbelly."

Rudy followed Dane's departing form out the galley door, noting the man avoided his last question. Dane had issues.

CHAPTER SEVENTEEN

Required to scamper topside every haul to monitor the contents of the nets, Rudy's minor seasickness disappeared. By week's end, the bycatch remained under five percent, which was good, but still higher than warranted. Rudy detested the sight of the unwanted fish being returned to the sea, the fulmars and gulls massing at the stern in search of a free meal.

Back at the observer table, he grew numb sorting out the different species. Jellyfish the size of frying pans, and skates as large as doormats, littered the floor boot deep, making movement through the area difficult. He slipped once, landing on his backside as the squish of marine life beneath him parted like a crowd shopping in a mall, threatening to engulf him before they let him go.

Although Dane sliced fish a table over, his attention remained focused on the conveyor belt churning more and more pollock into the hatch. Dane's experience superseded any bleeders Rudy had watched perform before, and the man's work ethic amazed him. With the precision of a machine, Dane removed the roe from the fish bellies and collected the eggs in a tray. He speared the unwanted species and tossed them down a chute in a smooth, mechanical rhythm. Glances up were rare, his mind engaged elsewhere, as though his thoughts rode the surface of his forehead like waves. Did he ever think of McKenna?

Rudy's shift rotation prevented seeing the man again at meals and they had only communicated with lifted eyebrows or a nod during work hours. Intent upon his task, Dane focused on his work, his quiet personality an asset to getting the job done. The noise from the equipment prohibited most oral communication, shouting and hand signals a secondary means to relaying messages between them. Frustrated, Rudy prayed for an opening.

One afternoon a few days later, during a lull between hauls, a hissing sound penetrated Rudy's earplugs. The frantic whistle of steam escaping somewhere nearby raised an alarm in his head. He scanned the work area, searching for the source of the noise. He spotted a trickle of vapor rising from the boiler next to his work station. Rudy searched the area for a fireman, but seeing no one, he tapped on Dane's table.

The bleeder glanced up, startled, his knife poised over a fish he was working on.

Rudy pointed to the boiler, indicating the steam pouring out of the hole.

Dane's eyes grew wide. He gestured as he shouted at Rudy. "Go use the phone in the break room. I'll find the engineer. Get out of here, now."

Rudy maneuvered around the maze of equipment between him and the crew room at the end of the deck. Once inside, he pulled out his ear plugs, found the phone, and alerted the crewmen topside. "Steam escaping an engine. Right next to the observer station." Rudy paused to catch his breath. "Dane Nichols went to find the engineer."

Rudy sat in a chair and waited. Within minutes the ship came to a stop and the once noisy vessel rocked as if falling asleep. He heard voices and shuffling feet, but little else, which meant the danger might have been averted. Staying here, he would be close to the exits. If the alarm sounded, he'd hit the stairs running. Time would be important if this turned into an emergency, time he might need to save his life.

His curiosity tormented him as seconds turned into minutes. He stood and peered out the door, trying to see what might be happening in the work area. Glimpsing Dane leaning against the machine that minced fish, Rudy stepped up beside him. "What did they find?"

"The leak was a bad valve. They're replacing it now. We'll finish the catch for today." Dane nudged him with his elbow. "Glad you saw that when you did. Could have been a lot worse."

"I heard it before I saw it. The scream of the steam pierced my ear plugs."

"No doubt." Dane pointed toward their work stations. "Looks like we're back on duty."

Soon the engines creaked to life, the eerily silent mincing machines returning to their constant clamor. Pulleys lifting heavy nets outside clanged their chains and Rudy resumed his sampling at the observer table. A leaking valve worried him, the force behind the steam enough to start an engine fire. One that could sink them. His mother often quoted the verse from the book of Matthew about not worrying about tomorrow, for today carried enough trouble of its own. Here he had the proof. But the information didn't reassure him.

Hours later, he fell into his bunk, praying for a few hours' sleep. His mind drifted to the past right before slumber claimed him. "Rudy!" He opened his eyes and peeked around. The room was shrouded in fog, and he couldn't make out the walls or doors. Beyond him the first step of the stairway beckoned. He tried to stand, but he couldn't find the floor. He grasped for something to help him up, but the chair beside his bed collapsed under his weight.

"Rudy!" The voice sounded further away now. Up. He had to climb the stairs. Shoving himself to his feet, he groped for the handrail, trying to pull himself to the next floor.

"Romelle. Don't play games." He placed his foot on the first step, but the board splintered. "Romelle, come down." Falling to his knees, he gasped at the pain. "Get out of the closets. Now."

"Rudy!" The voice grew faint. Where was she? The upstairs had so many closets. Which one did she choose this time?

"Romelle, please come down." He heaved himself forward and fell against the wall. The small room around him came into focus. His blanket hung from the bunk of the cabin, his pillow crammed against the locker. He shook his head to clear his mind.

The dream had returned, as it always did after a crisis. Would he ever be free of the memory?

"We're heading back to Dutch." Dane grabbed the bench beside Rudy two afternoons later. "Catch is secure. Need to refuel and unload our cargo."

"And evaluate that aging engine." Rudy tapped the table. "If that seam ruptures, we might not be so lucky next fishing trip."

"Didn't take you for a man who puts much stock in luck." Dane lifted a coffee mug near his face, steam wafting past his nose. "Saw you at the Bible study."

"Yeah, I managed to slip in late last night. Glad I went." Rudy shoved a basket of rolls Dane's way. "Have some. The cook gave me too many."

"Can't eat them." Dane drained his cup and set it down with a thud. "I already finished a plate of salmon and mashed potatoes. I'm stuffed."

"How many days to port?"

"Two, maybe three." Dane waved at a guy circulating with the coffee pot. "We'll be a day in harbor, possibly two. Then we head back to another fishing spot north of here."

"I'm spending the time in my bunk. I'm exhausted." Rudy glanced around the room. "These sixteen-hour days are tough on an old guy like me." He mimicked a yawn and grinned.

Dane poured cream into his coffee, an amused twist on his mouth. "We can't be much different in our ages. I'm twenty-seven, almost twenty-eight."

Rudy grabbed another roll and buttered it. "Twenty-nine in January."

"You got family waiting when you go home?"

"Only my worried mother." Rudy nibbled on the bread. "I promised her I wouldn't come back here because of the danger. But my supervisor at Pacific Seacoast Observers needed someone to finish the season, and my job at home was between assignments, so I came."

"What do you do?" Dane twisted his chair away from the table, leaned against the edge, and stretched his legs.

"I'm a port inspector right now. Seasonal work." Rudy turned to face Dane, straddling his chair so he could unwind his spine. He stretched and twisted, letting out a groan. "I go looking for trouble along inland waterways and at harbors."

"You the law?" Dane's eyes narrowed, a half-grin lifting the right side of his mouth. "Didn't take you for a deputy type."

Rudy laid his butter knife on the table, giving a snort. "Mostly I inspect catches and such and report it. Then the law follows my paper trail."

"You work out of Newport?" At Rudy's nod, Dane set his coffee cup down. "My wife moved there in July."

Rudy kept quiet, lifting his eyebrows as if he were surprised at the news, waiting for Dane to tell him what he already knew.

"Her father retired and put her in charge of his gallery. *Lady Marie's*. Ever heard of it?"

Nodding, Rudy sat up straighter, sensing opportunity before

him. Take it slow. Play it cool. "My mother works at a sandwich shop right across the street from there."

"My wife is McKenna."

"Yes, I know who McKenna is." Rudy paused, searching for the right information to reveal. "So Sydney must be yours?"

Dane's eyes narrowed, his jaw clamping shut. "Yes."

"She's a little doll."

Dane looked away, letting his gaze wander around the room before he focused again on Rudy. "I appreciate your tact, but Sydney is *not* a little doll."

"You sure about that?" Rudy leaned forward and fixed his eyes on Dane. "When was the last time you saw her?"

"A couple of years, I guess. She's not exactly the kind of daughter you go running home to see." Dane drummed his fingers on the table, a look of disgust in his eyes.

"Maybe if you did, you'd know Sydney is growing, changing, and struggling to figure out her world." Rudy kept his voice level, his breathing sharp and staccato against the pulse pounding in his head. He capped his rage behind his tongue. "She needs her daddy."

"All she *needs* is an institution." Dane stood and slammed his fist on the table. "McKenna is too stubborn to admit it." He pivoted on his heel and stomped away, leaving Rudy sitting there, voice caught in his throat, and heart banging against his rib cage, ready to burst. Good thing Dane left. Rudy wanted to strangle him.

CHAPTER EIGHTEEN

By the end of the second week in school, McKenna's nerves had frayed to the point of breaking.

Sydney had declared war on anyone associated with her public education, including her own mother. Though McKenna transported her to school, Sydney resisted leaving the house every morning. Tantrums escalated in volume as they approached the building. Neither coaxing nor calm reassurances made any difference. After fifteen minutes of settling the child into her place, McKenna left the school with a growing sense of dread.

Andrea's calls increased in frequency, often filled with unanswered questions about Sydney followed by a barrage of ideas on how to make school work for the child. The frustrated teacher's bag of tricks grew emptier with each attempt to help the child fit into the classroom.

Sydney's attention flitted from the building blocks waiting in the corner to the lizards sunning themselves in the terrarium under the window, but learning letters and numbers from a lesson on the wall didn't capture her interest.

"Her curiosity knows no bounds." Andrea's strained chuckle couldn't hide the underlying aggravation in her tone. "She's obviously intelligent, her fingers and hands have touched every object in the room, twice."

"But she's disruptive." McKenna closed her eyes and absorbed the unspoken criticism coming from her friend's lips. "She distracts the other kids, bouncing along the walls."

"I think with enough time she will grow disinterested in the room." Andrea's effort to put a positive spin on the conversation only reinforced McKenna's sense of failure. "Janice got her interested in the alphabet cards today. She clearly likes the pictures of the animals. Her spontaneous speech, as she recognized those creatures she's familiar with, took a giant leap upward."

McKenna bit her tongue, suppressing the question neither of them addressed. How many weeks could the teacher compromise her classroom for one little girl? McKenna sighed, the time for excuses long past. "Andrea, would Sydney do better with a private tutor?"

"Probably." Defeat tinged the edges of Andrea's voice. "She really needs one-on-one reinforcement. In a classroom with twenty other children, even with an aide, Sydney has too much time on her hands to get into mischief." Andrea's sigh cut through the phone line. "And when the classroom gets noisy, she folds up like a salted snail."

"I have a volunteer to help me, and I've ordered curriculum." McKenna's heart raced at the thought of what she was about to undertake. She'd studied art and photojournalism, not teaching. She didn't know the first thing about writing lesson plans or coordinating curriculum. But Sydney's future hung in the balance. She forced the words from her heart. "With your input, I want to try teaching her at home."

"I'll provide everything I know to give her." Andrea's eagerness made McKenna smile. "Sydney needs an environment change, and you can provide that for her."

"An aide at the clinic for sound training where I took Sydney last year said the parents who educated their children at home were much more satisfied at the end of five years than those who opted for public education." McKenna swallowed, praying she was making the right decision. "What happens if I can't make this work?"

"I have every confidence in your ability. Besides, you have the motivation to see it through."

"I do?"

"She's your daughter."

The gallery traffic had slowed after Labor Day, for which McKenna gave thanks, if only to allow time to adjust to Sydney's return home. Andrea had mapped out a schedule with the school speech and language specialist for Sydney to meet with the woman twice a week. Sessions with Janice playing games in the gym with other first graders were scheduled as well. McKenna and Andrea had worked two weekends going over curriculum choices and finding the kinds of materials which would appeal to Sydney's learning style.

"She's a visual learner, McKenna. Which is why the classroom doesn't work for her. So much of what we teachers do is in the front of the room while we talk. Sydney responds to things she can see and interpret."

"Sound has always been a problem." McKenna could list incidents where a noisy room had triggered a meltdown. As she connected the dots, the cause of her daughter's outbursts became clear. "Now I understand why."

"Removing the noise factor may speed up her ability to grasp concepts." Andrea pulled out a box of felt figures. "I brought these for you to use. Sydney can touch these, see them, and say them using all three senses together."

"I can build concepts with them, too." McKenna held up the apple. "Not just an apple, but a red apple. It hangs on a tree. We can eat it when we're hungry."

"You're going to make a great teacher."

She resisted the temptation to scoff.

Now McKenna sat beside Sydney, building a tower of blocks using the colors for a pattern. No tantrums had surfaced this week and Sydney seemed to enjoy the time with her. Sydney understood the organizational concept of what they were building, reaching to correct McKenna's attempt to insert a yellow block into the field of green they'd completed together. Sydney narrowed her eyes and held up a different block. "Green."

McKenna nodded, chuckling at her daughter's stubborn will. Still, Sydney was learning—despite McKenna's fears. Grateful her daughter had returned to a steady state of calm rather than the agitated, unhappy child she'd been the first two weeks of school, McKenna prayed the rest of the year could achieve similar results.

The bell on the shop door jingled and McKenna stood, ready to greet the person.

Livy smiled and waved, a tote bag over her arm. She strode to the back where they were working. "How's *Lady Marie's* first grade class going?"

"Actually, we're establishing some groundwork on which we can build future lessons." McKenna smiled at the older woman. "Any word from Rudy?"

"He called over the weekend. His ship had some sort of engine problem, so they finished their catch and headed back to Dutch Harbor for repairs." Livy set the soft bag down on the table. "He doesn't know if he'll go out again on that boat."

"I wouldn't want to risk engine trouble on the Bering Sea." Last week McKenna had viewed a program on fishermen in the northern seas and found herself frightened to the point she couldn't sleep. "I hope he gets assigned somewhere else."

"You and me both." Livy reached into the tote and pulled out a handful of slender ribbons. "I knew you were working on colors and patterns, and I thought these might intrigue Sydney."

"What a great idea!" McKenna fingered the delicate slips of

color. "We've been using the blocks and her crayons, but these will be fun to play with."

"I also brought you lunch." The woman lifted a sack from the now skinny bag on the table. "Sydney's usual is in here, and I brought you a container of soup and half-a-turkey sandwich."

"How thoughtful of you." McKenna gestured to the table. "Let me get Sydney's hands washed." When she returned, she drew out chairs for Sydney, Livy, and herself, one of the legs squealing when she dragged it across the floor. "Can we share?"

"I have my own." Livy scrunched down on the small seat, emitting a grunt. "I'm definitely not a kid anymore."

McKenna giggled, helping Sydney unwrap her sandwich. She lifted the lid on the soup and sighed. "Smells magnificent."

"Clam chowder with lots of potatoes."

"Yum." McKenna sat beside her daughter.

Livy looked thoughtful. "I'd like Sydney to spend a couple of afternoons at the sandwich kitchen. Afternoon business is slow, now that the tourist season has ended. I work in the back. She can experience utensils, food preparation, and maybe we can teach her the basics of cooking."

"She doesn't like to be in the kitchen when I'm preparing meals." McKenna didn't want to disappoint this wonderful woman, but cooking was not something in which Sydney showed any interest. She'd run and hide if McKenna made anything which required several steps. Give her a bowl of cereal and a spoon and she was fine. Ask her to help make cookies, and she'd act as if she were being tortured. "I don't know why."

"I imagine it's a combination of the noise of the pots and maybe the smells." Livy's smile turned mischievous. "I'd still like to try."

"You're so good to me."

"Sydney is too bright a child to leave behind." Livy nodded as if she already had the answer she sought. "With all of our input and prayers, she'll shine. You'll see."

McKenna bit back the doubt which always lay at the edge of her thoughts. Any activity which increased Sydney's vocabulary was worth a try. McKenna wouldn't refuse any help she was offered, especially from this gracious and loving woman. "If only her father would pay as much attention." Her sigh sounded exasperated. "She needs a daddy."

Livy patted her on the shoulder. "He'll come around."

"Did Rudy say something?"

"Only that he has met Dane." Livy smiled. "And he is a good worker."

McKenna gripped the edge of the table, unsure she'd heard the woman right. Dane had been located? He wouldn't stand a chance against Rudy. For the first time in two years, McKenna's heart sang.

The next afternoon McKenna entered the Tidewater Takeout on tiptoe, anxious to see how the cooking lesson went. The little café was empty, save for a lone diner sipping coffee at the counter. Giggles sounded behind the curtain dividing the main restaurant from the kitchen area behind. McKenna heaved a sigh of relief. At least Livy's sense of humor was still in place. Lifting the curtain and peering into the back area, she spoke to no one. "Livy?"

"Over here, McKenna." The woman's chuckle came from the other side of the range. "Just cleaning up."

McKenna traipsed to where the pair waited and gasped at the scene before her. Sydney sat on the floor in a mound of flour, sifting what looked like sugar through her fingers. Her jeans and t-shirt were covered with spilled ingredients. Traces of flour dust circled her mouth and her curls resembled the branches of a flocked Christmas tree.

"What happened?" McKenna couldn't wait for an explanation, stepping closer. "Let me guess! A recipe gone belly up?"

"No, a hands-on demonstration of the ingredients that make a kitchen." Livy bent over the knoll of flour and scooped with a dust pan. "I left to help a customer and when I came back, I found her like this."

"Oh, Livy, I'm sorry. Let me pay you for the wasted materials."

"No need." Livy dumped the dust pan into the trash. "Sydney likes to taste and touch her cooking lessons."

"Not to mention wear the results." McKenna eyed the muddle of tipped over canisters and spoiled staples, arching an eyebrow in the woman's direction. "How do you feel about that?"

Livy shrugged. "We had fun."

"Flour." Sydney blew a cloud from her fingers. She lifted a handful of sugar, the tiny crystals catching the light and shimmering as they drifted to the floor. "Pretty."

"Messy." McKenna reached for the portable brush and swept the mound toward her.

"Nonsense." Livy stood up straight, her dust pan brimming. "I've never had such a good time, nor have I entertained such a willing pupil. Sydney was happiest when she was touching the ingredients." The woman winked and smiled, ducking her head toward the little girl. "Weren't you?"

"Cooking." Sydney made circles in the pile remaining on the floor. "Make cake."

McKenna shook her head. "Reminds me of myself when I cook. I get ingredients everywhere." She pulled Sydney to her feet and brushed the powdery materials from her clothing. "She obviously grasped the concept."

"Increased her vocabulary as well." Livy pointed to the counter where a dozen different items sat in their containers. "Test her. She knows what all of those things are."

"You are amazing." McKenna noted the chocolate chips, nuts, marshmallows, butter, and baking powder. "And a lot of fun."

"Wait until you taste our results." Livy lifted a pan of crisped rice treats from the stove. A square had already been cut. "Rice is one of those things that doesn't trigger food allergies."

"You made these?" McKenna stared at the confection, then at her daughter.

Livy nodded. "Sydney cut the butter and added the cereal."

"Rice treats." Sydney held up her hands.

Livy leaned over the child, tapping her lower lip. "What do you say?"

"May I please have a rice treat?"

McKenna gripped the counter. Unbelievable. "Livy, you should have had a daughter you could teach to cook. She would have been a chef."

Livy smiled. "Romelle didn't like cooking much, either."

"Romelle?"

Livy turned to leave. "My daughter."

CHAPTER NINETEEN

Dutch Harbor received a dusting of snow the day the *Bering Explorer* returned to port. Rudy dug out his warmer flannel shirts and thermal underwear, readying himself for the onslaught of winter weather. Storms off the Bering Sea could arrive unannounced and with the fury of an approaching wild animal. He trudged over to the NMFS station to check in with Hawk and see if his assignment had changed.

"The *Explorer* is going out again on Monday." Hawk tapped his clipboard. "I'm putting you back onboard because they'll be gone two weeks and that will finish both their early pollock season and your time here." Hawk narrowed his eyes. "Can't convince you to stay for the winter season, can I?"

Rudy groaned. "Nice try, man." He fist-bumped the man's shoulder. "But my other boss on the mainland expects me the third week of October."

"I had to ask." Hawk leaned back in his chair. "We've got a good group of trainees coming in first of the year. A couple of them have gone through the program before, so they're practically guaranteed to make the grade."

"Nothing like experienced help." Rudy had passed the training his first time through the program, but not all were so fortunate. Possessing his North Pacific Groundfish observer license became a ticket to more employment and future expeditions. He'd enjoyed the money and the adventure for a handful of seasons before returning to the mainland for warmer work.

"Except when they get tired of the cold and go home to warmer climates." Hawk's expression suggested he hadn't quit recruiting.

"Much to be said about warmth." Rudy shook his head. "See you around, Hawk."

The door squeaked on its hinge as he left the headquarters and headed toward the hotel. A gift shop operated on the ground floor. He entered and nodded a greeting to the small, round woman at the counter, guessing her to be native Aleutian. Glancing around the shop, he spotted Dane looking at a display of beaded headwear across the room. Not sure of what the man's response would be, Rudy moved toward him, smile in place.

Dane looked up as he approached, a mixture of emotions playing across his face. The man almost appeared sheepish, his gaze darting around before examining the floor beneath his feet. Finally, he fixed his gaze on Rudy and nodded. "Hey."

"How's it going?" Rudy pointed to the assortment of beaded items the man had been looking at when he arrived. "See anything you can afford?"

Dane shook his head. "These native craft designs are beautiful, but they're expensive." He leaned against the counter, his expression troubled. "I wanted to apologize for my outburst on the ship a few days ago."

"Already forgotten." Rudy didn't want an apology. This man needed to pull himself up by his bootstraps and face his responsibilities.

"When I last saw my family, Sydney was totally out of control. We couldn't take her anywhere without a screaming fit." He glanced away as if caught in the memory. "McKenna tried to share what she'd learned about autism, but I thought Sydney needed more discipline."

"That's a natural response for fathers." Rudy shifted his weight onto his right leg. "We think we should control our kids."

"Sydney defied everything I tried to do." Dane clenched his fist. "And spanking made her worse. I'd never seen anything like it." He shook his head. "She'd disobey and then bend over for her swat."

An image of Sydney poised for battle flashed through his memory. Rudy bit back his chuckle.

Dane raised an eyebrow. "She'd watch me to see my reaction." He straightened, sticking his hands in his jacket pockets. "How do you cope with something like that?"

"One day at a time."

"I just decided to leave. I know that makes me sound like a deserter, but I was afraid I'd overreact and wind up hurting my daughter. I'm not that kind of guy."

"Neglecting her is not the answer, either." Rudy swallowed, searching for words that could help this man accept his daughter's disability. "McKenna misses you. She's handling this all by herself. She's running the gallery and coping with Sydney's problems alone. Remember, she didn't ask for this task, either." He paused, watching the man's reaction. Dane was listening, his face a mixture of regret and what? Hopefulness? A need for a second chance? Rudy couldn't decide, but he continued. "She needs your strength to lean on. Struggles are easier to bear when shared. That's what marriage is supposed to be."

Dane inhaled and pressed his lips together, his gaze on the ceiling. "I don't know. I'm not sure I'm the man for McKenna anymore. I do support her. I send her all I can since my day-to-day needs are pretty much met onboard."

"A paycheck doesn't hold her at night when she's crying. Nor does it fill the emptiness of her days alone with a child she desperately wants to understand." Rudy clenched his jaw, fighting back the pounding of his pulse as he struggled against antagonizing this man further. "Didn't you promise to love, honor, and cherish McKenna when you married her? Through sickness and health, for richer, for poorer, for as long as you both shall live?"

"But I didn't know we'd get a handicapped child." Dane's voice sounded feeble, as though his spirit had been broken by his circumstances. "I wanted a little girl I could love, one who looked like her mother, and would run into my arms and call me daddy." Dane inhaled, swallowing as he stared at the ceiling. "Instead, we got the monster from hell. A demon disguised as a little red-headed girl." Dane looked up at him, his eyes steeled against the moisture trying to escape. "All I wanted McKenna to do was find a good place for Sydney to grow up, and we'd have another child. But she wouldn't even consider the option."

"So you left McKenna to raise Sydney by herself." Rudy fought the urge to shake this man's teeth loose from his gums. "She's strong, but with you by her side, she'd be an unstoppable force."

"Sydney will never be whole, Rudy. She'll never be the daughter I dreamed of."

"Life doesn't come with guarantees." Rudy ached for this troubled man. Dane wanted what they all wanted—a wife, a home, a quiver of kids. But life had dealt him a hand he didn't know how to play and so he folded, leaving the cards on the table. Admitting to a stranger he couldn't deal with Sydney's problems took courage. "What if your second child came disabled? Would you farm that one out, too?"

Dane's eyes narrowed. "McKenna won't listen to reason, so there won't be a second child. Not for me. Not with McKenna." He pivoted away from Rudy and strode to the door of the shop. Yanking the door open, he stomped outside, slamming the exit closed as he went.

Rudy clenched his fist. *Lord, help me reach that man. For McKenna's sake. And for Sydney's. But most of all, for You.*

The *Bering Explorer* remained in port an additional two days. Rudy busied himself scouting the landscape, visiting the old church in the center of the village, and checking in with the main office. He prayed for another encounter with Dane. The man's bitterness was a cover for his own failures, his inability to find love for his daughter. Rudy's resolve to speak truth to Dane unleashed a torrent of bitterness in Dane that Rudy hadn't expected in its intensity. Somewhere inside Dane lay an individual Rudy believed wanted to love his family but thought he lacked the skill set needed to cope. If Rudy could convince Dane of his own strengths, this family might be re-united.

His cell phone buzzed in his pocket as he left the church grounds on Tuesday. Hawk.

"Yeah? Did the agency decide to send me home?"

Hawk's voice sounded subdued. "We have an issue you and I need to discuss. Can you drop by this afternoon?"

"Uh, sure. I can be there in five minutes if you want."

"Great."

Rudy stashed the phone and strode across Dutch Harbor to the NMFS office. When he entered, Hawk was on the phone, his tone all business, brow set in a perpetual frown, and pen poised to take notes. He gestured for Rudy to take a seat while he finished.

"What's up?" Rudy leaned back in his chair and eyed the big man as he hung up the phone and made a few more notes on the clipboard he carried. "And no, I won't work an extra month. My contract with the agency ends the middle of October."

Hawk didn't smile, only grimaced. Something was up. "I have a request for a transfer from an observer on a trawler to the *Bering Explorer*. It means you'd be through in a week, rather than two, and you'd be home to port every night until your time here runs out." Hawk set down his clipboard and gazed at Rudy. "What do you think?"

Rudy's disappointment riddled him like a deflated airbag. He'd lose another opportunity to talk with Dane. Maybe his last. They hadn't parted well and Rudy was determined to keep the dialogue going. McKenna's future depended upon it. As did Sydney's. Yet he was temporary, not full season. How could he refuse?

"Will that work best for you?" Hawk's orders were the law and Rudy had to cooperate, even if it meant losing traction with Dane. "I came to help you out. I'd say I'm at your disposal."

"Truth is, the captain asked. Apparently, he discovered his bleeder is upset over a discussion you two had." Hawk narrowed his eyes, his pencil tapping the clipboard. "I've never known you to be incompatible with another fisherman. What's going on?"

Rudy should have seen this coming. "I met his wife in Newport before I came north."

"Dane has a wife? He's worked up here for the past eight years. He hasn't left Dutch for two!"

"Yes, he has a wife. And that's where the problem lies." Rudy chose his words carefully, not wanting to divulge Dane's personal affairs. He looked intently at his boss. "I told him his wife is missing him and that he should make time to go home." Rudy leaned forward in his chair. "Didn't sit well with him."

Hawk frowned, the furrow between his brows deepening as he studied Rudy. "I know you. There's more to this than you're saying." He sank back into his chair and tapped the table with his pencil. "I'll work this out with the captain. If Dane needs to go home, you'll be the one to convince him. But don't get yourself thrown overboard, okay?"

"Trust me. I'll be careful." Rudy shifted in his chair and propped his ankle across his knee. "My mother would have your hide if something happened to me on the Bering Sea."

Hawk raised his hands in mock horror. "Are you sure I can't transfer you? I've met your mother, and she's a force to be reckoned with."

"As unbelievable as this sounds, Hawk, I don't want to perish in the Bering Sea, either."

Hawk stood and extended his hand. "Then make sure you don't."

CHAPTER TWENTY

WHILE RUDY STOWED HIS GEAR IN his compartment the next day, he heard a knock at the door. Turning, he saw Dane in the opening. Pulse notching up, he forced a smile. "Hey! Ready to sail?"

Dane's gaze swept the hall before he zeroed in on Rudy. "Can we talk?"

"Sure. There isn't much room here." Rudy braced himself for a verbal attack. "You want to go to the galley?"

"No. This is private." Dane stepped into the small space and closed the door. "I want to keep this discussion between us." Dane's jaw muscles rippled under his skin, like a man who worked to control his temper. His eyes, though, were shuttered, the twinkle replaced by a lingering emptiness. Guilt haunted his gaze.

"You must think me a coward." Dane leaned against the wall, one foot on the bunk.

"A coward?" Rudy prayed for the right words to help this man deal with his pain. "What do you mean?"

"Me hiding out here in the North, leaving McKenna at home to fight the battles I don't know how to tackle." Dane stared at the floor, knuckles tapping his thigh. "I know it looks like I've deserted her."

"Is that what you're doing?" Rudy sat on the lower bunk. "I understood from McKenna you were supporting her and Sydney with a paycheck every month. That's not a man who has forgotten his responsibilities and fled."

"I could never do that." Dane glanced up. "What you said the other day made me think."

Rudy waited for the man to unload his burden.

"You said a paycheck wouldn't warm her at night, nor would it hold her when she was crying." Dane swallowed and breathed deep, his gaze aimed at the ceiling. "That really hit home." Dane focused back on him. "I have loved McKenna since she was sixteen. I never looked at another girl after I met her. I wanted to be everything she needed. Her knight-in shining-armor, protector, lover. To think that she spends nights alone at home crying, broke me up."

"She still loves you." Rudy had witnessed the woman's faithfulness, her devotion to the man who captured her heart. He pulled the picture from his wallet. "She gave me this photo of the two of you to help me find you when I came up." He held the image out to Dane, who stared at it as if he'd been bitten. "You both look very much in love."

Dane sank onto the bunk beside him and put his head in his hands, the photograph dangling from his fingers. His breathing labored, an occasional sniff met Rudy's ears. They sat there for several moments without speaking, Rudy staying quiet to let Dane gain control. Dane lifted his gaze and pressed his lips to the picture. "I can't tell you how much I miss her."

"You don't need to tell me." Rudy placed a hand on Dane's shoulder, squeezing him gently to reassure him. "You need to go home and tell McKenna." Rudy pulled another photo from his wallet. "And this little girl needs a hug from her daddy."

Dane's eyes widened as he took the picture. "Wow! She's really grown. And she's so beautiful!"

"She is." Rudy leaned closer, pointing to the sparkling eyes and trace of a smile. "Inside and out. You just need to get to know her."

"I don't know if I can." The man studied the ceiling of the room, his mouth open as he breathed huge gulps of air in and out. "You can't imagine the tantrums and rages we endured."

"Yes, I can." Rudy studied the floor. When he raised his gaze,

Dane looked puzzled. "My little sister was autistic. My parents went through the same things you and McKenna are facing."

"Really?" Dane's eyes fixed on him. "How did they cope?"

"Holding hands with each other and aiming their prayers skyward." Rudy stood and gripped the top bunk for courage. What he had to say hurt him as much as it would Dane. "My dad would tease Romelle and flirt with her and get her to laugh. Mom was the nurturer, the one who helped Romelle discover herself."

"How old is she?"

"She was eighteen and doing well. But she died in an accident." His voice broke, pausing to find composure.

"When was this?"

"Eight years ago." Rudy closed his eyes, the memories flooding his thoughts. "She'd be twenty-six now."

"The same age as McKenna." Dane pulled off his seaman's cap and raked his hands through his hair. "Oh man, I'm sorry."

"Yeah." Rudy inhaled and let the air out slowly. "Like I said, life has no guarantees. You have to live each day as it comes. Romelle had eighteen good years with a family who loved her. Her death still gives me nightmares, but I know she spent her days happy until God took her home."

"You really think I could make a difference?" Dane stood and faced him. "I have no idea where to start."

"Start by going home." Rudy stood and clapped him on the shoulder. "Just be her dad."

"This is a lot to take in." Dane pulled his stocking cap tight around his ears and shoved his hands in his pockets. "I'm not convinced I'm the man for the job." He glanced about the small cabin, his gaze furtive, as if he sought to look at anything but Rudy. Finally, he nodded. "We sail in the morning. I'll see you then." Dane stepped out into the corridor and disappeared.

Rudy sat on his bunk and prayed.

The next morning Rudy wandered into the galley, his revelation to Dane still weighing heavily on his mind. Grabbing a cup of coffee, he loaded his plate with food and found a table at the end of the room to sit down. The table trembled, and he glanced up to find Dane setting a plate next to him. "Good morning."

Dane laid his fork on the plate and sank onto the bench. "Morning."

"Ready for another tour?" Rudy couldn't read Dane's mood, but the circles beneath his eyes and the pallor on his skin suggested the man had not slept well the night before. Fatigue, big time.

"You mean my last tour this season." Dane's frown deepened, his gaze wandering the room as he took in the men entering the galley. He sighed and twisted Rudy's way, lips pressed in a fine line.

"Beg your pardon?"

"I've mulled what you said over and over in my mind. I'm haunted by my actions."

"It's nothing you can't fix, Dane." Rudy stuck his fork in his scrambled eggs. "If I had a wife as devoted to me as McKenna is to you, I wouldn't leave her alone for anything."

"You're right." Dane nodded. "I've decided to go home once this season finishes. There's only two weeks left on this boat. I might have to work another boat for a week or so. But then I am going home."

Rudy high-fived Dane. "Write and tell her."

Dane grinned, the first hint of a smile since he'd entered the room. "I sent her an e-mail this morning. If she doesn't die from the shock, I'll be hearing from her soon." Dane pulled a receipt from his pocket. "Remember when you asked if I could afford one of those beaded headdresses the Aleuts make?"

Rudy nodded. "Can you?"

"I had enough in savings." Dane waved the receipt in the air. "I went ashore last night before they closed and bought one. I'll have them send it home." He looked up, his eyes twinkling, his smile wide. "Can't you see those beautiful blue and yellow beads against McKenna's dark hair?"

"She'll love it." Rudy's heart raced, his joy for Dane genuine, but his happiness for McKenna overflowing. Sydney would have her daddy back. McKenna her man. *Thank you, Lord, for making me an instrument of your work.*

CHAPTER TWENTY-ONE

McKenna stared at the message waiting in her inbox, index finger poised above the mouse. The subject read "Hello", the sender Pacific Fishermen and Company. Heart throbbing in her throat, McKenna fought to breathe. Her hands trembled and beads of perspiration chilled her forehead. She leaned back in her chair and covered her face with her fingers.

"Dane must be dead." Just whispering the words to the empty room brought tears to her eyes. The company had no other reason to contact her, unless Dane had perished somewhere at sea. "He won't be coming home. Sydney will never know her dad. I am alone."

She sat there for several minutes trying to regain control, but the strength to click on the e-mail message wouldn't come. She couldn't face it. Not now. She'd lived with the reality of her fear ever since Dane left for Alaska the last time. He hadn't returned, but she'd always had hope that he would. Now before her was a message she was certain would confirm her worst fears. Dane's boat had capsized or caught fire, and he hadn't been rescued.

The bell over the door to the gallery tinkled, and McKenna sprang to her feet. A giggle and a thump alerted her to someone coming through the front entrance. She clicked off the message screen and started toward the front.

"McKenna?" The voice was Livy's, the giggle Sydney's.

"Back here, Livy. In the office." McKenna pasted on a smile and straightened her shoulders.

Within seconds, the pair shuffled through the door, Sydney carrying a little plastic box of food. She set it on the desk and popped the lid. Smells of oregano and pepperoni wafted from the interior.

"What did you make today, Sydney?" McKenna peeked over her daughter's shoulder, forcing herself to act interested, even though she could feel the cursor pulsing, the message waiting, the words begging to be read. Later. She'd have to read the message later.

"Pizza." Sydney pointed to the food. "Pizza."

McKenna bent down for a closer look and pretended to take a deep breath. "Umm. Smells good. You want it for dinner?"

"Eat pizza." Sydney poked a finger in the warm cheese and stuck it in her mouth.

"I think she planned it as a snack." Livy winked, her deep-set eyes locking with McKenna's for a moment. "It's just a little one, made for a single serving. Do you have napkins?"

"Sure. By the coffeepot. Sydney, let's take your pizza to the children's table, and you can eat it there." McKenna scooped up the pizza box and strode to the play area, avoiding Livy's gaze.

Once they had Sydney settled at her spot, Livy laid a hand on McKenna's shoulder. "What's wrong?" She brushed her cheek. "Has something happened?"

Tears pooled in McKenna's eyes. "How did you know?"

"Your face is as long as a rolling pin." Livy squeezed her arm. "Tell me what's going on."

"There's a message on the computer from Dane's company. I'm afraid to open it." McKenna reached for a tissue, her cheeks damp. "They never contact me."

"Let's open it together." Livy took her hand and led her back to the office. "It could be something else, you know."

McKenna stopped. "Do you know something? Has Rudy contacted you?"

"No." The woman shrugged. "But a message is only a message until you read it. You're letting fear reign over your heart."

McKenna sat before the computer and pulled up the screen again. The subject line popped out at her, bold in black letters. She clicked on the item and held her breath as she moved the cursor down the screen. "Oh, my goodness!" She stared up at Livy waiting behind her. "It's from Dane! Can you believe it? Dane wrote me a message!"

"Good news, I hope?"

"I haven't read that far." McKenna wrapped her arms about her middle and rocked. "I'm speechless. A message from Dane." She giggled. "I thought he was dead." She waved a hand in front of her face. "I think I'm going to faint."

"McKenna! Read the message."

"What?" She glanced up at the perplexed look on the face of the older woman who stood beside her. "Oh. I'm sorry. I'm just so excited." She returned her gaze to the screen and read the e-mail to its end. She sat there stunned, mouth open, breathing erratic. Tears coursed down her cheeks, and she pressed her lips together to keep from sobbing. She looked up at Livy, her shoulders shaking.

"Well?"

"He's coming home." She fell against Livy's hip, feeling the woman's arms encircle her shoulders, warm hands stroking her temples. "Dane is finally coming home."

"Here, Sydney. You carry this." She led her daughter up the steps to the front door, McKenna's arms full of packages. She unlocked the deadbolt and swung the door open, turning sideways to get her purchases through the entrance. Dane's return could be anytime in the next two weeks, and she wanted to be ready. She'd purchased new linens for the bedroom, and stocked the cupboard with ingredients for all of Dane's favorite foods. A menu for their meals for the next month waited by the refrigerator. She hadn't cooked much since he'd left and planned to make up for the time lost by cooking and freezing meals they could eat when she had to work late at the gallery.

Sydney set her bag on the sofa and scooted to her bedroom, disappearing from sight. Sounds of the child playing with her talking story book wafted from the bedroom.

McKenna headed to the kitchen to put away the groceries, dropping the sack of linens in the hall for delivery to their closets later. She turned back to the task at hand and stacked the shelves with more staples. Stomach knotted, her hands trembled as she filled the snack drawer with Dane's favorites. How long had it been since she bought peanuts, black licorice, and wafer cookies? What if his tastes had changed? What if he no longer loved her?

Shoving the nasty thought aside, she folded the grocery sacks and tidied the kitchen. Her handsome husband, her knight-in-shining armor, was coming home. They would be a family again. He'd appreciate the changes in Sydney since he left. His daughter could actually say words now. Her increased ability to communicate had decreased the ever-present frustration she experienced trying to get her needs met. Dane hadn't understood the problem, and blamed McKenna for their daughter's eruptive personality. Now the tantrums were fewer and farther between. McKenna prayed Sydney's behavior would remain stable for a few days before something set her off. Dane's homecoming needed to be peaceful and joyous, not filled with the wails of a belligerent child.

"Oh please, Lord, make it so."

A crash sounded from the bedroom. McKenna hurried to the door and stopped. Scattered over the floor lay an assortment of books and an overturned chair. Sydney swung from the closet door, her feet gripping the knob and her hands clasping the top.

She smiled as her weight provided the momentum to keep it swinging from its hinges. Where did she learn to do that? McKenna closed her eyes. If Dane came home and found Sydney hanging from the rafters, he'd never stay.

"Come on, little monkey." McKenna reached out to her daughter. "Doors are for closing, not swinging."

"Swing." Sydney kicked her feet as McKenna lifted her down. "Sydney swing."

"Not today." McKenna knelt beside her daughter and handed her one of the books. "Let's pick up this mess, and then we'll go to the kitchen to make supper." She pointed to the shelf. "Stack them straight."

Half an hour later, McKenna had restored order to the room. She'd insisted on Sydney's help, though her daughter had to be coaxed to put each book on the shelf. McKenna righted the chair and placed it back at the desk. She turned to Sydney. "How about some dinner?"

McKenna reached for Sydney's crayons and a coloring book, took her daughter's hand and led her to the kitchen. Lifting Sydney to her booster chair, she laid the book down and handed over the crayons. "Color while I fix our food." Taking a minute to turn on the television, she returned to the kitchen and propped the door open so she could hear the news.

"Spaghetti tonight?" When Sydney glanced up as if she understood, McKenna busied herself getting the pasta and sauce ready to cook. Though she couldn't hear much of the program humming in the next room, having people noise around was comforting. She cut vegetables for a salad, turned to offer a piece of celery to Sydney and stopped. Not again!

Sydney stood on the chair, arms outstretched, reaching for the top of the kitchen door which stood ajar only a foot away from her daughter's precarious perch. Sydney stepped onto the doorknob and with a shriek sailed into the doorjamb.

McKenna shot to the rescue, but she was too late. As her daughter's tiny fingers smashed into the space where the door should have gone, the wail reverberated through the kitchen. McKenna lifted Sydney down and carried her to the sink. She filled a bowl with ice and plunged the bruised hand into the cold, stemming any swelling that might follow.

Fifteen minutes later, Sydney stopped sobbing, her hand pink from the ice cubes. McKenna checked each digit and couldn't feel that anything had broken. "You need to stay off the doors. This is not a gymnasium."

The smell of scorching food drifted past McKenna's nose. Spaghetti! Setting Sydney back in her chair, McKenna grabbed a potholder and shoved the pan off the burner. The remains of their dinner lay melded to the bottom of the cooking pan. She lowered the pan into the ice water she'd used for Sydney's bruises and added detergent to soak the burned food. Opening the refrigerator, she retrieved the peanut butter and jelly.

Images of Dane slamming the door as he retreated from a scene such as this filled McKenna's mind. Handing her daughter a sandwich, McKenna rested her chin on Sydney's head. Maybe Dane's homecoming wasn't such a good idea after all.

She fought back words she wanted to scream at Sydney. What would this child think of next?

The next morning McKenna drove Sydney to her appointment with the speech and language therapist at the elementary school. Sydney no longer cried as they approached the building, and her sessions with the pathologist seemed to be going well.

The teacher, Cheryl, greeted them as they entered. "Good

morning, Sydney."

McKenna waited, the greeting she and Cheryl both wanted still not forthcoming. McKenna patterned it for her daughter. "Good morning."

Sydney frowned, clinging to McKenna's hand.

Cheryl smiled. "Don't worry, she'll get it eventually. Come on in." Cheryl often sent home practice sheets for McKenna so she could reinforce the speech patterns the teacher had covered in their current lesson. Not every concept had been grasped. As Sydney entered the room with the teacher, McKenna turned to leave.

Janice approached. "We're trying out some new equipment today." She led McKenna to an anteroom behind the gym bleachers where a trampoline and gymnastics apparatus stood. "Think Sydney might find it appealing?"

McKenna couldn't contain her enthusiasm. "I was going to ask you about some kind of climbing exercise. You won't believe what she did yesterday." As McKenna explained the doorknob excursions to the amazed teacher's aide, she pointed to her knuckles to describe the bruises Sydney now bore. "If we can satisfy her need to climb and explore here, maybe she'll remain on the floor at home. Her dad is coming sometime in the next two weeks, and I want him to find our family environment peaceful and more normal than when he left."

Janice raised her eyebrows. "That's a tall order, but I'll see if I can get her interested." So far, Sydney had enjoyed watching the children move around the room but hadn't joined in the activities, frustrating everyone involved. "We'll give it our best shot."

McKenna waved and hurried to her car. She'd use this hour to drop by the shop and pick up the books for last week's sales. Sydney usually readied for bed early after a day spent at the school. More time for McKenna to get her bookkeeping caught up and her sales records in order. She didn't want the work hanging over her when Dane returned. He would have her undivided attention—well, as much as she could give him without interruptions from their daughter.

As she drove the short distance to the gallery, McKenna prayed. "Lord, I've waited for Dane to return for so long. Please make his homecoming special and our family reunion peaceful. May he want to love his daughter this time. Help me to make this happen."

For the first time since Dane left two years ago, McKenna lived with the hope he might return and be satisfied. He had to come home and stay. He just had to.

She parked the car in front of the gallery and gripped the steering wheel until her knuckles turned white. Like a guarded prison tower, the wall of hurt she kept stashed inside threatened to crumble, releasing the dam of emotions hidden away. Hot tears rimmed her eyes, and she blinked faster and faster. She reached for the door handle and stopped, losing the battle to a salty cascade rushing down her cheeks.

CHAPTER TWENTY-TWO

Traveling further north to find the fishing spot needed for its last catch of the early pollock season, the *Bering Explorer* ate up three days in transport. Though the ship had been given a clean slate and all its systems checked and repaired, the questionable reliability on the last trip still haunted the crew, making the long journey stretch on forever. Rudy shoved those worries to the back of his mind, catching up on his sleep, playing cards in the galley, and attending Gonzales' Bible study.

The study leader still sported his red and yellow bandanna, his tattooed arms bulging with well-defined muscles. When he spoke, his enthusiasm for the lesson he'd come to share seemed to animate him, making the gold earring on his ear sparkle in the ship's lamplight. "God said he would bless and multiply Abraham." Gonzales glanced around the room. "He made that promise to Abraham and said his descendants would number like the stars. Old Abe waited patiently for God to deliver the goods."

Gonzales turned and circled the galley. "God kept his promise. Sarah delivered a son in her nineties." He lifted his hands toward the ceiling. "Imagine that!"

The murmurs in the room grew louder.

"Wait. There's more." Gonzales grinned as if he held a deep secret. "We have been given the same hope."

One fisherman whom Rudy recognized from the wheelhouse blurted out. "I don't want another kid, man." The room exploded in laughter.

Gonzales pointed at the man who spoke. "*Our* promise is the gift of eternal life if we believe in God's son, Jesus. God doesn't lie. And

His son is our ticket to Heaven." He raised his Bible and read from the passage. "He wanted to show the heirs to his promise that his purpose was unchangeable. He delivered an oath, so that we would know God cannot lie and we would be encouraged to grab hold of the hope set before us. That's found in Hebrews, sixth chapter."

The big man paused, his gaze drifting from one face to the next as he studied the men in the room. "This hope, fellas, is an anchor on our soul. It's sure and steadfast, and one we can cling to." Gonzales smiled like he'd seen Heaven itself. "Jesus was the forerunner for us. He became a high priest forever and He is the one who will guarantee us passage into Heaven."

Across the room, Dane listened, his gaze intent upon the unconventional Bible study leader. Rudy prayed the message made its way to the man's heart. The stoic countenance Dane wore yesterday had disappeared, and a ready smile brightened his face. He flashed a grin Rudy's way and nodded—the decision to return home and get reacquainted with his wife and daughter apparently agreeing with him. Rudy returned the smile. Dane had found his way back.

Midweek the ship ground to a halt, the Bering Sea calm as the crew prepared to haul in what everyone expected to be a great catch. No word of any early season storms threatened the peace, and the crew came to life as the fishing regimen returned. Rudy took his place beside Dane in the hold, his log book ready. "One more tour, and we're headed south."

"Can't wait." Dane grinned. "Thanks for fishing me out of the abyss."

"God hooked you. I just reeled you in."

Dane laughed and nodded as the sound of chains signaled fishing had gotten underway.

The first net unloaded an alarming number of skates and one six-foot halibut, along with the requisite catch of pollock. The long journey from the bottom of the ocean to the ship's hold left no tails or fins twitching as the fish joined the journey to someone's sandwich on the mainland. Rudy pulled the skates and halibut out as fast as he could, shoving them to the side for sampling.

Beside him, Dane wrestled the unwanted species to the floor, helping Rudy get the bycatch out of the way. When they'd done all they could, Dane pulled out his knife and trimmed the roe into the catching trays while Rudy recorded his findings. The engine hummed, the eerie whistle of the last voyage missing.

As the hours dragged on, Rudy gave thanks his tour of service was almost complete. He'd kept his word to Hawk, and he'd found McKenna's husband—both tasks gave him satisfaction. His gratitude to God for using him in this way could have filled a universe. Now all he had to do was ride out the next few days and catch a plane home.

As the tonnage mounted in the hold, and the days remaining on this tour dwindled, Dane grew quieter. Rudy could only guess the reason. Going home and facing McKenna took courage. Admitting he'd made mistakes and finding his place again in his family would take time.

Rudy had no doubt McKenna still loved the man with all her heart, but he prayed she would realize how much being on her own had changed her. The spark of love that first brought the couple together still burned bright in each of them, but she and Dane would have to start over in finding common ground. Throw Sydney into the mix and the home waters might churn as rough as those of the Bering Sea under storm watch.

By the weekend, the catcher processor approached capacity, the captain estimating another day or two of fishing would end the tour. Rudy sighed in relief. The sixteen-hour days were taking their toll, and he needed some serious sleep time. He headed to his bunk after a grueling day of sampling, followed by three hours of paperwork and entering data on the ship's computer. Sleep didn't come right away, an odd whistle faint in the darkness. Rudy wrestled with the sensation he'd heard that sound before, but in his fatigue, he couldn't place the source. *I'm just exhausted.*

Daylight brought the sound of running feet. Rudy groaned and poked his head out in the hallway to check out the commotion. A man he didn't know hustled by, his dark skin and curly hair suggesting he'd come from Samoa, as so many of the fishermen had. Rudy didn't know if he could make himself be understood. "Hey, man! What's going on?"

"Boat stop. New leak in engine. Engineer, he repair." The man waved and hurried down the stairs.

Not again. Rudy wiped the sleep from his eyes and returned to his bunk. Dressing for the day, he wandered toward the galley, the smell of breakfast giving him hope that the damage in the engine room wasn't too great.

Dane sat at a table, nursing a cup of coffee. He grimaced when Rudy entered, gesturing for him to come sit. "You heard the news?"

"Another problem with the engine?" Rudy glanced around the room, fishermen lounging at tables, waiting for word to return to work. "I thought they fixed the problem when we were in port."

"A crate as old as this one can pop a problem without a reason." Dane swirled his coffee. "I wish we weren't so far from shore."

"Three days' travel on a good day." Rudy's heart rate accelerated. "That's not reassuring if the boat catches fire."

"At least we've had several safety drills if we need them. We may get to test our learning ability." Dane stood and clapped him on the shoulder. "Better get some grub while we still have food. We could be here awhile."

Rudy followed Dane through the buffet line, loading his plate with eggs and sausages. He filled his coffee cup and returned to the table where they'd been. "Think we'll be towed back to shore?"

Dane shook his head. "No. The engineer is confident he can fix the problem. We'll finish our catch and head for home a day late."

"I hope he's right."

Dane glanced at him, eyes narrowed. "This is not a good place to be stranded."

Midday the fishermen were summoned back to their posts and the engines surged to life. No strange sounds came from the boat's powerhouse.

The immediate threat removed, the men relaxed. With Dane at his side harvesting the roe, Rudy gauged the catch. The rhythm they'd developed working side by side these past few weeks created a compatibility for which Rudy thanked God. A good relationship with Dane would allow Rudy to help the man with pointers on how he could understand his little girl and rejoin his family.

Rudy saw himself as a mediator between Dane and Sydney much like Queen Esther when the king had signed a death warrant for all the Jews. Esther questioned her role when Mordecai pressed her to seek the king and plead for her people exactly as Rudy questioned his.

"Have you not been chosen for such a time as this?" Mordecai reminded her.

The woman surrendered to the calling. "If I perish, I perish."

Like Esther, Rudy had been placed in the lives of McKenna and Sydney at a time when God could use him to restore Dane to his rightful place as head of the family. Who else would have an autistic sister and also be an observer on an Alaskan fishing boat? The coincidence was not lost on him. Rudy understood autism in a way others would not. He also knew fishermen. Only a mighty, loving

God could have ordained such an encounter.

As Dane's shift ended, he waved at Rudy and yelled. "So far. So good." He gave a thumbs-up sign and left the work area.

Rudy finished his sampling, gathered his data, and headed to the ship's computer. Another three hours of inputting information awaited before he could call it quits for the day. Fatigue burned at his eyes and hunger gnawed at his stomach. Every time he'd been on a crew, the hours were the same. Rudy's resolve to be finished with observer work strengthened. Next time his company needed someone to fill in, Rudy would not be available, not even if Hawk were behind them begging. Only a call from God would get him back on a boat. No matter how little money he had.

Never had the bunk felt so welcoming as it did when Rudy crawled in three hours later. Almost midnight, the cold of the Bering Sea bore down on him as he donned a second flannel shirt and zipped his sleeping bag. The hum of the engine propelling the ship, and the noise of the night shift crew fulfilling their tasks lulled him to sleep. Even the listing of the ship didn't bother his rest tonight. Six hours wasn't enough, but it would have to do.

A siren blast jolted Rudy out of bed two hours later. The loud ringing of the alarm and the banging of doors and running feet could mean only one thing—the ship was in trouble. Grabbing his evac suit, and another oversized flannel shirt, he tucked his pocket-sized Bible inside and hit the deck running. Sounds of feet pounding the stair wells echoed in the night. Remembering the captain's words, he accelerated his pace—a vessel could sink in less than a minute.

Order reigned as the seasoned fishermen sought their assigned raft. Rudy had learned the drill half-heartedly, never thinking he might find himself in a real-life crisis. But now men sped across the deck, roll was called, and evac suits donned. He wriggled into the giant Gumby-like covering, the protection fighting his every move. He should have practiced getting into his suit more. Once he had the cumbersome enclosure all the way up, he glanced around the deck seeking Dane but didn't see him. What was keeping the man?

Smoke billowed around the ship, a red haze streaking across the water. How much trouble were they in? A loud explosion answered him—the ship's hull was probably involved. Minutes remained before the vessel sank, taking all remaining personnel to the bottom of the Bering Sea.

Closing the flap of his suit, Rudy said a prayer for all the crewmen to be rescued as his life raft dropped into the water. Inflating on impact, the flimsy craft looked like a tarp covering a giant tire. The outward appearance didn't give him confidence. Without questioning their fate, the other men jumped into the frozen darkness, scrambling to board their assigned contraption and await their rescue.

Rudy summoned his courage and leapt over the side. The eerie, black water surrounded him. He focused, seeking the edge of the raft. Bobbing like a cork on the water, Rudy propelled himself with small arm strokes to the waiting lifeboat. A red mitten-like hand reached down and grabbed his suit, yanking him up over the side. Gonzales smiled, his white teeth eerie in the darkness. Rudy crawled in, cold water dripping off him. He activated his emergency beacon and turned to help another sailor into the boat. Within seconds, their raft filled, all the assigned men accounted for. So far, so good. Find the others, Lord.

Rudy helped paddle water from the side of the craft, moving them away from the ship. Above him, other rafts still waited to drop. What was taking so long? Those men would be trapped if they didn't hurry. As if in answer, another loud explosion sounded and the ship groaned, listing sideways in the water. The lopsided hull hovered over the water, much of the bottom exposed, the deck and remaining rescue units tilted away from him.

Clinging to the side of his raft, Rudy anguished over the men still leaving the deck, pleading with God that no one else would suffer. As if in answer a shriek and a boom escaped the ship, the hulk of the vessel sliding into the night. The wake of its passing rocked the lifeboats. Never had Rudy been so alone.

The wind picked up an hour into their ordeal. The icy water, its earlier surface a sheen of blackness, now turned angry, lapping at the sides of the raft, making it bob like a cork. Though the Bering Sea was deadly, its shallower depth from other oceans prevented the high swells and rocking waves another body of water might have generated.

Rudy checked his beacon every few minutes to make sure it still worked, letting the light drift over the craft, illuminating the faces of the other men floating with him. In the darkness, the forms of the others on board disappeared, only the sound of their voices assured him his crewmates still remained. Never had he felt so isolated, the black depths like a monster lurking nearby.

The choppier the sea became, the more they bounced. Stuck in his memory was the image of the last raft still at the top of the ship when it listed sideways. Men could easily have been trapped on top if the lifeboat didn't drop or inflate. Rudy prayed everyone got out. He wouldn't know more until the rescuers arrived. With the adrenalin rush over and the fatigue of the last few days catching up with him, Rudy fell into a troubled sleep.

Sometime later, a shout from Gonzales jerked Rudy awake. The sky remained dark, and the faces of the crewmen were still lost in the murky shadows of the choppy sea. Rudy blinked, trying to make sense of the man's fervor. Pointing out over the water, Gonzales screamed. "Body floating!"

Rudy sat up straighter, squinting to see what the other fellow saw. His breathing grew shallow at the sight of a man in a survival suit drifting nearby. "Let's get him!"

Using their arms to propel the raft over the water, the men bobbed closer to the floating mass. The lead crewman issued orders for those on the side nearest the stranded sailor to hoist him up and land him in the boat, while they moved to the edges to allow room. For several tense moments, Rudy held his breath as the men tugged the evac suit, eventually raising the fisherman from the water. Once inside, they rolled him to the center for a better distribution of his weight.

Gonzales opened the suit's mask and groaned. "Lord, have mercy. He's wet inside."

Rudy's heart sank. Water inside the suit meant certain death if they couldn't get the fellow dry and warm. "How could that have happened?"

"Tiny hole somewhere is all it takes. He may have caught it on something sharp when he jumped. As long as he's been in the water, he could be wet all the way to his shoes."

The lead crewman shoved his arms up out of his own suit and tugged at the rescued fisherman's coverings. "If he's wet, we have to get him dry. Help me strip him."

"Out here?" One of the crewmen sounded as flabbergasted as Rudy felt. The man grabbed at the fisherman's legs. "If he wasn't cold already, this should finish him off."

"He's a dead man if we don't." The lead crewman spoke to the victim, whose body shook like a blender gone mad. "It's okay, buddy, we'll try to help."

The man's words slurred, his teeth chattering in the cold. "Muh, muh, muh, needs me."

Recognizing the voice, Rudy stopped breathing, his body pulsing with horror.

Dane.

The men gathered around the shivering form, stripping Dane of his wet clothes.

The lead crewman shouted. "Men, don't take any chances with your own lives. If you can't get any clothing out of your evac suit, don't risk it. One false move and we could all be pitched into the water."

One fisherman pulled off his own t-shirt, another offered a vest. Rudy slipped out of the lined flannel shirt he wore. Together they rubbed Dane's arms and legs, while the lead crewman performed chest compressions. "His pulse is slow and his breathing shallow." The lead looked around. "One of you will need to hold him against you, while the rest of us lean against his torso to keep him warm in this wind."

Rudy pushed out of the rest of his evac suit. "Let me give him my jeans. They're flannel lined. I have thermals I can wear under the evac suit."

The lead nodded. "Make it quick. You're in terrible danger without your suit."

Rudy jerked off the jeans. While he struggled back into the safety gear, the men dressed Dane in the clothing they'd volunteered.

Gonzales moved behind Dane and opened his arms wide. "I'm the biggest one here. Set this fellow in my lap and lean him against my chest. The shirts and my warmth should block most of the wind."

Two other crew members lifted Dane into position. The big man wrapped his muscled arms around Dane and pulled him gently against his chest. "Pull my sleeves down and stick his arms into the shirt with mine. There's plenty of room."

The men worked Dane's arms into Gonzales' shirt while the big guy followed with his own arms down the sleeves. Tight but insulated.

Rudy sidled up beside the Bible study leader and leaned against Dane's right side, feeling warmth from the other two bodies. Another crew member leaned in from the left. The lead crewman laid himself across Dane's legs. The only part of Dane remaining unprotected were his feet, neck, and face. A fifth crew member sat at Gonzales' feet, wrapping his legs campfire style over Dane's.

Gonzales nodded. "He's as warm as we can get him, men. If he makes it, it will be the hand of the Almighty what saves him."

The crew leader spoke from his spot on Dane's legs. "If any of you start feeling cramps in your legs or arms, we'll shift positions. Especially you." He glanced up at Gonzales. "You have to be able to move when help arrives."

The man nodded and glanced over the group. "Let's pray. God Almighty is out there waiting to hear from us." His dark eyes landed on Rudy. "You start."

Rudy closed his eyes. "Lord, send us rescuers soon. Make my beacon strong, so they can find us easily."

Each fisherman followed him.

In his evac suit, Rudy wasn't cold, despite the missing shirt and jeans. Dane, though, only had a pair of jeans and an assortment of shirts. The shivering had stopped, which indicated the hypothermia may have grown worse. Dane had lost consciousness, but Rudy couldn't tell if the man slept or had slipped into a coma. *Please, Lord. He was going home.*

Everyone grew silent as they kept vigil over the rescued man, his presence a reminder of the fate they all faced if not rescued. Like hungry demons seeking prey, the sound of waves lapping at the sides of the lifeboat filled the darkness.

The promise of dawn peeked at the horizon when Rudy heard the sound of helicopter blades whirring above the water.

One of the men in his raft shouted. "I told you having the observer on board would get us preferential service. It's the bloody Coast Guard honing in on his beacon."

A cheer rose from the rest of the fishermen, and Rudy found it humbling to be the hero. The approaching roar of the airborne rescuers could as easily have been a symphony orchestra, the sound was so sweet to his ears. Having the Jayhawks circling above meant his certain return home. Thank God, his mother did not have to lose a second child. He'd lived to recount another adventure. Two hours before he hadn't been so sure.

A cage-like basket dropped from the chopper, and a man in a Coast Guard uniform slid down with it. "Let's get you men started into the helo. Anyone injured?"

The lead crewman shouted at the officer, pointing at Dane cocooned in the circle of bodies. "This guy took on water. He needs immediate attention."

Rudy moved aside as the rescuer reached for Dane, flashing a light into his eyes, and reaching inside his shirt to check for a pulse. The man's grim face reflected what Rudy already suspected. Dane was in deep trouble. "Help me shove him into the cage. He's going to need every second we can give him."

Slowly the basket wound upward, pulling Dane to the waiting chopper. Rudy held his breath, the rescue effort protracted when

Dane needed haste. Soon all of the men on his raft were lifted to the waiting belly of the helicopter. Rudy slid in beside Gonzales, the big man's head bowed as he prayed.

Rudy glanced around, grateful that another Coast Guard officer had already wrapped Dane in dry blankets. The men beside Dane were rubbing his limbs, trying to warm him.

Not able to move closer to his friend, Rudy looked out the open door at the ocean below, searching for other rafts waiting rescue. Two ships chugged across the water, headed toward a cluster of white in the distance. Another Jayhawk headed their direction. More men would be rescued. He prayed no more had been lost in the night awaiting rescue.

Though the noise inside the helicopter prevented conversation, Rudy's eyelids grew heavy, his overwhelming fatigue, coupled with the terror of Dane's ordeal, making him drowsy. The long night had taken its toll. As the Coast Guard flew them to safety, the roar of the blades hummed Rudy to sleep. When he awoke, the chopper was setting down. "Welcome to Anchorage, gentlemen. Land of the giant snowdrift."

Rudy sat up, blinking. How long had he slept? The other men were shedding their evac suits as they prepared to de-board. Rudy tugged at the tight-fitting garment, the cocoon unwilling to let go. Finally, he got the cumbersome thing down to his ankles and stepped out. He looked around for Dane. The man was gone. "Where's the hypothermia victim?"

One of the crew men pointed to a departing ambulance. "He didn't have a moment to lose."

"Where will they take him?"

"To the regional hospital here first, then he may be airlifted to Seattle." The lead crewman shook his head. "His hypothermia is the worst I've seen. And I've been on the water twenty years."

Rudy's heart sank. "What are his chances?"

"He could still live, but at this point his life is in God's hands." The man studied Rudy. "We did everything we could, even to the point of risking our own safety."

Rudy nodded. "I know. Are we going back to Dutch?"

"Our boat sank to the bottom of the Bering Sea." The lead crewman now spoke to the entire group. "The pollock season is over until December. No reason to go back. We can all head home."

Rudy bit back a retort. Without Dane, going home might not be the happily ever after he'd hoped to find in Dutch Harbor.

CHAPTER TWENTY-THREE

MCKENNA SQUINTED AT THE DIGITAL READOUT on the clock. Why was the alarm ringing at five o'clock in the morning? She'd had a busy day at the gallery, and Sydney had created another problem at school. Exhausted, McKenna had gone to bed early. She must have hit the wrong button when she set the alarm.

She reached over to snap the switch off, but the ringing continued. As her foggy, sleep-filled brain crept from the dream in which she'd been wrapped in Dane's arms on a sandy beach, McKenna registered the sound she heard as a phone ringing. Her cell phone had been turned off when she crawled into the covers at seven, so the piercing wail jarring her awake had to be the landline her parents kept in the house for emergency.

Emergency?

Jolted awake, aware every second that passed could be someone calling to relay an important message, McKenna sat up, shook her head to clear her brain, and stood.

Please, Lord, let it be a wrong number. My day left no room for anything more.

But even as she prayed, the only two parties who might call the number were her parents or Dane. Feeling the truth punch her in the middle, she groped her way through the living room, knocking over an end table as she staggered into the sofa. She found the swinging door leading to the kitchen, and switched on the light, reaching the phone on its sixth ring. The persistence could only mean one thing. She wasn't going to like the news. Hand shaking, she lifted the receiver. "Hello?"

"Hello, this is Chaplain Arthur Mellor, of the US Coast Guard station in Anchorage, Alaska. I'm trying to locate the whereabouts of McKenna Nichols."

"This is she." McKenna swallowed down the metallic taste rising in her throat, the calm she sought eluding her. "How may I help you?"

"Mrs. Nichols? Oh, good. The number we had on file for you had been disconnected and this number was listed as an alternative. I'm glad to find you so easily."

"I moved to Newport this summer." McKenna grabbed the back of a kitchen chair, turned it toward her, and sat. Pulse throbbing at the base of her throat, she fought the mounting panic in her head. Dane was coming home. Due any day. Why was the chaplain calling her? Had Dane been called out to sea again? Finally, she found her voice. "What do you need from me?"

"Mrs. Nichols, I'm afraid I have some very bad news." The chaplain paused, his breathing heavy into the phone. "I'm sorry to tell you your husband has died in an accident at sea."

"Dead?" McKenna gripped the phone, her knuckles white from the strain. "No, this can't be. He was headed home."

"Your husband's ship caught fire and during the emergency evacuation, men were forced to jump into the water and claim their lifeboat."

"Dane didn't jump?" McKenna's breathing grew shallow, numbness spreading through her limbs. This couldn't be happening. She'd waited so long for him. And now he was dead?

"Dane didn't make it to his lifeboat. He floated for hours before a raft picked him up His evac suit had been damaged somewhere in his travels. When crew members pulled him out of the water, he was shaking from the cold, speech slurred, and breathing shallow."

"Oh, poor Dane." McKenna's knees wobbled, absorbing the shock of the chaplain's words. "What happened?"

As the chaplain explained the accident, each detail of the rescue more unbelievable, McKenna's composure crumbled.

"A life flight airplane was waiting for him in Anchorage, but he died an hour after he was rescued." The chaplain paused. "Do you have someone you can call to come be with you?"

"I...I don't know." McKenna's voice broke, sobs threatening to erupt. *No. I must be strong.* "I thought my husband was coming home." She swallowed, fighting for control. "I'm having a hard time believing you."

"Mrs. Nichols, I know this news comes as a shock. There are families in Newport who are with the Coast Guard. May I call one of them to have someone come and be with you?"

"Thank you for the offer, Chaplain. I think I need to be alone." McKenna swiped at wetness on her cheeks, steeling herself against the shock. "This is all too sudden. You understand."

"Do you have a pencil handy?"

McKenna glanced around the kitchen. Sydney's crayons sat on her booster chair seat. McKenna picked up the red one. "Yes."

"This is the number of the Coast Guard chaplain nearest you. Write it down in case you change your mind and need someone to talk to."

McKenna turned and wrote the number on the wall—huge, angry, red numbers scarring the surface like the rage within trying to destroy her. Dane was coming back to her and Sydney. Dane would be the husband and father he'd promised to be. Dane was supposed to come home, not die. "Thank you for the information." She gritted her teeth, ice filling her veins. "I will call if I need anything."

"We'll be in touch regarding arrangements for transporting your husband's body." The chaplain's words grew faint. "I'm truly sorry for your loss, Mrs. Nichols."

"So am I." She hung up the phone, slipped off the light, and slid down the wall to the floor. *So am I.*

Knees pulled up, she wrapped her arms around her legs and buried her face against the cotton nightshirt she wore. The shock of the news left her numb. This had to be a nightmare. If only she could wake up, the last few minutes would disappear. She couldn't let go. She didn't dare. She'd spent so much time over the last two years being strong that if she did, she'd shatter.

Alone in the darkness, she shivered, breathing shallow and pulse racing—the silence of the kitchen broken only by the hum of the refrigerator. No tears came, no sobs sounded, only the dull throb of her heart proved she yet lived. Dane was dead, and she couldn't even cry.

McKenna remained immobile, unaware of how much time passed, when a knock sounded at the door. Shivering in her nightshirt, she glanced up from her spot on the floor and saw the digital readout on the microwave. Six-thirty. Who would be coming to her door at this hour? Tempted not to answer, McKenna wrapped her arms about her waist and tiptoed to the side window, allowing a glimpse of whoever stood outside. Under the street light a small compact car had parked at her driveway. A short figure waited on the porch—a woman—whispering through the door. "McKenna? It's me. Livy."

Rudy! Oh no, please God. Don't let him be on the same ship as Dane. I can't bear any more tragedy tonight.

Using the pale light of dawn as a guide, McKenna walked away from the window, slipped down the hall to grab her robe, and tucked the warm velour around her as she returned to the entry. Bolstering her courage, she flipped on the porch light, and opened the door to the waiting woman. "Please don't tell me something has happened to Rudy."

"Rudy called and asked me to come." The older woman reached out an arm and touched McKenna's shoulder. "May I come in?"

Nodding, McKenna stepped back from the doorway, allowing Livy to enter. "Rudy knows, then?"

Livy held out her arms. "He was on the life raft with Dane." Livy's tears glistened in the shadows the early morning light created. "The men took off their survival suits and gave Dane their clothes, trying to save him."

McKenna stepped into the woman's embrace. "They risked their lives to save Dane's?"

"Yes."

McKenna couldn't contain her grief any longer, the wall built around her heart crumbling at the kindness of strangers. She let out a cry and sobbed into the older woman's shoulder. "Oh, Livy. I loved him so much." She gripped Livy tighter, her body shaking in agony. "He was coming home. To me. To Sydney."

"I know, honey. I know." Livy's hands rubbed her back and whispers of prayers came from her mouth. "Jesus, hear us. Take our pain. Take our sorrow. Your child is hurting, Lord. A knife has sliced her heart. Her soul bleeds. Hold her and heal her, Father."

McKenna let the tears flow, rocking in Livy's arms. Nothing had prepared her for this. She'd survived the loneliness. She'd survived months of not knowing where her husband was. She'd survived the challenges single parenting created. But the death of her husband was not something she'd ever truly imagined. Men like Dane didn't die. In her eyes, he'd been invincible. Always out there, somewhere. His warm, brown eyes, dark brown hair, teasing kisses. Gone. Forever. At least when he was fishing, she knew he existed. His checks reminded her he still thought of her. All that gone. Alone became a new word she didn't want to try.

She shuddered, then straightened, swiping at her cheeks, trying to stem the pain. But the wetness continued to flow. Even to her ears, her wails sounded like a wounded animal. When finally her insides ached and her throat felt raw, she looked at Livy, pulling in a long, shuddering breath. "I didn't even think. Is Rudy okay?" She hiccupped. "You said he called to tell you about Dane?"

Livy smiled and gestured toward the kitchen. "Let's go make tea, shall we? You look like you could use a cup."

McKenna followed the woman, glad Livy felt so comfortable leading the way to McKenna's kitchen. Heart aching, her soul raw, she didn't have the strength to play hostess. She glanced at the wall where she'd written the chaplain's number, a painful reminder of the earlier phone call that changed her life forever. "What would I do without you?"

"You're strong, McKenna." Livy pulled out a chair for her. "You are an amazing mother and a talented young woman. Dane's death is a terrible blow, but you will rise from the ashes of your loss."

"How can you be so certain?" McKenna leaned both elbows against the table, supporting her wearied torso in the chair. "I don't feel strong at all."

"Because I've been where you are." Livy filled the teapot and set it on the stove to heat. She faced McKenna and leaned against the counter, quiet for several moments—the sound of the water heating filling the void. Finally, Livy glanced at the ceiling before gazing at her. "I lost my husband and daughter to tragedy."

McKenna sat up straighter, stunned. "What? What happened?"

"Eight years ago, our home in Astoria caught fire." The steam whistled from the teapot. Livy moved it to the center, then reached into the cupboard and retrieved two cups. "Earl Grey?"

McKenna nodded, anxious to know more about Livy's past, while another part wanted nothing to do with it. That part simply wanted to curl up in a ball and pretend nothing else existed. Nothing else mattered. Nothing did, did it? Other than Sydney. Oh, Lord. Sydney. Now they were truly alone. *She* was alone—never to have the hope of a husband coming home to help her again.

"My husband insisted on going into the house to get Romelle, even though Rudy said he knew her favorite hiding place." Livy set the cups on the table and sat down next to McKenna. Silent, she stared into the steam rising from the tea. "My daughter Romelle was autistic, much like Sydney." She inhaled a deep breath and blew it out. "When the firemen found them. . ." She paused, taking another deep breath. "When the firemen found them upstairs, Ivan, my husband, was on the floor in front of the closet where Romelle liked to hide, her body in his arms." Livy picked up her tea and sipped. "They both perished."

"Oh, Livy. I'm so sorry. I didn't know."

Livy set her tea cup down. "I thought the loss would kill Rudy. He blamed himself for not insisting on going into the house to get his sister." She looked at McKenna, eyes brimming. "When he decided to work in Alaska, I knew he was trying to run away from the pain." Livy drew in a ragged breath. "But his going helped me refocus my prayers on him and learn to live with my loss. If I'd lost Rudy, too, I wouldn't be here. There's not enough of me to grieve that much."

McKenna understood. "That's the way I feel. I had so looked forward to Dane's return." She paused, bracing herself against the grief. "To lose him now leaves me shattered inside. It's like I've lost him twice." She sipped her tea, the agony of her situation threatening to make another appearance. "I'm so glad I can lean on you. With my parents in Europe and Dane's parents uncommitted to their granddaughter, I'm very much alone."

She closed her eyes, contemplating the next action she needed to take. Hearing Livy's story helped—McKenna wouldn't suffer alone—not in terms of losing Dane or in raising Sydney. McKenna's mouth popped open as the impact of Livy's revelation dawned on her. "That explains why you and Rudy know what to do with my daughter."

A giggle caught McKenna's attention. Sydney stood in the doorway, a mass of curls framing her face. "Cocoa?"

McKenna drew Sydney into her lap, pulling the small body close. "Did we wake you?"

The child's eyes blinked in the light, sleepiness not yet faded from her face. She leaned against McKenna, fingering the lace of McKenna's robe. "Cocoa?"

Livy stood and retrieved a mug. "Which cupboard?"

"Far end."

Livy opened the cupboard and found a cocoa packet. Pouring the mix into the cup, she added hot water, the teaspoon clinking the side as she stirred. "Romelle grew up to be a beautiful young woman, but she never lost her timidity. Her fear." Livy turned to look at McKenna, setting the cocoa on the table. "Rudy spent a lot of time with her, watching out for her safety, calming her when she was upset, making certain she lived a happy life. Romelle trusted him and went wherever he took her."

"Did you teach her at home?" McKenna lifted Sydney into her chair, setting the mug of cocoa in front of her daughter.

Livy nodded, sitting again. "The classroom noise was something she couldn't tolerate, either. She learned to read and write. Math enabled her to manage a checking account. But Romelle didn't like cooking. The only dinners she made were pizza and baked chicken." Livy stared at the table, a smile on her face as if she'd entered a fun memory. "Rudy took her to restaurants to ensure her ability to get food from another source." Livy tilted her head and whispered in a conspiratorial tone. "But between you and me, Rudy liked chocolate milkshakes as much as she did, so taking Romelle guaranteed he'd get to order a burger and shake."

McKenna tried to smile, then sobered at the thought of Rudy. "You said Rudy called. He risked his life to save Dane?"

"All the men on the life raft did." Livy touched McKenna's arm. "Dane didn't die alone. He was loved and cared for even though he suffered."

"Did the men make it to safety?" McKenna shuddered at the thought more might have lost their lives tonight.

"Yes. A helicopter picked them out of the sea. Apparently, the ship's crew is accounted for. After Rudy gets checked for hypothermia, he's coming home." Livy raised her hands heavenward. "Thank you, Lord."

Remembering the chaplain's words, McKenna glanced at the calendar. "I need to ask a favor of Rudy."

"Whatever it is, he will be glad to do it." Livy folded her hands in front of her, leaning on the table and rattling the salt and pepper shakers. "He feels he let you down."

"Let me down?" McKenna stared at Livy. "He went to Alaska and found my husband. Dane said in his e-mail Rudy convinced him to come home. Why does Rudy feel as if he let me down? I owe the man a huge debt of gratitude."

"What is it you need him to do?"

CHAPTER TWENTY-FOUR

RUDY BOARDED THE FLIGHT BOUND FOR Seattle, his mind numb with all that had transpired in the last five days. His boat had sunk, his new friend had perished, and his mission to restore McKenna's family had failed. The emptiness inside gnawed at him; the ache for the little girl waiting at home with her grieving mother needling his mind.

What would McKenna do now? Her source of income vanished with the death of her husband. He didn't know how much money she made at the gallery, but he suspected the profits varied with the tourist season. If Dane had worked since high school, his social security might contain enough employment quarters to support a surviving child. Perhaps the couple had squirreled away money in a savings account. Though McKenna's problems weren't his concern, he'd welcome them if they were.

Through the window next to his seat, Rudy watched the luggage and cargo being loaded. One large box was loaded into the hold, the airline personnel struggling with its bulk. Rudy grimaced—the container held Dane's body. McKenna had sent word through the Coast Guard that she wanted Rudy to accompany the man's remains home, so he'd delayed his return until the funeral parlor in Newport could make the proper arrangements and fly Dane back to the lower forty-eight.

Rudy appreciated the faith and trust she placed in him, but the guilt of his failed attempt to bring the fisherman back to his family haunted him. He wasn't one to question God's sovereignty, but Rudy certainly figured God could have handled this a little differently. What was the mighty creator of the universe doing, leaving a woman alone and her child fatherless, when God could have spared Dane? Rudy would have volunteered if it meant Dane could go home.

Rudy checked his thoughts. His own mother counted on his return. She'd suffered her share of losses already, and though she'd bounced back from the grief over time, losing him to the unrelenting ocean might have stilled her spirit once and for all.

No. God was in control, His reasons for not seeing Dane to safety were His to make. In the scheme of things, Rudy could only bow his head and thank God for sparing the lives of all the crewmen, save one. The disaster could have been so much worse. Dane's time was up and God called him home. McKenna would go on, God guiding her through the rigors of single motherhood in the years to come. In theory, it all sounded like a neat and tidy package, a pious promise to a painful problem, but in the physical realm, it meant agony for those left behind.

Rudy withdrew a notepad from his shirt pocket and made a list of ways he might help McKenna. He'd have to be careful. Before Alaska, she'd been a married woman, waiting for her husband to return. Keeping his involvement friendly and helpful, he'd managed to stay clear of any impropriety on his part.

Now, though, McKenna lived the role of grieving widow. She needed time to find her way, to plan for Sydney's future as well as her own. Having him too near might muddy the waters and confuse her thinking. He couldn't deny being attracted to her. But his desire would make matters worse. He'd have to steer clear of McKenna, offering help or advice only when it was requested. Otherwise, he might scare her away forever. Rudy wrote in the notepad before stashing it back in his pocket. *Fools rush in where angels fear to tread. Think before you act.*

The flight attendant came down the aisle, checking seat belts and assisting passengers, stopping to straighten the back of the seat next to him. The trip to Portland would last almost four hours. All his gear and reading material perished in the bottom of the ocean. He had nothing to do but fly home. For only the second time since his life raft hit the water five days earlier, Rudy leaned back and slept a fitful sleep.

Seated at the back of the funeral home waiting for Dane's memorial service to begin, Rudy stared at the program in his hand. Statistics leapt out at him—dates, places, names—fragments of the dead man's history verifying he once existed. Little else darkened the folded page—where Dane spent his time, how he viewed the world, who or what filled his last thoughts as God called him home. Had Rudy not met the man and worked alongside him aboard a doomed ship in a lonely sea, the program in his hands would tell him nothing of the man Dane was.

"Do you have anything to say to McKenna after the service?" Beside him his mother lifted a handkerchief from her bag, clutching the fabric in her fingers like a weapon against the emotions he guessed waited to burst from her inner being. "I know she'll want to speak with you."

Rudy slumped in the pew. He hadn't been to see the widow upon his return to Newport. Riding home with her husband's body housed in the belly of the plane, Rudy had skirted the waiting personnel at the airport, walking away from the scene of the hearse and its attendants. The funeral home, not the family, had come to pick up the body, for which he was grateful. He couldn't yet face McKenna, his failure to complete his mission weighing heavily on his heart. He glanced at his mother. "I don't know what I'd say, Mom. Sorry seems inadequate."

"You gave her hope, Rudy. Preparing for Dane's homecoming

energized her. She had two weeks of anticipation. I've never seen her so happy or so content."

"Then, slam dunk, he's dead." Rudy swallowed, aiming his gaze at the slats of wood forming an arch over the funeral home auditorium. "I raised her spirits, only to leave her vulnerable against an agonizing blow to her heart. Not exactly hero material, here."

"But she knew Dane still loved her."

The canned music piping into the silence increased in volume and a door on the left of the podium opened. The funeral director entered, followed by McKenna. The sight of her made Rudy gasp as if he'd taken a knife to the gut. Dressed in a black jacket and flared skirt, McKenna carried a bouquet of white roses. Her hair swept up and away from her face, caught beneath a narrow-brimmed hat from which a dotted black veil hung. She walked to the end of the first pew and faced forward in front of the coffin. Even from the back of the room, Rudy couldn't miss her trembling shoulders rising and falling with each breath, head tilted forward, and free hand dabbing at her nose. His overpowering sense of guilt pecked at him with each shake of the hat's veil. He fought the urge to leave.

Following McKenna to the front pew, an older woman with silvered hair worn in a braided knot at the back of her head joined a tall man dressed in a black suit. Though at least twenty years older, the woman could have passed for McKenna's twin. The man carried Sydney, who hid her face in his shoulder.

Rudy looked at his mother. "Her folks?"

Nodding, his mother touched her eyes with the handkerchief. "Flew in from Italy as soon as they heard. Didn't arrive until last night."

A second couple entered. A man bent at the shoulders and toting a cane led a short, plump woman who sniffed into a tissue. Her reddened eyes and pursed mouth belied a feeble attempt to hide her grief. A young man and a pregnant woman followed, sitting beside the older couple.

"Dane's family?"

"Sister and husband. Mom and Dad."

Rudy inhaled deeply, the accident weighing on his heart as though an elephant sat on his chest. Death affected so many people—loved ones who can never again talk or hug or enjoy the dead man's company. Never share a meal. Never discuss politics. Never seek his opinion. "Such a waste."

His mother read his thoughts. "They'll be reunited in heaven."

A man Rudy recognized as the pastor of his local congregation entered and walked to the podium. He nodded to family members seated in the front and then scanned the rest of those in attendance. "We are here today to celebrate the life of Dane Ferguson Nichols, son, brother, husband, and father, a friend to many of you and a brother in Christ to those who knew him from Waldport Community Church.

"Born November 23, 1988, Dane married McKenna Leanne Danielson, June 21, 2008. He was the father of Sydney Marie Nichols, born September 6, 2010. He died in Anchorage, Alaska following an accident on the Bering Sea on October 10 of this year."

"He is survived by his wife and daughter, his parents, Ross and Rita Nichols, a sister, Diane Nichols Fenwick and husband, Richard, and a nephew, Gavin."

The pastor's words blurred to a drone as Rudy relived the horrors of that night only a week before. What happened to keep Dane from jumping off the ship when he should have? What tore his survival suit? Why did all their efforts fail to save him? Rudy couldn't weep, not here, but his heart bled. The depth of his failure ripped through his soul like a jagged knife slicing his inner core. He'd never be able to face McKenna again, never help Sydney grow up, never trust his own strengths. The need to run from the room pressed against his thoughts, the only anchor his mother's gentle hand on his knee, her fingers patting his thigh in reassurance.

When the service ended, McKenna laid her bouquet across the top of the coffin which remained closed.

Rudy stood with others in the room, the invitation to come forward and pay last respects to the deceased offered. Many worked their way to the front of the room, touching the casket and bending low to whisper words of encouragement to McKenna. As Rudy's row moved last into the center aisle, he shook his head and glanced at his mother. "I can't do this, Mom."

She gave his arm a squeeze. "Wait for me?"

He nodded, stepping to the back wall as his mother reached the casket, pulled a single rose from her tote, and laid it on top. She turned and greeted McKenna, who stood and wrapped her arms around his mother, the young widow's sobs audible in the silent room. The two women spoke quietly, his mother stroking the cheek of the grieving widow.

Something she said made McKenna look up, her gaze meeting his. She stared for a moment, her head inclined toward his mother, the ghost of a smile on her face.

He glanced down, not willing to see the anguish in her eyes, nor the sorrow she wore like a shroud, suffering he should have prevented. He turned and walked toward the exit.

After listening to Livy's explanation as to why Rudy hadn't come forward, McKenna's gaze followed the man as he exited the auditorium. She turned to her mother. "I'll be right back. I have to catch someone before he leaves." She nodded toward the back where Rudy had reached the door.

"Is that a friend of Dane's?" Her mother frowned. "Do I know him?"

"No. He's the observer who convinced Dane to come home. I have to thank him."

"He's my son." Livy extended her hand to the woman. "I'm glad to finally meet you."

McKenna hurried down the aisle, skirting a couple of well-wishers talking together. She glanced over her shoulder to where Livy stood speaking to her parents. Livy would fill the space of time for her as she sought Rudy. Her first responsibility was to her family and Dane's, but the need to see the man who last saw Dane alive drove her. "Excuse me." She stopped at the door. "Rudy?"

The man glanced up at his name, turning toward her. His face held no smile, his eyes had lost their glimmer. He opened his mouth as though to speak, but shook his head and waved her away. Dropping his gaze, he continued down the sidewalk, shoulders rounded and head down.

"Please?" McKenna stepped outside to the sidewalk and waited.

Rudy stopped, tilted his face upward and turned, walking back to where she stood. "I'm sorry, McKenna."

"Thank you." McKenna resisted grabbing his hand. "And I don't mean for coming today. Thank you for traveling home with him." McKenna reached out and touched his shoulder, giving it a squeeze. "It meant so much to me."

"I'm sorry I didn't bring him home alive." Rudy gazed away from her, releasing a deep sigh. "You knew he was coming, didn't you?"

"Yes. He e-mailed me twice. His messages were full of hope, saying how much he missed me. How much he still loved me." McKenna paused, a lump in her throat threatening to make her cry. She took a deep breath and continued. "He said he'd been wrong and was excited to be returning. He told me you made him see things differently. He sounded like he was ready to be the father Sydney needs." She touched Rudy's shoulder again. "I have you to thank for that. Knowing he still loved me and wanted to make things right in our marriage gave me closure when he died. I'll always be grateful to you."

Rudy gazed at her, the twinkle she'd always seen in his eyes missing. He pulled out his wallet. "I wanted to return the photos to you. Dane never left them anywhere, once he had them. They're crinkled because I pulled them from his wet shirt the night he. . ." Rudy stopped and swallowed, drawing a ragged breath. He handed over the pictures. "I am so sorry, McKenna. We tried to save him. If we'd been rescued only an hour sooner . . ." His voice broke and Rudy stared at the sidewalk, his chest heaving as he fought for control.

"Hear me, Rudy Taylor." McKenna placed both her hands on his shoulders. "I will never forget what you did. You cannot know how much your friendship and your unselfish quest for me and my family meant. You went above and beyond the call of duty for people you hardly knew. There is *nothing* to forgive." McKenna cupped his chin with her hand, forcing him to look at her. "You have been a true friend to me."

"I've enjoyed every minute I've spent with you and Sydney."

"And we with you as well. I look forward to having you around again."

Rudy shook his head. "I've been offered a position with the fisheries service." He studied her, a rueful smile on his lips. "Apparently surviving a sinking ship makes me an expert on safety. My boss, Hawk Bishop, recommended me to the training group in Seattle."

McKenna gasped. "But what about your mother? How will she fare with you gone?"

"I need employment. I'm tired of working part-time here and there. This is an opportunity to finally find a position that pays well and requires full-time hours. My boss, Hawk, called me last night.

He recommended me when he learned he has to take a leave of absence for health reasons. The position is permanent as it now stands."

"But Rudy—" McKenna swallowed hard, the shock of his words stealing her voice. "I'd hoped you and I—"

"McKenna, *we* can never be. Every time you look at me, you'll think of Dane's death. You need time to process your grief. To discover your new identity. You are a widow—an attractive young woman with a great future."

"Can't that future include a friend?"

"Could you really endure another relationship with a man who makes his living working out of town? Who may have to be gone for weeks at a time? Live with the uncertainty yet again, the danger, the loneliness." Rudy's eyes met hers, a look of regret on his face. "Think about it."

McKenna remained silent, processing the truth of his words. She'd already lost a husband to the Bering Sea. Living through this nightmare, or a similar scenario involving the ocean, a second time would shatter her. The possibility made her stomach churn. Once again, she'd be a lonely woman, standing at the water's edge, wondering what danger her husband might be in today. Tears pooled in the bottoms of her eyes as the reality of Rudy's words sank into her memory. She couldn't do this again. No matter how much Rudy meant to her. She would not let the Bering Sea continue to factor into her life.

Rudy nodded at her, and without saying goodbye turned in the other direction and walked away.

Her gaze followed the man's retreat. McKenna hesitated before returning to her waiting family. They had moved out of the auditorium and huddled together near the funeral home entrance. Her parents spoke in low tones to Dane's folks, grief evident on each face. As McKenna joined them, she glanced once more toward the emptying parking lot.

Rudy had reached his car and was unlocking the passenger side for his mother. He looked up and met McKenna's gaze, lifting his hand to wave before he climbed in.

She pressed her lips together, willing herself to join her circle of mourners. Julia and her new husband had driven over from the valley. Andrea had come alone. Today McKenna needed to grieve her dead husband and offer solace to his parents in their loss. The hurt nagging her, though, wasn't only for the husband she'd lost, but also for the wounded man who had given so much of himself to be her friend. The man who had accepted Sydney without reservation, and who had followed Dane to Alaska to bring him home. He'd risked his life to restore her family and she couldn't even thank him. Rudy was hurting, too, and it would be unseemly for her to reach out to him right now. Saying thank you might never come because she doubted she would ever see the man again. The loss loomed larger than her spirit could bear.

She stepped up the sidewalk and leaned into her father's embrace even as her heart screamed to run the other way. When she looked to the parking lot again, the car was gone.

At least here, no one would question more tears.

CHAPTER TWENTY-FIVE

TWO AFTERNOONS AFTER DANE'S SERVICE, RUDY entered the Tidewater Takeout where his mother worked, heading toward the curtained door that kept patrons from wandering into the kitchen. His mom's voice wafted from the food preparation area, her laughter reminding him of earlier times when she'd spent afternoons cooking with his sister. The sound made her seem younger than her fifty years. He rounded the casing and froze.

Sydney, tongue caught in her teeth and fingers gripping a small knife with his mother's help, stood on a stool cutting slices of cheese at the counter. She lifted each little square to a waiting saltine, then topped the snack with another cracker. Stacking the finished product on a plate already covered with her creations, she smiled at his mother.

"Perfect." Mom nodded her approval to the child, glancing his way. "Care to join us?"

Backing up, he shook his head, retracing his steps in an attempt to disappear. He wasn't ready for this. Rudy's heart ached at the sight of the child, guilt needling his subconscious. She'd never know her father, the memory she might hold of him now would fade with the years. Dane would become a face in a picture and not the warm, caring human being who had wanted to love his little girl, if only he'd been given another chance. If Rudy could trade places with the man, he would. He turned to go.

"Rudy. Swim?" Sydney's voice stopped him.

Looking over his shoulder, he smiled at the child, her sweet gaze so intent Rudy's cheeks burned. If only Dane could have seen her like this. "Not today, Sydney. But soon." He reversed direction and stepped closer. "Is this a cooking lesson?"

Mom nodded, brushing the child's curls away from her eyes and stroking her cheek. "Sydney is making great progress. She can fix peanut butter on crackers, or substitute with cheese." She directed her next question to the girl. "Shall we have a tea party now?"

Sydney climbed down from the stool and carried the plate of crackers toward the door. When she neared Rudy, she glanced back at his mother.

"He might be hungry." Mom knelt beside her. "Shall we share our crackers with him?"

"Rudy. Crackers." Sydney took his mother's hand and the pair walked past him into the café, his mother inclining her head toward the door, indicating he should follow. Sydney claimed the table beneath the ship's wheel while his mother set the plate of snacks down and reached for a pitcher of water from the front counter. The little girl stared at Rudy.

"What brings you here today?" Mom helped Sydney climb into her seat. "Jim ready for you to return to work?"

"Yep. Was afraid he'd lost me."

"In a town this size, that's bound to be news." Mom gave Sydney two crackers on a napkin, then offered the plate to him.

"I suppose." Rudy took a cracker and set it down. "Anyway, he wanted to send me to Coos Bay and the south coast until Christmas." The distance suited him. He wouldn't have needed to worry about running into McKenna. No questioning fishermen to make innocent inquiries, either. Maybe there he could have come to terms with his failure, leave his grief behind. "I told him no."

"Why?" His mother stopped what she was doing and stared at him.

"I'm going to Seattle." Rudy bit into his cracker. "Hawk recommended me for what will probably be a permanent position training recruits."

"You almost perish on the Bering Sea and you immediately go to work for the company that nearly cost you your life?" His mother raised her hands and brought them forward as if to slap something. "Are you determined to leave me alone? I give up on you."

"Mom, I can't make it here." Rudy willed her to understand. "I'm going to Seattle as a trainer. Hawk will let me fly home for Christmas. He's going to have surgery the first of the year and I will double up to fill his shoes as well. I have to get away."

"I don't need you? McKenna doesn't need you? Are we not important?"

"Of course you are. But staying here I'm destined to be a guy who drifts from job to job. In Seattle, I can finally settle into a permanent position."

"Especially since you're hiding from McKenna." His mother poured three glasses of water and distributed them around the table.

"I'm not hiding, Mom."

"Of course you're not. The job makes a convenient way to escape." His mother studied him, her silence loud in the empty afternoon café. "She's going to need friends to help her through this loss."

"True. But I'm the friend who promised to bring Dane home. And I failed." Rudy finished his snack. "We have no future together."

"I know how you operate, Rudy. This is the same kind of behavior you exhibited when your father and Romelle died."

"It's the only way I can cope, Mom. I'm sorry if it bothers you." Rudy fist-bumped the table. "But at least I'm consistent."

"What about Thanksgiving?"

Finally. A change of subject. Mom had backed off.

"Christmas is all I can promise you. I can drive to Carrie's and meet you there." He shifted in his chair, making a scraping sound that Sydney blocked out with hands over her ears.

His mother shook her head. "You're hopeless."

"That's why you still love me." He pointed at the plate near him and rubbed his middle. "Good. Sydney."

"Good. Sydney." The little girl crammed half the cracker into her mouth. His mother pulled the plate away from the child. "Table manners are next."

Ignoring his mother's keen insight, he changed the subject again. "I'm surprised McKenna has Sydney back into her routine this soon. McKenna can't be ready to move forward already?"

"She's not." His mother studied him. "But you and I know Sydney will do better keeping to a schedule. McKenna and her mother are out today looking for a place to rent until her parents can return to their itinerary after Christmas. Several houses standing empty here in Newport."

"Speaking of empty places." Rudy reached into his pocket. "I'm giving up my house. The lease goes through the end of the year. Not much furniture, but I could leave it for them to use."

His mother bit her lip, tears pooling at the bottoms of the lids. "You aren't going to return, are you?"

He touched her shoulder, leaned in to kiss her temple, and turned. The bell over the door rang hollow.

After she dropped her mother off for lunch with her dad, McKenna returned home. A package waited, the postal carrier climbing into his truck as she drove into the driveway. The return address belonged to a gift shop in Unalaska, Alaska, the official city surrounding Dutch Harbor. Most fishermen, Dane included, referred to the place as Dutch, so seeing Unalaska printed in the address unsettled her. As light as the package was, she believed she might be the victim of a joke—she'd open the whatever-it-is and discover a gotcha inside. Or a clown would pop up with a note from a marketing agency claiming she'd won her choice of a gift from nowhere land.

Or maybe Dane really meant it when he'd said he planned to make up for his absence when he returned.

McKenna shuddered, too late catching herself in a half-sob. She dropped the box on the kitchen table and snatched up a tissue, the unbidden tears making her nose run. Her grief was too new, the loss too fresh, to deal with unbidden memories. Would her heart ever stop bleeding?

At least when Dane had been gone and she'd never seen him, she'd had hope he would one day return, her loneliness an empty spot in her chest with which she could cope. But death had closed up the vacant chest cavity, covering it with a layer of bittersweet sorrow through which hope could not dig. No matter what size the shovel.

Tossing her fourth tissue into the waste can in as many minutes, she returned her attention to the package. Dropping it on the table made it rattle, fueling her curiosity. Being inquisitive was better than being sad, so she lifted the box once again and shook it. Something answered back, an almost imperceptible clink muffled by what might be packing material.

Please let it be something that won't make me cry.

She glanced at the clock. Her mother was showing her dad the apartments she had found to rent until after the new year. They'd be back in time for dinner. If she opened the package now, they wouldn't question her about it when they returned.

Livy had borrowed Sydney for a cooking lesson. She'd need to leave soon to pick up her daughter. Her gratitude overflowed for Livy's generous offer to keep life normal for Sydney while

McKenna struggled with her grief. Livy understood what she was feeling, had suffered loss of the same magnitude, and by example was leading her through the maze of bereavement. How would she ever repay her friend for her kindness?

McKenna found scissors in the drawer and cut into the corners of the mailing wrapper, taking care not to poke the box itself in case the lightweight whatever-it-was inside was fragile. Working her way through the layers of tape, she found the edge of the lid and freed the top from its bottom. She lifted the cover and stared.

Inside lay a cluster of brightly colored beads—reds, blues, and yellows—woven together in an intricate design. She lifted the piece and examined it with her fingers, working around the outer edge in a circle. What was it? She'd never before seen anything so delicate and yet so sturdy.

She noticed a small note in the bottom of the box and opening it, read.

McKenna,

I saw this and thought how beautiful the beads would look in your black hair. When I get home, we will renew our vows and this will be a symbol of my devotion to you. I pray we will get a brand-new start.

With all my love, Dane

Why had she thought she couldn't cry anymore?

McKenna entered the Tidewater Takeout two hours later. Livy had phoned and asked if she needed to bring Sydney home, but McKenna had declined the offer, saying she'd been detained by an unexpected delivery. She hadn't lied—not really—because the beaded jewelry and Dane's note left her in a puddle in the middle of the floor for more than an hour. When she thought she could again breathe, and her stomach stopped cramping, she stood, washed her face, and applied emergency makeup.

Entering the café, she resisted popping her compact to see if her reddened eyes and puffy cheeks had faded. Even if Livy noticed, the woman wouldn't mention it. If anyone understood McKenna still had grieving issues, Livy did. For once, McKenna had an alibi which no one challenged. As a grieving widow, she could tear up any time the situation called for release. Lately, it seemed that's all she did.

The café was quiet, no patrons lingered at the counter or nursed a cup of cold coffee. "Livy?"

"Back here, McKenna."

She followed in the direction of the voice, pushing aside the curtain separating the customer area from the food preparation.

Livy stood at the cupboard, a clipboard in her hand, making notes as she inspected the food stores.

Sydney lay on a flour sack on the floor, asleep.

McKenna bit her lip, guilt finding its way into a frown on her face. "I'm so sorry to be this late." She lifted the box from her coat pocket and held it out to Livy. "This arrived from Unalaska today. Dane sent it." She set the package down and lifted the beaded gift within.

"Your husband's love still lives." Livy fingered the beads and pursed her lips. "What a great day. Isn't God's timing perfect?"

"If you'd seen me an hour ago, you might not think this such a great surprise. I opened it and found a note from Dane inside. He wanted me to wear these beads when we renewed our vows." McKenna swallowed. "To start over."

Livy smiled. "How wonderful. Now you know how much he really cared. "

"If Rudy hadn't gone to Alaska, I might never have known."

"Speaking of Rudy," Livy laid down the clipboard on a table

nearby, "he came by earlier today to say goodbye."

"Goodbye?" McKenna's pulse quickened.

Livy faced her, sorrow written in her frown. "He's on his way to Seattle."

"Already?" McKenna wilted. "He said he was going when I saw him at Dane's service. Livy, no."

"He's running from his pain again, just as he did when Romelle died." Livy smiled, her face wistful as she nodded. "But this time he's found employment that will be permanent. I have prayed for that for so long. I can't be sad. But I had hoped he'd work here in Newport." Livy pointed to Sydney stirring from her nap. "I can only believe God knows what He is doing."

"I didn't think he'd really go." McKenna returned the headdress to its box, studying it, the gift so unlike any Dane had ever given her. He'd always been more practical than impulsive. To Dane this flash of color was nothing more than wasted dollars, money spent on a trinket. She guessed Rudy's influence played a part in the purchase.

Her chest ached at the thought of Rudy gone. Forever. Why did he have to go? She might never see him again. He'd become such a dear friend. She'd hoped for so much more. But maybe she'd read more into their friendship than he cared to give. Once her parents left again, she'd be truly alone. How she would navigate uncharted waters, she didn't know. But she had no hold on Rudy. Like the Lone Ranger, he'd swooped into her life, made a difference, and moved on to new deeds.

Though she couldn't believe she had any more tears to shed, her eyes pooled along their rims. She pushed the tears back to spare Livy any more pain. What had happened to the steel veneer under which she'd had to operate alone for so long?

"Sydney, let's get your coat on. We need to go home and have supper with Grandma and Grandpa."

On the way home, McKenna chastised herself at her wayward thoughts. She had no right to speculate on Rudy's interest in her two days after she'd buried her husband. Sure, Dane had been absent physically and emotionally for the last two years, leaving her almost a widow by default, but his recent emails and intention to return home had shown his change of heart. So why were her traitorous feelings swinging like a pendulum whenever she thought of Rudy? She shook her head. It had to stop. The man had made it clear he thought of her as a friend, and that was all. Livy said he wouldn't be back. End of story. *Lord, is this Your doing? Perhaps then it is best.*

CHAPTER TWENTY-SIX

Rudy's aunt Carrie had outdone herself with the decorations. When he arrived on Christmas Eve, twinkle lights outlined the Victorian's massive porch, shimmers of red and green circling each column and rimming the big bay windows. This wasn't the first time she'd gone all out dressing her house up for Christmas. He remembered many past holidays where green and red sparkled from every corner. He'd spent the day anticipating the splendor, allowing memories to occupy him as he crossed the Astoria-Megler bridge into Oregon. Seat weary, his expectations kept him at the wheel. He wasn't disappointed.

Images of Christmases past paraded through his mind—warm evenings of laughter his family shared with his aunts, uncles, and his grandmother, for whom Carrie, the unmarried sister, had taken responsibility until the woman succumbed to old age ten years before. With his grandmother's passing, the house fell to Carrie. Her older sisters and brothers—aunts and uncles to him—moved on to private celebrations with their individual families. After his father and sister perished, only he and his mother remained Carrie's guests.

Carrie stood in the doorway, his mother, having driven up a day earlier, at her side. Carrie's pink bunny slippers and lime green housecoat added to the festive look of the house. She didn't appear fatigued—she must have enlisted Mom's help.

He trekked up the stairs to the door, the long banister evoking a mental image of his sister Romelle's insistence she slide down. Rudy had helped her—a fall to the ground two stories below might have killed her.

He kissed his mother first, then turned to his aunt. He embraced her and whispered in her ear. "You always know how to make us feel comfortable coming back to Astoria for Christmas."

"Your house may have been lost in the fire, but your heart is still attached to this city." Carrie kissed him on the cheek before turning to her sister. "Am I right, Livy?"

"So many Christmases spent here with you, Rudy, Romelle, and Ivan." His mother's voice wobbled, as though the memories threatened to rob the season's joy from the moment. "Thank you for continuing a cherished tradition."

"Christmas wouldn't be special without my sister's family here." Carrie stepped back from the entry and gestured for him to pass through the door. "I've got hot spiced cider and lemon-ginger scones waiting for us."

Rudy followed the cinnamon scent filling the house into the parlor. A tall fir graced the corner, more lights and ornamental balls adorning its branches, the fresh forest smell permeating the space. Sprigs of green outlined the mantel of the fireplace at the other end of the room. Red candles in glass lamps sat spaced evenly across the span of oak gracing the top of the firebox. The wicks blazed like molten gold, illuminating the area in soft hues of light. A small fire in the hearth added warmth, an occasional spark popping like a kettle drum punctuating a musical score. He never tired of celebrations here with his aunt, her ability to bring tradition to life in this stately house a gift. "You girls have been busy."

The wall of windows through which he and McKenna had watched the Columbia earlier this summer were outlined in tiny icicles of white twinkle lights. He still remembered her ashen face when she revealed Dane's status as a fisherman. Offering to find the man while Rudy worked in Dutch Harbor had seemed like a God-appointed duty at the time. Never would he have imagined such a tragic ending to an innocuous request.

"I can't believe you've stayed here alone for so long." Mom took a cup of cider from her sister. "When our mother left the property to you, I don't think she intended you to remain here forever."

Carrie handed Rudy a napkin with two scones tucked inside. "Where would I go?" She helped herself to the pastries, taking a bite and dabbing the powdered sugar from her lips. "This has been our family home since you and I were old enough to tumble down the front stairs. When I walk through the rooms, I remember the hours of fun we shared with our older siblings. The six of us filled these bedrooms with laughter, heartaches, and good-natured rivalries." She swept her arm in front of her as if to encompass the room. "If I sold the house, I'd move into something smaller with no sounds to remember, no images from the past to fill my thoughts, no memories to ponder." Carrie gazed at his mother and narrowed her eyes. "*That* would be alone, sister. Quite empty and most depressing."

Mom nodded. "I understand." She blinked twice. "If my house had not burned, and I'd continued to live there without Ivan and Romelle, I'd at least have the memories."

Rudy winced at the discussion. His mother had moved with him to Newport, insisting she wanted to be close to her remaining child. He'd been happy to accommodate her, keeping a family member nearby. But if Mom had moved in with Carrie, she could have shared in the recollections Carrie kept alive. Now that he lived in Seattle, his needs loomed selfish in the shadow of his mother's sorrow. She had become the one left alone.

But without the sandwich shop and his mother's involvement, he might not have connected with McKenna or Sydney. They'd become important threads in the tapestry of his existence. If only he hadn't failed his quest to bring Dane home. Pain ticked inside his chest.

"Where's that sweet girl you brought here in August?" Carrie's gaze pierced his, as if she'd read his mind, her large brown eyes intent. "McKenna, wasn't it? She had that adorable, strawberry-curled child."

Rudy's throat closed. He swallowed, trying to move the scone lodged there. "She's..."

"She's the one I told you about who lost her husband to tragedy six weeks ago." Mom shook her head. "Her loss almost undid the poor thing."

"That's too sad." Plopping in a nearby chair, Carrie focused on him. "You going to catch her on the rebound?"

"I doubt it. She's still mourning." Rudy sipped his cider. "I'm now living in Seattle. My Alaska boss is facing surgery the first of the year and needs me to cover for him, so I will be working double duty soon. This is an opportunity to become a permanent employee for the fisheries service."

"Running, are you?" Carrie set her cup on the table, folding her hands in her lap. "You two were friends. Obviously attracted to each other. What are you afraid of?"

"I tried to do her a favor by finding her fisherman husband and sending him home. I'm sure Mom told you our ship sank before I could make that happen. I survived. He didn't." Rudy clenched his fist. "I let her down. I doubt she wants anything to do with me."

"Nonsense!" Carrie's voice cracked like a horsewhip behind a sleigh. "You found the man, didn't you?"

He nodded.

"You convinced him to come home, didn't you?"

Another nod.

"You didn't sink the boat, did you?"

He shook his head.

"According to your mother, you were fortunate to escape the tragedy yourself."

"That's just it. I survived. He didn't. Some hero I turned out to be."

His mother cut in. "Her parents are still here. They interrupted their trip to Europe to come home for the funeral and be here for McKenna while she grieves."

Carrie harrumphed. "They won't stay forever, I'm guessing." She tapped the table with her fingers.

"I think they've made plans to return to the Mediterranean after the new year." His mother touched his shoulder. "McKenna will be very alone then."

"She needs the time. Seeing me will only remind her of Dane's death. She's had enough men working oceans in her life." Rudy straightened his shoulders. "I need to clear my head as well. I won't be on the ocean this time and I'll make a lot of money." Rudy met his mother's gaze. "That should alleviate your fears."

Carrie leaned forward in her chair. "Let me tell you, son. I've spent my life alone, trying to do the noble thing. When I agreed to care for my mother after my father died, I set my suitor free, not wanting to burden him with my responsibilities. I told him we needed time." She settled back and sighed. "What a tragic mistake. He found someone else, and I missed out on the joys of my own family, tending to my mother's needs." She glanced out the window, staring into the darkness. "I've not suffered. But, if I could go back and do it over, I'd have listened to my Charlie and married the man when he begged. We could have shared the burdens." She sat up, her face a picture of resolute will. "Don't follow in my footsteps."

"Even if I did seek her out, not enough time has passed for her to sort out her emotions." Rudy bit off another piece of scone, catching the crumbs in his fingers. "Staying away is the best thing I can do for her right now." He chewed a minute. "In a year, she'll have a grip on her situation and grief will be less likely to impact her decisions."

"A beautiful girl like that will not last a year." Carrie stood to her feet. "Act, Rudy. Or you'll lose her to someone else."

"Then it wasn't meant to be." Rudy brushed the crumbs off his hands. "I have to trust God to lead."

"How can God lead when you're unwilling to move your feet?"

Rudy stared at his aunt, searching for a sensible reply. Nothing came. McKenna needed time, and he'd determined she should have space. The thought she might fill the emptiness with another made him pause, but it didn't change his resolve. He sighed. If she did, they were never meant to be together as a couple.

Carrie lifted the carafe of cider. "Seconds, anyone?"

While McKenna held the front door, Mom and Dad carried in two large baskets filled with packages and set them in front of the Christmas tree. Dad sat on the sofa, pulling one basket between his feet, and lifted out gifts, handing them to her mother.

Sydney's eyes grew round as the mound of brightly-wrapped surprises with glittering bows spilled into the living room, tumbling around her on the floor. McKenna couldn't suppress her laughter. The child's birthday party had been sparse, waiting to see if Rudy found Dane, and if he didn't, delaying the festivities until Rudy came back and shared in them. But in light of the tragic turn of events, celebrating anything had been out of the question. Though Sydney didn't understand how her life had been altered in the wake of her father's death, McKenna understood the ramifications. Ordinarily, she wouldn't overdo the amount of gifts, but this Christmas, considering all that had happened, the generosity seemed to ease the pain she felt.

Still, the numbers of packages seemed staggering. She folded her arms across her chest. "You two spent way too much."

"Not as much as you might think." Her mother straightened the boxes and stacked them into a neater pile. "We picked up a few things while we were in Europe and decided to give them as gifts, rather than souvenirs." She lifted out two small ones from the bottom of the basket and set them in front of the pile. "We missed Sydney's birthday, remember."

"Mom." She closed the door and joined Sydney on the floor. "I can't reciprocate in kind. I'm not certain what my finances are going to look like, now that Dane is gone."

"We don't expect you to, dear." Mom sat on the sofa. "But we intend to support you in whatever way you need until all of this gets resolved."

"Don't think me ungrateful, but I'm determined to carry on. Dane's life insurance is invested. Sydney has a trust fund. Social security will make dependent child payments. The gallery is certain to pick up with the tourist season. I should be fine."

"Financially. Yes. But emotionally, you need time. Your husband's death will replay itself over and over for a while. I'm not convinced you've finished mourning."

"Trust me, I've already shed an ocean of tears. But knowing Dane loved me and intended to come home has made it easier to move forward. I missed him before, but now he's forever gone. I have no reason to pine for him. A lot of my grieving had already been done during his extended fishing excursions. I've lived with the loneliness and the questions of his absence for two years. In many ways, he was already dead to me. I know that sounds hideous, but it is the truth. After Sydney came, our marriage never returned to the level of love we shared in our earlier years. In many ways, Dane used Sydney's problems to destroy us. Now I need to make a new life for Sydney and me."

"You won't discount marrying again, I hope?" Mom linked hands with Dad.

"Maybe I will. Sometime in the future. I want to, but not every widow does. Dane had trouble accepting Sydney's challenges, and he was her father. Finding another man to take on that responsibility may not be possible." She wrapped an arm about her daughter and drew her close. "With the gallery, Sydney's education, and the moniker of head of household now on my shoulders, I'm not sure what kind of time I'll have to pursue a relationship."

And that's only if I can find a man of Rudy's character. Someone who can embrace a child like Sydney and give her the love she needs. No one else need apply.

"Well, promise me you won't get involved with someone who earns his living on the ocean." Her mother leaned forward and touched McKenna's knee. "You've been alone too much."

"On that, I will agree. I can't risk my heart to this kind of tragedy again." She smiled. "As long as he comes home to me, I'll be happy with a dumpster diver."

Her father leaned forward. "A banker or a teacher would be good." He touched his chin as if thinking. "You know, someone who shines his shoes, combs his hair, and wears a suit."

"Have you already picked him out?" She gave her father a suspicious smile. "I can't believe you're already plotting."

"It's only because we love you."

His duffle bag loaded in his truck, keys rattling in his palm, Rudy faced his mother as they stood at the bottom of Carrie's stairway entry. Now that Christmas was over, he had to reach Seattle before nightfall, a six-hour drive. Mom wasn't making leaving any easier.

"Won't you send McKenna a note, wishing her a happy holiday

season? Let her know you think about her and Sydney."

He sighed. "We've been over this. McKenna needs to come to terms with her loss. She's vulnerable right now. What if she forms an attachment to me because she's desperate for answers? Her emotions are raw, and she could easily mistake affection for me when it's gratitude she's really feeling. I've got broad shoulders, but I don't want to be hurt, either."

"You already care, don't you?"

He opened the door of the pickup, put one foot up on the floorboard, and cast a glance over his shoulder. "Probably more than I'm willing to admit. But if I care for McKenna, then everything I stand for is a fraud. I told her I would help her as a friend. Nothing more. She was Dane's wife, and he obviously loved her, but his attitude toward his precious daughter made me furious. All I wanted to do was protect them both." He stepped into the cab, then closed the door, rolling the window down. "But if I rushed in, McKenna might later think I took advantage of her vulnerability. An opportunist waiting for my chance. The Bible makes it clear we are not to desire another man's wife. Seeking McKenna out before she's had a chance to sort out her feelings would make me just as guilty as a man who's had an affair. I know there are others who would think so."

Mom gripped the edge of the window. "I'm proud of you, Rudy."

"Why? Nothing has changed." He inserted the key in the ignition. "I attempted to help. Hoped I could make a difference. Sydney deserves the kind of understanding you and Dad gave Romelle. If Dane had returned home, he may or may not have become the father he should have been. And now, we'll never know."

"McKenna has closure. She can turn this page of her life and move forward." His mother leaned against the door. "You say nothing changed, but for McKenna, everything has."

"That's why she needs time to sort out her feelings." He started the engine. "I may only have been God's instrument to facilitate her next chapter. But that doesn't mean I'm included among the pages."

"I'll be satisfied for now, then, but I know she values your friendship." Mom stepped away from the truck. "You like this new job?"

"Yes." He stuck his hand out the window, and she grasped his fingers. "After I've been there for a while, I can come home and help you move back to Astoria, if you'd like."

"As much as I'd like to be with Carrie, I can't leave McKenna." She squeezed his hand and let go. "Her parents will finish their trip soon, and she will be left alone. She needs me."

Rudy bit back a grin. "She's fortunate to have you nearby." At her shrug, he slipped the truck into gear. "Love you, Mom. Got to go."

As he pulled out onto the highway, he glanced in the rearview mirror. His mother stood waving with her right hand. In her left, she held a handkerchief to her nose. *God, this is so hard. Protect her. Help McKenna. Help my decision be the right one. For all of us. But especially for You.*

CHAPTER TWENTY-SEVEN

The grey skies matched McKenna's depressed mood as she drove her parents to the airport at the end of January. Both of them were eager to finish their world tour and with warmer temperatures ahead of them, her father faced less chance of health complications. Their high spirits only served to drive McKenna deeper into the despondency that had shadowed her like a shroud since Dane's death.

"We'll be back soon, dear." Her mother hugged her, whispering in her ear. "We'll be praying for you every day." Mom touched her shoulder. "God has a plan."

"Thanks, Mom." She kissed her mother's cheek. "I'll be too busy getting ready for the tourist season to think about anything else."

"Don't hibernate in that shop." Her father wagged a finger at her. "You've got good help. Take a day off. Visit the valley. Make friends. Find a new love."

"To what end?" She grabbed his hand and kissed his forehead. "If you haven't noticed, men don't seem to stay in my life."

"Men are like trolley cars." Her dad chuckled, grabbed the handle of the wheeled carry-on, and slid his arm around her mother. "Another one always comes along."

As she headed back toward Newport, the car enclosed McKenna like a tomb. The emptiness and silence enveloped her, everyone she'd held dear, gone. Even Sydney seemed to sense the quiet.

She'd been living with her parents when she married Dane. When he went to Alaska, her college friends had been close, her needs met by Dane's faithful financial support. She'd moved to Newport to run the gallery for her folks, keeping it profitable always a challenge. Her greatest gift had been meeting Livy and Rudy. Now, Dane would never come home, her parents were traveling the globe, and Rudy had moved to Seattle. The elements that had sustained her vanished—all but Livy. She'd never been this alone before.

McKenna shuddered, the fear of all she faced causing her to tremble. Going home to an empty house would be more of the same. Her mind played tricks as she thought ahead to the life that awaited her. Scenarios of disasters pranced across her thoughts, performed in panoramic color. Illness. Poverty. Losing Sydney. Her heart raced and her breathing grew erratic. Moisture beaded her forehead. Keeping the car on the road became more difficult as her concentration wavered. Afraid of making a mistake and causing an accident, she pulled to the shoulder and turned the key. For several minutes she sat there, lungs burning as she fought to breathe. Her eyes awash with tears, she fought the terror consuming her.

"Dane, why couldn't you have come home to us?" She yelled at the windshield. "Why?" She hit the steering wheel. "Couldn't you have found enough love for both of us?" She leaned forward, her arms folded as she sobbed into them. "And you, Rudy. My *friend*." She spat the word out so forcefully she choked. "Did you think I could suddenly manage by myself? Did you even think what leaving would do to Sydney?" Her fists clenched. "You're no better than Dane. Leaving us alone." The pain claimed her and she wept silently in the stillness. "So, so alone." She found her voice. "Oh God, what am I going to do?"

No answer came. No calming voice. No easy answer.

Sydney remained quiet, her interest in dot-to-dot books and a new gel pen keeping her busy. Alone in her thoughts, McKenna explored her options. Marriage had promised one thing and delivered another, men had failed her, and motherhood had left her exhausted. The only resource she'd returned to over and over again was her faith. That's what she had now. Would it be enough?

A knock on her window startled her. She looked up to see a uniformed policeman smiling at her through the glass. She rolled down her window. "Officer?"

"I saw you parked and wanted to be sure you're all right."

"I will be." She glanced at the mirror to see how red her eyes were. "I lost my husband not long ago and was besieged by memories, so I pulled over to compose myself."

"My condolences, ma'am." The policeman looked in the back at Sydney. "How far do you have to travel?"

"Newport."

"That's a winding stretch of road ahead." He looked concerned. "Is there someone I can call to make sure you get home safely?"

She shook her head and forced a smile. "No. Trust me, there's no one to call."

The following day McKenna prepared to spend the day at home teaching Sydney vocabulary words. Livy had suggested using cookbooks with pictures of the foods as a teaching tool. McKenna headed to the kitchen to retrieve the few recipe cards she owned and the complimentary bread guide the yeast company had sent.

She opened the drawer and recoiled. She'd forgotten that this was where she'd deposited all the snacks she'd purchased for Dane's homecoming. She stared at the assortment of peanuts, black licorice, and wafer cookies crammed into the space—items that neither she nor Sydney would ever want. What had she been thinking?

She clenched her fists and squared her shoulders, taking a deep breath as she headed to the broom closet. Time to remove the reminders. A stack of grocery bags sat folded on the top shelf and she grabbed one. Shaking it open, she dug deep into the bulging drawer, stuffing the bag with every last package of Dane food she found.

One forgotten bag of peanuts dropped onto the floor. She picked it up and like an exclamation point on the end of a dramatic sentence, she threw the package at the wall. "I'm setting myself free." The bag split and the peanuts dotted the floor, scattered like the fragments of love she'd so long guarded close to her heart.

CHAPTER TWENTY-EIGHT

RUDY STOOD ON THE EDGE OF the pond where the recruits waited to test out their safety equipment. Of the original twenty who flew here for training two weeks ago, only ten remained. Two had gone home after watching the video of ships that had sunk. Two others decided this wasn't their dream job. The final six failed to pass the intense, two-week course in observer sampling and recording of data.

After yesterday's practice run of putting on the survival gear in a room where the lights flashed, and the darkness of a distressed ship was simulated, making it difficult to see, the real test came today. Each of the remaining ten held their evacuation suit in their hand, waiting for his instruction.

Rudy swallowed several times as he prepared to share survival techniques in a disaster. Images flooded his memory of the *Bering Explorer* listing to the side as the explosions blasted the night sky. The long wait for help in black, churning waters haunted him. The vision of Dane shivering uncontrollably in his evacuation suit weighed like an anvil on his chest. Part of his job as trainer was to remember that fateful night and recount for these recruits how an evacuation unfolds, detail safety procedures, and share responsibilities for other crew personnel. Knowing they had to work together could save a life. Rudy's heart pounded against his breastbone, his breathing short and irregular. Reliving the nightmare reinforced his terrors.

"One of the worst things you can face as an observer is an emergency evacuation of your ship. Mechanical problems, menacing storms, and engine fires can occur without warning.

Being prepared is the best way to protect yourself and help save the lives of those around you. Always keep your beacon close by."

Rudy stopped and breathed in. He looked at each of their faces, gauging the panic rising behind the calm, exterior demeanors. "I survived a ship disaster. But a friend of mine did not." He walked down the line, studying each one. "It's not something you soon forget."

The recruits stared at him, exchanging glances with each other as they absorbed his words. More than one looked frightened, as if the information he was about to deliver could spell their demise.

"The best thing you can do to protect yourself is learn to put on your evac suit in a hurry. Yesterday you saw how hard it is to climb into these things when there's no light, sirens are blaring, and crew members are running around you. But those are the conditions a disaster brings."

"The captain of the ship I was on enforced emergency drills on a regular basis. We were given one minute to rush to the deck of the ship from wherever you were, pull on a suit like the one you hold in your hand, and jump into the cold, dark waters of the Bering Sea. Today you will perform that test here, so you know what to do."

"Remember the gear unfolds like this." Rudy held up his evac suit. "You climb in like this." He opened the top. "If you've played with Gumby as a child, you may find the suit feels like that. Bends about the same, too."

A nervous twitter passed among the trainees. Their attention to his words said they were learning a valuable lesson.

"Let's see if you can improve on your record." Rudy held up his stopwatch. "Ready. Set. Go."

The recruits unfolded their evac suits, shaking them right and left, trying to find the opening to climb into. One tall young man managed to get a leg in before losing his balance and landing on his backside. A girl wriggled into hers only to find the front was now facing backward. As the minute hand swept toward the twelve, only three of the trainees were in their suits. The other seven were stranded at various stages of donning the unmanageable outerwear.

Rudy clicked the stopwatch and shouted. "Time!"

The ten gazed at each other, laughing at the different levels of skill each one had failed to perform.

"Seven of you just died." Rudy remained stern. "Look around you. Your ship is sinking and you are not prepared to hit the water."

The faces of the trainees sobered. One girl's cheeks drained of all color.

"Finish putting on your evacuation gear." Rudy waited as the seven who hadn't completed the task scrambled into the orange garb. He gestured for them to follow him to the edge of the dock where a freshwater lake stretched before them. "You are all officially dead because you didn't get your equipment on in time, but for the sake of practice, I want you to jump into the lake."

One girl gasped. "That's at least fifteen feet to the surface."

Rudy studied her. "You'd rather ride a burning ship into the ocean?"

Another raised his hand. "Will these things float?"

"Yes." Rudy assured them. "But you are looking for a life raft to climb into. The raft will help get you out of the water. Not everyone who hits the water will be spotted in the dark, but a raft is easier to see and recover."

Rudy gestured toward the lake. "Ladies, first."

The tallest girl turned, and holding her nose, jumped off the dock. The evacuation suit did its job, and she bobbed on the surface like a cork. The young men, not wanting to be outdone by a female, jumped as one to the waiting water. Soon nine of the ten were in the water.

The girl who had objected to the distance, stood paralyzed at the dock's edge. She hung her head, arms wrapped tightly about her middle. "I can't do this." She strangled on the words. "I just can't do this." She started to sob.

Rudy went to her side. "It's okay. Take a break." He touched her hand. "You'll get another chance tomorrow."

"And if I can't?" Her reddened eyes squeezed shut as she tried to control her tears.

"You won't pass the training." Rudy patted her shoulder. "I can't risk you losing your life in the Bering Sea." He inhaled deeply. "And contacting your parents is not something I care to do." He clenched his fists. *Again.*

Nor do I want to leave a little girl and her mother alone. Thoughts of McKenna raced through his mind. How was she faring now that she navigated life alone? Did she think of him? Had she met someone? Would he ever see her again? He looked at the frightened recruit beside him.

"I have to pass this." The girl stood rigid as she eyed the water below her. "I have to." With a cry, she raced toward the edge of the dock and leaped into the water. She landed with a splat, the sound of the belly flop breaking the calm of the harbor.

Rudy looked down, afraid she'd hurt herself. "Are you okay?"

She looked up at him, triumph on her face. "I think my technique needs work."

Rudy laughed for the first time that afternoon.

An hour later, Rudy dismissed the trainees and headed back to the headquarters. Evaluations and recommendations needed to be completed now that these ten recruits had achieved observer status and would be transported to Alaska at the first opportunity.

As he opened the door and entered the building he was hailed by his supervisor.

"Taylor?" The man waved a piece of paper in his hand. "An urgent message came in at the main office for you."

"Who from?" Rudy couldn't think of anyone who needed to contact him.

"The medical center in Newport, Oregon. Your mother was taken there this afternoon."

"I'm leaving now." Rudy grabbed the note and turned toward his locker. "I'll take the evaluations with me and have them ready on Monday."

"Are you heading south?"

"I'll catch a commuter. Driving will take too long."

"Monday, then."

McKenna jumped when her phone rang mid-afternoon. She checked the caller ID and saw the number for the Tidewater Takeout in the screen. Strange. Livy usually called from her own phone. She answered.

"Is this Mrs. Nichols?" A young girl's voice she didn't recognize shouted into the receiver, the unmistakable sound of Sydney crying in the background.

"Yes. Who's this?" McKenna's heart rate elevated as she spoke to the stranger.

"I'm Molly, Livy Taylor's afternoon replacement." Behind her, McKenna heard another clear, identifiable wail. "She's fallen and cut her arm. We had to send her to the medical center. Can you come and get your daughter? She's not happy."

"Be right there." McKenna closed her phone and sprinted for the door. She passed her assistant coming for the afternoon shift. "Take over for me. A new delivery of children's materials to sort. Emergency."

Entering the café two minutes later, she heard Sydney crying in the kitchen. She burst through the curtain and seeing her daughter in the corner, she bent down and wrapped her arms around the child. Sydney's cries tapered off and McKenna questioned Molly. "Is Livy okay?"

"I don't know. The owner was here and loaded Livy up in her car." Molly appeared shaken. "We think she might have hit her head. But the cut on her arm will probably need stitches."

"I'll go see her." McKenna stood and led Sydney toward the door. She stopped. "Did anyone let her son know?"

Molly shrugged. "I doubt it."

McKenna prayed all the way to the medical center. *Please, Lord, don't let this be serious. Let the x-rays show nothing but a concussion.*

Or less.

Sydney sat in her car seat, singing a Sunday school song she'd heard on a video. "Zacchaeus was a eee wittle man. . ."

McKenna resisted joining in, her thoughts on Livy. Spring break was only two weeks away. Would Livy recover in time? Tourists always swarmed into Newport that week, and a sandwich shop like the Tidewater Takeout would be teeming with customers seeking a fast sandwich and drink on their way to the beach. Livy spent a lot of time on her feet during the break because the entire café crew had to work extra hours making to-go sandwiches or they couldn't keep up during business hours. Knowing Livy as she did, the woman wouldn't like being sidelined without a good reason. McKenna had to reach Rudy. He'd know what to do.

McKenna switched gears, focusing on her own challenges. She needed to make arrangements for Sydney because gallery business kicked into high gear with the arrival of the tourist season. Lost in her thoughts, she drove blind, not searching the highway for some sign of a medical clinic.

A car honked as it passed. *Concentrate on your driving.* She hadn't been to this facility since she'd returned to Newport. Sydney had stayed well all winter, as had she, not prompting a visit to the local medical center. Finding the place seemed easy enough. The road through Newport only ran north and south. She spotted the square little building. Driving into the parking lot she hurried Sydney to the entrance.

"Olivia Taylor?"

The receptionist scrolled down her computer screen. "Are you family?"

McKenna shook her head. "Have you called her son?"

The receptionist nodded. "We left word at his work number. Do you have another number for him?"

McKenna's throat felt dry. "If I can see Livy, I can probably get you a number."

"She's in triage right now." She pointed down a hall. "I understand she's in a feisty mood."

McKenna laughed. "That sounds like Livy."

She heard Livy before she found the room. A doctor stood in front of her discussing her chart. "Livy?"

"Ah, McKenna. So glad you are here. Will you tell this young man I'm able to take care of myself and I want to go home?"

"What's happened?" She stepped into the room, Sydney's hand in hers. Her breath came in short spurts, as if she'd run the hallway to get here. The pace of her heart matched her erratic breathing. "Is she all right?"

"She's slipping in and out of wakefulness." The doctor shrugged, his face unreadable. "She says she didn't sleep well last night. I've continued to probe, unconvinced that's all this is. Her arm needs stitches, but I think she hit her head."

"What are you suggesting?" Cold sweat swept across McKenna's forehead.

"I'd like her to spend the night so we can observe her."

"McKenna, tell him I don't need that." Livy folded her arms across her chest, her face a pout.

McKenna looked at her friend. Livy's color was good, eyes bright, and smile radiant. "Is Rudy coming? He might shed light on the situation."

"He called my cell phone after the clinic left a message at his work. He said he'd catch a flight to Portland and then drive from there. We probably won't see him until five."

The doctor wrote on his chart. "And we need to make a decision before he gets here."

McKenna struggled to offer advice. "Livy, if it were my mother, I'd want her to spend the night to be safe. I know how Rudy feels about you. Don't you think he'd insist on the same?"

Livy sighed. "Probably. Only he wouldn't be as nice as you." She leaned back against her pillow. "Well, doc, it seems like everyone is on your side in this, so I'll stay."

"Good, Mrs. Taylor." The doctor strode toward the door. "I'll get you assigned to a room."

Livy smiled at Sydney. "How's my little munchkin?" She held out her hand to the child who snuggled closer to McKenna's leg and whined.

McKenna stroked the top of her head, understanding her distress. Confusion clouded her daughter's face. She spoke to Livy. "Right woman. Wrong place."

Livy nodded. "Listen, if I get discharged in the morning, I don't think the doctor's going to let me do anything tomorrow, but—"

"Don't you worry about it." McKenna stepped to her bedside and grasped her friend's hand in hers, pulling Sydney closer as well. "Sydney can spend the day with me at the gallery."

"Are you sure?"

McKenna nodded. "Absolutely."

CHAPTER TWENTY-NINE

RUDY FOUGHT THE URGE TO SPEED as he hurried from the airport, checked out his rental car, and aimed down the road to Newport. On the phone the doctor had assured him his mother's injuries were minor, but the weekend offered him an opening he might not have had otherwise, and he wanted to see for himself. After securing the leave from his boss, he'd caught a flight to Portland, and now burned the miles beneath his tires.

He found the medical center and parked. The receptionist stood at her desk as if she were leaving for the day.

He hurried forward. "Olivia Taylor?"

The woman smiled. "You must be Rudy." She pointed to a door that led to the main part of the clinic. "She's in room 10. The doctor is with her now."

Rudy paused at the door, the man in a white coat speaking in low tones to his mother. "Mom?"

The doctor turned and his mother sat up behind him. "Rudy. So glad you're here."

The man introduced himself and filled Rudy in on his mother's afternoon. "We've convinced her to stay the night because she keeps drifting in and out of wakefulness. Does she ordinarily have spells where she is mentally pre-occupied?"

"Spacey?"

The doctor nodded.

Rudy shook his head. Not his mother. Rock solid. Stubborn like Gibraltar. "Like she hit her head?" At the doctor's nod, he became alarmed. "Never."

"Your mother came in disoriented. We suspect the trauma may

have left her in a state of shock, but we're not certain her head missed the floor when the rest of her landed." The doctor studied Rudy. "We'll know better in the morning."

"I really don't think this is at all necessary." His mother folded her arms across her chest.

"Mom." Rudy went to her and laid an arm across her shoulder. "You've already agreed to stay. I'll swing by in the morning, pick you up, and take you out to breakfast at the Chalet to celebrate." He gave her a squeeze. "I'd feel a lot better knowing you were completely checked out. Do this for me?"

"I'm sure I'm fine." She sighed, shaking her head. "But I'll stay."

"Thanks, Mom. I'd be lost without you."

The doctor tapped his chart and headed for the door. "I'll be back to check on you."

As the door swung closed, Rudy turned back to his mother. "Can I bring you anything from home or pick up something at the shopping center?"

"I'd like the book I'm reading." Mom pointed to her purse. "Look in there and see if my glasses are inside or if I left them at the café, would you please?"

Rudy rummaged around in the bag. "I'm not seeing your case. It's still the neon pink one with the glittery surface?"

"Yes." Mom glanced around the room. "I must have left them. I don't remember needing them today, though." She focused on him. "You look tired."

"I'd already put in a full day when the clinic called my boss. I skedaddled out of Seattle like a bank robber in danger of hanging."

Mom laughed. "Take the key to my house and spend the night. How long are you here?"

"Long enough to get you checked out and safely back home." He pressed her gently against the mattress. "Now get some sleep."

She put a hand to her head. "My head hurts."

"Let me get the doctor." Rudy hurried to the door, relieved when he met the man on the other side coming back in. "She's complaining of a headache."

The doctor took one look at Rudy's mother and stuck his head out the door. "Nurse. Bring me a gurney, STAT." He refocused on his patient, taking her wrist and checking her vital signs. "Are you dizzy, Mrs. Taylor?"

"A little." Mom's eyes widened, her gaze meeting Rudy's as the doctor continued his examination.

The gurney arrived amid a clatter of wheels and wall bumping, the technician sidling the rolling table alongside Mom's examination bed.

The doctor wrapped an arm around her and motioned for Rudy to do the same. "Help me move her here, will you?"

Rudy stepped up beside his mother and following the doctor's lead, transferred her to the waiting gurney. *Please, Lord, watch over her.*

"Let's get you into x-ray, Mrs. Taylor." The doctor wrote notes on her chart and handed instructions to the technician as he filled him in. "She's assigned here to room ten, bed one. But I want her to get an MRI before we bring her back here."

The technician nodded and shoved the gurney out the door and down the hall away from the entrance.

The doctor turned to Rudy. "You can go with her, if you want. It'll take fifteen minutes or so to get what I need."

"What do you think it is?" His pulse notching up with every breath, Rudy flexed his hands to relieve the growing panic. *Not Mom. Not now.*

"I suspect it's a concussion, nothing more. But I'm making sure she doesn't have a subdural hematoma I can't see from the outside of her skull."

"So you really do think she hit her head?"

"Considering she slipped on a crumpled mat, caught herself on the way down, and hung on to the knife she was using at the time, she wouldn't have anything left to break her fall." The doctor squeezed Rudy's shoulder. "I'm just glad the knife didn't do more damage to her arm. This could have been a whole lot worse."

An hour later, with his mother settled in her bed while they waited for the results of the x-rays, Rudy prayed. *A concussion is bad enough. A hematoma could kill her.*

Exhausted, whether from the injury or the excitement of her afternoon, Mom slept as he sat by her bedside. He planned to call his aunt Carrie as soon as he knew something more specific.

Mom's eyes blinked open, and she stared around the room before her gaze landed on him. "Where am I?"

Disorientation. Not a good sign. She's too young. Lord, are you listening?

Rudy leaned nearer her bedside, noticing her color had improved with the nap and her eyes seemed clearer and more focused. "You're still at the hospital, Mom. Playing tiddlywinks with the clock while the x-rays develop."

"You play tiddlywinks, I'll count holes in the ceiling tiles." She chuckled, a yawn breaking through her laugh.

Joking was good. More like the woman he knew and loved. "Do you expect to be here long enough?"

"I can't stay. McKenna has to work at the gallery tomorrow, and she told me not to worry about Sydney." She groaned. "I need to let her know one way or the other. Poor McKenna."

"I doubt you're going to get out of here that fast." He handed her his phone. "Better call her."

"You have her number?"

"Speed dial three."

His mother grinned as she punched in the number.

McKenna left early the next morning, hoping to stop by the medical center and see Livy. The woman's call the night before sounded positive, the doctor and Rudy both insisting she spend the night. McKenna hoped she might cross paths with Rudy and catch up on what he'd been doing.

She entered the hospital room and found it empty. A nurse stood on one side, tucking a sheet beneath the mattress. McKenna smiled. "Did Mrs. Taylor already go home?"

"Her son took her to breakfast, then home."

"She must be okay, then?"

The nurse laughed. "She's too ornery to be anything else. I've seen healthy family members leave with less energy than she had as a patient. "

"Thanks for the good news." McKenna didn't have time to search, so she took Sydney by the hand and headed to the gallery. She'd missed seeing Rudy, but maybe that was better for everyone involved.

On Sunday, McKenna dared to go by Livy's home. The woman's car sat in the drive. She didn't see any other vehicles around. She knocked.

Livy appeared at the door and smiled. "McKenna! So glad you dropped by. Come in." She glanced at Sydney. "Do you know me today?"

Sydney smiled at Livy, recognition in her eyes. "Cookie treats?"

Livy laughed. "You bet, sweetheart."

McKenna followed her daughter and Livy into the neat kitchen, glancing around the small house for signs of Rudy.

Livy took the pan of cookie bars out and sliced a couple Her eyes twinkled. "He's gone."

McKenna nodded. "I figured he'd have to get back to Seattle by tomorrow. Did you two have a nice visit?"

"He spent the night at the clinic, sleeping in a chair. Saturday, he took me to the Chalet for breakfast as soon as the doctor released me, then home. He spent some time at the aquarium, letting his supervisor know he's now in Seattle and not available for spring break shows."

"The children will miss him."

Livy handed her a plate. "He will miss the kids. He loved being the resident shark."

"He was good in the role." McKenna helped Sydney to a stool near the counter. "Is he happy?"

Livy studied her. "Time will tell."

CHAPTER THIRTY

Four Months Later, Summer Break,
Heceta Head State Park, Oregon coast

WHILE KURT BACKED HIS RIG INTO the space at the furthest end of the parking area, Rudy stashed his phone and his wallet into the jockey box of the pickup, pulling out his seasonal pass to leave on the dashboard. No need for a ticket while they played along the ocean's bottom.

Though they'd arrived early, the beachfront park already showed signs of life. Summer break brought out all the tourists, especially on a day like today where the sun shone overhead and the wind gusts blew mild. Beachcombers climbed the rocks at the northern tip of the cove and explored the two sand caves at water's edge. The breakers crested a great distance from shore, making the immediate waters safer to play in. Picnickers had already claimed most of the tables lining the lawns.

"Good thing we're early." Kurt removed the chain on which his key hung around his neck and slipped it into his wetsuit. "This parking lot may be double-parked by the time we finish our dive."

"At least you're at the road's edge so you won't get trapped." Rudy pointed to the curve leading to the highway above them. "We can make a fast exit."

"Let's pray we don't finish our dive like we did last fall. I thought we were going to need a quick getaway in an ambulance last time. You go out too far today, and I'm going to leave you to the sharks."

Rudy chuckled and opened his door, locking it behind him. "I deserved that. I don't plan on making the same mistake twice." He hustled around to the back of the truck and recovered his scuba gear.

At Kurt's suggestion, they had both brought tanks and breathing apparatus. Rudy wanted to explore the waters beyond the inlet and after his near drowning episode last fall, he and Kurt agreed that taking tanks would reduce the risk of swimming out too far.

"Feels good to be back here." Kurt grabbed his fins. His goggles rested on his forehead, and he zipped his wetsuit to his neck. Shrugging into his tanks, he adjusted the weight across his back. "Ready to hit the water?"

Rudy followed his friend along the grass to where they could navigate the rocks to the sand beyond. He dropped his shoes behind a large chunk of driftwood and completed his change into diving mode by stepping into his fins. Waddling into the surf, both he and Kurt tested their air supply and then submerged when the water grew deep enough to disappear.

Today's dive filled Rudy with expectancy. He hadn't explored the water since last summer. The observer job that almost cost him his life stole the fall. His opportunity to stand in for Hawk Bishop in Seattle had claimed the rest of the pollock winter season and lasted until the end of the spring. This time with Kurt was long overdue and he swam with excitement, anxious to be in the water again. Newport felt like home, but the entire Pacific coastline beckoned him.

His mother had welcomed him last Friday, his position as personnel supervisor over for now. Hawk had recovered from his surgery, and with summer ahead in Dutch Harbor, the man expected to return to full status. Fall would mean training new recruits for the fishing seasons to follow. Rudy would return to Seattle, a full-fledged instructor. He delighted that he had finally found full-time employment even if it took him away from Newport and the ability to check on his mother.

Her fall at the café and injury to her arm in February had given him an opportunity to visit his supervisor at the aquarium, informing her of his change of status. The woman had asked him to let her know if he had any time off during the summer. She could always use a trained shark. Consequently, Rudy had obligations at the Oregon Coast Aquarium this week, playing his shark role for the scheduled summer children's programs. Next week, he'd check out Newport again to see if the job market had changed since he left, but with a specialized job waiting for him, he doubted he'd give the possibility much time. He'd look for a rental if he found something semi-permanent. Until then, Mom was glad to have him.

He still had to pinch himself at this sudden change of fortune. His biology degree had taken five years to complete, but the need for men like himself hadn't translated into permanent work. Several janitors employed at the science center had upper division degrees in marine science, all hovering, waiting for an opening to use their training. If a job posted, he'd fall in line behind them. He didn't want to return to Dutch Harbor again. Now that he had specialized training that didn't require him to work on the ocean, his mother would quit worrying. He regretted he couldn't be close to her, but he couldn't be picky. Work was work, and he'd needed something permanent quite a while.

Paddling along behind Kurt, he probed the sandy ocean bottom like a seal searching for a place to fish, his mind wrestling with his options. Kurt tapped him on his tanks, pointing to a well-lit area along the sand to their left. Rudy nodded and followed his friend. Waves were stronger here, and he could feel the rush of breakers above them as they paddled along below. They'd have to exercise caution or they'd swim beyond the protection of the coastline. He didn't want to repeat last fall's scenario, with or without scuba gear.

The rocky shoreline flattened out, leaving great stretches of sand dotted with shells. Rocks clustered here and there, sea stars clinging to their surfaces. As Rudy swam around a larger boulder sticking up above the ocean floor, a flat head sole darted away, disappearing beneath the protection of the protruding stone. Rock fish swam nearby, their orange scales bright in the shaft of sunlight probing the water's depth.

Rudy relaxed as the current carried him along, Kurt at his side. He'd been out of the water too long, making this dive a much-needed reprieve from his daily routine. Nothing like the ocean to remove a man from his struggles. Down here he could forget everything that hassled him topside, the nightmares about Dane, his tortured thoughts over McKenna's welfare, and the all-too-familiar job uncertainty. Too bad the tanks on his back had a limited air supply. He wouldn't mind staying down here a day or two.

McKenna hummed as she and Sydney headed down highway 101 en route to their former home in Eugene. Summer vacation meant a break for both of them. McKenna's newlywed friend Julia had invited Sydney to come play with her children while the two mothers spent some girl time catching up on their lives. McKenna had worked the gallery all weekend, with tourist season beginning to pick up in the coastal areas. But today she had garnered the help of an artist who would manage the store so she could get away with her daughter.

As they neared the entrance to Heceta Head State Park, McKenna's heart sank, recalling the last time she'd been here, the day she'd met Rudy Taylor. The day he almost drowned. The day Dane's homecoming began. Rudy had invited her into his life, the friendship helping a lonely woman and her disabled daughter cope with the emptiness of their lives. She hadn't seen Rudy since Dane's funeral in October, and his absence left a void she hadn't been able to fill. She'd learned from Livy that Rudy came home for a day at Christmas, but he hadn't been to see her.

"Ocean?" Sydney banged the seat with her feet. "Rudy? Swim?"

McKenna's shoulders sagged. Even her daughter remembered this as the place where they'd first met Rudy. Perhaps she shouldn't stop. Sydney again kicked the seat and McKenna surrendered. Pushing her signal blinker on, she slowed for the abrupt right turn into the park, steering around the handful of curves leading to the cozy little inlet. She glanced at her watch. They had an hour before they'd have to head for the valley. "We can play in the water today. For a little while."

"Ocean?" Sydney's agitation knew no boundaries. "Rudy. Swim?"

"No Rudy." McKenna rounded the last curve of the drive and stared at the parking lot teeming with visitors. No empty spaces waited to be filled. She gulped. There had to be one. There had to be. Without a parking space, she'd have a fight on her hands all the way to Eugene. Her daughter's disappointment could match a volcanic eruption.

She drove slowly down the pavement, pausing every few feet to see if a small space were available between the larger vehicles. Nothing. She reached the pay station, hit reverse, and angled her way back toward the other end. Every spot taken. McKenna's despair made her head throb.

A pickup sat at the edge of the road where vehicles rounded the last curve and headed into the parking area. The truck was backed up far enough to allow another car to sit right in front of it, barely clearing the roadway. Doing so would block the pickup's exit, and she'd risk someone entering the park and taking the last curve too fast, smashing her front bumper. But she had to take a chance. An hour of playtime in the water would mean two hours of quiet driving to her destination. She'd need to keep an eye out for the vehicle's owner. She didn't want to wind up in a dispute with strangers because she'd blocked their exit.

She hurried Sydney to the pay station, then found the sand toys in her trunk and helped her daughter maneuver the rocks lining the park's edge. Glancing back over her shoulder every minute or so, McKenna made certain she could still see the pickup from where she stood. If its owner showed up, she'd need a quick getaway up the slope.

Her hands flapping as though delighted to be at her favorite little stream, Sydney pulled off her own shoes and waded into the quiet ripples of the narrow creek. She splashed, stomping her feet in the water, the spray wetting her shorts. She picked up small rocks and tossed them into the water, her hands waving when each one made a plunking sound as it disappeared into the depths.

McKenna removed her shoes and stepped into the stream beside her daughter. She shivered in the breeze rolling off the ocean, pulling her hooded sweatshirt tighter around her shoulders. Raising the hood up over her hair, she called to Sydney. "Move over here, honey." She held out her hand and guided her daughter away from the shady trees lining the creek.

Out in the open, the sun warmed the spot. Shallower waters waited as well because they neared the juncture of the creek with the ocean. She sat on the sand, letting her feet dangle in the water. She alternated her gaze between the pickup behind her and Sydney, who played a few feet away.

Opening her tote, McKenna remembered the book she'd brought to read and lifted it to her lap. The bright sun blinded her, making the page impossible to see. She rummaged in the bottom of her bag for her sunglasses. Checking once more for the owner of the pickup, she directed her attention to the story before her. Set in the early days of the nation, the tale grabbed her interest, and she was soon lost in a world from long ago.

"Rudy. Swim?"

Sydney's question jerked McKenna from her book, and she glanced around for the owner of the pickup. Checking her watch, she gasped. The hour at the beach had long since ended. She sprang to her feet, brushing off as much sand as she could while she donned her shoes. "Let's get your shoes on, baby. We've stayed here a little longer than I planned. Come on."

"Rudy. Swim?"

McKenna fought to keep the frustration out of her voice. "Not today, sweetie." She brushed Sydney's feet clean and helped with her shoes. Taking her daughter's hand, she headed for the car. Her pulse quickened when she spotted someone throwing gear in the back of the pickup, the man looking around as though trying to figure out who had hemmed him in. Dragging Sydney up over the rocks, she hurried toward her car, rehearsing all the polite excuses she could think of to assuage the man's anger if she needed to. She approached the pickup and cleared her throat. "I hope I didn't keep you waiting too long. I lost track of time. We'll be out of here in just a second."

The man turned toward her, sunglasses in place and a towel over his head. He'd obviously been in the water, droplets dripping from his trunks. "Take your time, I'm waiting for my friend to catch up." Grabbing a towel from the back of the truck, he propped his foot against the wheel and dried his feet.

"I'll hurry, I promise." McKenna reached in her tote for her keys and popped the trunk, lifting Sydney's sand toys into the car. Slamming the back closed, she opened the door for Sydney. "Get in, sweetie. We need to get on our way."

Sydney glanced back over her shoulder at the ocean. "Rudy. Swim?"

"Honey, there is no Rudy swim today." She pulled on her daughter's hand, forcing her voice to remain calm. "That was last time. Get in!"

Sydney started to cry. "Rudy. Swim."

"Not today." McKenna breathed deep and counted to ten. If she lost her temper, the scene could go ballistic. Once upset, Sydney could turn a minor explosion into World War III. McKenna held her breath, praying the fuse had not been ignited. She tempered her tone, dropping her voice to a whisper. "Sweetie, he isn't here this time."

"Are you sure about that, McKenna?" The male voice behind her almost made her jump out of her shoes. Shaking, she whirled around and stared.

Rudy, carrying a scuba tank and wetsuit on his arm, stood at the back of the pickup, grinning like a circus clown. In need of a trim, his copper hair covered his head in an explosion of ringlets, the sunlight darkening the wet curls. Bare-chested, his muscular arms rippled beneath pale winter skin, patches of red no doubt left by the coldness of the water in which he had been swimming. He glanced at his friend and together they laughed before he fixed his gaze on her. "You remember my swimming partner, Kurt?"

The other man pulled the towel off his head and lifted his sunglasses. "Long time no see."

A rush of heat throbbed its way up McKenna's neck and along her chin. All her carefully rehearsed words wafted away on the wind, her mind like an erased slate as she stood staring. She shook her head, allowing herself to laugh. "Sydney kept telling me you were here. But I thought she remembered this place from last summer's near-fatal incident."

Rudy heaved his gear up over the side of the pickup bed and turned toward her, coming within a few feet of where she stood. His green eyes searched hers, a warm smile spreading across his face, the look one of a dear friend. "How are you doing?"

A thousand inappropriate responses flitted through McKenna's mind, but only one reply made it to her lips. "I've missed you."

Rudy studied the black-haired beauty smiling at him, fighting the urge to wrap his arms around her and kiss her breathless. All winter he had imagined this moment, his first encounter with McKenna since her husband's funeral and the ensuing months she'd had to come to terms with her loss. His pulse ramped up a notch, and he struggled to breathe, future possibilities igniting a fire in his imagination. He focused his mind on the present, managing a quiet and safe response. "How's Sydney today?"

"Rudy. Swim?" The little girl had unhooked her seat belt and climbed from the car, her unruly mane exploding in softness around her tiny face. "Ocean?"

"Yes, Sydney. I did swim today." Bending down, he held his arms out. "Can I have a hug?"

Sydney glanced at her mother before stepping into his embrace. She smelled like baby powder and shampoo, her fragile frame dwarfed by his shoulders. He wrapped her in a gentle squeeze, kissing her forehead before releasing the child to her mother.

He glanced at McKenna. "Mom said she's done well this year."

McKenna beamed. "She's reading a little, and she knows her numbers."

"Must have a good teacher." He winked, then stood, rubbing his hands on his arms. "Wind's picking up." Stepping back a pace, he reached for his t-shirt in the pickup cab and pulled it over his head. The fabric settled down around his torso. "You still managing the gallery?"

"Mom and Dad left for the Mediterranean at the end of January.

I'm on my own." She studied him. "Are you no longer in Seattle?"

"I finished teaching the last of the recruits until fall, so I opted for some time home. The aquarium can't seem to manage without their resident shark." He grinned. "I also wanted to check on Mom and see how she is doing since she fell and hurt her arm."

"I'm sorry I missed you when you were last here. Are you staying with her?"

"Bunking on her sofa."

"I'm glad to see you." She glanced at her watch. "Sydney and I are meeting friends in Eugene for dinner, so we need to get on the road."

He straightened, holding out his hand. "It's good to see you, McKenna."

"And you." She grasped his hand, giving it a gentle squeeze. "Hope to see you around sometime."

CHAPTER THIRTY-ONE

WHAT HAD SHE BEEN THINKING? MCKENNA'S composure dwindled as she drove out of the park and headed south on 101 to Eugene. With each mile, she relived the beach scene with Rudy over and over again in her mind, but the more she thought, the warmer her cheeks became. Her brain had fallen asleep, her mouth had dried up, and her tongue had twisted itself into knots as she tried to say something intelligible.

This had been Rudy. Her friend. Sydney's buddy. Livy's son. McKenna had stood there like a mute, her gaze frozen on his biceps, and her heart thumping like a Taiko drum out of sync with the rest of her body. How could she have behaved like a mindless idiot? Shaking her head and biting her lip, she pounded the steering wheel with her fist, careful not to wake Sydney who now slept in her car seat.

Because you still hold out hope Rudy will be more than just a friend.

McKenna inhaled a sharp breath, afraid to give the thought life. What about Dane? He'd now been dead for almost nine months. Was that a sufficient mourning period? Once he had been a devoted husband, the father of her child. He'd loved her, provided for her needs, and owned her heart. She'd honored her marriage vows by being faithful.

But he left you alone for two years. You wear your loneliness like a banner of fidelity.

When the voice wouldn't be quiet, McKenna prayed for wisdom. "Father, I know I'm free to move forward. Keep my lonely heart from jumping in where it doesn't belong. Rudy has been a true friend to Sydney and me. I don't want to spoil our relationship with desires beyond what our friendship holds. Nor do I want to marry a fisherman again. But if there is a spark there, a slight chance for happiness between us, show me how to make it happen."

The silence in the car left McKenna free to think. As the miles disappeared beneath her tires, she focused on the upcoming meeting with Julia. Her friend would have insights into McKenna's dilemma. Julia had recently married for the second time, having lost her first spouse in an accident. Julia could help her make sense of these feelings and would know how to move forward in her life. McKenna needed someone's reassurance that she wasn't crazy.

An hour later McKenna pulled into the driveway of a spacious home on the north end of town. Gabled windows lined the expansive roof, and McKenna guessed each of the five panes opened into a bedroom on the other side. Julia's two children by her first marriage and Doug's son by his late wife would need room to co-exist as brothers and sister in their blended family. For all McKenna knew, Julia and Doug might have another addition to their family on the way. Had it really been ten months since she had photographed their wedding?

The front door opened and Julia hurried out, a big smile on her face and arms opened wide. "You're here. You're finally here."

McKenna stepped from the car and embraced her friend. "I'd forgotten how long a drive it is from Newport. I stopped at Heceta Head State Park for an hour so Sydney could wade a little before we headed on down." She shut her door and opened the passenger side for Sydney. "I hope I haven't made you wait." She walked around to the trunk for her overnight bag.

"Not at all. Doug won't be home from work for an hour." Julia reached for the bag. "Let's get you settled so we can talk."

McKenna took Sydney's hand and followed Julia into the home. After a brief trip upstairs to leave their things in the guest room,

Julia ushered them into the kitchen. Settling Sydney at the table with a glass of milk and a plate of cookies, Julia pulled out another chair and gestured for McKenna to sit while she set the teapot to heat.

"So how are you holding up since Dane's accident?" Julia's eyes held warmth, moisture welling at the rims. "I know it must have been a terrible shock to you."

McKenna nodded, her mind searching for what she could honestly tell her friend. "I had been alone so long, that when he e-mailed me he was coming home, I couldn't believe it."

"And then he didn't make it." Julia removed a casserole from the refrigerator and set it near the stove, pushing the oven control to preheat before sitting beside her. "McKenna, I am so sorry."

"I filled the cupboards with everything I could think of to make him happy." McKenna shook her head at the memory. The joy. The anticipation. "I'd forgotten the snacks I bought for his homecoming. When I found them in a drawer, I bagged them up and tossed them in the garbage." She sniffed, the impact of what she'd endured these past few months threatening to make another appearance. "It hurt to lose him, but knowing he was coming home helped give me closure I wouldn't have had if he had died at sea with no word." She gazed up at her friend, afraid of seeing censure in her eyes. "He hadn't been a part of our lives for two years. His death, in some ways, released me from a prison in which I'd been held captive."

Julia squeezed her hand. "I understand. You won't hear any rebuke from me."

McKenna sucked in a deep breath. "When I stopped at the park today, I saw Rudy for the first time since the funeral."

"Rudy?"

"He's the biologist who left for Dutch Harbor the day of your wedding. You probably don't remember me mentioning him."

Julia sat up straighter, the expression on her face one of deep thought. "Actually, I do. You pointed him out at the funeral as the man who convinced Dane to come home. Right?"

McKenna nodded. "He's been gone since the funeral working in Seattle."

"He's the one you couldn't stop talking about at the wedding." Julia stood when the oven beeped and opening the door, slid the casserole inside. "Lasagna needs about forty minutes to heat, doesn't it?" She set the timer and faced McKenna. "I suspected you had feelings for him, then. Remember?"

McKenna nodded, her friend's insightfulness sending warmth across her cheeks. "But my only interest in him was as a friend."

"Things haven't changed between you, have they?" Though Julia inclined her head, her lifted eyebrows said she'd guessed McKenna's dilemma. "He's still hovering?"

"Not exactly. Sydney adores him. But he's become distant and reserved."

"He's afraid. Suddenly you are available, and he's not sure how to proceed."

"But Dane's only recently died." McKenna glanced at her daughter, who sat taking apart an Oreo one lick at a time. "I can't hop on the romance express, can I?"

"Dane left you alone for almost two years. Your heart has been running on empty. You are overdue for a fill-up. It's no sin to seek someone who pays you attention." Julia reached for McKenna's hand. "Flowers don't bloom in the darkness, they need to be where there's sunlight and nourishment. God didn't intend for you to live your life in a closet. You're a beautiful woman, sweetie, with normal desires and needs."

"But Dane's death is so fresh."

"Physically." Julia stood and grabbed the teapot which now whistled. She poured two mugs full and set them on the table. "But emotionally, he's been dead to you far longer." Julia handed her a plate. "Here, have a cookie."

"I loved him."

"Yes, you did. Your faithfulness is a testimony to your character." Julia bit into an Oreo. "But Dane's death has set you free, as you said. If this Rudy guy is worth your time, don't let him get away. He may be afraid to pursue you for the very same reasons you're afraid to go after him."

"You think I should initiate this?"

Julia sipped her tea. "From where I sit, it sounds as if the ball is in your court."

McKenna picked up a cookie. "Your answers really surprise me."

"You didn't know me when my first husband died."

"But you've shared some of what you went through."

"I thought I'd never breathe again." Julia set her teacup down. "I was pregnant. I saw my husband every day. We'd made love that morning. It took almost two years before I was ready to even leave the house." Julia glanced at her. "You've already put in the two years, McKenna. Dane's death is closure to a marriage he'd already deserted for reasons I find deplorable. It's your turn to move on. From what little you've told me, Rudy sounds like a wonderful man. Not many of us get two chances at love in this life. Don't miss your window for happiness."

"Your memories don't get in the way of loving Doug?"

"Not at all. Doug has become my everything." Julia cocked her head, an amused smile on her mouth. "Speaking of Doug, we'd better finish dinner. Can you make the salad?"

McKenna tore lettuce as the three Allen children, who had spent the day with friends at an amusement park, arrived a few minutes before their father. They worked around her, each one doing his or her part in setting the table. As she sliced tomatoes the children laid out silver, glassware, and plates.

"Mom, does Sydney need to sit by her mother?"

Answering Doug's son with a nod, Julia smiled at her. "He's been calling me Mom for awhile now, but I never tire of hearing it."

Sydney covered her ears as the noise of shuffling chairs and clinking dishware filled the room. To reassure her, McKenna wrapped an arm around her daughter and found her a stool next to the salad makings. The children disappeared into the dining room, the cacophony of sound generated by their conversation and their assigned chores traveling with them. Sydney appeared to wilt, the combination of strangers, noise, and a long day taking its toll.

Julia brought out a huge dictionary and held it up. "I stored my highchair in the attic when we moved. Think this will do?"

McKenna nodded. "She probably won't last long, she's so tired."

Chopping onions, peppers, and celery, McKenna finished the salad as Doug arrived, the kids surrounding him like a hero at homecoming, chattering about their day. Doug listened to each one's tale before greeting his wife. They kissed like newlyweds, the kids protesting with groans and rolls of their eyes at the two lovebirds. An ache rose within McKenna.

Julia laughed at the threesome. "Someday you'll find out this isn't so bad." She clapped her hands. "Find your places. Dinner is ready."

McKenna carried the salad and the dressings to the table while Julia set the homemade lasagna near the stack of plates. While McKenna helped Sydney up on her chair, Julia returned to the kitchen and soon appeared with a basket of garlic bread.

After Doug's blessing, plates of food circled the table, the children supplying bits of conversation between them. The banter among the newly blended siblings grew spirited, some friendly competition making McKenna smile. She hadn't eaten dinner in a family setting in such a long time, the lively conversation among siblings made better entertainment than a movie. The room blurred as she compared her life with Sydney to the warmth she witnessed here.

Sydney remained quiet, chewing on her garlic bread and tasting her salad.

Julia smiled McKenna's direction. "Are we losing her?"

McKenna nodded. "I'll probably take her upstairs right after dinner."

"Let me get the dessert." Julia nodded at her daughter, who grabbed the salad bowl and bread basket while she carried the lasagna to the kitchen. Within minutes, she returned with an ice cream cake, her daughter following with plates.

Squeals of approval made the rounds, Doug's son staring at the dessert. "Is this a special occasion?"

Julia winked at Doug and cut him an extra-large piece. His eyes twinkled as he stood and took Julia's hand. "McKenna, we're glad you and Sydney were able to join us tonight. We waited so you could hear our announcement." He looked at the three children staring at him. "Kids, our family is about to grow." He smiled at McKenna. "We are going to have another baby in November."

McKenna gasped, her surprise lost in the excited babble coming from the children. When each had expressed good wishes to their parents, McKenna stood and gave Julia a hug. "You are going to be one busy lady."

Julia studied her. "Let's get some happiness going for you."

McKenna felt an unexpected rush of heat warm her neck. If nothing else, Julia was quite direct. If only joy came that easily in her own life. But the possibility of finding love again even made McKenna smile. When she closed her eyes that night, only one face filled her dreams—a smiling, copper-topped man with green eyes and a lop-sided grin.

She could only imagine what he might think of Julia's advice. One way to find out. She rolled on her side and prayed for courage.

CHAPTER THIRTY-TWO

Rudy couldn't get McKenna out of his mind. As he hauled in groceries to restock his mother's cupboards the next day, he relived the scene at the beach in his head, replaying the brief encounter like a vinyl with a scratch. He'd spent the winter months imagining their first encounter, accepting the possibility she'd find peace with her past and move on. But her comment had surprised him.

"I've missed you."

What had she missed? His friendship? His corny jokes? His inability to deliver on his promises? Dane's death changed everything between them. Was it possible for them to move beyond friendship?

"See you around, Rudy."

He could still feel the squeeze of her hand. Could recall every angle of her face, every wisp of her black hair blowing on the breeze. Could smell the powder and shampoo she'd used on her little girl.

Nothing would please him more than to see her, but he couldn't be sure if what he had in mind for their future matched what she saw in their relationship. They'd become good friends. He'd put his life on the line to save her marriage. He'd made every effort to get Dane back into her arms. But God hadn't seen it that way and Dane perished. With her husband dead, McKenna's status changed.

Available. Vulnerable. Desirable.

He stopped. Everything they'd shared as friends could be lost if he misread her intentions.

Am I ever in trouble here.

He shook away his thoughts, arguing with himself. She was too recently widowed, her grief too fresh to climb aboard his agenda. Wasn't she?

Or had Dane's death been the end of a long and lonely wait for something better to happen in her life? She'd loved her husband, of that Rudy was certain. But even the strongest love can be trampled one too many times. McKenna had remained faithful, had never given up hope, had carried on in the face of overwhelming circumstances. Dane had played the fool. With him out of her life so long, she might be ready to move on.

Rudy inhaled and reached for his car keys. Mom would know.

When Rudy entered the Tidewater Takeout a few minutes later, the place bustled with customers, summer tourists eager for a quick sandwich and a drink to carry with them to the nearby beach. He glanced around for a table and found a small, square space for one near the back corner. Seated, he amused himself watching the patrons as they made their selections, readymade sandwiches beneath the glass disappearing like ice cream on a sunny afternoon. His mother smiled as she worked, bagging the food and handing over the drinks like a vending machine.

When the rush died down, Mom came to where he sat. "Are you here to order?"

"The usual." Rudy studied her face. Lines of fatigue creased her mouth, and gray half-circles underscored her eyes. "Busy day?"

"Summer is always busy on the coast." She scribbled on her order pad. "Ginger beer?"

"If you have it." He squirmed in his seat, trying to find a more comfortable position. "Take your time."

"You off work?"

"Until tomorrow. Got another shark show at the aquarium."

"Ah, summer catches up with you, too." She placed both hands on her hips. "How long before you return to Seattle?"

"Depends." A certain raven-haired beauty could make or break his decision, but he didn't voice the thought. "Can't pay my bills without a paycheck."

"Why don't you look here again? I continue praying you'll find work in Newport." She set down his beverage. "God can still work miracles, you know."

"God knows, like I do, no work means no pay. And you know how much I like to eat."

His mother chuckled and walked back to the curtained door leading to the main kitchen.

Rudy sighed deep enough to air out his socks. He leaned back against the wall and stared through the front window of the diner. The front of McKenna's gallery up the street sparkled in the coastal sun, the door opening and closing as the tide of tourists explored the shops in Nye Beach. After their chance meeting yesterday, when she'd told him she was headed to Eugene, she wouldn't be working the gallery today. He could go in and snoop without being caught if he wanted to.

I'd rather go when she's there.

The thought made him smile. At least his mind knew what was important, even if his body remained too cowardly to act upon his feelings. After he probed his mother about what she knew, he'd decide his next move.

"Here you go. One kielbasa with sauerkraut and mustard." His mother set the plate down, alongside the bottle of ginger beer. "You want a glass and a straw?"

"Nah, I'll chug it." He closed the bun with his fingers and lifted the sandwich to his mouth. Tipping back so as not to lose the sauerkraut, he moaned. "I've missed these working up north all winter.”

“I haven't lost my touch.” His mother sank onto another chair and rolled her shoulders. “What a day.”

“You look spent, Mom.” Rudy chewed on his sandwich. “They ought to bring in more help during tourist season.”

“We worked doubles this morning, making enough sandwiches to take us through the afternoon.” His mother tapped the table. “As long as I have a ready supply of the most popular ones, I can keep up. If I had to stop and make a kielbasa for every customer, I couldn't do it.”

“I appreciate the extra effort on my behalf.” Swigging the ginger beer, Rudy swallowed and cleared his throat. “How's Sydney doing in your cooking class?”

“She's a trooper. Made those rice cereal and marshmallow bars with her this week.” Mom smiled as if recalling the experience. “She likes those. One of the few things we make she'll actually eat.”

“Are you telling me Sydney did the work?”

“No, silly. But she counts the marshmallows and measures the cereal. She knows where the third cup measure is on a stick of butter.” Mom inclined her head, a goofy grin on her face. “She's only seven. That's what kids her age learn to do.”

“How's McKenna holding up?” Rudy studied his mother, waiting for a reaction to his question. He wasn't disappointed.

“She's moving forward. Once her parents left again, she focused on work and teaching Sydney. McKenna is very organized. Keeps up her books, writes school lessons, spends time running the gallery.” Mom gazed at him. “She's staying ahead of her pain, though her heart hasn't healed.”

“Is she missing Dane terribly?”

Mom sat up straighter and leaned forward, elbows on the table. “Dane wasn't part of her life for more than two years. Knowing he was coming home to his family helped her find closure. Letting him go didn't require a lot of effort."Mom stood and slapped the table. "It's her friend who flew north with the fishing boats she's missing. Should I draw you a picture?" She walked to the counter where a customer waited.

Rudy choked on the sausage in his mouth. He coughed for a minute, eyes watering and lungs wheezing, as he fought for air. When he could breathe normally, he took another swig of the ginger beer and chuckled. That's what he got for asking his mother what she thought.

Forward ho!

CHAPTER THIRTY-THREE

MᴄKᴇɴɴᴀ ᴀʀʀɪᴠᴇᴅ ɪɴ Nᴇᴡᴘᴏʀᴛ ᴇᴀʀʟʏ ᴀꜰᴛᴇʀ leaving Doug and Julia's that morning. With summer tourist season bringing in lots of foot traffic, she dropped by the gallery to check on the sales activity while she'd been gone.

Sydney had played with toys the Allen children offered her, but spending time with them as peers didn't happen. She'd sat in her spot, enjoying the novelty of a can of marbles and a Chinese checkers board, but playing a game with the kids didn't appeal to her. Instead, she'd played with her collection of blue and red cat's eyes in a corner of the board while the Allen siblings fought to construct marble pathways across the board. Shrieks of laughter would make Sydney jump, but understanding that someone's marble had hopped its way out of the main path and was stranded didn't register. Such was the play life of an autistic child.

The gallery clientele had dwindled to a handful of patrons when McKenna entered late afternoon, Sydney in tow. She worked her way to the receipt book mid-store, waving at the two artisans waiting on the customers. She took the sales copies to the children's table to tally them while Sydney played. The number of receipts since the beginning of the weekend surprised her, and totaling the sales in her head became an exercise in futility. She went to the office and retrieved the calculator, resuming her seat beside her daughter. The bell at the front door jingled often, but she ignored the sound, engrossed as she was in getting the sales figures right.

Satisfied with her final count, McKenna sat up and straightened her back, easing the kinks sitting at the low table had produced.

She found a red block under the calculator and handed it to Sydney.

Her daughter shoved it back, and tapped the table. "Presents?"

McKenna tried to think of something appropriate. "Box of marbles?"

Sydney shook her head. "Presents?"

The tension of working with figures the past hour had left its calling card. Her forehead throbbed. "I don't know, honey."

"Coloring books?"

At the sound of the male voice, McKenna twisted in her chair and stared. Short on air and heart galloping like a runaway horse, she gasped. Above her, Rudy held out a blue block, lop-sided grin in place, eyes twinkling, waiting. He's here. He's smiling. Say something.

Sydney beat her to it. "Presents?"

Rudy bent down and squatted beside her daughter, handing over the blue block. "Marshmallows?"

"Cookie bars."

"I had one of your cookie bars today." Rudy rubbed his stomach. "Sydney is a good cook. Mmm."

McKenna found her voice. "Your mother is an amazing teacher. Sydney is doing so many new things she never would have tried before." She swallowed, attempting to clear the words sticking in her throat. Her panic sent chills up her spine which threatened to undo her. "I don't know what I'd do without your mom."

Rudy fixed her with his gaze, a sad smile on his face. "She had a lot of practice with my sister."

McKenna rolled her lips together and breathed deeply. "I was really sorry to learn that part of your history. Neither you nor your mother ever shared what your family had endured. I can't imagine how hard that must have been for both of you."

Rudy nodded, lifting his gaze to the ceiling. His jaw muscles flexed as he studied whatever it was he looked at instead of her.

"Mom took their deaths the hardest."

"That's not what she says."

Rudy glanced her way, a rueful smile stretching his mouth. He was silent for a moment. "I believed I could have found Romelle in the smoke, instead of Dad. I knew her habits. When they both perished, I had to get away. Guilt was killing me."

"Your mom told me." McKenna inclined her head and chose her words with care. "Is guilt the reason you took the job in Seattle?"

His gaze was direct, his face stoic. "Yes." His eyes searched hers. "I didn't keep my promise to bring Dane home to you."

"That was God's responsibility, not yours. He saw it differently." McKenna folded her arms and narrowed her eyes. "But you broke a promise you could have kept and didn't."

"I did?" Rudy sat up straighter, frowning. "Nothing like batting a thousand."

McKenna nodded. "We were supposed to celebrate Sydney's birthday when you returned. You skipped out."

He slapped his forehead and leaned back. "I totally forgot."

"I know." McKenna tapped the calculator with her fingertips. "So what are you going to do about it?"

He wrapped his arm around Sydney. "I am going to go find this little darling some really nice presents and eat birthday cake until I'm dizzy."

McKenna laughed and extended her hand. "I'm holding you to this, you know. And so will Sydney."

He took her hand and squeezed it. "Of that I am certain. Name the day. I'll be there." He rustled Sydney's hair. "Come to think of it, I'm working as a shark tomorrow at the aquarium. Why don't you bring Sydney, and we'll grab lunch between shows?"

Sydney stared at Rudy. "Otter. Swim."

"That, too." Rudy laughed, tickling her daughter. "What a memory."

"She never forgets a good time." McKenna gathered up the receipts and put them in her tote. "The day she spent with you and Livy at the aquarium last summer is etched in her memory."

"What about your memory?" Rudy's gaze searched her face.

Red. Pink. Crimson. McKenna could feel the wave of heat creeping up her cheeks. "I haven't forgotten the events of the day either. It's the day I learned you were an extraordinary man."

Rudy shook his head. "Just a lot of painful experience to fall back on." He glanced at his watch. "Tomorrow then? Say, eleven-thirty? Backstage door?"

"We'll be there." McKenna followed Rudy's retreat all the way to the front of the store, nodding and smiling when he turned and waved. Only then did her heart stop pounding.

This is Rudy, stupid. McKenna mumbled to herself as she stood before her mirror the next morning, trying to figure out what to wear to the aquarium for her lunch with Sydney and Rudy. *He will be working.* She argued before the mirror. *This isn't a date.* She turned, first right, then left, giving herself a once-over. *It's an outing for Sydney.* She tossed the yellow peasant blouse on the bed. *Who am I trying to kid?*

She walked to her closet and pulled out the new maroon, v-necked shirt she'd purchased. The piece had two layers—an under shell of form-clinging rayon overlaid with a covering of maroon eyelet. The neckline scooped in all the right places, and the color enhanced her hair. She smiled. "But if this *were* a date, he'd love the color."*And now I'm speaking to mirrors!*

Her hands trembled as she brushed her hair. She'd always felt so safe with Rudy. Conversation had been easy, like talking with an old friend. So why did this meeting at the aquarium have her so rattled? She laid the brush down. *You're free. He's single. Sydney likes him.* The realization hit her like a brick. *Rudy is everything you wished Dane could have been.* "No wonder I'm nervous." McKenna said to no one. She retrieved her skinny jeans from the closet and draped the top down over the belted waistline. Adding a set of gold earrings and a pendant which dangled below her throat, she returned to the mirror. Pleased with what she saw, she strode to Sydney's room to get her ready. A lot of time had passed since McKenna enjoyed dressing to please a man. "This may not be a date, but it sure feels like one." She ignored the rise in her pulse, the lightness of her step.

An hour later, they entered through the backstage door Rudy had indicated and passed into the crowded theater as the wetlands presentation finished. Summer always brought out the crowds and today was no exception. Sydney covered her ears as the audience trickled out, her gaze aimed at the floor.

The cast of players retreated from the stage, the shark waving before he exited. McKenna moved forward in the room, leading Sydney by the hand.

Soon Rudy appeared back on stage, costume draped over his arm, hair in need of a cut.

McKenna fought the urge to fluff the unruly locks, the curls squished flat against his head by the shark suit.

 Rudy strode toward them. "Hi, ladies. Ready for lunch?"

Sydney dropped her hands to her sides and looked at the man expectantly. "Rudy. Otters?"

He knelt before her and tweaked her chin. "We can take a quick look now. Or we can get our hamburgers and look when we come back."

"Hamburgers?"

Rudy smiled and lifted Sydney in his arms. "I thought I might persuade you." He nodded toward the entrance they'd used to get in. "My truck is outside. There's a neat café on the public docks down the road. We can get a good lunch there." He glanced McKenna's way. "I have another show at one."

"We'd better hurry, then." She followed the man, admiring the broad shoulders and the confident stride as he carried Sydney out to the waiting truck. Stocky. Strong. Adorable. Soon the three of them were seated at a little table outside a ramshackle hut claiming to be Dockside Restaurant—*all the fresh seafood you can eat*. The breeze had picked up and McKenna shivered.

"Here, take my jacket." Rudy pulled off his lightweight slicker and hung it over her shoulders, his fingers brushing her arms as he pulled the front forward. "The sun is playing tricks on us today. Lots of sunshine and little warmth." He glanced at Sydney. "Is she cold?"

"I doubt it. She has on a long-sleeved shirt underneath her hoodie."

And I'm getting warmer by the minute.

Satisfied, Rudy hailed a waiter who came out of the restaurant to help other patrons. The man, dressed in a seaman's cap and a striped shirt, could have doubled as a pirate. He waddled over, menus stuck beneath his arm, a day's growth of beard outlining his double chin. "Need a menu? Or have you eaten here before?"

Rudy fist-bumped the guy and laughed. "Howie. I'd like you to meet my friends, McKenna and Sydney." He nodded at the imposing figure beside him. "This guy makes the best chowder in the world."

Howie nodded and harrumphed. "I don't know how he knows that. He never eats anything but a burger." The waiter turned his attention on McKenna. "But I'm willing to bet he'll eat something different to impress you."

McKenna fought the grin forming at the edges of her mouth. "I certainly hope you're right. He always smells like onions and fries.

A little chowder might offset the obvious."

Rudy gasped, his jaw hanging open, eyebrows meeting in the bridge of his nose.

Howie howled. "What's a class act like you doing hanging with a sea horse like him anyway?"

McKenna inclined her head and winked at Rudy. "He's risked his life on my behalf a time or two. I intend to repay the favor." She reached up toward the waiter, opening her palm. "I'd like a menu, please."

Howie handed over the plastic-coated sheets, offerings printed on both sides. "Be back in a minute while you decide." The man lumbered away, his striped shirt hitched up on his belt in back.

"He's a study in charm, isn't he?" McKenna peeked over the top of her menu at Rudy.

"Reminds me of Hawk, my former NMFS coordinator boss in Dutch."

McKenna sat up straighter, the mention of Dutch Harbor zinging her with memories. "Which brings up a decision I've made. My parents suggested a vacation when school let out to help me move on. They even paid for it. Do you think Livy would consider going with me on a cruise?"

"Mom?" Rudy's face skewed, eyebrows raised and mouth puckered. So cute. "Where?"

McKenna laid her menu on the table and drummed her knuckles against the surface. "Alaska."

CHAPTER THIRTY-FOUR

Rudy sat silent for a minute, his eyes searching hers. "Alaska?"

"I want to see the land that claimed my husband's loyalty." McKenna pulled a brochure out of her tote. "Ever heard of the inland passage cruise?"

"Beautiful scenery, but not Dutch Harbor by any stretch of the imagination." Rudy tapped the table, thinking. Was she serious? "The cruise doesn't take you to the Bering Sea."

"True, but I think seeing the glaciers and touching the land where he lived would give me peace. I might even hop a plane to Dutch Harbor. The final nail in the coffin of my marriage."

Rudy considered how to get McKenna safely to Dutch Harbor so she could experience the seaport for herself. The town, Unalaska, now had a visitor's center and tourists could visit by boat, car, and plane. People traveled there to see the scenery in the summer months, or they went to work. The planes he'd ridden were small and flew low over the water, but they were the fastest way to the port. The roar of the small twin-engine crafts, though, would send Sydney into fright and flight mode. McKenna would spend the entire trip calming her down. Rudy folded his arms and leaned on the table. "Stick with Alaska. The plane ride to Dutch would have Sydney screaming."

Howie reappeared, order pad in his fingers, a grin on his face. "You convince him to eat the chowder?"

Rudy shook his head and wrapped an arm around Sydney. "My little buddy here and I would like the hamburger baskets." He glanced across the table, challenging her to change the order. "McKenna?"

"I'll have the chowder and hot tea."

Howie nodded and punched the order pad with his pencil. "Coming right up."

"Are there fishing ports elsewhere?" McKenna replaced the brochure and pulled out a pad of paper and a pencil. "Spill."

"We have a fishing port right here in Newport." Rudy pointed the direction of the Hatfield Science Center down the road. "NOAA anchors in Yaquina Bay. Trawlers come and go. You can get a good feel for what goes on in Dutch Harbor simply by visiting your own home port."

"A cruise, though, would offer relaxation, along with the scenery." McKenna jotted notes on the page. "Sydney and I could make new memories. I'd like to clear out the fear and anxiety still haunting my thoughts. Create new images of Alaska and snow-packed lands to anchor my heart."

As Howie approached, Rudy smiled at her. She needed this to heal. "Mom would be delighted to go with you." He leaned back to allow room for the big man to set down their food. "How soon will you ask her?"

"I need to check a few more details and then I'll know more."

Rudy nodded, a warm, fuzzy feeling growing in his gut. Mom might get over her memories of him in Dutch Harbor if she rode a boat up the coast to Alaska. With his opportunities for employment here limited, Dutch Harbor remained an open door. But a cruise piqued his interest. Only one question—why couldn't he come, too?

That afternoon Rudy finished two more presentations for the wetlands education program at the aquarium. As he pulled off his shark costume after the final performance, he heard his name.

Glancing around, he caught the wave of the aquarium personnel manager. The woman often hired him to work the school day presentations, along with the educational entertainment here at the aquarium. She smiled as she approached him. Rudy inclined his head. "What's up?"

"We're in need of a full-time marine biologist here at the aquarium. Vacancy opening at the end of July. With your background and work experience, I thought you might be interested in the job."

"Where do I apply?" Rudy couldn't believe what he'd heard. Somewhere other than Seattle wanted him? Nothing he'd rather do than work at the aquarium. His degree had landed him all sorts of odds-and-ends kinds of employment related to his marine studies, but nothing permanent had come his way. Nor had any of the positions fully made use of his biology training. He'd even entertained working as a janitor so he could be close to the labs and the ongoing research.

"It's working with the fish." She gestured for him to follow her to the exhibits at the end of the causeway. The jellyfish tank stood before them surrounded by wall aquariums with various species in each exhibit. "Care and feeding."

"Would I work with Dr. Clarkson?" The noted marine biologist oversaw the research projects of the aquarium. His team often made discoveries which affected the entire world of marine science. He doubled as an academic advisor to the public exhibits, making certain the fish on display were properly treated.

She nodded, leading him into her office. "You'd be his lackey." Studying him, she leaned forward on her desk, palms down. "His demands have sent more than one assistant storming out the front door. Think you're tough enough?"

Rudy chuckled, laying his shark suit in a box. "I've worked with sea captains and NMFS supervisors. They are all a bunch of crusty sea barnacles. I'm pretty sure I can handle Dr. Clarkson."

She grinned, holding out a file folder. "The application is inside. Fill it out and report on Monday. I've already approved you for the job."

Rudy stood there, stunned. No more piecing jobs together here and there. No more stints in Alaska. He was finally anchored in Newport. His hometown. His favorite haunts. His mother. An image of McKenna's face flitted through his mind. Yeah, her, too. He couldn't think of anywhere he'd rather be. Time to go spread the news. "Thanks, I'll get this back to you later this week."

CHAPTER THIRTY-FIVE

THE NEXT MORNING MCKENNA LOADED SYDNEY in the car, ready to head for work. Today was Livy's day to take Sydney and with Rudy here, both of them were stopping by. Humming as she drove to the gallery and parked her car, McKenna's mood reflected her anticipation in seeing Rudy again. Looking into his green eyes. Wishing she could ruffle his wavy hair. He always kept it short, unless his job occupied more time than his schedule allowed and haircuts fell to the wayside. Like it was yesterday. Half inch. Curly. Framing his rugged face. Not overly handsome, but wholesomely appealing.

His farm boy looks paled in comparison to the size of the man's heart. Humble and warm, he always considered others before himself. Considered her needs. Sydney's. Made sacrifices above and beyond the call of the moment. McKenna's eyes burned. Even when she and Dane had first married, and her husband thought only of her, she didn't remember feeling so connected in spirit to him as she did to Rudy. His unselfish concern had captured her soul. If only she could tell him.

The gallery door squeaked when she inserted her key, competing with the tinkle of the bell hanging above. Saltwater and ocean air corroded the best hinges, despite efforts to keep them lubricated. Her father maintained the locks and hinges while he ran the gallery. She'd need to do the same. Somewhere in the office the three-in-one oil still lurked. Finding it might be the challenge.

Tugging at Sydney as she entered the shop, she flipped the light switch on and strode to the back of the store. While Sydney sat at the children's table, McKenna entered the office and rummaged around through the shelves and opened the wall cabinet. At the top, she spied the oil can. The front door bell tinkled. She stepped out of the office, her pulse quickening. Rudy.

"McKenna? We're here."

"Coming." She grabbed the oil can in her left hand and, despite the child's whining, took Sydney's hand in her right, dragging her to the front of the store. Forcing herself to breathe normally, McKenna inclined her head and smiled. "Did Livy make you volunteer to help her today?"

"No, I wanted to see Sydney." Rudy glanced at her left hand. "You using three-in-one oil to control Sydney's complaints these days?"

McKenna giggled, sticking the oil can behind her back. "Uh, no. I noticed the hinge is starting to squeak when I open the front door and thought I'd try to fix it." Her face felt as hot as the griddle she'd heated Sydney's breakfast on this morning. "Let's go see your mother."

Rudy stuck out his hand, his green eyes twinkling as he studied her. "Give me the oil can, and I'll see if I can fix the noise."

She handed over the greasy tin. "You don't have to fix my door."

Pulling off the stopper on top, he examined the can and made a face. "Where did you find this stuff?"

"In the office."

"How old is it?"

McKenna shrugged. "Probably as old as my father. Why?"

"For one thing, it's almost empty. For another, it smells like something else—maybe paint thinner—has been put in the can." He tipped it upside down. Nothing emerged. "Definitely empty." Rudy tossed the container into a nearby trash can. "You go visit my mother. I'll look around the office and see if there's a newer version. If not, I'll pick up a can of lubricant for you today when Sydney and I are out and about. Can you wait until later for the door to be fixed?"

McKenna grinned. She'd wait all day if it meant seeing Rudy back in her store. "Sure."

She'd appeared so embarrassed. Rudy worried as he drove his mother and Sydney to his mom's house. He relived the scene at the gallery in case he'd made her uncomfortable. The blush in her cheeks, her hesitancy to give him the oil can, the rush to go see his mother waiting in the pickup. As if McKenna couldn't bear to be near him. He sighed—maybe she didn't think of him as any more than a friend, a guy who had helped her find closure with her husband.

"Penny for your thoughts." Mom glanced his way as he drove, the probe of her stare prompting him to think fast. When he didn't answer, she spoke again. "She's certainly a beautiful girl."

"Her husband couldn't stop talking about her when I met him." He shot a look his mother's direction. "Said he'd loved her since they were in high school."

His mother harrumphed. "You're not fooling me, Rudy Michael Taylor. McKenna is on your mind. Her husband has been gone nine months. And she thinks you're the best thing that's happened in her life since sliced bread."

"Great. I'm a bag of whole wheat." Rudy maneuvered the pickup down the lane to where his mother's house sat. "Not making me feel real glamorous here, Mom." He parked in the drive and smiled over his shoulder at Sydney. "Hey, little one. Ready to have some fun?"

Sydney stared back at him, confusion in her eyes. "Rudy. Swim?"

He shook his head no. "We'll do puzzles and make cereal cookies and help Livy." He stepped from the cab, moved to the other side of the truck, and opened the passenger door for his mother. "You get the door. I'll help Sydney."

His mother slid out of the cab and rattled her key at him. He opened Sydney's door and helped the child from her car seat, following his mother into the house.

"Now that we can talk, I received a different offer yesterday." Rudy grinned as his mother whirled around and gaped at him.

"What kind of offer?" She stood rigid in the middle of the kitchen. "Please tell me it's not about Dutch Harbor again."

"It's not." Rudy took Sydney's hand and led her to the living room, kneeling before the book cabinet. He glanced at his mother, still standing at the counter, waiting for him to answer.

"Rudy, if you don't tell me this instant, I'm going to clobber you."

"The aquarium director caught me as I was leaving the shark show and asked if I would like a job working with Dr. Clarkson, the head biologist."

"Here? In Newport?" Mom crossed her arms over her heart. "That's the kind of news I needed." She walked to the refrigerator. "Shall I make coffee to celebrate?"

"Nothing like coffee and some of your cookies for a party."

She raised folded hands toward heaven. "I've been praying something like this would come along for months." She spread her arms out from her sides, palms waving. "For I know the plans I have for you, says the Lord. Plans to give you a future and a hope." She lowered her hands and focused on Rudy, chin up. "Jeremiah 29:11. My ongoing prayer verse."

"Well, relax, God has answered you."

"He always does. He may be slow, in our opinion, but He's never late." Mom glanced at Sydney. "Sydney's cereal cookies are here."

"Perfect with a cup of coffee." He pulled out the bottom drawer and retrieved a boxed puzzle, setting it on the square coffee table nearby. Sitting on the floor beside her, he patted the top of the box.

"Puzzle?"

Sydney opened the box, dumped the pieces, and leaned over the table top. Soon she was engaged in fitting the pattern together.

"Mom. Look." Rudy pointed at the table. "She's putting the puzzle together upside down, exactly like Romelle did."

His mother carried a cup of coffee to where he sat beside the child. "Doesn't surprise me at all." She stood and watched for a few minutes, smiling as he helped Sydney find pieces.

"What are you thinking?" Rudy could only imagine the thoughts running through her head. "This brings back memories of Romelle?"

Mom's smile faded for a moment, then returned like a sunburst after a shower. "Yes, she reminds me of Romelle. But what I really notice is how much Sydney looks like she could be your daughter."

Rudy glanced at the child. He'd noticed the similarities before. Having met Dane, with his deep brown hair and moody dark eyes, Rudy remembered thinking Sydney didn't resemble either of her parents. He didn't mind people thinking she was his daughter. The way McKenna stirred his heart whenever he came near her, he might someday make Sydney his step-child. Every man had his fantasies. This might be a dream come true.

CHAPTER THIRTY-SIX

McKenna closed the gallery at five and hurried home to meet Rudy when he brought Sydney. She stepped out of the car, her heart skipping into a wild, erratic rhythm at the sound of the wall phone ringing. She sprinted up the stairs, unlocked the door, and scurried to the phone, counting the rings. One, two, three, four, five, six. Snatching the handset on its sixth ring, McKenna already guessed the caller. Mom or Dad. No one else would have been that persistent. Not on that phone.

"This is McKenna." She waited for one of them to answer, but all she heard was a sniff. "Mom?" What was wrong? Her already racing heart notched up a beat, light perspiration beading her brow. "Mom, are you there?"

"Sorry, McKenna." Her mother's voice wobbled, the telltale echo of ragged breaths from crying punctuating her words. "I had to compose myself."

"What's going on?" McKenna squeezed her eyes closed, steeling herself with prayer as she waited for her mother to surrender the news. *Not Dad. Please, not my father.*

"It's your dad." Her mother croaked out the phrase before inhaling another stuttered breath and sniffing. The silence loomed, as if they had been cut off. "He's not well."

The words hit like an anvil against McKenna's temples. Her mind sped ahead of her mother's explanation, imagining every horrible scenario possible. Heart attack? Stroke? Pneumonia?

"We visited the Great Wall. The wild plum trees are in bloom, causing him terrible congestion, kicking in his asthma. I'm afraid this damp climate is going to give him pneumonia." Her mother exhaled, the sigh long enough to leave a trail of vapor across the Atlantic. "Did you know they turn off the heaters here March fifteenth? He's not only cold, but we can't find the right inhalers for him. So we're coming home."

"How much of your trip will you miss?" McKenna looked at the itinerary pinned to the bulletin board. Beijing? Yangtze River?

"Only Australia is left." Her mother sounded more and more tired as the conversation lulled. "But we can make that a separate trip another time."

A knock at the front door caught McKenna's attention. "Just a second, Mom. Sydney's coming home from her day with the Taylors." She laid the phone down and hurried to open the front door. Rudy and Sydney smiled at her, and she gestured for them to enter. "My mother is on the phone, calling from Beijing."

"As in China?" At her nod, Rudy's eyes grew wide.

She smiled, waving as she trotted back to the phone. "Mom, you still there?"

"Yes, honey, but I have to go. We'll be catching a flight Friday. Should be in Portland by Sunday."

McKenna glanced at the calendar on her wall. "Should I be looking for a house?"

"Don't do anything until we get there." Her mother's voice caught, the line growing faint. "Love you."

McKenna hung up the phone and turned to find Rudy and Sydney standing in the kitchen, staring at her. She pressed her temples between her thumb and ring finger, blowing out the breath she'd been holding.

"Everything okay?" Rudy's gaze met hers, concern written in the frown lines that wrinkled his forehead.

"I think so." McKenna studied the floor for a minute, trying to make sense of the call. "They're skipping Australia and coming home." She gazed up at the itinerary on the wall once again, running her finger down the list of dates and places. "Dad visited the Great Wall and got congested." She refocused on Rudy. "Between Mom's attempts to hide her crying, and her vague information about Dad's asthma, I'm not sure." McKenna spied a pen on the counter and marked the following Sunday with a circle.

"Is she always so elusive?"

"Only when she doesn't want me to worry." McKenna bent down and drew Sydney to her, wrapping her arms around her child's stiff shoulders. How fitting, since her mind was on her mother and this is something she would do, if she were here. McKenna's frustration grew. Someday her little girl would return the hug. Someday she'd call her Mommy. Someday. She held on to that hope. "Mom thinks I have enough worries on my plate without adding hers."

"She wants you to move?" Rudy pulled up a chair and sat as McKenna stood back up, lifting Sydney to her booster seat.

"Not yet." McKenna went to the refrigerator and retrieved a pitcher of fruit punch. Grabbing three glasses from the cupboard, she transferred all to the table. "Drink?" She handed Sydney a glass of juice, then poured one for Rudy and herself. Sitting, she sighed. "She said not to do anything until she and Dad get here, which will be Sunday." She glanced at her mark on the calendar. "But the arrangement has always been temporary. I lived here to keep the house occupied while they traveled. I'll still manage the gallery, but live somewhere else."

"I know it's none of my business, but do you make enough to pay rent?"

"I don't know." McKenna cast him a rueful smile. "Remember, this plan originally included Dane and his return from Alaska. We would have purchased our own home when he showed up. Bought furniture." She huffed at the memory, the irony of her situation making her smile. "Paying rent never occurred to me." She looked up at him again. "Funny how things change."

"Want me to keep my eyes open for something?"

McKenna leaned forward, setting her glass on the table, and folding her arms across the familiar surface. She didn't even own a table. She and Dane had eaten at a kitchen island in their apartment. "I'd be grateful." She studied the smiling man across from her. So nice. Great green eyes. Deep dimples. *I am in over my head.* She sat up abruptly, reining in her thoughts. "This day has been coming for a while. I'm not at all prepared."

"Something will turn up." Rudy touched her hand. "If I weren't living with Mom, she'd let you move in with her."

"How is your mother today?"

"Cocky." Rudy set his glass on the table and rose from the chair. "She stayed home and read her book while Sydney and I explored the beach." He shivered. "Don't be in a hurry to wade in the water. The surf is still pretty cold."

"Did Sydney wade in?" McKenna had tested ocean water in June before. Not always warm.

"Yeah. We stayed until our feet turned red." Rudy gave her a cheesy grin, worry in his eyes. "I hope that's okay."

"With Sydney, you rarely leave the beach without red feet. Numb toes, too."

"Romelle was the same way." He turned to go, looking over his shoulder at her. "I promised Mom I'd bring her a celebratory dinner, so I'd best be going."

"What are you celebrating?"

"I was offered a job at the aquarium. Full-time. Permanent."

McKenna's heart bounced up to her throat, surprised it fit. "When do you start?"

"I interview on Monday. But she said I had the job if I wanted it."

"Your mother must be ecstatic."

"That's one way of putting it." Rudy grinned, patting Sydney on the head. "Thanks for loaning us your daughter today."

McKenna searched for something to say. The man was leaving. Right when she'd hoped he'd stay. "Before you go, could you look at something Dane sent me from Alaska?" Did she sound as desperate as she felt?

Rudy's mouth puckered in an amused grin. "I wondered if it ever came."

"You know what it is?" McKenna stared at him. "How do you know?" She went to the cupboard and retrieved the box, lifting the beads for him to see.

Rudy took the piece from her and fingered it. "He was looking at this right after he and I had a heated discussion about your welfare. I guess I got through to him." He turned the beads in the light, capturing their sparkle. "He didn't think he could afford it."

"You didn't pay for it, did you?" McKenna held her breath. Dane had never been cheap.

"No." Rudy spread the beads apart and placed them on her head. "He said the colors would look beautiful on you." He studied her, adjusting the strands circling her face. His touch made her tremble. "He was right."

McKenna's cheeks grew warm at the compliment. Rudy thought the beads looked beautiful on her. She swallowed hard, ignoring the flutter in her breastbone. "But what is it?" McKenna touched the beads against her hair.

"It's an Aleutian wedding cap." Rudy tilted his head. "Did Dane send a note or anything?"

"Yes. He said he wanted to renew our wedding vows when he returned." Her voice caught, tight, painful.

"And he wanted you to wear this." Rudy lifted the cap, fingers brushing her cheek, and returned it to the box. "Take care of this. He used his savings to buy it. Believe me when I say this shows how much he really loved you."

"I do." McKenna closed the box. "The gift was so unlike any other he'd bought for me, I knew it had to be special." *Your influence is written all over the present.*

"Treasuring it will keep Dane's memory alive." Rudy sighed, flashing her a sad smile, and glanced at his watch. "I really need to be going."

With Dane's gift between them, McKenna couldn't detain Rudy any longer. The moment required her to be the widow she was, not the eager girlfriend she wanted to be. She found her professional voice."Thanks for taking Sydney today. Business at the gallery turned brisk this afternoon."

"Oh, I almost forgot. I picked up a bottle of oil for your lock and hinge. I'll swing by early tomorrow to fix your door. That work?"

"Yes." She fought her pounding heart, remaining calm and collected. She'd see him again.

Rudy waved and exited.

With reverence, McKenna returned the box to its cupboard, her husband's last act of love touching her spirit.

Thank you, Dane. I will cherish this gift in memory of you. But I'm moving on. My heart is lonely. I know you understand.

McKenna went to see where Sydney had disappeared, humming her way down the hall. She couldn't wait for this day to end and tomorrow to arrive. Though she wasn't scheduled to work, she'd go in to see Rudy. She could justify her presence simply being the boss. No one would ever suspect she'd showed up for ulterior motives, least of all Rudy. Only she would know her secret.

Rudy worked the doorknob several times after oiling it, making sure the squeak had disappeared from the lock. He swung the door back and forth, adding a drop of oil to each angle of the three hinges as they moved in a half-circle. Considerable corrosion had collected on the top axis, exposure to falling moisture the most likely culprit. When the sound ended, he gazed up at McKenna, who stood watching him. "I think it will be good for awhile." He capped the spout and handed the can to her. "Keep this in a safe place. We'll probably need it again before long."

Her smile made his heart flutter. She took the container from him, her fingers brushing his. He swallowed hard to contain his breathing. McKenna's new status as widow, her sudden availability, and her genuine beauty played havoc with his sense of reason. *Get a grip, Taylor.*

"Thank you, Rudy." McKenna stepped away from the door. "Now the squeak of the hinge won't compete with the tinkle of the bell."

"Anything else need fixing?" Rudy glanced around the gallery, noting another woman helping a customer at the counter. "Looks like you have help today."

"She's the regular artist on duty." McKenna's face flushed, and she dropped her gaze to the oil can. "I'm taking the books home, so Sydney and I can spend time together."

"You didn't have to come in today?" At the shake of her head, Rudy fought the grin forming at his mouth. "I wondered where you'd stashed Sydney."

McKenna thumbed the direction of the children's table. The little girl sat building Christmas trees with her blocks.

"Hey, Sydney." Rudy waved, the reality of McKenna's presence making him smile. She'd come in to meet him, rather than telling the relief help to expect him. Hmm. "I would have been happy to fix the door without bothering you." Though having her here made the task much more pleasant. She must have thought so, too.

"Oh, it's no bother. Really." Her eyes brightened as she gazed at him, expectancy written on her face. "I had to pick up the receipts anyway."

Rudy looked beyond her to the children's table in the back. "Do you think Sydney would enjoy a day at Cape Perpetua?" The park, built atop one of the northern coast's highest points, overlooked the Pacific Ocean, allowing a wide sweep of beach, both north and south. Hiking trails through the dense forest abounded.

"She loves places she can climb and run." McKenna inclined her head, a dozen questions in her eyes. "But you spent the day with her yesterday. Are you seriously considering another outing with a cantankerous seven-year-old?"

Rudy shoved his hands in his pockets. *No, I'm considering a day with her mother.* He gazed at McKenna, heart pounding loud enough to hurt his ears. "Well, I thought maybe she'd like to tag along while I showed her mother the view from the top of the park. I can't think of any spot more breathtaking on this stretch of coastline." Rudy shrugged, waiting for her reaction. *Nor was there any place more romantic.* But he didn't voice the thought. "Unless those books are really behind and in need of attention."

McKenna stilled, her gaze searching his, lips parted as she inhaled an almost imperceptible breath of air. A smile, so slight he might have missed it, crossed her face. "The books can wait. Sydney always needs a new adventure."

Rudy grinned, the breath he'd been holding seeping out between his lips. A new adventure, indeed. For all of us. He nodded to the back of the store. "Let's get loaded up. I might even spring for lunch."

McKenna laughed, the sound like bells tinkling from a wind chime. He followed her to where Sydney sat stacking blocks. This day grew better by the minute. And to think all of it began with a two-dollar can of oil. Hardware stores had suddenly elevated themselves to the realm of matchmakers. You never knew where romance might spring.

McKenna held Sydney's hand as they stood with Rudy at the top of the Sitka National Forest overlooking the Pacific Ocean and Cape Perpetua campground. She breathed in the moist, cold, ocean air, filling her lungs. "My dad will be so much better off when he gets here. He's always said he can breathe along the Oregon coast."

"Did he live in the valley once upon a time?"

She nodded, directing her gaze to him. His hair bounced with the rippling breeze, his profile shadowed by whiskers he'd not taken time to shave. Rugged. Boyish. "Dad grew up in Portland and decided he'd had enough of big city life when he married my mother. They moved here and opened the gallery. Mom worked there days while Dad taught school in Lincoln City."

"Teacher?" Rudy's eyebrows lifted at her nod. "What? Art?"

"History, mostly. At the high school level."

"Did he give you perfect grades?" Rudy's lopsided grin captured his mouth, the twinkle in his eye assurance he teased.

"Actually, I never had him as a teacher. I only attended school in Newport. Dane went to Waldport High until he transferred in as a junior."

"That's when he met you."

Nodding, McKenna bit her lip, that first encounter with Dane flashing through her memory. He'd caught the attention of every girl in the high school. Yet he'd only had eyes for her. "Yes. I was sixteen." How long ago that now seemed.

"Just yesterday, right?"

McKenna squinted at him, trying to be clever by making a growly face. "Right."

Rudy grinned and shifted toward the ocean, raising his hand to his forehead, as if blocking out sunlight. "I think I saw a whale spout." He pointed to the north. "This is migration season."

McKenna cupped her hand above her eyebrows, hoping to catch a glimpse of white spray aimed skyward. "I missed it. We need binoculars up here."

"Let's hike the trail for a ways." She started to protest, but he interrupted. "If Sydney gets tired, I'll carry her on my shoulders."

"That will be fun." Surprised again by how he read her thoughts, McKenna joined him as he walked down the incline, Sydney's hand in hers. Rudy grasped the child's other hand. The huge Sitka trees loomed above them, alternately shading them and illuminating them as the sun passed between the giant pillars. McKenna breathed in the scene. "How many acres in this forest, do you know?"

"More than two thousand, I heard. I know the trails cover twenty-six miles."

McKenna gasped. "When you said we'd go for a hike, you meant we'd *go* for a hike."

"I didn't mean hike the entire trail today. We'll walk along the path that overlooks the ocean. Parts of it are lined with stone set by the Civilian Conservation Corps back when Roosevelt was in office. There's an observation post that served as a shelter once upon a time."

"Made of stone, too?" McKenna had been here before, but she didn't remember a spot like that. "I've never seen so much rock."

Rudy nodded, pointing ahead of them. "I think it's right around the next bend." He glanced her way. "You grew up here. You haven't walked these trails before?"

"Long time ago." McKenna stared out over the churning water below them. "Dad and Mom were always busy with the gallery on weekends. Family outings were rare."

"I love the outdoors. I've hiked all over Lincoln County since I moved here." Rudy gestured to a stone shelter that came into view.

"There it is. Kind of an outpost for observation."

"It's lasted a long time. But then I guess when it's built of stone, it would." McKenna slowed her steps as she approached the rocky structure. Inside the air grew cooler, a gust of wind whipping through and chilling her. She pulled her arms close to her sides. "I'll bet this offered a lot of protection once upon a time."

"The roof still doesn't leak. Says something about stone." Rudy pulled off his windbreaker and wrapped it about her shoulders, the garment warm and smelling of spice. "If you're cold, we can head to the pickup."

"No, this helps. Thanks." She stepped through the open door into the sunshine, her sense of his nearness driving her. Such a thoughtful guy. Always attentive. Taking Sydney's hand again, she imagined it were his. "The sun helps, even if the breeze is a little brisk."

Sydney whined as they started down the trail again.

Rudy stopped and bent down. "Sydney. Cold?" He shivered, his lips stuttering as he imitated being cold. "Brr." He crisscrossed his arms across his chest and shuddered, grinning at Sydney's stare. "Sydney. Up?" He patted his shoulders and held out his arms. When she stepped forward, he stood and lifted her over his shoulders, settling her at the back of his neck. He took her hands and placed them on his head, wincing when she grabbed a handful of curls. "Hold on to Rudy." He slid his hands down her legs and grabbed an ankle in each. "Sit tight, Sydney. I'll give you a horsey ride like we did before."

McKenna fought the giggle bubbling at the top of her throat, and fell into stride next to him. Glancing up, Sydney was smiling, tiny hands gripping Rudy's hair as she shifted right and left from her lofty perch. McKenna tried to match Rudy's gait, but his long legs made his hips pitch side to side as he headed down the path, bouncing Sydney on his shoulders with each step. McKenna had seen elephant riders jostled in much the same way. Sydney didn't seem to mind.

As the path wound upward again, Rudy stopped and waited for her. "Need a break?"

"I'm doing okay. You?"

His breathing sounded labored, the uphill climb, coupled with a child on his shoulders, taking its toll. "Let me catch my breath." He inhaled and blew it out. "I'm winded, is all."

"She's bigger than she looks." McKenna's gaze followed the trunk of a huge Douglas fir towering above her. "This tree, too."

"We'll have to return and pay our respects to the Sentinel." At her frown, he pointed to another section of trail above them. "It's a giant Sitka spruce known as the Silent Sentinel of the Siuslaw. A few years ago the State of Oregon designated it the Oregon Heritage Tree."

"Old?" McKenna marveled at how Rudy knew so much about so many things. Biology served him well, his mind a loaded sponge.

"Only six-hundred years." He turned and climbed upward again. "Stands one-hundred eighty-five feet and has a forty-foot circumference at its base."

"That would be something to see."

Rudy stopped as the trail ended at the parking lot. "We'll see it another day." He reached up and lifted Sydney over his head, setting her near her mother. "I'm ready for lunch." He squatted in front of Sydney. "Ready to eat, kiddo?"

Sydney looked up at her. "Eat?"

"We should have brought a picnic."

Rudy stood and studied her, smile warm, eyes twinkling. "Next time we will." He walked toward his truck. "I remember your potato salad."

"I'm happy to make more." McKenna made a face. "But you start work Monday."

"Your parents will be home." Rudy wagged his finger. "They might not approve of you keeping company with a fisherman."

"How did you know about that?" McKenna put her hand to her mouth.

"Didn't. But if you were my grown daughter, I'd want a more stable lifestyle for you, after all you've been through." Rudy squeezed her shoulder. "Smart, aren't I?"

"Only if you know it doesn't matter what the man's employment status is, if he can love my daughter. Not every man is that self-less."

"Those men are the ones who lose." Rudy smiled. "The Sydneys of the world are heaven-sent."

McKenna resisted the urge to wrap her arms around Rudy and hug him. If only he could know the kind of treasure he was. What she wouldn't give for a lifetime of Rudy-filled moments. She found her voice.

"But you won't be a fisherman after Monday. You have to report for work at the aquarium. My parents won't say a word."

"That's assuming I get the job."

McKenna punched him playfully in the arm. "Either way, there won't be time to make you potato salad and share a picnic."

"Then I guess we better head to the dock and pick up more of Howie's chowder." Rudy unlocked the truck and opened the door for her. Lifting Sydney to her car seat, he buckled her in. He shut the door and stepped up to where McKenna sat in the passenger seat. "At least at Howie's we can eat outside and make it feel like a picnic. Until we can enjoy the real thing."

McKenna smiled as he shut her door. This feels like the real thing. Lord, slow down my eager heart.

CHAPTER THIRTY-SEVEN

MONDAY MORNING, RUDY STRODE TO THE aquarium personnel office, application in hand and anticipation in his heart. After three tours in Alaska as an observer, a stint as a port inspector, and numerous days as a team player in the aquarium's outreach program to schools, Rudy set his sights on this new position. Working here, he could stay in Newport. Find stability in his life. Get married. Start a family. Whoa. Where did that come from?

Dr. Clarkson's reputation as a no-nonsense specialist who routinely devoured the spirits of his co-workers didn't faze Rudy. He'd worked for boat captains whose glare could pickle an inexperienced sailor in a nanosecond. His various positions had toughened him—being chewed out for minor infractions came with the territory. Sensitive types didn't last in what often made up the dogfight world of marine biology. Rudy had come through unscathed, with his own battle scars to prove it. Let Dr. Clarkson give it his best shot. Rudy was prepared to handle whatever the man delivered.

Kelly sat at her desk as he rounded the corner and stopped at the door. "Good morning."

Her greeting was cut short by a ringing phone. She waved, motioning him into her office while she took the call. She pointed to a chair. He sat as she listened in the handset, making notes on a yellow notepad. She hung up and smiled. "Sorry about that."

"No problem. I brought the application." He opened his portfolio and handed her the form. Nothing like being eager.

"Good." Kelly read over the page, marking the sheet at different points. "You're a perfect fit for what we need."

"That's nice to know." Rudy leaned back in the chair. "I hope there's a roster of duties somewhere."

Kelly glanced up. "You'll report to Davis after we finish here. He will show you the ropes." She tossed him a pad of paper. "Make notes from the get-go. Dr. Clarkson will expect you to know the impossible and to never forget what he failed to tell you in the first place."

Rudy fought the urge to roll his eyes.

Kelly leaned back in her chair. "Most of the employees who work for Dr. Clarkson don't think ahead and that gets them into trouble. Try to anticipate what's coming and be ready for change."

"He wants a yes man." Rudy steepled his fingers, thinking of the many ways men with power tried to intimidate. "I am good at being positive and upbeat, but I won't let him wipe his shoes, using me as the polishing cloth."

Kelly agreed. "He'll respect you because of it."

Rudy stood. "Where do I find Davis?"

That afternoon Rudy headed to the sandwich shop. He heard his mother's laughter as he walked through the door, along with the sound of a tiny, little voice chanting, "Oh, no! Oh, no!"

Sydney.

He passed through the curtain and broke into a belly laugh at the scene before him.

His mother stood by the mixing counter, her apron covered in what looked to be chocolate. In her hand was a handle, the missing pot that had been attached to the object upside down on the table.

Beside her Sydney stared, face scrunched up and eyes wide.

"And what has happened here?" Rudy inclined his head and snickered. "New cooking technique?"

His mother quirked an eyebrow. "Smart aleck. My pot lost its handle just as I was about to pour melted chocolate over my peanut bars. Fortunately, melted chocolate isn't really hot, only warm. I'm not harmed, and Sydney is fine."

"Sydney and I would be happy to scrape your apron for you." He glanced at the little girl, winked, and ran his pointer finger down the front of his mother's apron. Sticking a glob of chocolate in his mouth, he moaned. "Umm. Good."

His mother shook her head but turned to face Sydney, offering her apron.

Sydney followed his example and gathered her own glob of chocolate. She smiled at him as she stared at the warm, gooey confection on her finger. "Umm. Good." She wiped it off on the apron.

Rudy laughed. "Speech and language therapist extraordinaire, at your service."

"You missed your calling." His mother set the handle on the counter and lifted the apron over her head. She grabbed another from inside the nearby closet and tied it around her waist. "Let me get this mess cleared." She handed him the chocolate-covered apron. "It was clean when I put it on. Grab two spoons and you and Sydney can share the bounty, but I doubt she'll eat any. There isn't that much. Most of it hit the table."

Rudy took Sydney's hand and led her to the other side of the counter, setting her on a stool. He reached into a utensil drawer and retrieved two spoons. Laying the apron out on the table, he ran Sydney's spoon down the front and handed her another glob of chocolate. "I hope this doesn't make her hyper." He scooped up another bit of chocolate for himself.

Sydney handed him the spoon. "No."

"McKenna says Sydney only eats the chocolate when they get hot fudge sundaes." His mother grunted as she scrubbed the table and wiped up a spill from the floor. "How was your interview?"

"Didn't happen." Rudy scraped the last of the chocolate from the fabric and handed the spoon to Sydney. At his mother's questioning glance, he smiled. "Kelly read my application, gave me the job, and sent me to work."

"You're permanent?" Mom's face lit up like a newly decorated Christmas tree. "That's wonderful."

"Pray I can stay on Dr. Clarkson's good side. I didn't have to work with him today. The man who's leaving trained me. Lots of technical stuff to remember."

"Technical?"

"Procedural protocols. Fish food formulas. Schedule of water changes." Rudy rotated his head in a circle. "My brain is still spinning from all the notes I made."

"You like it?"

Rudy nodded. "I'm excited. It's what I trained for, something I'm uniquely qualified to do. Plus, I know Dr. Clarkson. I had him for a couple of undergraduate classes."

"The best part is this job will keep you here in Newport." His mother clasped her hands together as if they were permanently glued from hours of prayer. "No more floating on the Bering Sea."

Rudy looked down at Sydney, still holding her spoon. "Definitely a plus."

McKenna finished locking the gallery and hurried across the street to the sandwich shop to get Sydney. The pickup parked in front made her heart skip a beat—Rudy had come to see his mother after his interview at the aquarium. She'd prayed for him all morning, doing her best to ask for God's divine providence in Rudy's life, though part of her prayers for him to stay in Newport stemmed from selfish wishes. She couldn't help herself. Every minute with the man made her like him more. If only she could summon the courage to tell him.

The buzzer sounded, announcing her arrival, but the only sound in the empty café came from the ice machine rattling next to the drink dispenser. Voices, low and murmuring, wafted from behind the curtain. She stuck her head through the opening and heard her name.

"McKenna will be here soon, so you two better finish up your scraping."

Scraping? Her curiosity piqued, she stepped further into the preparation area and sniffed. Chocolate. And peanut butter. Definitely decadent, whatever it might be. Her stomach growled. Tiptoeing toward the main counter, she stifled a giggle.

Rudy and Sydney sat before an unhandled pot on the table, scraping the inside of the cookware with spoons. Rudy ran his spoon down one side and lifted a gob of something brown, holding it up where Sydney could see. "Yum. Now Sydney do it."

Sydney shook her head. "Rudy do it."

Rudy took her hand, spoon in her fingers, and scraped the pot, removing a second gob of brown goo. "Yum. Bite for Sydney."

Sydney kept one set of fingers pressed against her ears, eyes fixed on the wad of chocolate inches from her lips. "No."

Rudy coaxed the child, making smacking noises with his lips. "Good. Sydney like it."

Sydney turned her head. "No."

Livy stepped from the pantry. "You can lead a horse to water, but—"

Rudy popped the chocolate blob in his mouth. "—you can't make her like chocolate." He inclined his head as he studied Sydney. "Child, you are a rare breed. If you were a fish, the aquarium would stick you in a tank all by yourself and turn on the spotlight."

"Otter swim?" Sydney laid her spoon on the table, wiggling down from her chair. "See otter swim?"

Rudy touched the end of Sydney's nose, rubbing his fingers along her chin. "You never forget a thing, do you?"

McKenna stepped into the light, glanced from Sydney to Rudy, and finally to Livy, spreading her arms. "Looks as if you two had quite an afternoon. Did Sydney spill something again, Livy?"

The woman shook her head, untying her apron. "The chocolate mess falls to me, I'm afraid." She hung the apron on its hook near the pantry door. "Rudy and Sydney cleaned up the apron, and I gave them spoons to finish off the pan, too. But Rudy is getting the greater benefit."

McKenna grinned at the man licking his spoon with an air of triumph. "Sydney is not the kitchen licker type."

"Good." He caught his thumbs on either side of his collar. "Save me all the dirty beaters, leftover spoons, and mixing bowls. I love to do clean-up." He inclined his head. "In fact, I'm now the official clean-up at the aquarium, among other various and sundry duties."

McKenna clasped her hands together. "You got the job?" At his nod, she raised her palm for a high-five, and he met her mid-air. His touch tingled all the way down her arm. "This calls for a celebration of some sort. Don't you think?" McKenna looked to Livy for support.

Livy nodded, her pleasure evident in the smile across her face. "I can't tell you the number of hours I've spent praying Rudy would find something close to home, full-time, and permanent."

McKenna pivoted toward him. "Tell you what. I've got all the makings for tacos at my place, and I have Sydney's favorite cake in the freezer waiting for you to come to her birthday. Why don't we celebrate tonight, at my house?"

Rudy smiled, his lop-sided grin in place. The twinkles in his eyes spoke mischief. "Don't tell me you can cook, too?" At her suspicious stare, he raised his hand, touching each finger as he counted off. "Photographer, teacher, gallery manager, *and* cook? Is there nothing you can't do?" He waited, tapping on his thumb. "Must be something to attach to this digit."

Rudy dreamer? She squelched the thought, folding her arms across her middle and clearing her throat. "I've been known to burn a perfectly good pizza to a crisp without even trying."*Whew.*

"I'll take the tacos."

She frowned at him before turning her smile to Livy. "See both of you in an hour?"At the woman's nod, she took Sydney's hand and headed for the kitchen's exit. Pausing at the door, she spoke over her shoulder. "And I have something important to discuss with you, Livy."

"Me?"

McKenna nodded, winking at Rudy. "I already ran the idea past Rudy, and he thought it a good one."

Returning her wink with a smile, Rudy plunked his spoon in the pan and stood. "We'll be there."

His mother's excitement over his new job oozed out of every word as she chattered beside Rudy on their way to McKenna's place later. "I can't believe you're going to be permanent in Newport. It's too good to be true."

Rudy had trouble believing his good fortune himself. Not that he hadn't earned the position. Hours of labor in different scenarios filled his résumé—skills he'd acquired by the sweat of his brow. His university education had only been the beginning.

"You think you'll buy a house?" His mother's question interrupted his thoughts.

"Better see how Dr. Clarkson and I work together before I make too many plans." Rudy turned down McKenna's street. He'd admit a house would be nice, with a view of the ocean. A wife and family wouldn't be far behind. He'd already chosen the woman he wanted, along with her darling, curly-headed daughter. All he lacked was the courage to pursue her.

He parked the truck and opened the door for his mother. As he locked the vehicle and proceeded up the sidewalk, a tiny voice sounded from the porch. He glanced up to find McKenna laughing, Sydney's hand in hers. "What did she say?"

"Guess." McKenna's smile lit up her face. "You've obviously worn your wet suit a few too many times around her."

He looked down at his black jeans and shirt, the only clean clothes he'd had in his closet. "I suppose it does look about the same to her."

"Dinner's ready. Come on in." McKenna stepped inside, gesturing for him and his mother to follow her into the kitchen. Garlic, oregano, and cayenne, a mixture of scents fit for an Aztec god, wafted up from the pan of browned meat simmering on the stove. Chopped lettuce, tomato, olives, and cheese waited in individual bowls on the counter. A pottery bowl on a back burner warmed a small stack of tortillas.

"If it tastes as good as it smells, I'm hungry." Rudy breathed in deep, appreciating the efforts made to celebrate his new job. "I didn't have much time for food today."

"Except for scraping chocolate from an apron with a spoon." Her laugh cheered him, like the chime of a triangle at the end of an energetic sonata. She strode to the cupboard and lifted four plates down, handing them to him. "Table, please." She opened the refrigerator. "To drink I have iced tea and soda." She straightened, the question waiting his answer.

"Water for me." His mother sank into a chair, patting the booster seat beside her, encouraging Sydney to climb up. "Hot kitchens dehydrate the body."

"I'll have tea." Rudy set the plates on the table. "Is it black?"

"Quite." After filling the glasses, McKenna set the bowls of fixings in the center of the table. She spooned the meat into a casserole and set it near the tortillas. "Sour cream? Guacamole?"

"Please." He surveyed the table, his mouth watering at the appetizing fare. "I know of restaurants that don't make their tacos this fancy."

"Restaurants are in business to make money. They don't have a new job and a birthday to celebrate, like we do." McKenna cast him a shy smile. "Would you honor us with grace?"

"Lord, we thank You for the gifts You bestow on Your children. Bless the hands which prepared this food. Thank You for the nourishment to our bodies." Rudy peeked up at McKenna, the hint of a blush warming her cheeks. "Thank You for the friendships which surround this table tonight. Amen."

Her eyes sparkled as she met his gaze, the longing he saw in them startling. Nine months had passed since Dane's death, but two-and-a-half years had disappeared in the wake of his absence. McKenna's loneliness hovered like an unanswered question. "Help yourself."

Rudy didn't need any more encouragement.

CHAPTER THIRTY-EIGHT

MCKENNA'S HEART ACHED AS RUDY AND Livy said their goodbyes later. Great people. Good friends. When she'd brought up the idea for Livy to join her on the Alaskan cruise, the woman didn't respond, as if the notion of traveling on a boat was more than she could comprehend. "I like adventure, but for me this would be similar to your parents touring Europe."

Rudy enjoyed his party, sharing it with Sydney's overdue birthday. The triple chocolate cake McKenna served brought raves from the man. "I'm so stuffed, I'll never eat again."

"Until tomorrow." Livy winked at McKenna, hugging Sydney one last time as she headed for the door. "Rudy's not been known to go without food long, unless he's trapped on a fishing boat."

"Mom." Rudy feigned an exasperated face. "Fishing boat cooks are known for their abilities. Hungry men resort to desperate measures if not fed well. Cooks could find themselves bait, if they aren't careful."

She swatted at him and huffed. "I'll be in the truck." Livy traipsed down the sidewalk toward the pickup, opened the door, lifted out her stool, climbed up, and deliberately closed the door.

Livy's attempt to give them privacy warmed McKenna, and a sudden flush burned her cheeks. Being alone with Rudy made her flesh tremble. If only he would kiss her.

Rudy focused his attention on McKenna. "Thanks for the party. You really outdid yourself on those tacos. I appreciate all your efforts."

"Very simple fare. Impromptu parties are like that." McKenna could feel the heat climbing her neck as Rudy's gaze penetrated her own. "I'm glad the cake stayed fresh enough. I froze it last September in case..." She caught herself, gulping back the sudden wave of pain the memory evoked, the special moment with Rudy lost."Sorry. Images of the accident pop up at the worst moments."

"Dane was your husband. Don't regret missing him." Rudy flashed a smile, grabbing her fingers, eyes full of tenderness. "Healing will take time."

"That's not it, Rudy." McKenna studied the rugged features of the man as his lop-sided grin appeared, loving how the little dimples popped into place. *Tell him*. She inhaled her courage. "That accident could have taken both of you. I put the cake in the freezer last fall for you, because I never thought you'd find Dane. I knew when you returned, you'd help Sydney celebrate her birthday. That's not something Dane ever did. He was never here in September."

As if stunned, Rudy's face blanched in the fading daylight at her declaration, the trickle of freckles she'd never noticed before dotting the sides of his cheeks near the hairline. He swallowed, glancing down at the ground, shaking his head. He lifted his gaze, pain in his eyes. "How could he do that? His own daughter?"

"Dane couldn't handle her diagnosis. It was easier to disappear than face it."

Rudy's grip on her fingers tightened, and he stepped closer, breath faint on her face. "I am never going to let that happen. I promise I will be here for you, so you don't travel this road alone."

McKenna forced herself to breathe, Rudy's nearness making her pulse run wild. Could he feel her heart pounding through his grip on her fingers? "I appreciate all you've already done." She swallowed, forcing down the lump that had lodged in her windpipe. "It means a lot to know I'm not alone, that I have someone I can call when the going gets tough."

If only it could be all the time.

Rudy stepped back a pace, releasing her hands and sticking his in his jean's pockets. Silent for a moment, he looked at her, eyes intent as if searching for the right answer. He breathed deep and exhaled. "I'm going to be honest, McKenna, even if it means risking our friendship."

"What is it?" She couldn't imagine what could be troubling him. If she lost Rudy's friendship, she didn't think she could remain in Newport. *Lord, don't let that happen.*

He focused beyond her, staring out toward the now darkened skyline, the sound of the tide rolling in not far away. "I don't want to be friends with you." At her gasp, he held up his palm, fingers pressed against her lips, eyes dark and intense upon her face. "I want to take our relationship to a different level. If you hadn't been married when I met you last summer, I'd have moved us forward before now." Dropping his hand to his side, he scuffed the porch with his shoe as if the spot were the most interesting thing he'd ever seen. "And I may be asking too soon as it is." He lifted his gaze to hers, looking every inch the part of a little boy who'd found a kitten he wanted to keep, but was afraid to ask. "Would you consider dating me to see if we have something more than friendship between us?"

McKenna fought the urge to squeal, putting her hands on his shoulders and giving him a kiss on the cheek. "I thought you'd never ask."

His jaw popped open, eyes wide. "Seriously?"

She pressed her forefinger to his chin, closing his still gaping mouth. "Seriously." She summoned her courage and spoke from her heart. "Rudy, I loved you as a friend last fall when you saved my daughter from the aquarium tunnel. I loved you more when you put yourself on an airplane and flew to Alaska in search of my husband. And when Dane lost his life and you came back to say you were sorry you didn't fulfill your quest, I fell head over heels. That probably sounds wrong." She paused. No, she had to tell him. "I loved Dane. I did. I was elated he was coming home. God, though, had other ideas. Dane is not coming back. And I've been lonely so long. And there's this guy who spends his life being a hero. How can I say no to the gift God has sent me?"

He grabbed her about the waist and pulled her against him, lips meeting hers in a tender peck. He drew back, searching her eyes, seeking permission for more. "Then you'll date me?"

She tilted her head, pressing his mouth with hers, removing any doubt.

He deepened the kiss, the feel of his heart against hers beating as hard as hers had been a moment before. When he pulled back, he kicked his lop-sided grin into place. "I'll even provide the babysitter."

She splayed her palm on his chest, dipping her chin. "Is she reliable?"

"She serves chocolate from her apron."

"Even better." She wrapped her arms around him, leaning into his embrace, his kiss answering a thousand questions her heart wanted to ask.

On the drive home, Mom remained quiet. Rudy cast her a sidelong glance, trying to read her thoughts. She stared out the window, as if the city street they traveled held great fascination. If she hadn't seen the sights on this thoroughfare hundreds of times, he might have accepted that explanation. Not a chance. Mom had something on her mind. And when she was quiet, it usually involved him.

"What did you think of McKenna's invitation to cruise the Alaskan inland passage?" He waited, his mother's mouth twisting as if she sought an answer. "Think you'd enjoy the adventure?"

Mom smacked her lips, the popping sound her signal she'd heard him and she'd come to a decision. "You should make the trip."

"Me?" Swerving on a curve in the road at her statement, Rudy gripped the steering wheel, yanking the pickup back onto the asphalt. "I can't travel with McKenna. She's single. As am I."

Mom twisted his way, eyes narrowed in the darkened truck. If he could see them, they'd be twinkling. "You could do something about that, you know."

Rudy fought the grin forming. Plotting again. The rascal. "McKenna and I have an understanding."

"Is that what you call it?" His mother's shoulders rose, dropping as she exhaled a sigh big enough to reroute the truck. "From where I sat tonight, I'd say you both are waiting for the other one to make a move."

Rudy slowed as he approached his mother's drive. Parking behind her car, he killed the engine and swiveled his knees right, facing her. He stretched an arm along the back of the bench seat and put a hand on her shoulder. "You don't think it's too soon for us?"

"No, I don't." Mom reached up and clasped his hand in hers. "That poor girl has lived forever without anyone to catch her when she falls. Her husband died. Another nine months to suffer. That's more than two-and-a-half years of waiting, Rudy." Mom let go and rested her hands in her lap. "Long enough, in my book."

"Would it help you to know I love her?" Rudy held his breath, anxious to hear what his mother would say to his declaration. "And I kissed her good-night?"

"Sweetie, you aren't telling me anything I don't already know." Mom gazed up at him, patting his cheek. "The moon has a way of casting shadows on her porch." She tweaked his chin. "Now do something about it."

CHAPTER THIRTY-NINE

Sydney babbled cartoon scripts, content in her car seat, as McKenna drove to the Portland airport Sunday to pick up her parents. The three-hour trip required planning, Sydney's stash of coloring books and crayons tucked in the pocket back of the driver's seat. Her favorite radio station played through the speakers.

Mom had been evasive when McKenna drilled her about her father's condition before they flew out of Beijing yesterday. Mom had said he'd been coughing, but they'd purchased an inhaler to help if his airways became restricted.

McKenna prayed the long trip wouldn't complicate his congestion, but riding sixteen hours in controlled cabin air promised to tax his lungs. When they touched down in Seattle, they had to change planes. The fresh, seaport atmosphere could improve things if her father stepped outside the airport, if only for a moment, before catching his flight to Portland. Driving him back to Newport, McKenna could make as many stops as he needed, the coastal air a welcome reprieve. His lungs would thank her, as would he, with a hug and a great, big kiss.

She rubbed her thumb across her lips, Rudy's good night kiss still on her mind. She hadn't talked with him since the impromptu party, but she'd seen his mother at the café. Livy said his new job demanded his full attention, every waking minute spent learning the aquarium routines. Exhaustion sapped his strength when he finished his shift, and the man returned home to his bed and collapsed. But, according to Livy, he loved what he was doing, the opportunity to work full-time in his field in his favorite city buoying him through the fatigue.

McKenna smiled. Rudy would remain here for the foreseeable future. He wanted to date her. She couldn't wait to share the news. Her parents should be thrilled.

The airport loomed ahead. She checked the digital readout on her dash. She'd arrived almost thirty minutes early. Plenty of time to park, find a restroom, and meet her folks at the gate. She followed the signs through the parking structure and spied an empty space.

Taking note of her surroundings, she helped Sydney climb out and led her to the back of the car. McKenna reached in the trunk for the new earphones Andrea had suggested. A busy airport meant lots of noise and stimulatory activity, both triggers for a royal meltdown. Sydney's eyes grew round as the sounds disappeared. She tilted her head first right, then left, testing the headgear. McKenna smiled. Maybe they could navigate the airport without a scene.

Satisfied when Sydney didn't protest, McKenna took her daughter's hand and together they walked into the terminal. After using the facilities, they found the reader board listing gates of incoming flights. Her parents' flight from Seattle was delayed. McKenna's spirits sank. The sooner her dad could get into Oregon weather and inhale, the sooner he could breathe again normally.

Sydney tugged at her hand, eyes on a concessionaire selling sandwiches.

"You hungry, Syd?" At the point of a finger, she followed her daughter across the thoroughfare and reached into her purse for the bills to purchase two hot dog baskets with fries. She carried the baskets to a table where she could see the reader board. Sydney ate her fries as McKenna kept vigil on the incoming flight changes. *Don't let them be delayed too long.*

A few minutes later, the hot dogs consumed, and the fries all but bathed in ketchup, the status for her parents' flight changed, the flight schedule display flashing *on time*. Catching her breath, she wiped Sydney's fingers clean, tossed the empty cardboard containers in the trash, and strode with her daughter to the gate.

Sydney sipped her soda as she walked, the straw making noisy gurgles as the cup emptied.

McKenna didn't intervene. In an airport like this, one little girl making rude noises with her straw wouldn't be heard. The people she cared about at the moment waited to land on an incoming airplane.

One steward with a wheelchair and two airline employees waited outside the jet bridge opening before disappearing down the long tunnel. Someone aboard the plane needed assistance.

McKenna's breathing accelerated, worry niggling at the back of her mind. Dad? She dismissed the thought and focused on the gate. If the passenger could be debarked without delay, the rest of the travelers could make a speedy exit, Dad and Mom among them.

She squeezed her hands into fists, bouncing a little on her toes. Mom and Dad were just a short distance from home. She had news to share. Much had happened since they left in January for the last leg of their journey. Would their excitement match what she felt?

Passengers emerged from the jet bridge, carry-on luggage in tow. She caught a glimpse of her mother, hustling up the bridge with the others. The steward who had pushed the wheelchair before followed her mother. Where was Dad?

McKenna's heart stopped. Seated in the chair, eyes closed and wearing an oxygen mask, her father bounced along the segmented corridor. Skin pale, hair askew, he appeared to be wrung out.

"Dad!" McKenna grabbed Sydney's hand, lifted her off the chair where she'd been swinging her legs, and tugged her forward. Travelers parted as she pushed through the throng, calling out, "Dad!"

A hand grabbed her arm, slowing her progress. "McKenna, he's all right."

She turned to stare into the strained face of her mother. "What happened?"

"He had an asthma attack on the flight from Beijing. The airlines insisted on the oxygen to fly on to Portland. He just needs to be home."

"Hey, sugar." Holding his mask and smiling, Dad gasped for air, his wheeze proof of his condition. He chuckled, the sound like one of Sydney's twisted straws, the rattle ragged and labored. "I really know how to make an entrance, don't I?"

"Not funny." McKenna bent and gave him a hug, then wrapped her arms around her mother. "I'm thankful you're home safe."

"So are we." Mom leaned down and touched Sydney's shoulder. "Hello, darling. Remember me?"

Sydney slipped behind McKenna's leg, head down, eyes peering up at her grandmother. Her gaze darted to Dad in the wheelchair. "Ride?"

"I think that's allowable." Mom addressed the steward as if they'd become fast friends. "Are you pushing him to the car or do you want it brought around?"

"Have it brought to the loading zone." He pointed to a set of elevators. "I'll take him there."

"Can my granddaughter ride with him?"

The steward glanced Sydney's way, her earphones askew, and her arms secure around McKenna's legs. "Probably shouldn't, but let's do it."

Dad helped Sydney into his lap, and McKenna walked beside the chair as far as the loading zone. "I'll go bring the car up. Give me a few minutes. I parked in section T."

A glance passed between Mom and Dad. "Do you think Sydney will wait with us?"

"Syd, I'm going to go get the car. Do you want to stay or go?"

Sydney hopped down and took McKenna's hand.

"I guess we have our answer. Be back soon." She hurried away, pulling Sydney along at a greater pace than when they'd arrived.

Conversation dwindled to whispers as McKenna drove home to Newport. They stopped twice as they traveled, Dad's insistence on fresh air prompting the delays. Sydney fell asleep in her booster seat first, then Dad reclined the front passenger seat and dozed. From her rear-view mirror, McKenna kept eye contact with her mother who chose to ride in the back with Sydney. Whenever Mom asked her a question, she'd nod where appropriate, or shrug her shoulders when she didn't know. Neither of them wanted to disturb the sleeping passengers.

"Rest stop ahead." McKenna turned on her blinker and slowed to make the turn. "I need to stretch my legs."

"A rest would be good for all of us." Mom leaned forward over the reclining seat and tapped Dad's shoulder. "Need a bathroom break?"

Dad roused as if in a sleepy stupor. "I need ocean air more."

"Plenty of that here." McKenna killed the engine. "You two go ahead, and I'll stand outside the car and watch over Sydney."

"Does she need to use the facilities?" Mom popped her door open. A gust of wind caught the door and banged it closed.

Sydney's eyes fluttered, and she stretched. "Ocean? Rudy swim?"

McKenna's cheeks burned. Leave it to little mouths to utter big news. She braced for the inevitable reaction. She wasn't disappointed.

"How does she know Rudy?" Mom's eyes widened, and she

studied McKenna's reaction. "Are you keeping company with the man?"

"He's taken a special interest in Sydney. He grew up with a little sister exactly like her."

Dad scowled. "But he's a fisherman, right?" He folded his arms across his chest. "Haven't you had enough of life with ocean-going men?"

McKenna inhaled and gave her parents what she intended to be an understanding smile. "Rudy is a marine biologist, not a fisherman. He's tired of doing observer work for the government, so he recently accepted a position at the aquarium, making Newport his permanent home."

She opened her door and climbed out, turning to open Sydney's door. As she did she delivered the punch line with a smile she couldn't contain. "Which really pleases his worried mother." *And me.* She didn't voice the elation she carried inside, but it probably showed on her face. She couldn't hide her happiness.

"And he's become special to you, hasn't he?"

Yep, it showed. Either that or her Mom knew her well enough to read between the lines.

"McKenna?"

"Yes. He and I have a special bond because of what he did for Dane and what he's doing for Sydney." She left so much out of the statement it almost sounded like a lie. She wasn't sure her parents were ready for the rest.

"Sounds like a reasonable young man." Dad opened his door, taking a deep breath. His breathing had grown steadily stronger, his need to fill his lungs improving with each stop. "I want to smell salt air and use the facilities. I'll be back." He stood and staggered away from them, swinging his arms from side to side, stopping to bend and stretch. Straightening, he followed the sidewalk to the restroom.

Mom popped out behind her husband. "I'll go with him." She leaned against the car and whispered. "You're not fooling me, young lady. I've known you a long time, and I see more than friendship with Rudy written on your face." She winked, closing the car door.

McKenna giggled. If Rudy knew what they were saying, he'd probably return to Alaska. No, his eyes had told her much more than his words, standing together like they had on her porch. And his kisses? She couldn't go there. Not now. She'd really give herself away if she did.

Even though her parents insisted she and Sydney continue living in the upstairs of the bungalow while they occupied the daylight basement for their living quarters, McKenna decided she needed to find a new home for Sydney and her. Mom could probably endure the environment of the downstairs apartment, but she wasn't convinced Dad would remain healthy there. However, her dad had never been one to give in easily, and his stubborn streak wouldn't allow her to take his place. Where she would live, she didn't know, but a change was necessary.

On her day off the following week, she had loaded Sydney in the car to go house hunting when Rudy pulled into the drive and parked his truck.

"Did they fire you already?" McKenna couldn't imagine why he might be here.

"I've found a house I want to lease. I thought you might like to see it." Rudy glanced at Sydney. "Want to go for a look-see?"

McKenna glanced at her watch. "Sure. I'm in need of space myself."

"Your parents don't want you staying here?"

"They don't want to disrupt Sydney by moving her downstairs. I don't want Dad in the basement, either." McKenna raised her hands in exasperation. "I've tried arguing."

"This may be the answer, then. Hop in."

The house stood at the north end of town, a small cottage with a fenced yard. Rudy helped McKenna out of the pickup and lifted Sydney to the ground. Together they walked up to the door.

"I've got the key." Rudy unlocked the entrance, stepping back to let McKenna in. The foyer opened three ways—left to the kitchen, right to the bedrooms and straight ahead to a brightly-lit front room.

"How did you find an empty house with a view of the ocean?" McKenna strode into the sunlit space and twirled in a circle. "At such an affordable price."

"I went to see my old landlord in Depoe Bay." Rudy leaned against a door casing, his hands in his pockets. "He'd recently evicted the tenants here and refurbished it. Thought he might sell because he's had trouble with unreliable renters at this location. Partiers love the proximity of the ocean."

"He trusted you, though." McKenna walked toward the windows. Light poured in through the biggest glass. A littering of windswept bushes and gnarled trees formed a break in the shrubbery outside that opened onto the Pacific. I'd be tempted to make this the bedroom. Waking to a view of the ocean every morning would be heavenly."

"The openness may not last long. The lot below has been cleared for a new dwelling to be built." Rudy grimaced. "I might soon get a view of the roof."

"What a shame." McKenna turned from the view and faced him. "I used to be able to see the ocean from Mom and Dad's house, but the building boom ruined that."

"What do you think? Should I take it?" Rudy's eyes glimmered as he waited for her answer.

"Wish I'd found it first." McKenna wandered toward the bedrooms, her attention on the size of the spaces. "The bathroom is nice with a door to the master bedroom and a door to the hall."

"Did you check out the kitchen?" Rudy pointed to a swinging door leading out of the front room.

She walked through the opening and gasped. "It's all windows!" Low cupboards ran the length of the outside wall beneath a tiled counter of buttercup yellow. A motif of daisies on a blue background formed the backsplash. Above the floral display, paned windows overlooked a stretch of beach in the distance, the ocean beyond. On the opposite wall the appliances waited between both upper and lower cabinets. "Oh, Rudy!"

He stepped behind her, wrapped his arms about her waist, and rested his chin on her shoulder. His breath on her neck made her tingle. "You like it?"

"How could I not?" She turned and gazed at him. "This feels like it came straight out of a storybook."

"Tell you what." He grabbed her fingers in his. "My mother is not ready to lose me yet, and I'm dating this gal who has expensive tastes." He grinned when her jaw opened to protest. He put a finger to her lips. "Why don't you and Sydney take this house? It's close to the gallery, her school, Mom's diner."

"That doesn't seem fair." McKenna frowned. "You need your space as much as I do."

"But you have to admit this is perfect for you." He tilted his head. "Am I right?"

She nodded.

"And I have an in with the landlord." Rudy narrowed his eyes. "You could live here, keeping the space reserved, until I can move in."

She sighed. "But that means making Sydney move again."

Rudy pursed his lips and studied her. "Not if I have any say in the matter."

McKenna stared at him, speechless. The heat creeping along her jaw could only mean one thing. She'd blushed pink all the way to her toes.

After Rudy surprised her by letting her rent the cottage, McKenna prepared to move. Her parents tried to change her mind, asserting the bungalow they shared was big enough for the four of them. But McKenna insisted the basement apartment would not be good for her dad's lungs.

McKenna made their homecoming as comfortable as possible, cooking dinner on her days away from the gallery. Mid-week she prepared tacos again, the memory of Rudy's celebratory dinner, before her parents returned, making her smile. She hadn't seen him since the day he'd taken her to the house. He'd bought them dinner in Depoe Bay, warning her his schedule would be tight for a while. He'd sent roses to the gallery the next day in celebration, the note said, of her new freedom as a paying tenant. The guy continued to astound her with his thoughtfulness. She could only believe this display of affection proved what she'd known all along. Ordinary would never describe Rudy. He was considerate and attuned to her needs. Still, she missed him.

At dinner, her parents had asked if she was ready to take her cruise yet. She'd told them about the trip to Alaska with Livy, but confessed she'd only made the initial contacts. The cruise line should be answering her soon. Maybe tonight there'd be a reply.

Her parents had headed to their quarters and she had put Sydney to bed a few minutes earlier, returning to the kitchen to clean. One main pan to scrub. Four plates. Nice thing about tacos.

Easy. Quick. She'd have time to check for e-mail messages if she hurried.

A few minutes later, McKenna heard an engine die and saw headlights fade almost at the same time as the knock sounded on the door. A visitor this time of night, and unexpected, alarmed her. She tiptoed to the front window and glanced at the porch to see who stood there. Whoever had come knelt on one knee, as if looking for something they'd dropped. She hesitated. Opening the door to an unannounced arrival didn't appeal to her. She waited, watching. Still on one knee, the visitor knocked again. Louder. More persistent. "McKenna?"

Rudy?

She flipped on the porch light and opened the door. Rudy looked up at her, one knee on the wood slatted surface, the other bent as he leaned forward, smiling. She stifled a laugh, his odd behavior fueling her curiosity. "What brings you here at this hour?" *Another kiss? Mom and Dad might not be asleep.*

Rudy kept one hand behind his back, lifting his iPod up to read with the other.

"What are you doing?" She giggled, putting a finger to her mouth, lest her parents hear them.

He winked at her, pointing to the blue screen glowing in the darkness. "In Hebrews, the writer tells us of two unchangeable things in which it is impossible for God to lie. We who have taken refuge in Him have strong encouragement of the hope set before us. This hope we have as an anchor of our soul, a hope both sure and steadfast.' Stuffing the electronic device in his pocket, he brought his hand from behind his back and held out a small velveteen box. "I want to share that hope with you and with God's help, be an anchor for your heart." He reached for her hand. "I love you. Will you marry me?"

McKenna gasped. "This is so...so..." She searched for the right words. Sudden?

Unexpected. "Wonderful." She laughed. "I guess we're skipping the date-me-for-a-while part?" She grasped his palm and pulled him to his feet, shaking her head in bewilderment. "You are full of surprises."

"You don't think it's too soon?"

In the shadows the moon cast over the porch, his countenance fell as if he feared her answer. The little boy with the question on his face had resurfaced. What a kind and loving man—always thinking of her first.

"I love you, Rudy." McKenna wrapped her arms around him. "As I told you at the aquarium the day Sydney ran screaming out of the underwater exhibit and you caught up with her, you are like the Christmas present I never got. Marrying you, I will finally open the package

I've needed for a long time."

Taking a step back, Rudy took a ring from the box and slipped it on her finger. The diamond solitaire glittered under the porch light. He lifted her chin with his fingers and drew her close. His kiss felt warm and soft on her lips, full of promises she'd never believed would ever be hers again. Her eyes misted, happiness complete.

Voices sounded behind them, along with a giggle. She peered over Rudy's shoulder to see her parents standing at the bottom of the steps. Her mother smiled. "We heard something and decided to check it out. I'm guessing you two have news to share?"

McKenna laughed. Even in the dim porch light, Rudy's cheeks flashed red.

The bow of the cruise ship plunged through the deep, blue waters of the Pacific, pushing its way up the coastline of Canada en route to Kodiak Island. Rudy wrapped his arms about McKenna's waist, burying his face in the scent of her hair. She leaned against him, her cheek warm against his. "How is Mrs. Rudy Taylor this morning?"

She circled his arms with hers, lifting her face to the sky. "I'm living a wonderful, unbelievable dream. By my side is a man who claims to be crazy in love with me and who also cares for my daughter. A new view of Alaska awaits me, memories of another time left behind." She angled her face so she could look at him the chill of the air brushing her cheeks with pink. "I couldn't be happier."

He kissed her neck, loving how she trembled in his embrace. The beat of her heart sped a little faster, her breathing ragged and uneven, her form relaxed against him. "How do you think Sydney is doing without you?"

McKenna lifted her shoulders, air rushing from her lungs when she exhaled. "Livy probably has her cooking a seven-course meal by now. Nothing would surprise me."

"Let's see . . . carrots for appetizers, burgers for the entrée, fries by the basketful, chocolate shake for the drink, and cereal cookies for dessert. That's five. What did I forget?"

"A soda for the chaser and pizza squares with the carrots."

Rudy squeezed his bride closer. "Got to give the girl credit for creativity." He kissed her ear. "At least she's learning how to take care of herself. Your mother probably has her doing the laundry, just to keep up."

"Until we get home and she'll want to be waited on again."

Rudy stood straighter and leaned his head against McKenna's. "I don't mind. She needs all the affection I can give her. Helping her make sense of this crazy world is going to take both of us."

McKenna twisted in his arms, tears pooling at the rims of her eyes. "You are the most amazing man, Rudy Taylor. I love you with all my heart."

"I am the one blessed. I married the bravest, most determined mother, and ever faithful woman, in the world. That she's also the sexiest chick I ever met is frosting on the cake of life."

"God knew our story from the beginning. He's the one who anchored us with hope."

"An anchor for eternity." He leaned in and smiled when she met him halfway, the kiss promising many, many more to come.

NOW A SNEAK PEEK AT
BOOK TWO

LOVE CALLS HER HOME

Chapter One

Lissa Frye jolted upright, listening for the strange noise that had broken the stillness. She squinted into the darkness as dawn's approach grayed the black interior of the room. The dresser and nightstand took shape, but still no clue to the sound's origin surfaced.

What was it?

A sharp claw, attached to a softer paw, touched her arm and she jumped. Sorrel's rough tongue licked her chin, the swish of a wagging tail a sign the noise had baffled the dog, too.

"Did you hear that?" At her question, Sorrel yipped. The dog panted, pushing her nose into Lissa's lap.

She stroked the dog's curly ears and petted her head. "Lie down, girl. It isn't time to go." The dog whined and retreated to her rug, wispy snores the only sign the animal existed in the shadows.

The room again fell silent. The hush lingered like a menacing spirit, a ghostlike apparition that made Lissa uncomfortable. She'd regained her land legs since returning from the Navy three months ago, but the missing hum of the ship's engines and the ever-present roll of the vessel as it sailed had not been replaced.

The quiet here roared louder than any ship ever had. Fifteen years of living with that reality would take time to fade. If ever.

Lissa stood and stumbled toward the dresser, stubbing her toe on the travel bag she'd left on the floor last night. The luggage, packed and ready to load in the Suburban for her trip over the mountain today, waited to be stowed after she helped Sorrel into the passenger seat later. Hopping on one foot as she massaged her injured digit, she reached for the lamp. As she did, a light flashed to the left of its base, the strange buzz rattling the water glass beside it.

Her cell phone. On vibrate.

Oh, no. Not at six-thirty in the morning. She moaned as she read the time. Nothing good could come of a call this early. Unless it was Dad. Or Eily. Or Kurt? No, that was too much to hope.

She picked up the phone and stared at the readout. Sheriff Matthew Briggs. Her boss. On a Saturday, no less. She'd worked the last three, all filled with emergencies her new job required her to handle.

What was it this time? A herd of cows that had pushed over their rotting fence and now blocked traffic as they trotted along Highway 20? A raptor shot by some inexperienced hunter? A ram who'd led his flock into a ravine and couldn't get out?

She sighed. Whatever crisis awaited her meant she wouldn't be driving home anytime soon. Her trip would be postponed, maybe all weekend. She punched the screen to answer the call. Might as well get this over with.

"Don't you believe in sleep?" Lissa stifled a yawn as she waited for Matthew to respond. "Must be some emergency."

"I was afraid you'd leave for your folks' place before I reached you." His words, laced with warmth, made her smile. Matthew deserved her respect. She could picture him in his uniform, broad shoulders packed into his neat tan shirt. From beneath a massive crop of brown hair, grey eyes pierced the edges of her soul. Ever the gentleman, Matthew had treated her like an equal, accepted her into the sheriff's department without hesitation, and made her feel welcomed in an office of six other men. Too bad he was happily married. "You're not on the road yet, are you?"

"No. I planned to leave around nine." She waited for the other shoe to drop. "What's up?"

"Missing person report from a concerned storekeeper. Might be animals involved. Do you have time before you head out?"

Lissa sighed. Animal welfare pervaded her job description and, though the trip she'd planned today to her father's home in McKenzie Bridge had waited too long, she had to respond to Matthew's request. Fifteen years in the Navy had kept her from Dad and his new wife, Eily, and now that Lissa lived closer, they expected her to visit as often as her new job allowed. This renewed connection to her father, after so much time apart, warmed her. But Matthew wouldn't ask if the case wasn't urgent. He knew how much she needed to reconnect with her family.

"How long do you think this will take?" Lissa worked to keep the impatience out of her voice. "I've got a four-hour drive ahead of me. Can we check this out before noon?"

"Depends on what we find. But I doubt it will take more than an hour." Matthew must have read her mind. "Bring your file on ranchers available to foster animals. We may need it."

"Got it." Lissa kept the file in her rig. "I'll meet you at headquarters at eight."

"That's fine. Wear your tall boots."

Clicking off her phone, she went to her closet and retrieved the last clean uniform she'd hoped to save for her return to work next Tuesday. If this call went well, she could replace the uniform in her closet when she finished. She grabbed a towel and headed for the shower. Duty called.

Mueller Ranch, Harney County, Oregon

Rain pelted the filly's bony back like gravel thrown from the roadway shoulder. The shower's chill burrowed into her hide. Beyond the fence, spring precipitation had greened the barren hillside, begging shoots of grass from the frozen soil. In the paddock where she stood, the downpour only added to the mud and manure, rendering the sludge sticky and deep. In the corner, a layer of green floated on the surface of the water trough.

As the filly stepped through the muck, her legs ached from the cold, her hooves heavy with packed dung. Though her coat shimmered with a cinnamon glow in the summer, the filth of the pen dulled it to a dirty brown. Her skin itched, and the shedding hair clung like ticks on a coyote. The soupy ground beneath her offered no place to lie down and roll.

She longed for the growing forage beyond the fence, her stomach a tight knot of hunger. One blade had popped up near the fence post, but the meager shoot did little to satisfy the growling inside her belly.

Her mother wobbled on shaky legs beside her—coughing, wheezing, the breaths staccato and shallow. Mucous dribbled from the mare's nostrils. Her lungs whistled with every breath, similar in pitch to the fierce wind blowing in from the canyon adjacent to the ranch—the canyon where her mother had watched her prance last summer.

The filly's ears twitched. She studied the ranch house not a hundred yards away. The old man's dilapidated machine, which bellowed loud enough to scare a rattlesnake, sat like a piece of scenery in the drive. Where was he?

The man had fancied her last July, a foal learning to run, gamboling on newborn legs. He'd allowed her freedom to roam, to frolic along the creek basin, never out of sight of her watchful mother cropping grass and weeds. The tough, tasteless fodder couldn't compare to her mother's sweet milk. As the summer progressed, however, the mare's supply of nourishment dried up, like the meadow under the summer sun, and she was forced to eat what her mother did.

The old man had provided hay all winter while snow covered the ground. On occasion, she'd snatched the sweetened grain he rationed out for her mother. The molasses, corn, and oats made a welcome treat on a frosty day. But then he'd disappeared. No hay, no grain, no anything. Starvation became a reality.

She missed the man's chuckle. The way he scratched in all the right places behind her ears and between her eyes. She could still hear him boasting to his friends.

"Ain't she a beauty? Cinnamon like her mama. Tail and mane like her daddy. I saw him. Wild Kiger stallion snuck in right beneath my nose and got the mare pregnant. Didn't think ol' Bets could carry a foal to term. But, by gum, I'm glad she did. Ain't never seen a more beautiful filly. See the stripe down her back and on her legs? She's worth a mint, if you ask me."

Why didn't the man come? If nothing else, he could tether her mother against the hillside as he had last summer. The mare had grazed in the dried pastureland, nibbling at milkweed and snipping off thistle tops. The winter snowmelt had left the grasslands ripe for growing. Recent rains encouraged the meadow to soak up all the sky could muster. The new green shoots beckoned her. She and her mother could forage to satisfy their appetites once they escaped the paddock. If only he would come and open the gate—let them beyond their prison, into the spreading carpet of green.

Her mother groaned, shuddered and bent her knees, sinking into the mud. Her breathing rasped now, loud and grating, like the file of the farrier who trimmed her hooves. Her head sank lower, her muzzle drifting into the mire. The filly nickered and nudged her mother, trying to get her to stand. She inched closer, the mud sucking at her legs. Hovering over the mare's back, she nuzzled her mother's neck, massaging the length of it with her chin.

A noise caught her attention. The filly raised her head, ears forward, nostrils flared as she checked the scent. At the top of the hill an engine rumbled. She tried to nicker, but no sound came.

The little horse bumped her mother with her muzzle. Help might be coming.

Lying down, the mare already sounded better. Even the wheezing had stopped.

Unable to sleep, Jayden Clarke stared at the ceiling anxious for this day to break. Fingers of grey dawn crept in through the windows like burglars seeking a score. The sound of rain pattered against the glass.

He bolted to the window and lifted the blind. A fine mist fell, covering the driveway. Rain? On the first day of summer? Puddles occupied the spot where his mother's car should be. No! She'd promised to drop him at Bennie Mueller's ranch today. Why did she leave without him? He looked around his room and spied her note on his dresser.

Jayden, left early for groceries. Have some toast and juice. I'll take you to Mr. Mueller's when I return, or you can ride your bike. George is sleeping. Let him. Mom

He put the note back. Riding his bicycle to Bennie's would take forever in the rain. Jayden groaned. This couldn't be happening.

With school out, he'd barely slept last night, excited to re-unite with his old friend. He hadn't seen the elderly rancher since last September. Bennie suffered from arthritis and, even though Jayden was only ten last summer, Bennie had needed his help with the extra ranch chores warm weather brought.

Jayden couldn't wait to hug Duke, the black and white collie, or send the dog chasing the Frisbee after chores were done. He probably wouldn't recognize the yearling foal. He'd played peek-a-boo with her last summer, burying a carrot chunk deep in the hay. She would snort her way to the bottom to find the crunchy reward. He'd cleaned stalls and pitched hay until exhaustion claimed him. The three of them—he, the filly, and Duke—had been inseparable all summer. Nine months of school and a grueling winter left him eager to return. The ranch, the man, and the animals filled a void inside Jayden nothing else could satisfy.

His new stepfather, George Barnes, might be the reason his mother had left earlier than planned. The long-haul truck driver had arrived home last night after completing a cross-country delivery ahead of schedule, surprising Mom and upsetting Jayden. George had stopped by the bar en route and walked into the house edgy, irritable, and unstable. Jayden's heart sank, remembering the way his stepfather's speech slurred. If George had continued downing the booze as he often did on his weekends off, he could be anywhere—bedroom, sofa, kitchen table—drunk and mean. Jayden needed to be on his guard.

George's abusive temper made life at home a powder keg. When drunk, the man raged at any little infraction. Last night Jayden had made the mistake of asking his mother a question before she served George's dinner and received a slap to his arm. The blow lingered like a nasty bruise. The act had surprised Jayden because his stepfather had never been physically abusive.

Next time he might break something. Jayden wouldn't wait around.

He tiptoed to the kitchen and fixed a light breakfast. Still in his pajamas, he wandered into the living room. He barely cleared the door when an empty Jim Beam bottle zinged by him, missing his shoulder by mere inches and landing on the couch. He whirled around, the buttered toast and orange juice shaking in his hands.

"Where is she?" George glowered at him from the recliner, bulbous nose puffed red and cheeks splotched with pink. At his feet lay another empty bottle next to an opened pretzel box. Breakfast. "You deaf, boy?"

"She said we needed groceries." Being alone with this man in his drunken state made Jayden tremble. "Mom left before you woke up?"

"Melanie's not here, is she?" The words rode on George's tongue like a hissing snake, ready to coil and strike at the slightest provocation. "So I guess she's gone, stupid."

Jayden couldn't believe Mom had left him like this. She hadn't before—especially when George had been drinking. If his stepfather had slept in as his mother had written, she didn't see George this way before she headed to the store. Since she knew Jayden would visit Bennie this morning, she'd trusted he would be safe—not facing a mean and nasty drunk. The vacant house echoed like a cave in the hills, the missing woman torching George's anger. The blame fell to Jayden.

"If you weren't such a wimpy, sniveling kid, your mother wouldn't need to shop so often." George's sneer, combined with the smell of booze on his breath, made Jayden's stomach churn. "She's always buying this shirt for you, or those shoes, saying, 'Wouldn't Jayden like that jacket?' My money, your gifts." He snorted. "I married her, and who do I get stuck with? A measly eleven-year-old who sucks all her affection away from me."

George slammed his fist on the edge of the recliner. "Where is she anyway?" He tipped a third Jim Beam toward the ceiling, tossing the bottle to the floor when it emptied.

"Getting groceries."

George growled, kicked the pretzel box and the bottles away from his feet, and swiveled the recliner toward the window.

Jayden edged closer to the wall, waiting for a chance to slip out to his bedroom. He didn't know how soon his mother would return. She had her own money, resources she kept secret from George. Jayden's real dad's life insurance funded her shopping expeditions, paid for the clothes her son needed, and left a little for splurges. Jayden suspected Mom grew weary of the verbal abuse and, like him, found reasons to be gone.

When George sobered up, he'd morph into a different person, the sweet and generous guy she thought she married after Dad died. The trucker would hit the road again for another cross-country haul and leave Jayden and Mom alone for a week or two. After last night's encounter, why hadn't she waited a little longer to take Jayden with her today? He didn't understand.

Snores interrupted his thoughts. George had passed out. He would sleep like this for hours, the effects of the booze crippling his ability to function while the alcohol laced his system. When he awoke, he'd hold his head, seeking sympathy for the hangover he claimed pounded him like a prizefighter. If Mom was doing a big shop, she might not return for two or three hours. By then George would have slept the booze off, sobered up, and taken meds for his headache. Jayden would stay away as long as possible.

During the winter months, classes and homework kept Jayden busy. He stayed out of George's way whenever they were both home. School offered a barrier of protection since his stepfather was well aware of the watchful scrutiny teachers kept over their charges. He worked longer hours in the winter, sometimes staying away for a month at a time. Worsened driving conditions kept him from returning home, even when the hauling slacked off around the first of the year—a welcome respite to Jayden. He and Mom enjoyed each other's company without the threat of George.

Now school was out. No homework. No classes. More George.

The snores grew in intensity. Seizing the opportunity, Jayden sneaked out of the living room with his breakfast, closing the bedroom door with a soft click. He sat on the edge of his mattress, trying to swallow the toast over the lump in his throat. Sunlight poked through the blinds, begging him to come outside.

He downed the orange juice, slipped into his clothes, and wrote a note to his mother. Leaving the missive on his bed with a prayer she'd find it, he grabbed his denim jacket and tiptoed into the hallway leading to the garage. He passed through the kitchen and checked the refrigerator for more to eat, but found nothing. Cereal would rattle in the bowl, waking George, and without milk, the dry flakes would be tasteless. Satisfied he could last until dinner, he slunk to the back door. He twisted the knob, hurried down the steps, and donned work boots. His bicycle beneath him, Jayden pedaled out through the open garage door like he'd been set on fire. He couldn't wait to see Mr. Mueller. If he never saw George again, it would be too soon.

Two miles of straight stretch burned beneath his tires, and soon he faced the rising elevation leading to Bennie Mueller's ranch. He peered over his shoulder to make sure he hadn't been followed, sighing in relief when the empty road trailed like an asphalt ribbon behind him. Summer vacation awaited. Boy, horse, dog.

He stashed his bike in a roadside thicket, wiped his rain-spattered face, and hoofed it the rest of the distance. Panting as he arrived at the top of the hill, he frowned at the scene below.

Things at the ranch had changed. Mr. Mueller's pickup sat crooked in the driveway, exposed to the elements instead of protected by the overhang of the barn like the rancher preferred.

Not seeing the horses where they should be—grazing in the pasture—Jayden turned his gaze toward the barn. Coat muddied and head down, an animal stood alone in the rain, mired to its knees in the muddy round pen. Was this the foal he'd played with? The creature raised its head. No welcoming whinny. Mr. Mueller would never have left an animal like this. Never.

When Duke didn't barrel up the hill barking like a windup toy on steroids, Jayden considered turning back. He sensed trouble. Should he go home and get his mother? That meant facing George again. No, if Mr. Mueller's truck sat in the driveway, the rancher couldn't be far away.

He summoned his courage and scrambled down the hill. He checked every nook and cranny while calling for Duke. No sign of the dog. He hurried faster to discover the reason. As he neared the ranch buildings, an engine sounded out on the empty highway he'd left twenty minutes before. The vehicle slowed, and Jayden's pulse soared. He didn't want to be discovered snooping around when Mr. Mueller appeared to be gone. He had to hide.

Lissa checked her uniform, grabbed her tote, and led Sorrel to the kennel run behind the house. "Sorry, girl. You'll have to wait until later. Emergency." After locking the gate, she stroked one of Sorrel's front paws as the dog stood on her hind legs, begging through the fence. "I'll be back soon. Promise." She returned to the Suburban, her tall boots waiting on the seat beside her, praying she'd spoken the truth.

Lissa closed the door of the SUV and did a final visual check to see if she'd left anything undone before she headed out. The rented house she now called home waited in the quiet, shutters closed, drapes drawn. The small yard, green from spring rains and receding snow, sported dainty iris blooms popping up near the juniper tree. Nestled beside a rock outcropping, the last daffodil blossoms hung in weary silence, ready to sleep until next year.

A buzz at her side vibrated in her pocket. Anticipation fueled her fingers as she pulled out her cell phone. Might it be Kurt? Every ring of the phone nourished her hope he'd contact her. They'd met at a family Thanksgiving dinner two years before and had spent their week of leave visiting the ocean, shopping in Portland, and sharing a meal and a movie. He had promised he'd keep in touch when he left. He kissed her goodbye at the airport, sent her a handful of e-mails, and disappeared. That was a year ago. He hadn't kept his word. She wanted to know why.

She studied the screen. Matthew again. "Change your mind?"

Matthew chuckled into the phone. "I'll be five minutes late. Don't shoot me."

"I should, after rousting me out before my morning coffee. Slave driver."

"Guilty as charged."

Coming Spring of 2018

A Word from the Author

When my son, Jonathan, graduated from college with a degree in Marine Science and found a job as an observer biologist for the National Marine Fisheries Service, I was excited. But when that job swept him away on a plane to the Aleutian Islands in the middle of winter where he would be working on the Bering Sea, I was terrified. The next few months would keep me on my knees praying for his safety.

He returned home with all sorts of tales about his great adventure. I discovered in his stories the setting for what I thought would be a compelling novel, especially when Jon told me some fishermen often travel to work in the Bering Sea to leave problems at home behind.

I had previously written part of a novel about a woman whose husband wasn't willing to partner in raising their child because of her disability but had abandoned the plot because the circumstances weren't fitting. Instead, listening to my son's stories, I created Dane Nichols, a fisherman who has a legitimate reason for leaving his wife and child behind when he goes to work in Dutch Harbor, Alaska. When the job becomes an escape rather than a means of supporting his family, trouble brews.

As I further researched Dutch Harbor, I discovered the nation's largest fishing port does have a season other than winter. In fact, the townspeople now have a Port of Dutch Harbor Travel and Convention Bureau. Dutch Harbor and its companion city, Unalaska, are both located on Amaknak Island and connected to each other by a bridge. Unalaska is considered the tourist destination, while Dutch Harbor captures the fish. During the short summer season, visitors can drive there if they choose, but access by plane and boat are still considered the most convenient choices.

See www.unalaska.info.

McKenna was an easy character to envision. I had seen her in countless women with whom I had attended autism support groups. These women loved their autistic child with a passion, but received no support at home. As the mother of an autistic daughter, I sensed their despair at trying to do this job alone, and my heart went out to them. I was fortunate to have married a man who took his responsibility in rearing our daughter seriously. He is not alone—a lot of fathers deserve special praise for sharing in a role they never envisioned. But to the man or woman who must shoulder the task alone, I offer my deepest respect and admiration.

The coastal town of Newport, Oregon is a real city, and the places mentioned in the story are favorite haunts of my family. Many of the scenes involving Sydney are based on real life incidents my husband and I experienced rearing our daughter. These episodes are unique to our family's history. Not every parent of an autistic child will identify with some of the behaviors here. Many will have their own stories to tell.

I did choose to home school my daughter because she reacted to the overstimulation of the classroom the same way Sydney processes it in the novel. I will forever be grateful to my homeschooling friend Jeanne Wallace, my first speech and language consultant, who welcomed my daughter into her home. As my daughter touched and moved every object that first visit, Jeanne pointed out how very intelligent Rachel was. A special thanks also goes to speech and language specialists in our school district, Cheryl Lockard and Carol Holbrook, for the roles they played helping me help our child. My daughter is a happy, functioning adult who has learned how to cope with her world, and not the fearful child who once made everything a challenge.

One word of note: Autism and people on the autism spectrum scale keeps changing. When my daughter introduced me to autism,

I had never heard of the condition before. At that time, only three types of autism were documented. Now, almost three decades later, autism spectrum disorder is recognized as a condition that affects people in all walks of life and with different degrees of dysfunction. Some people are brilliant, some are the class nerd, some can barely function at even a preschool cognitive level. Many can talk, some never do. No *one* therapy has been found to treat autism as a whole. Each individual must be served at his or her level of function, which makes the disorder difficult to treat. As a Christian, I believe each person is a unique creation of God and deserves our respect. Each of us should try to walk a mile in their shoes.

Thank you for taking this journey with me. I hope to see you again soon.

If you'd like to connect with me you can find me at the following places:

Website: www.authorpatricialee.net

Blog: www.authorpatricialee.net/blog

FB: www.facebook.com/patricialeebooks

Twitter: @lee_patricia

Rachel is Pat's daughter, an adult autistic artist who loves critters of all kinds. She's yet to find an animal she doesn't want to attempt to draw. Her card collections and calendars have blessed customers since she opened her business in 2005. Check out her creations at:

www.crittercornercards.com

Discussion Questions

1. McKenna is determined to remain faithful to her marriage vows, even though Dane has not returned home in two years. If Rudy Taylor had not volunteered to try and find her husband, do you think she should have gone on waiting for Dane? At what point should she have felt abandoned and free of her commitment, if ever. What does the Bible say?

2. Rudy is not comfortable spending time with a beautiful married woman. He declares that those wedding vows she made are sacred and that anything he does for her is based on friendship. Do you think men and women can just be friends in these kinds of circumstances? Should Rudy have removed himself from the situation altogether?

3. Have you ever met a woman like Olivia who loves unconditionally and who embraces each person she meets as someone who needs her special kind of devotion? What would the world be like if there were more people like Olivia in our lives?

4. At the beginning of the story, the reader is led to believe Dane is a poor father and has shirked his responsibility. When we meet Dane, we see a young man who is bewildered by the circumstances he finds himself in and doesn't know how to handle the situation. Do you find Dane more likeable as the story progresses, or should we, like the boutique owner said, paint him yellow? Were his actions cowardly? Are you sorry when he decides to return home? When he dies? Why?

5. If Dane hadn't perished at sea, what kind of challenges would he

and McKenna have had to overcome to sustain their marriage? Would their relationship be stronger or marginal, based on the kind of counsel Rudy gave Dane in Alaska?

6. Rudy runs away from the scene when Dane dies. Now that Dane is dead, he is afraid McKenna will feel he took advantage of her sorrow if he pursues their friendship at a different level. Do you believe he showed wisdom in walking away, or is he merely adding more pain to McKenna's situation, especially when she is left bereft of friends?

7. Have you known people with disabled children? Have you attempted to learn about their disability? Have you offered to help the parents when they need a sitter or a night out? Finding someone you trust to care for your normal child while you run errands, go out to dinner with your spouse, or visit the doctor can be difficult at best. Have you considered making yourself available for a child who is challenged? What would stop you from doing so?

8. Stretching ourselves to help those in need is what Christ asks of us. Both Rudy and Olivia set that example for us. How can you help someone in need today?